DEEPEST COVER

Still feeling fine and without thinking about it he opened the door to the Oval Office.

Bill recognized Chief of Staff Edgarton but the other man was a stranger. Not the President but an impostor with a stack of papers on his lap. Both of them looked up and the man who should have been President said, "What is it, Bill?"

The impostor knew his name. Odd, Bill thought as he drew his gun. Something wrong now. He winced as his head exploded in pain. Shoot the—arrest the impostor, no *kill* the impostor. A blinding headache, a white light—

Clarity returned and he realized with a shock that the stranger was the President. And the gun—in his hand, the barrel pointed at the President's feet. He thrust it quickly back into its holster. "I'm sorry, sir."

Also by Richard Aellen

FLASH POINT*
CRUX
REDEYE

*Available from HarperPaperbacks

THE
CAIN
CONVERSION

Richard Aellen

HarperPaperbacks
A Division of HarperCollinsPublishers

HarperPaperbacks   *A Division of* HarperCollins*Publishers*
10 East 53rd Street, New York, N.Y. 10022

Copyright © 1993 by Richard Aellen
All rights reserved. No part of this book may be used or reproduced in any manner whatsoever without written permission of the publisher, except in the case of brief quotations embodied in critical articles and reviews. For information address Donald I. Fine, Inc., 19 West 21st Street, New York, N.Y. 10010.

A hardcover edition of this book was published in 1993 by Donald I. Fine, Inc.

Cover design and illustration by Designed To Print

First HarperPaperbacks printing: November 1994

Printed in the United States of America

HarperPaperbacks and colophon are trademarks of HarperCollins*Publishers*

10 9 8 7 6 5 4 3 2 1

Barry Siegel

Godspeed

THE
CAIN
CONVERSION

PROLOGUE

Moscow
October 30, 1962

The child would never kill. Not without careful intervention and training. He was only five years old, a handsome, loving little boy whose father had sown the seeds of destruction from which Dr. Marina Sorin planned to cultivate an assassin, if her growing affection didn't sabotage her resolve. Watching him through her office window, she tried to convince herself that her efforts would give the boy the kind of positive and healthy life impossible with his father.

Positive and healthy until it killed him.

The boy, whose name was Mischa, was in the courtyard of the psychiatric clinic where Marina worked. The courtyard had once belonged to a church, torn down in the 1930s during the Stalin regime. Mischa, bundled against the November chill, was feeding a flock of sparrows, pulling crumbs of bread from a lunch box decorated with a picture of Soviet Hero and Cosmonaut Yuri Gagarin. As he worked his way around the courtyard he picked up a stray feather and tucked it into the box. When the crumbs were gone she knew that he would place the feathers between his clenched fingers and stand, arms outstretched, face to the sky, turning slowly as the birds swirled and rose swiftly around him . . .

Marina's assistant knocked gently. "The car is here."

The assistant's eyes followed her with a new respect, and when she stepped outside Marina saw why: the limousine was a glossy black Chaika used only by high-ranking members of the Politburo or the KGB. Idiots, Marina thought. After all the dire warnings and insistence on secrecy they send a car that draws attention like a ballerina on center stage.

Fifteen minutes later they slid behind the walls of the Kremlin, where a special assistant named Fedorchek greeted Marina with a look of lengthy disapproval. She was not the image of Soviet propaganda films but a short, square woman with a Mongol cast to her features and straight ink-black hair cropped short and parted down the middle. Red nail polish drew attention to delicate hands, but her thick black eyebrows had not been plucked and she wore no makeup.

Fedorchek hustled her through the security checkpoint and past stone-faced guards to a reception room where a half dozen men in business suits waited. They grumbled their displeasure when, after a quick consultation with the receptionist, Fedorchek motioned Marina forward. "Are you nervous?"

"No."

His gaze lowered and he flicked an imaginary grain of dandruff from her shoulder. She would have slapped his hand, but he had already turned away and opened the door to the highest office of the land.

Premier Nikita Khrushchev was standing. He regarded her with bright, intelligent eyes. A round, bald man, with a mole on his nose and a roll of fat draped beneath his chin, he looked like a butcher or a chef, not the leader of a world power recently on the brink of war with the United States. He poked a thumb at a chair. "Sit, Dr. Sorin. Sit down."

Smaller than he looks on television, she thought. And nervous, if the broken and irritated skin bordering his thumbnail was any indication. Khrushchev crossed his arms. "Well?"

"Sir?"

"The Ipatyev Project. You have studied the program?"

"An impressive beginning."

"Cows piss on impressive. Will Colonel Guneyev's team succeed? Your opinion."

Marina blinked but did not show surprise. In a profession dominated by men, she had learned that unless she projected an aggressive, tough image her superiors didn't find her credible. She was prepared to trade profanity with Premier Khrushchev if that's what it took to convince him she was tough enough for the job. Keeping her voice low and authoritative she said, "Not using these techniques."

Khrushchev leaned forward and his eyes narrowed to tiny dark spots. "Guneyev tells me you have a patient, a boy with a split mind whom you control like a puppet. Is it true?"

"He exaggerates. I have only begun my work with the boy."

"Can you train him to kill on command, yes or no?"

"I would be privileged to try."

"You will be pleased to accomplish it. You are now in charge of the Ipatyev Project. Colonel Guneyev will report to you."

Marina hid both her surprise and pleasure. With a rush of confidence she heard herself say, "On the condition that the project is named after me."

Fedorchek gasped. Khrushchev's head moved forward like a turtle's. "You are not a member of the party, Dr. Sorin. Why not?"

"I am a scientist, Comrade Premier. Party affiliations do not alter the Babinsky reflex or change the specific gravity of urine."

"I'll bet you repair tractors, too. Do you know why we call it the Ipatyev Project?"

"After the man who began it?"

"Blind to history as well as politics," he said scornfully. "One year, Doctor, and if your results match your arrogance you can have your . . . Sorin Project." He nodded his dismissal. Fedorchek took Marina's elbow and hurried her out of the office. Now that it was over, she felt the sweat trickling down her spine. Fedorchek shook his head and whispered, "You are a foolish woman. Comrade Khrushchev named the Ipatyev Project himself."

Marina felt a thrill of alarm. "But who was Ipatyev?"

"Even a scientist must remember what happened July 16, 1918."

It was a date every Russian learned in grade school. "The Czar was executed at Yekatrinburg."

"Bravo, scientist."

"And Ipatyev?"

He glanced up and down the hallway. "The house where it happened."

Marina Sorin was thirty-three, old enough to have moved to the forefront of her profession and young enough to be confident of her ability to do the impossible. Flush with victory, she returned to the clinic where she found Mischa sitting on a couch, elbows clutched close to his body, rocking, rocking. Marina joined him and put an arm over his shoulders. The body kept moving and didn't stop until she began the English song that always calmed him:

> *Where have you been, Billy boy, Billy boy?*
> *Oh, where have you been, charming Billy?*
> *I've been to seek a wife,*
> *She's the joy of my life,*
> *She's a young thing and cannot leave her mother.*

As Marina sang, the boy relaxed and became aware of the world around him. His face turned toward her and she saw herself reflected in huge brown eyes flecked with gold like captured sunbeams.

"*Where have you been, Billy boy, Billy boy?*" His finger reached tentatively to her cheek. "*Where have you been charming Billy?*" She intercepted his hand and cradled it in her own. "*I've been to seek a . . .*" Marina paused and the boy tensed. New words slipped slowly, softly, from her lips. "*I've been to find a knife, which will end my baby's life, he's a young thing and cannot leave his mother."*

The boy smiled and corrected her by singing softly, *"I've been to seek a wife—"*

"—find a knife," Marina insisted.

He stared at her, puzzled. Marina repeated the line. *"I've been to find a knife . . ."* She stroked the back of his hand. "Come on, sing it with me." The boy joined her, tentatively at first, then with growing certainty. *"I've been to find a knife, which will end my baby's life, he's a young thing and cannot leave his mother."*

Not yet, anyway, Marina thought. Her hand curled around the boy's, closing his fingers into a fist within her own, like the petals of a flower clutched tight around the seeds of new life.

They began the song again.

CHAPTER

1

Washington, D.C.
199–

Matthew Sullivan was twelve years old and trying to please his father. He held the gun in both hands, just the way he'd been taught, and braced himself as the crowd surged forward. He was looking for an enemy, an assassin, what his father called the Hink. Because he expected a man, Matt didn't notice until too late the woman with a clutch purse, her arm rising, a pistol pointed at him—

Matt fired twice, the high-pitched *beep* of the laser pistol drowned by the explosion of the woman's gun. The smiling people projected against the wall froze in position while two blinking yellow lights registered the location of Matt's "bullets," one in a building behind the crowd, the second in the knee of a man ten feet from the assassin.

"You're dead," Bill Sullivan told his son.

"It's not fair, it's a woman."

"So was Sara Jane Moore."

"Who?"

"A woman who tried to kill President Ford."

"Who's President Ford?"

"He was between Nixon and Carter. 'I'm a Ford, not a Lincoln'—that's what he used to say."

Matt made a face and shrugged broadly, a childish response that emphasized his immaturity. He was small for his age, with red hair and an eager smile that strangers thought was cute and Bill thought was too eager. The boy had inherited his father's solitary nature, but lacked Bill's confidence or sense of purpose. Today's visit to the Secret Service training facility outside Washington, D.C., was an attempt on Bill's part to recover an intimacy they seemed to have lost.

Bill thumbed the reset button. "Next threat, get ready."

"I'm no good at shooting."

"Sure you are. Okay, what are you looking for?" The scene projected on the wall shifted to a ballroom filled with people in formal dress who sat at banquet tables. "Quick now, what?"

"Eyes, face, hands . . ."

"The kitchen door, watch it, watch—"

It was only a video image, but Bill could feel his hands twitch and legs tense. After fifteen years in the Secret Service he responded instinctively to a fixed expression in a crowd of hero-worshipers, a heavy coat worn on a summer afternoon, a hand thrust into a shopping bag or a rifle barrel sliding through the kitchen door, now slightly ajar . . .

The rifle and Matt fired at the same time. Matt's amber strike light showed he was high. Three more shots from the rifle before one of Matt's wildly erratic shots found its mark and froze the image. By that time the wall was peppered with amber strike lights and the imaginary diners had taken cover on the floor. The boy looked sheepish. "It's hard."

"That was great, you got him."

"But I got a waiter, too."

"Probably an accomplice." Bill was rewarded with a grateful smile. "You ready?"

"You do it this time."

"I already passed the course."

"My arm is tired."

Bill hesitated, then took the laser weapon. It was the same size and weight as the Smith & Wesson Model 19 that most of the agents carried. He snapped the gun into his breakaway shoulder holster and handed Matt the reset button. "Any time."

The next sequence was a motorcade, the camera positioned in a follow car. Twelve years ago they used pellet guns and a film projector for this exercise, but now it was like a life-size video game. But the psychology was the same, as were the likely positions an assassin might choose. Bill spotted the movement in the open window and whipped out his pistol. He got off two quick shots, one of which illuminated the window in amber and stopped the projection.

"You got the Hink," Matt cried, self-consciously using the unofficial term for a potential assassin.

Bill felt a surge of satisfaction, even though he knew that a handgun fired from a moving car at this distance would hit its target only with luck. He offered Matt the gun, but the boy shook his head. "I don't want to do any more."

"This is a half-million-dollar facility," Bill reminded him. "Better than those video games at the mall."

The boy rolled his head back and forth as if stretching his neck muscles, a noncommittal kind of response that Bill found irritating. No judgments, he reminded himself. This was Matt's day, whatever he wanted to do. They had already toured the classrooms where lawyers once taught Bill just how far he could breach the constitutional safeguards protecting an individual's liberty; they had visited the kennels where dogs were trained to detect explosives; and at a Technical Services lab the technician made a mold of Matt's outer ear, the same process they used to custom fit the radio receiver each Secret Service man wore in his right ear. All morning Matt had been excited, but now the hesitancy that so often held the boy in check had returned. He was ready to go home.

"So how'd you do?" the technician asked Matt when they stopped at the control booth.

"Okay," Matt mumbled.

"He was great," Bill said with forced enthusiasm that caused his son to wince.

The Beltsville Training Facility was like a well-guarded campus. Bill handed the guard his pass and they turned onto Interstate 95 south. It was October, and the air was crisp with the scent of autumn leaves. They drove with the top down on the Mustang convertible, a classic 1968 model on which Bill lavished much time and attention. Outside the facility Matt seemed to relax. The slipstream kicked his red·hair into the sun as he tilted his head back to watch a helicopter passing overhead.

"Have fun?" Bill asked.

"Yeah."

"What'd you like the best?"

"The dogs."

Oh, great, Bill thought. I wrangled special permission for a tour of Beltsville and you'd rather play with dogs.

Bill Sullivan was a man of immense self-confidence with one exception: He was not a natural father. As they drove to Washington he made a couple of conversational forays, vainly seeking the sort of father-son rapport depicted on television shows. Finally they both fell silent.

The afternoon's activity was less of a strain. They met Claire and Megan at the Arena Theater and watched a British farce called *Noises Off*. At least Bill and the kids watched it; Claire was working the show, a special matinee for the hearing impaired. Dressed in black slacks and a turtleneck sweater, she stood to the left of stage and used her hands to interpret the dialogue.

"This will be a tough one," she warned them beforehand. "It's a comedy, and timing and inflection don't translate well through the hands."

Not true, Bill thought. Everything translated well through Claire's hands. Even now he found his attention drawn from the actors to the white hands sculpting the air in a pale downwash of light. With her broad face and generous mouth she was not pretty in the conventional sense, but the transcendent expression she wore when signing imbued her with a special grace. "The perfect medium," she laughingly described herself. Afterward she would remember little of what she interpreted.

Megan sat on Bill's left. She was a raven-haired eight-year-old, energetic and fearless as a tiger, as open and gregarious as Matt was guarded and defensive. During the performance Bill saw her hands dancing above her lap, trying to keep pace with her mother. From one generation to the next the silent skill had been passed down. Claire's mother was deaf, and Claire had learned American Sign Language as a child. She supported herself in college by working as an interpreter and Bill always said that he fell in love first with her hands. Had he been given to introspection he would have discovered something else: a distrust of words, which didn't apply when they were translated into movement.

When the play was over, Claire was glassy-eyed with excitement and the kids were hungry. They stopped at a Burger King, where Matt surprised Bill by giving his sister a glowing account of their activities at Beltsville. They sat at a table whose immovable plastic seats were too close to it and Megan asked her brother, "How come you call him the Hink?"

Without meaning to cut off Matt, Bill answered automatically. "A man called John Hinkley tried to assassinate President Reagan. So that's our nickname for anyone else who tries it."

Matt's enthusiasm evaporated. "I don't think I could shoot anybody, not even a Hink."

"You could if it was your job."

"I wouldn't have a job where I had to kill people."

"How else would you protect the President from a killer?"

Matt toyed with his straw, rotating through the plastic cover into the milkshake. "I don't believe killing solves anything, that's all."

Megan said, "If you kill a mosquito it solves getting bitten."

"We're talking about people, not insects like you, weegus," Matt said.

Claire said gently, "I don't like that term, Matt."

"Tell her not to be stupid."

"So what would you do, Matt?" Bill persisted. "If someone pointed a gun at the President how would you handle it?"

"He'd tell a mosquito to bite him," Megan said with a giggle.

Matt ignored her. "I'd try to talk to him."

"Words can't stop bullets. How're you going to talk to the barrel of a gun?"

The boy jumped to his feet. "At least I wouldn't sing about it." He grabbed his tray and marched to a trash bin.

Claire shook her head: *Let it go.* But Bill was puzzled. Singing? What was he talking about? Walking to the car he kept his tone casual and said, "Who was singing, Matt? What did you mean?"

"It doesn't matter."

"No, I'm curious. What song are we talking about?"

"When you were waiting to shoot the Hink. What you were humming."

"What was it, the 'Marine's Hymn'?"

"I don't know the name."

They reached the Mustang, which still had its top down. Rather than open his door, Bill perched on the frame, scissored his legs inside and dropped to the seat. When Matt attempted it on the passenger's side, Bill stopped him. "You've got jeans on. The rivets will scratch the paint."

"I can do it," Megan said, "I don't have jeans."

She perched on the frame and flipped backward into the backseat, feet flying into the air.

"Great technique, Megan," Matt said. "You should join a circus—the human beanbag."

He slid into the backseat beside his sister. Driving home, they didn't speak of the song, but it seemed to fill the rushing air above Matt's head, another example of his father's need to find fault and contradict him. After all, he could still hear the single lyric that Dad sang slowly under his breath while scanning the video crowd: *"He's a young thing and cannot leave his"*—pausing until the Hink appeared—*"mother."* And pulled the trigger.

CHAPTER

2

Little bastard, Vasily Amenov thought as he swung the heavy sledgehammer into the tombstone. A crack appeared, a jagged line separating the boy's name, *Mikhail Vasilievich*, from *Amenov*. Vasily swung again: a spray of shattered stone against his leg. Another blow and a large chunk fell to the earth. *Vasilievich*—what a joke. *Mikhail Jeremievich* was more like it. He repositioned his feet and continued swinging the hammer.

It was an overcast, unfriendly day and the grass in St. Clement's Cemetery was damp and cold from last night's rain. Vasily's hands were protected by the fine kid gloves that were a legacy of his service in the Soviet KGB, now renamed the *Ministerstvo Bezopasnosti Rossii*, or Russian Intelligence Service, an innocuous designation Vasily despised and few people used. To the man in the street and the world at large, the unblinking eye and poised dagger was still the emblem of the *Komitet Gosudarstvennoi Bezopasnosti*, the KGB.

The wrong life, Vasily thought grimly as he delivered a blow that shattered the top half of the stone. I have lived the wrong life. Looking back he divided it into two halves, the first a series of successes accompanied by joy and satisfaction, the second one of pain, lost promise and tragedy. The line of demarcation was clear; he knew the day, the hour, the second it happened. He still had the evidence, banal and conclusive, a curly red hair found beneath his pillow.

The only other people in the cemetery were an old couple who had brought flowers to the grave of their granddaughter. Now the blows of the hammer caught their attention and the old man came toward Vasily. "What are you doing?"

"None of your business." He brought the hammer down on what remained of the base.

"Stop it." The old man grabbed the hammer.

"Get out of the way."

"Leave the dead in peace."

"There's nobody buried here, you stupid shit." He pushed him away, letting go of the hammer. The old man stumbled backward, tripped over the debris and fell. His wife, an old *babushka* with a worn sweater and shapeless skirt, came running, screaming her husband's name. For a moment Vasily felt the wild urge to kick them both to death, these stupid *kulaks* for whose sake the mighty Soviet Union had now been dismantled. But they were not the enemy. The faceless reformers in the Kremlin, they were the culprits.

Vasily tucked his hands into his coat, hunched his shoulders and walked a half mile to the trolley stop. While in the KGB he had been assigned a chauffeur-driven limousine, but no longer. Now he took the *electrichka* and sat in a long car crowded with housewives and students who sat three abreast on their way to the city. Two young men with greasy porcupine hair, dressed in torn leather jackets, were talking in obscenities, bothering the old lady next to them. Hooligans, Vasily thought with disgust. Such things would not have been allowed in the old days. He would have arrested them himself, on the spot, the authority of his KGB badge all that was necessary.

The badge was gone, thanks to the unsuccessful coup against

former Soviet leader Mikhail Gorbachev. Vasily had not been a leader of the coup, but for his support he had been stripped of his job, his rank and his pension, and sentenced to three years in prison. When he returned home he found that the Soviet Union had ceased to exist, Moscow had become the capital of the Russian Republic, and the KGB had changed its name and much of its staff. Like the country, it was now a cluster of separate divisions engulfed in the chaos of reorganization.

Vasily left the trolley and walked to a dismal 1950s-era prefabricated complex disparagingly referred to as *Khrushchoby,* a pun on Khrushchev and the word for slums, *trushchoby.* The elevator to his building had been stuck on the third floor for a week, so he climbed stairs that stank of boiled cabbage and cat shit. He was breathing heavily by the time he entered the overheated shoebox he had secured with the aid of friends who could help him but not be seen with him. He shared a common kitchen down the hall, but ignored it in favor of the hot plate he kept on his dresser. There were dirty dishes in the bathroom sink but he didn't care. Let the cockroaches take over the apartment; they had already taken over the country.

Vasily threw himself onto the cracked vinyl cushions of the couch and smoked a cigarette. In the old days it would have been an American Kent, but now, without salary, pension or privilege, he smoked Troikas, the oval Russian cigarettes that invariably sagged and fueled his bitterness toward the State that had betrayed him. The smoke dissipated slowly, like the cancer cells that had infiltrated his body so completely that no surgery or chemotherapy could save him. Vasily Amenov was terminally ill. That was why he had been released from prison two years early. *Humanitarian pardon* they called it, the new Russian government proving its liberalism to itself. They expected him to die in this miserable apartment, but Vasily had other plans. Betrayers must be punished.

At six o'clock there was a knock at the door. Vasily opened it to a thin, nervous woman who carried a large suitcase. Gavrila Roday, a lawyer, had once worked for the KGB but had joined the reformers at the politically correct moment. Now she was part of the RIS Investigations Committee, which was reviewing and categorizing old KGB files with classification SECRET or higher. She was an unattractive woman who had been infatuated with Vasily for years, but only after his release from prison did he make her his lover, feigning an attraction he didn't feel in return for the information he needed.

Gavrila came quickly into the apartment, placed her oversize handbag on a chair and pulled out a pack of Marlboros. The name of the KGB had changed but not the perquisites of power. Gavrila was a Marlboro woman—highly placed. Her hand was shaking.

"First the wrong numbers," she said. "Then the fucking elevator."

"What numbers?"

"An irradiated water experiment in Kazakastan, conventional designation Project Yellow Birch. Those were the numbers you gave me."

"I gave you the Sorin Project."

"The nine-hundred series six one sub Bravo five had a—"

"*One* five. Sub Bravo *one* five. I wrote it down."

"The way you wrote it, it looked like a slash, not a one."

"It's a *one* five."

"I know that now. But first I found sub Bravo five, Project Yellow Birch. The librarian saw it was wrong."

"You showed him?"

"He was at my elbow. They lost a file the other day and everyone is crazy with new procedures. A researcher must be accompanied by a librarian who must then sign for each article taken to the projector."

"Shit."

"When I saw it was wrong I had to explain it was the Sorin Project I wanted, not Yellow Birch. He's the one who realized the slash was a one, so you should be grateful."

"And?"

A thin jet of cigarette smoke shot from between pursed lips. Gavrila's hand dived into her purse and emerged with a palm-sized reel of quarter-inch magnetic recording tape. Vasily grabbed it. "This is the activation tape?"

Gavrila shrugged. "It was the only one in the file."

Not a cassette tape, which surprised him. He would have to find a reel-to-reel machine to play it.

"How? If the librarian was watching?"

"I spilled my cup of tea. He ran to find a rag, and I removed it from its container."

"And the file itself? The microfilm?"

"One hundred and eighty-one rolls of film, Vasily. How many times could I spill the tea? You said first importance was the tape, second the name, and third the files themselves."

"Then what about the name? Did you find it?"

"I read the files."

"And?"

She was staring at him with an expression of speculation and distaste. "The things you did. The psychiatrist's report about the boy—is it true?"

"I never read the report. I wasn't in charge of the program."

"But you . . . did those things?"

Vasily placed the tape on the table and crossed the room. Gavrila stood her ground until he was staring down at her. Now he could see the delicate network of blood vessels radiating from the corners of her eyes, the gray roots of her hair, the perpetually chapped corners of her mouth. He took the cigarette from her hand and slowly embraced her. For a moment she remained rigid. Vasily moved his lips gently over her forehead, across her cheeks to her lips. The first kiss was tentative, gentle. She sighed and opened her mouth, her body relaxing into his. He felt her hands on his back, drawing him close. Still holding the cigarette, he touched the ember to her neck. She yelped and twisted free, hand reaching behind her head. "You burned me!"

"An accident."

"Fuck you." She went to the bathroom and after a moment Vasily followed. He could not afford to make her angry. Gavrila held a cold washcloth to the back of her neck. She glared at him in the mirror, eyes glistening with tears. "You made a scar."

"I'm sorry, Gavi."

"Get away."

"Let me make it all right."

"Prison has made you mean," she complained as he placed

his hands on her hair, gently moved them down to her ears and took the lobes between middle finger and thumb. She was wearing her good earrings, tiny pearls in a gold pin, the ones she had on when he took her to dinner the first time. He leaned forward and kissed each ear, gently tracing each outer edge with the tip of his tongue. She shivered with anticipation. He kissed her. After a moment Gavrila's tongue flicked forward, dancing across his teeth and along the roof of his mouth. He trapped her tongue with his teeth. She shuddered like a butterfly pinioned by its wings. The wet cloth smacked to the floor.

Vasily broke free and saw that her anger had been replaced by the familiar hunger. She pushed toward him, but he put a finger on her lips. "The name."

"Later."

"Now."

Her expression became coy. She lifted the pen from his pocket. "I'll write it on your chest."

He stood silently as she unbuttoned his shirt and slid it from his shoulders. The nib of the pen was cold against his skin. When she was done she touched the name with her tongue and looked up with a smile.

"Read it to me," Vasily said.

Her chin tilted up. "No."

Vasily turned her so she faced the mirror and wrapped his fingers in her hair. Gently he pressed her head forward until her neck revealed the angry circular welt of the cigarette burn. He brushed it with his tongue.

"Ow, ow," she whispered, a quick-rising staccato whisper that mixed pleasure as well as pain.

He moved his lips away and pulled her head back until she was staring at the ceiling. "The blouse."

She did as he instructed, unable to look down, hands fumbling with the buttons. When it was free, Vasily slid the blouse over her shoulders and let it fall to the floor. Gavrila reached backward to unsnap the bra but he blocked her hand. "No."

He stood behind her and pushed his thigh between her legs. One hand draped over her shoulder, he curled a finger beneath the underside of the bra and began to peel it upward. They watched together as the elastic band compressed each breast in turn. She drew a quick breath as first one nipple then the other popped free. Her flaccid breasts were rippled with stretch marks. Vasily took her hands in his, moved them to his mouth and sucked on her fingers. Then, manipulating them as if they were his own, he moved her fingers to each nipple, circling, sliding, pinching.

"Vasily—"

"Make them kiss."

Gavrila let out a low moan as her own fingers forced the dark, puckered nubs together. Vasily watched the mirror with clinical objectivity. She was too thin, too eager for it.

Since his diagnosis and release from prison Vasily had been haunted by images of death and decay, which coalesced around their lovemaking. Hunched over Gavrila in the bed he was acutely aware of her ribs, her hips, the flat pubic bone pressed against his body, and an image arose of the bones beneath their flesh, two skeletons intertwined, barren teeth and empty eye sockets and a phallus made of vertebrae thrusting into the void of a gaping pelvis. His eyes never left her face. She bit her lip during climax, head twisting left and right. Vasily came and imagined his sperm as poison spreading quick cancer through her body, turning her orgasm to death throes.

Later he lay on his back and stared at the water-stained ceiling while Gavrila nestled close, seeking comfort from a body that had become a stranger to itself. The stain resolved itself into a child curled in a fetal position, one arm outstretched and distorted, bent back on itself. The image reminded him of Mischa, the child of betrayal who had sabotaged his past and stolen his future.

He got out of bed without waking Gavrila and went to the bathroom. In the cracked mirror the bastard's name was backward, ink smeared during lovemaking. Vasily wrapped a cloth around his forefinger and used a tile cleanser to erase the name from his chest.

Just as I will erase your life, he thought as the letters disappeared. But when the ink was gone the name remained in red-roughened skin, blurred and backward but still visible to Vasily's eye, the name they had given the bastard he wished he had strangled the day he was born: BILL SULLIVAN.

CHAPTER

3

The house is burning. His parents are asleep and Bill is running down a long hallway toward their bedroom. He screams a warning but scorched air sucks his words away and flames follow him, catch him, shoot forward. His hands are burning, but when he shakes them flames fly everywhere. He reaches for the door and it bursts into flames. His mother is coming toward him in her nightgown, but when he reaches for her the flames fly off his fingers and wrap themselves in her hair. His father stumbles backward into the room. Bill points at him and the flames shoot up his father's body, both parents now dancing and screaming and Bill slapping at the flames, trying to kill the fire. An inhuman sound from above them, the cry of a dying peacock, and Bill looks up just as the ceiling gives way and a mass of burning debris descends and engulfs him—

"Bill." Claire's voice woke him. He was lying in bed, his body damp with sweat, heart pounding. Her hand was on his shoulder. "You okay?"

"Jesus . . ."

"Was it the fire?"

"You could tell?"

"You were flicking your hands so hard the bed was shaking."

The fire dream, the twisted vision of his parents' death. Bill had not been there to warn or wake them the night they died. It happened during his first and only year he spent at Wichita State University. He had come home for Christmas and on New Years Eve went to a party where he got so drunk he passed out in the car. When he woke up it was six in the morning and he was shivering with cold. The heater had barely warmed the car when he turned onto the street where he lived and saw the red fire truck opposite the blackened ruins of his home, the firemen sifting the wreckage. An icy rain had come too late, drops making tiny hissing explosions in sea of ash . . .

Bill got up, stripped off his sweat-dampened nightshirt, and put on a fresh one. The nightmares had followed him when he left Kansas and transferred to the University of Maryland, tormenting him until he met Claire. After his marriage they became increasingly rare and finally stopped altogether. Until tonight.

He returned to bed, where he lay on his back while Claire snuggled close. "What is it?"

"I don't know. I've had this feeling all week, like somebody's watching me. The other day I thought someone was following me. I ran a yellow light to get rid of him and then circled the block and followed him to Tyson's."

"When was this?"

"Wednesday. That's why I was late getting home."

Tyson's Corners was the largest shopping center in the Washington area. Claire said, "It's the job. Working the White House turns all of you paranoid."

"Just because you're paranoid doesn't mean everybody's not out to get you."

Her fingers found his leg and moved in small circles upward. "Everyone is not out to get you—only I am."

"You already got me."

"Show me."

It was early in the morning, the children were asleep, and the world was theirs in a way they would never know again.

Vasily Amenov sat before a microfiche projector, its gray illumination emphasizing the pallor of his skin. He adjusted the carrier to display a listing of names until he found the one he wanted: *Sullivan, William, 16 Ernestine Circle.* The listing was for Lynwood, Virginia, a suburb of Washington, D.C.

"Will you be long?" A frail woman hugging a microfiche envelope gave him a toothy smile.

"In a jiffy." The colloquialism seemed stiff on his tongue. Speaking English after all these years was like returning to roller skates.

Vasily was in London. He had slipped undetected out of Russia, using a false Swiss passport under the name Maurice Seitz. The document was part of an escape package he had prepared while still working for the KGB. He spent one day in Zurich, where he emptied his bank account of the eleven thousand dollars in hard currency he had saved over the years. In a city with some of the best medical facilities in the world the money might buy Vasily a few more months before cancer claimed him, but he was not tempted. The eleven thousand dollars was earmarked for destruction, not salvation.

Vasily fed the microfiche machine a pound and it spit out a copy of the phone listing. He folded the address into a small notebook and left the Westminster Research Library. It was time to renew an old friendship. No, not friend, he thought as he walked to the Soho district where Guy Jurmon worked. Business associate.

London had changed since the days of his youth. The lowlying city of quiet confidence he remembered had lost its personality before an onslaught of skyscrapers, fast-food shops, automobiles and immigrants. Few people rode bicycles these days and fewer still could get across streets jammed with tourists and wrong-way traffic. The roomy, sedate black taxis were molting, taking on peacock colors and advertising slogans, while the distinctive red phone booths too often smelled of urine and were being replaced by open glass stalls.

Some things had not changed. The names of the underground trains—District, Circle, Piccadilly, Northern—brought familiar memories, as did the gaudy sex emporiums of Soho. The place he was looking for was called Bob Randi's on Great Windmill Street. The facade was black plastic with the name in pink neon. A video store occupied the main floor, and a sign pointed upstairs to something called the Kitty Krib. A plump girl wearing a blonde wig that fit her like a fishbowl peered from the entrance. "Live show, sir?"

Sir, like he was a gentleman. Leave it to the British to blend courtesy with pornography. "You work here?"

She eyed him seductively. "It's not always work."

"I'm looking for the manager, Guy Jurmon. You know him?"

She leered. "Gerbil Jurmon? Sure, everybody knows him. He's not in today. You interested in business or pleasure?"

"Neither."

"Give me an hour, I'll make a believer of you," she called after him.

Vasily had arranged for the reel-to-reel tape of the activation signal to be duplicated onto a cassette. If it *was* the activation signal; he hadn't heard the tape. There had been no time and the risk in Moscow too great. Now, on his way to pick up the tape, he found himself passing the Royal Opera House. This was where the Royal Ballet performed, Mecca for dancers like Yelena. How many nights had he waited outside the stage door? How many nights would she rather have gone drinking with other members of the company? Or home with her lover? *Jeremy, not Jerry.* That's how he had introduced himself. Jeremy Lawrence, a red-haired choreographer for the company.

Facing the Opera House was a bronze statue of a seated ballerina staring at her legs with a beatific look of satisfied exhaustion. Looking inward, Vasily thought, like they all did, lives spent looking in mirrors, just like Yelena.

Yelena . . . the name still carried the magic of their first meeting. It had happened a lifetime ago, back when the streets of Moscow still teemed with the maimed veterans of the Great

Patriotic War, when Vasily was only two months past graduation from the KGB Academy. His cover assignment was that of a Pravda journalist, and he had returned to his hometown of Obninsk to establish his credentials by writing an article about the new Cultural Palace. His friends and neighbors pretended to believe the fiction that he was a journalist, but his father wasn't fooled. "Since when do Pravda reporters have such boots," he asked with a wink.

"I work for Pravda, Papa, do not forget it."

"Da, da," father agreed. "And I work for the Church of Rome!"

As a prelude to the evening's entertainment, Madame Varvara, the choreographer, explained her interpretation of the opening night's performance of Stravinsky's *The Firebird.* Vasily moved his lips silently, translating her words into English. He had an excellent ear for languages and would soon be assigned a covert assignment in America or England.

Madame Varvara ended her speech, and Vasily, prompted by a nudge from his mother, joined briefly in the applause. The lights flickered, then blinked off. On stage an actor portraying Prince Ivan was prancing around in green tights and a hunting jacket. A flicker of orange light and a medley of eerie chords sent Ivan into hiding behind a tree. The Firebird appeared and Vasily almost laughed aloud at the garish costume. The red and orange plumage was made of some sort of industrial plastic and the feathered headdress was beet red. But when the girl moved, his smile faded. There was something about her, her lithe body, regal bearing, full lips—Vasily tilted his program to catch the light and read her name: Yelena Velaskaya. It was the last time his eyes left the stage. Unlike the fragile, tentative swans beloved of most ballets, the Firebird was powerful, a creature of strength and purpose. At one point Yelena spun to a stop and stared directly at him, crystal blue eyes piercing his fiction of a Pravda man, his superficial identity as a KGB officer, straight into his heart. It was an intimacy so intense that he put his hand on the chair in front of him to keep from falling forward. That this feeling was mutual he never doubted.

After the performance his parents went home, but Vasily

stayed for the reception. He waited in the People's Congress Room until Yelena appeared, her hair pulled back in a ponytail. She was younger than he imagined, a teenager with cheeks still full from fading childhood, but her poise was that of an adult. When Madam Varvara introduced him as a reporter from Pravda, she said, "A drama critic?"

"Sadly, no." His voice caught and he cleared his throat self-consciously. "I'm just covering the opening of the Cultural Hall."

"What did you think of our performance?" Her voice was pitched low and hinted at secret knowledge. He barely heard his own response. "Were there others in it?"

"Such gallantry, Mr. Amenov. You must have studied in Leningrad."

"Moscow, actually."

"Then you must have seen the Bolshoi."

"Not as often as I should have."

She tossed a shoulder. "Ballet should never be a duty."

"Tonight it was an unexpected pleasure. Particularly the twirling movement."

She smiled, white teeth all the more charming for their imperfection. "Which twirling movement?"

"Like this." He raised his arms and did a passable imitation of what he had seen on stage, making an exaggerated point of whipping his head around with each turn. She laughed. "You mean the entrance of the Firebird."

"Those movements, what were they called?"

"Coupé jeté en tournant."

"Coopay what?"

"Jeté en tournant."

He repeated the term and smiled. "I love it."

"The choreography?"

"The way you stared at me while doing them."

"Row G, seat twelve. That's where I spot."

"Spot?"

"A fixed point for the eye. Otherwise it's easy to lose your balance."

Yelena always insisted it was pure chance that she was staring at him, but Vasily never believed it. They married three weeks later despite the objections of Yelena's parents, who thought that at seventeen she was too young; the censure of Vasily's superiors in the KGB, who insisted that she join the Communist Party; and the reservations of his own father, who felt that a ballerina did not fit Marx's definition of a worker.

I risked my career for you, Vasily thought, and how did you repay me? The answer was hidden in a battered pocket watch that had once belonged to a German officer killed in the Great Patriotic War. The watch was a gift from his father. Vasily pulled it out and popped open the back. Inside was a thin sheet of cellophane folded once to embrace a clump of blonde hair. Removing the tuft, he held it to the light and pinched his thumb and finger, causing the individual strands to rotate, shafts of gold as pure and bright as his love for Yelena had been . . .

A curly red hair caught the light, garish and alien, coiled among Yelena's soft blonde hair. His fingers froze. The evidence of betrayal was no more faded after thirty years than the hatred it inspired. This was what he found in his own bed, the red hair that changed his life forever. He replaced the hair and snapped the cover shut. It was two o'clock.

He went to the Sound Works, where a young man wearing suspenders handed him the stolen tape along with the cassette. Vasily was alert to any sign of alarm, anything that might indicate the technicians were aware of the incendiary nature of the tape. The clerk's casual attitude reassured him even as it increased his worry that it was the wrong tape, that whatever it contained was not the activation signal for Bill Sullivan.

Vasily had no personal interest in whether the United States President lived or died; it was the consequences of the attempt that he wanted to see, the desperate attempts of the new Russian government to wriggle free of its responsibility, and Yelena's pain when she saw the final havoc her betrayal brought. Filled with both anticipation and suspicion he walked briskly to the River Thames, doubling back twice to insure he wasn't being followed. By the time he reached the broad promenade along the embankment his nerves had steadied. He sat on a bench near a group of tourists clustered around Cleopatra's Needle. Earlier he had purchased a Sony tape player. Now he fitted the earphones over his head, inserted the tape and turned it on.

At first nothing, then a Russian voice filled with dire warnings: the enclosed material was classified MOST SECRET; those without authorization were forbidden to utilize the tape; severe penalties for unauthorized use. A blizzard of KGB references followed, after which there was a pause before the material Vasily was waiting to hear: "Sorin Project remote activation Alpha One, four-second-preparation countdown begins now, *i razz i dva i tri i—*"

There was no *four*. In its place Vasily heard a voice say in English: "I see the President and he's been bad."

It wasn't the schoolboy phrase that stunned him, but the voice. His own voice. *But I never said that.* And then he realized what they had done—what *she* had done, the psychiatrist, Marina Sorin. From among the hundreds of words and phrases they had asked him to record so long ago she had constructed this phrase. Not for the boy's training, as she had led him to believe, but to make the activation code itself.

Vasily played it again. "I see the President and he's been bad."

He began to smile. This was what he had risked his life to steal? His own voice? He began to laugh, surprising the tourists who looked up from their guidebooks and smiled tentatively. I could have picked up the phone and called him myself, Vasily thought. A new wave of laughter brought tears to his eyes. The activation signal. His own voice.

CHAPTER

4

Unlike the FBI's imposing Hoover Building or the CIA's spacious campuslike complex in Virginia, the Secret Service headquarters is located just a few blocks from the White House in downtown Washington at 1800 G Street. It is a nondescript ten-story concrete building whose architecture suggests tax accountants and elevator maintenance companies. There are no statues in the lobby or bronze stars representing agents killed in the line of duty, and the uniformed doorman who perched on a stool behind a podium usually had a paperback novel flattened beneath his forearm. This was headquarters, a land of quiet corridors and calculated career moves, which Bill Sullivan had successfully avoided for fifteen years. He was here today only at Roy Patchin's request. The ultimate insider wanted to talk to the ultimate outsider and Bill had no idea why.

Bill and Roy Patchin shared a checkered history. They had

both transferred to the University of Maryland from other schools, Bill to begin his sophomore year, Roy his junior. It was while rooming together that Bill's determination to join the Secret Service had rubbed off on Roy, but for different reasons. While Bill relished the role of the guardian, Roy found fertile ground for the kind of political maneuvering in which he excelled.

The elevator let him off on the eighth floor. From behind a bullet-proof glass booth a crewcut guard with bulging ears nodded brusquely and buzzed Bill through a metal door into a long hallway whose dark blue rug and gray walls reflected efficient no-nonsense professionalism. Roy's secretary, a beautiful African-American with a swan neck and dazzling smile, ushered him into an office meant to impress. Roy had designed and funded it himself—the two words were invariably linked—in an amalgamated Santa Fe and Bauhaus style that affirmed the expectations of its occupant.

"That's new," Roy said, pointing to a cowhide rug. "You recognize it?"

"A dead cow."

"*That.* The brand. Here." His finger jabbed downward. "Double R Bar—it's a famous ranch in Arizona."

Roy had an Easterner's fascination with the American West. He spent his vacations on dude ranches in Montana and for weeks after his return referred to Washington as "back East." Roy was the youngest deputy director in the Service's history and conscious of it. He had a round face with a Boy Scout smile and neat, lifeless hair. His custom-fitted blue shirt had gray and maroon stripes so thin and well-harmonized they seemed to hover above the fabric. He motioned Bill to one of two matching leather chairs and took the other himself. After a few moments of small talk Roy said, "I want to offer you a new job. State Department Liaison. You'd be right down the hall working with Jim Lowry."

"Doing what? Running visa applications for senators?"

"There's more to it than that. You'd go up a grade, get a raise."

"No, thanks."

Roy frowned. "It's not the comparison thing, is it? You don't want to work for a guy who shared the same TV and toilet paper in college? Because I'd hate to think your career was stymied at my expense."

Bill remembered his amusement the first time he watched Roy spread a newspaper before cutting his toenails. "I don't think it's jealousy, Roy. I really don't."

"You're getting a little old for the Protective Detail, Bill. It's not healthy."

"I can still pass the physical."

"So can my dog. I'm talking about your mental health. Most guys burn out after two tours on Protective. You've applied for one waiver after another."

"And you've approved them."

"Not this time." He handed Bill a familiar form, the waiver request he had submitted last month. What wasn't familiar was the decision. Denied. "Sorry," Roy was saying. "New policy, nobody takes more than two tours on Protective without a rotation."

"Why?"

"I told you—new policy."

"Cut the shit, Roy. You and the director make the policy. Why?" He was surprised at his own vehemence and the whisper of panic that the thought of giving up Protective aroused.

Roy stiffened. "Birnbaum did a follow-up study, says it's not healthy."

Stuart Birnbaum was director of counseling and family services. A psychiatrist. Bill felt a familiar distaste. "You talked to Birnbaum about me?"

"Not just you, everybody. All part of the career evaluation program we did a few months ago. Birnbaum says adrenaline addiction is—what did he say?—a familiar pathology for those working Protective. He thinks we have to protect you guys from yourselves."

The phone rang. "Shit," Roy said, "I told Jeannie no calls." He yanked the phone to his ear. "What?" As he listened, his expression grew somber. "Where?" He glanced at Bill. "Get a blue and white at the entrance. Right now." He replaced the phone. "It's your boy, he's at the hospital."

"Matt?"

"Skateboard accident. They couldn't find Claire."

Bill was on his feet. "How bad?"

"He was unconscious when he arrived at Fairfax Memorial. I've got a siren coming to the entrance if you . . ."

Bill didn't hear the rest. He was already out the door.

The KGB. That was how most people still referred to the ever-changing Russian Intelligence Service. That was how Major Gennadi Khiza thought of himself—a KGB man—as he sat in his command car and stared through binoculars at the window to the apartment.

"I don't like it." He handed the glasses to his assistant. "She should have signaled by now."

Khiza was a short, wiry man with flat nose and cleft chin. His almond eyes hinted at a Mongol heritage, which was a drawback in the intelligence service but one which he had overcome with a blend of tenacity and ruthless efficiency. The tendons on his neck were naturally prominent, lending an impression of repressed anger that he did nothing to dispel. A short man needed his compensations.

Last night during a top-secret briefing held at the KGB's spacious new headquarters in the suburb of Yasenevo, Khiza had become one of five people to know the details of the Sorin Project. Its scope and daring left him awestruck. For thirteen years every American president had walked with death at his side, death available to any Soviet leader who found himself locked in a confrontation with the enemy where success was imperative and no other solution available.

"Still nothing," his assistant reported. Khiza glanced at his watch, a Seiko chronograph he had bought in Prague. Ten minutes since the sex-starved traitor Gavrila Roday had entered the building to meet her lover. Something was definitely wrong. Khiza raised the walkie-talkie. "All units, this is Goalie. The code is red. Repeat: code red."

Police stampeded the building. There were curses when they discovered the elevators were out of order, then a thunder of boots in the stairway. A little boy playing with an orange rubber ball lost it as his mother pulled him to safety. One passing policeman kicked the ball aside, then another, as it bounced downstairs. By the time Khiza reached the apartment the men had taken positions on either side of the door, their Kalishnikov rifles at the ready. Khiza reached tentatively for the doorknob and twisted. Not locked. Drawing his pistol, he glanced at his team to make certain they were ready. Down the hall a baby cried. Khiza took a deep breath and nodded. The floor shook as police rushed the room and flattened themselves against the walls. Gavrila sat on the floor, forearms resting on her knees, an envelope dangling from her fingers.

"Where is he?" Khiza demanded. "Where is Amenov?"

She shook her head slowly, the envelope slipped to the floor. Khiza nodded toward the bathroom and one of the policemen invaded it noisily, then returned. "Empty."

He crouched beside Gavrila, whose gaze remained fixed on the far wall. "You tricked us," he said harshly. "You knew he had gone."

Her lips twisted and she laughed soundlessly. The pain was real, Khiza decided. He picked up the envelope from between her feet. Inside were two items: a card that said, *Save yourself,* and a five-kopeck coin, the traditional subway fare. The woman's laughter had turned to something else; Gavrila Roday was crying.

Khiza found a phone in a neighboring apartment. He ordered the mother and her three children into the hallway while he made his call. The stench of unwashed diapers made his stomach churn. Hurry up, he thought as he waited for his connection. The familiar voice answered with only a phone number.

"It's me," Khiza replied. "The nest is empty."

"The activation tape?"

"Gone."

"You checked everywhere? It looks like a reel of film."

"I know what it looks like. We'll tear the place apart but don't expect anything. He stole it for a reason and he disappeared for a reason. Either he's going to sell it to *them* or he's going to use it."

They both understood that *them* referred to the Americans,

once their enemy but now a reluctant source of economic support. But the Americans retained enough military might to destroy the Russian Republic should the provocation become grave enough.

"Did you release the Hawk?" Khiza asked.

"Not yet but—"

"You waited? Why?"

"In case you caught our bird in the nest."

And while you delayed, Khiza thought angrily, Amenov's trail has grown colder. "Release him. Now."

"It may be too late . . ."

"Then I hope you like the taste of shit, because if Sullivan is activated you can kiss your ass goodbye."

He hung up and stood for a moment to regain his composure. Beneath his tough talk Khiza was afraid. It would not be shit but bullets they would be eating if the American President died.

Bill didn't wait for a Secret Service escort, but drove directly to Fairfax Memorial Hospital. All his life he had trained to avoid tragedy; he knew how to read a crowd for threat, how to scan the terrain with a killer's eye, how to form a human chain around the President, how to work a wounded man through a panicked crowd, how to apply enough first aid to keep most victims alive for the first ten minutes. Now none of it mattered. His vulnerability was that of all parents to the accidents of their children.

He arrived at the hospital, where a half-witted receptionist in a green sweater directed him down the hallway to the Emergency Room. His footsteps on the linoleum floor seemed to increase tempo of their own volition until he found himself jogging. Did every hospital take up a city block?

At the Emergency entrance a crowd of people speaking Spanish were gathered at the admissions desk. A large woman, eyes closed, lay on a gurney, whispering, "I'm all right, I'm all right." The nurse behind the desk was trying to explain how to fill out the admission forms. Without planning it, Bill found himself waving his identification badge over the heads of the crowd.

"Special Agent Sullivan, Secret Service." All eyes turned toward him. "You have a boy, Matthew Sullivan. Where is he?"

She gave him the room number and directions.

"Bill!"

Claire was hurrying toward him, long cotton skirt trailing behind her, eyes grave with concern. "Is he all right?"

"I don't know. Where's Megan?"

"Barb Fowler is watching her. We were shopping and when we got home . . ."

They took the elevator to the third floor and waited impatiently until Dr. Kasarian appeared. He looked Arabic and far too young to be a doctor, and Bill was filled with misgivings.

"He'll be all right," Kasarian reassured them. "Hit his head and suffered a concussion. We stitched the wound and took X rays of his skull and vertebra."

"Is he paralyzed?"

"No, no, nothing like that.

"Then why the X rays?"

"To insure there's no internal bleeding or fractures. It's standard procedure."

Matt was awake. He lay in bed, his head swathed in bandages, but when he saw his parents a look of relief spread across his face. Claire knelt and hugged him.

"Ow, Mom . . ."

"Did I hurt you?"

"It's okay." His eyes flicked to Bill. "Sorry, Dad."

"What happened?"

"The guys were running Mongo and I didn't want to do it but they kept ragging me. I mean really bad, like, 'His dad's got a gun but he's afraid to make the run' and stuff like that. So I was—"

"Wait a minute. Who's Mongo?"

Claire said, "The hill at the end of the lake, that's what the kids call it."

"Mongo Mountain," Matt corrected. "Anyway, I said 'No way' so Ron Lattimore started collecting bets until there was like twenty-three dollars that I couldn't make it. But I almost did it, only I hit this stone or something and like totally wiped out. I think I broke my board."

Claire pressed his hand. "That doesn't matter, nothing matters as long as you're all right."

Matt grinned sheepishly. "That's good because I never turned in my makeup assignment for math class."

Bill glanced at his watch; it was four-forty-five. "I'll be right back," he whispered to Claire.

There was a public phone near the nursing station. He called Roy and, after reporting Matt's condition, said, "What we were talking about earlier? It's a deal. I'll take State Department liaison."

"Hell, I already gave it to Doug Bell." His voice brightened. "Just kidding. Welcome back from the dark-glasses brigade. I'll tell Personnel to get the paperwork going. And when it's official we'll get together and celebrate, the four of us, you me, Nancy and Claire."

It was the right decision, but Bill had to fight a rising anxiety. The truth was that he could conceive of no other job. As a boy he had read a book about the Secret Service the same year that President John Kennedy was assassinated. He remembered his mother crying and his father staring hollow-eyed at the television as the horse-drawn casket moved slowly through the streets of Washington. Most of all he remembered little John-John, the President's son, bravely saluting his fallen father. At that moment he experienced a huge outflowing of sympathy and a fierce desire to protect the innocent. The Secret Service was not a job but a calling, the dream that sustained him in the aftermath of his parents' death, the goal that brought him to Washington: the heroic vision of a nameless man in dark glasses, the guardian who stood ready to sacrifice his life for the public good. And now it was over.

Not yet. The words rose from his subconscious like bubbles but they ran together and sounded more like *nuhyet*. But if not now, when? Protective Detail was a young man's game. He couldn't expect to work the White House until he retired.

"Don't look so sad." Doctor Kasarian was at his side. "The X rays show no damage."

They returned to Matt's bedside. It never occurred to Bill that the words that had popped into his mind a moment before weren't two words at all but a single word he heard correctly but simply didn't recognize. *Nyet.*

CHAPTER

5

Juho Ryti sat relaxed but Ramrod straight, eyes closed, slowly flexing his fingers to ward off the stiffness that he knew was an early indication of arthritis. Juho didn't know that his code name was Hawk nor did he care. He had never much liked Russians and liked them less now that the ruble was worthless. That was why, for this job, he insisted on payment in Swiss francs. His Russian control officer, Yuri Ulovsky, had not bothered to argue the matter, and Juho was sorry now he hadn't asked a higher figure. The Russians used him rarely, but when they did he knew it was a matter of international consequence, a matter they could not afford to be identified with should the assassination fail.

"Hot towel?"

Juho opened his eyes. A flight attendant leaned across the seat holding a towel between two tongs.

"Merci," he said with only a slight trace of an accent to betray his origin. Juho was a native of Finland and looked like the outdoorsman he was. His cropped white hair bristled like a porcupine's and his face had the expressionless quality of one who lived alone. There was a calm directness about him that inspired confidence in strangers, but unease in those who knew him better. It was a confidence born of physical prowess and little purpose, a view of life formed by the vast forests where silent snows covered the land much of the year and life was won day by day against odds that eventually would triumph.

Juho had grown up at Lake Kemijarvi, where his parents owned a hunting and fishing lodge. Once each fall a group of KGB officials stayed for a week to hunt moose. A burst of activity always preceded their arrival—special phone lines installed, stocks of vodka and expensive food laid in, the arrival of a private cook. Whether they numbered two people or twenty, the Russians insisted on taking over the entire camp. They never paid tips and never hired his father or Juho as a guide, so Juho amused himself by following them and leaving false trails. One year he witnessed an execution that determined his life's work.

It happened the summer he was thirteen. Two of the KGB men had gone hunting. The leader, Grishenko, was a man with V-shaped eyebrows who smoked foul-smelling cigars that drove the dogs to the far side of the room. Prozorov was gregarious and friendly and never without a joke or a bottle of vodka. Juho followed them along a ridge above the boulder-strewn river and saw Grishenko drop his rifle, apparently by accident. He couldn't hear the conversation that followed, but it looked as if Grishenko was concerned that the front sight was damaged. He gave it to Prozorov to inspect and received the other man's rifle in return. Without hesitation Grishenko moved the barrel of Prozorov's rifle beneath his comrade's chin and blew his head apart. Before the sharp report reached Juho he saw the KGB man fall. He was less shocked than struck by the similarity between a man's death and that of a deer, bodies collapsing as if the bones turned to water, leaving only a shapeless mass of flesh on the earth.

Juho slipped away and was back at the lodge when

Grishenko arrived with Prozorov's body and a sad story of how they had been crossing the river when Prozorov slipped on a rock and foolishly tried to use his rifle in an attempt to regain his balance. Whether the other KGB men believed this or not, none contradicted Grishenko.

Juho said nothing for a year, but thought a great deal about what he had seen. That winter he watched his parents grow more heavily in debt to keep the lodge operating and realized that there would come a day when the banks would own the lodge outright. When the KGB group returned the following year, Juho sought out Grishenko and told him what he had seen. The Russian grew ominously quiet, but Juho reassured him he had told no one and never would.

"Unless what?" Grishenko said suspiciously. "You don't tell me this unless you want something."

"A job. The next time you need it done, use me."

Grishenko stared for a long moment at the fourteen-year-old boy, then exploded in laughter. When he realized Juho was serious, he said, "How many languages do you speak besides Finnish?"

"Swedish and Russian."

"Learn German and English, then ask me again."

It was the beginning of a sporadic but lucrative relationship with the KGB. The Soviets had their own people for run-of-the-mill assassinations, but they preferred Juho for politically sensitive or particularly difficult assignments. Over the years he had made a lot of money, but now it was time to leave the business. These days there were too many newcomers crowding the field—wild-eyed Arabs, Italian terrorists, South American revolutionaries—amateurs whose methods were sloppy and indiscriminate, men who had never hunted meat for the table and who wouldn't last a week in the wilderness. Urban killers, children with machine guns who equated noise with power and machine guns with marksmanship.

Juho studied the picture of his quarry. Once they landed in Washington he would have to pick up the trail himself. He would have to track and find the target, then analyze the best way to ambush him. Juho stared at the picture and wondered for a moment what this man had done that his death was worth so much. Then he put the speculation aside and closed his eyes. He had only begun the hunt for Bill Sullivan and already he was tired.

It was Sunday afternoon. Lynwood Village was holding its annual Fall Festival at the mouth of a man-made lake around which the community had been built. Tents and booths and food stands spilled across a grassy hill, and a half dozen kites soared flashing in the sun above the gathering. Bill and Claire had come with the kids, their first outing since Matt returned from the hospital. They stood on a small pier beside a flotilla of paddle-wheel boats. As Claire took pictures of them, Bill helped the children into life jackets.

"I'm driving," Matt said.

"We have to share," Megan said.

"I'm in the left seat."

"Matt, it's not like a car, you don't have a steering wheel . . ."

As usual, Megan was right. The boat was nothing more than two pontoons spanned by a benchlike seat with foot pedals that operated a paddle wheel at the stern. Bill said, "You both can paddle."

"But I get to steer," Matt insisted, and the argument began anew. Bill glanced at Claire, who read his expression and with her free hand made the sign for *kids*. Bill signed back *crazy*. Matt caught the gesture. "What are you saying?"

"Nothing."

"They're talking about us," he told Megan, who instantly joined her brother in clamoring to know what their parents were saying. Bill nudged the boat into the water. "Anchor's aweigh."

"Daddy!"

Matt began paddling, and Ginger, their five-month-old Irish Setter, splashed along the shoreline, barking excitedly. The kids called her, and Ginger began swimming after them.

"Don't—" Claire began, then shook her head. "Poor dog."

She pulled a telephoto lens from the hunting vest and took a few more pictures. Photography had always been her passion, a private endeavor that didn't burden her with the responsibility she had known as a child when she was her mother's voice in the hearing world. Claire was the last of four children, twelve years younger than her closest sister. The family joke was that whenever Mom wanted a new voice she had another baby.

Claire looked for Bill and saw him standing motionless by a picnic table. His vacant expression was familiar and frightening—familiar because it had long been part of his personality and frightening because it was becoming more frequent. Last week she watched for seven full minutes while he stood on the small footbridge over the lake and moved not a muscle.

Lapses. That was Claire's name for them. Moments of hibernation when Bill seemed aware of his environment yet apart from it. It had been a powerful attraction when they first met, the philosopher's soul in the warrior's heart. She treated them as sacred moments and waited for him to share his thoughts. When he never did, she grew bold enough to interrupt one day. "What are you thinking?"

"I'm not thinking."

The response was neither a joke nor a way of deflecting her question. He meant it. More recently there was a half second each morning when he looked at her with his eyes momentarily blank, reflecting neither recognition nor rejection, like a computer screen just turned on. She went to him and took his hand. "You don't want to do it, do you?"

"What?" As usual, his transition to the present moment was imperceptible, apparent only to Claire.

"The move to Liaison. You keep getting that faraway look in your eye, like working headquarters is the death chamber."

He smiled. "You think you're so smart."

"I know you. All but this." She held a slight gap between her thumb and forefinger.

"What's that?"

"The part you don't let me see."

"If you don't see it, I don't have it."

"Maybe you just don't see it either."

Megan came running up, her feet muddy. "Can I get a hot dog?"

"Eat some of these," Claire said, lifting a bunch of grapes from a canvas bag.

Megan gave her an exasperated look. "Mom . . ."

"Now there's a picture." Bill indicated the lake, where Ginger sat like a king beside Matt, the slow flip-flop of the paddles tossing spray rhythmically into the air behind them. Claire grabbed her Nikon and went to the shore. Megan tapped Bill on the shoulder. "Daddy, can I have a kiss?" Her lips were distended and her words awkward.

"What have you got in your mouth?"

Fighting a grin she said, "I want a kiss."

"What have you got there?" Bill tickled her and with a burst of laughter a grape popped out and landed on the lawn. Imitating her mother's voice Megan wagged a finger and said, "Don't waste the earth's bounty, Daddy."

"Come here, Sugarbear."

She danced from his reach. "Try to get me."

Claire would chase her, Bill knew, but he had never been comfortable acting the child himself. It was a reserve he regretted when he saw other fathers wrestling and giving piggyback rides and making silly answers to serious questions.

"Come on, Daddy, get me."

"Too many people."

She spotted a nearby game booth and grabbed his hand. "Let's play the ring toss."

"Have you still got some money?"

"Of course. Come on."

Bill walked slowly, enjoying the impetuous tug of his daughter's small hand, her fingernails decorated with sequins. The ring-toss booth was an island of wood posts separated by five feet from the wood counter that surrounded it. A fat girl with a tentlike blouse and pink spandex tights moved back and forth inside the counter collecting money for wood rings whose diameter was barely large enough to accommodate a post. "Put a ring on the post, go home with the most, five tries a dollar."

Megan spent two dollars without result. When she had one ring left she insisted Bill try it. He leaned across the counter, emptied his mind of distractions and sent the ring spinning. It caught one corner, gyrated briefly, then settled over the post. "See Daddy," Megan cried triumphantly. "You always win."

"Another winner," the fat girl shouted with mechanical enthusiasm. As she reached to remove their ring, another one plunked down on top of it. A tall man with gray hair smiled at them from an adjacent counter. "Didn't mean to land on top of you."

"Double winners," the girl called as she flipped both rings free with a practiced motion. "Choice of prizes. You folks were first."

"You choose, Megan."

"I want the dolphin."

The operator pulled a stuffed dolphin out of an ocean of cheap prizes and called to the stranger, "You, sir?"

"Let me have the squirt gun."

She held both prizes like trophies and called out, "A dolphin for the little girl, a squirt gun for Daddy. A prize for every size, five throws for a dollar."

She thrust the dolphin with its lopsided eyes into Megan's hands then waddled across the booth to deliver the squirt gun.

"Do you have water?" asked the winner.

"Got a whole lake right down there."

The tall man raised the gun to eye level and pointed it at her. "But do *you* have any water?"

"Not here." She stepped out of the way and began retrieving rings. The gun swung slowly until the barrel pointed across the booth at the back of Bill's head. He was looking at the lake, where Matt was silhouetted by silver water reflecting a descending sun. When Megan saw the stranger he smiled and lowered the gun until it pointed at her. She hesitated before she made a pistol of her fingers and pointed back at him. The man grimaced in mock pain and clutched his heart. Bill, still looking away, let his hand fall absently to his daughter's shoulders. "Let's go see Mom."

Walking to the lake Megan glanced back over her shoulder, but Juho Ryti had disappeared.

CHAPTER

6

As Bill wired himself for work Monday morning he was aware that this was his last week on the Protective Detail. He stood in the bedroom and ran one wire from the Motorola radio on his belt down his sleeve to the transmitter strapped to his wrist, and another wire beneath his collar to the custom-molded receiver that would tuck neatly into his outer ear. Next came the shoulder holster with his Smith & Wesson hammerless revolver. He put on his coat and checked his appearance in the dresser mirror.

You won't need the gun working Liaison, he reminded himself. And what about the rest of the equipment neatly tucked in the aluminum briefcase he was required to have available at all times: handcuffs, tear-gas canister, passport, two speed-loaders, a flashlight, a book of government transportation requests good for flights on any major airline in the world, an extra set of handcuffs, aviator's sunglasses, an extra pair of wing-tip shoes with rubber nonslip soles, the identification pin providing access to Location Thunder Mountain, the underground bomb shelter in Virginia where the President would be sent in the event of an atomic attack. How much of this would he turn in when he left Protective for Liaison? He had always felt a certain disdain for the headquarters types in their temperature-controlled cubicles, and now that he was scheduled to join them he felt an undertow of resistance.

The phone rang. He answered it, holding the phone in place with his raised shoulder. "Sullivan residence."

A man's voice, slow and distinct: "I see the President and he's been bad."

Bill had a fleeting impression of exhilaration and alarm, as if he opened the closet door and found the Grand Canyon or a night sky free of familiar constellations. The phone went dead. A tingling sensation worked its way inward from his hands and feet, then disappeared, leaving him as secure and clearheaded as he had ever felt in his life. The bathroom door opened and Claire's face appeared in a cloud of escaping steam. "Who is it?"

Bill replaced the phone. "A crank call."

"Dirty words?"

"Silly kids."

She made a face. "Boring."

Bill went downstairs. Collecting the paper, brewing coffee, eating breakfast with the kids—everything he did was methodical and unhurried. He usually left the house before Claire, who taught a class in sign language at the high school three days a week, but today he was in no hurry. They left together, Claire in the Toyota minivan, Bill driving the Mustang. There was a traffic delay on the Roosevelt Bridge but he felt no anxiety or impatience. In the Mustang's polished hood he watched the reflection of a Boeing 737 on its approach to National Airport. He was suffused with a quiet euphoria that didn't desert him even when he scraped a pillar in the parking garage, bending the sideview mirror on the passenger door. Normally even a scratch concerned him, but this morning he didn't even take the time to inspect the damage.

He walked to the White House, where, across the street in Lafayette Square, the usual crowd of protesters and lost souls were climbing out of their sleeping bags and cardboard boxes to take up their protest signs. At the East Gate he flashed his I.D. at Lurene, the Uniformed Division officer, who waved him past with a smile of recognition. He felt her eyes follow him and on an impulse turned to look. She was talking to a man in a suit, paying no attention to Bill. The incident amused him. Why do I feel so good this morning?

The basement level of the White House contained the working offices of various staff and household personnel. There was a restaurant, barbershop, travel office and the Secret Service command post in room W-16. Bill passed his card key through a sensinometer and the lock clicked open. A bank of video screens lined the far wall, each trained on a different area of the White House, from basement to rooftop, like a photo montage. Agents arriving for the morning shift were checking their equipment and getting their duty assignments. Bill returned greetings, fitted his earpiece and adjusted the squelch on his radio, which linked him to his fellow agents like an electronic arterial system of some huge animal.

Shift Leader Jimmy Rodriguez stood up from his desk, touched his hair absently, then called out, "Okay, people, listen up. Today's schedule: the Man will be at the House until one o'clock, then will attend a luncheon at the Mayflower Hotel. Special Agent Cookson is advancing the luncheon and you'll receive assignments from him."

He glanced at his notes for the previous day's "lookouts," the Service's term for people considered a threat to the President. "A package for the President arrived yesterday from some limpdick named Jim Wilson, probably an alias. Said package contained a dog turd between two pieces of rye bread and a dinner invitation that was hostile in tone and content."

"Chihuahua or Great Dane?" someone whispered.

Rodriguez ignored it. "Second incident occurred twenty-three hundred hours last night when one Rowena Marshall showed up at the East Gate with a portable heat lamp seeking to warn the President about global warming. Marshall was committed to St. Elizabeth's for observation. She'll be there during the luncheon but there may be others of her group putting in an appearance. Watch for emblems like this." He displayed a button showing an orange earth melting. "We'll be using Tango frequency today. Okay, let's make the posts."

Bill took the stairs to the Oval Office. Throughout the day he would rotate to different posts where he would stand with arms at his sides or crossed or behind his back, shifting from one foot to the other while White House staffers, congressmen, senators, military officers, cabinet members, and political persuaders of every stripe rushed past, whispering fiercely and clutching briefcases whose combination locks sprang free at the correct rotation of a child's birthday or a wedding anniversary. None of them would speak to Bill except to ask directions to the nearest restroom.

Bill relieved Special Agent Tim Dwyer, a burr-headed young man who told him that the Chief of Staff had joined the President a few minutes ago. Bill nodded and raised his radio. "Sullivan relieving Dwyer on post five."

The information was redundant, since Command could see them on a video monitor. Bill stared at the door to the Oval Office. He had seen it a thousand times before, but this morning every detail stood out: the way the light crept through the space beneath the door, his own ballooned reflection in the brass doorknob, the incongruous plaque *Thank You for Not Smoking*. He felt both distant and incredibly attuned to the smallest detail of his environment. It was a feeling that should have alerted him that something was wrong, but he felt fine. Still feeling fine and without even thinking about it he opened the door to the Oval Office.

The two men were not at the desk, but sat across from each other near the empty fireplace. Bill recognized Chief of Staff Edgarton, but the other man was a stranger. Not the President, but an impostor with a stack of papers on his lap. Both of them looked up and the man who should have been President said, "What is it, Bill?"

The impostor knew his name. Odd, Bill thought as he drew his gun. Something wrong now. He winced as his head exploded in pain. Shoot the—arrest the impostor, no, *kill* the impostor, you must—thoughts, intentions, urges all burst like fireworks in different directions. A blinding headache, a white light—

The Chief of Staff jumped up, overturning his chair. "What the hell—"

The band of pressure against Bill's temples snapped. Clarity returned and he realized with a shock the stranger was the President. And the gun—in his hand, the barrel pointed at the President's feet. He thrust it quickly back into its holster. "I'm sorry, sir."

Chief of Staff Edgarton, red in the face, was stuttering curses. The President hadn't moved, but his eyes were fixed on Bill. With deliberate calm he said, "What seems to be the problem?"

Bill's mind was reeling. A moment ago everything felt predictable, inevitable, and now the world had splintered into a kaleidoscope of irreconcilable events. "I thought I heard . . . something."

The voice in his earpiece said, "Sullivan, where are you?"

His head cleared. He had to say something, had to make sense out of what happened, but there was no sense. The truth was alien, an enemy that would jeopardize his career and destroy him. *I need an excuse, something to tell them until I have time to think.* He raised the microphone to his lips. "Oval office. We have an incident. Jimmy?"

Rodriguez sounded tense. "On my way."

Bill turned to the two men. "I thought I heard breaking glass. The window."

He indicated the curved windows that opened onto the colonnade overlooking the White House lawn. In the distance a uniformed agent with an Uzi was already jogging toward them. The Chief of Staff said angrily, "There's no broken glass."

"I realize that. I made a mistake." He turned to the President. "I'm sorry, sir."

As he left the room he heard Edgarton say to the President in disbelief, "A mistake?"

Bill shut the door and took a deep breath. He could hear the queries and comments on the command network, agents asking what the false alarm was all about. Broken glass, Bill thought as Rodriguez rounded the corner. Broken glass.

CHAPTER 7

After making the phone call Vasily Amenov was too filled with anticipation to sit still. He left his London hotel and walked the streets, his mind alive with images of the events he had put in motion. Where was Sullivan now? In his car? Or at the White House with the President's blood already an angry spray on the wall? Or dead himself, killed in the attempt, eyes vacant, his body surrounded by shouting, screaming people.

Vasily found himself walking up Earl's Court Road, the path of betrayal, the same route Yelena took the day the world changed forever. The crowds became thick around the High Street Kensington Underground, but Vasily's eyes sought the rooftop of Derry and Tom's department store. The building was still there, but now it was occupied by a Marks & Spencer and a number of smaller shops. Years ago there had been a garden on the roof, a serene island of swaying trees, gurgling streams and pathways that meandered through an intricate and lush landscape far removed from the bustle of the streets below. It was still there, he discovered, open to the public through a door on Derry Street.

The rooftop restaurant was closed for renovation and the gardens were deserted. This was where he had taken Yelena for dinner on their wedding anniversary. "Our secret place," they called it. Later they met here for lunch. Because the restaurant was so expensive. Yelena brought sandwiches in the baby carriage and they ate in the gardens. He remembered the time when Mischa, two years old, fell into a pond when the cry of a peacock scared him. Good memories made bitter by betrayal.

Vasily crossed over the footbridge and wandered among the trees, ponds and thick foliage that hid the fifteen-foot-high walls. The peacocks were gone, but two flamingos stood single-footed and motionless in the pond, and ducks dozing in the middle of a flagstone path moved reluctantly at his approach. At the end of the Spanish garden Vasily found a narrow arched door set into the wall, its rusty padlock hanging open.

He entered and climbed a circular stairway to a small observation platform overlooking Kensington Park. From here he could see the Russian embassy, its roof bristling with antennas, one of the huge mansions bordering the park.

Did you stand here? he wondered. Were your feet once where mine are now? While I was working in the embassy was your lover kissing you and his hands adoring your body? Were his pants unzipped? Did he come into your hand? Did it add zest to your betrayal to meet at a place special to us? Or did you think you were safe because I had taken Mischa to visit his grandparents in the Soviet Union while you stayed to dance the last five performances of *Romeo and Juliet?*

He had been suspicious by then, of course. He returned secretly to London and followed Yelena. He hadn't planned to kill anyone. He had no plan at all, still hoping until the last moment when he saw them kiss that it wasn't true. Perhaps if they hadn't met in this special place or if the cricket players hadn't arrived—a half dozen young men in white, one carrying a bat that had been autographed by his teammates—perhaps no one would have died. He did not recall picking up the bat, but he remembered how the lovers had chosen a secluded bench and hadn't seen him until the last moment. Jeremy Lawrence had his back to Vasily. Yelena didn't see him until the bat was already raised high and Vasily had death in his eye. Without yelling or crying a warning she leaped back—a dancer's reaction, keep your body out of harm's way. Lawrence was unaware when he turned—a look of polite curiosity, then a bloody pulp.

A peacock had screeched, or maybe it was Yelena. Vasily could recall little after that. He read the accounts later, of course, but the next thing he remembered clearly was sitting at his desk at the embassy, a growing crowd outside his door peering in at him, at the bloody stick dangling from his hand. Rather than let a KGB man fall into the hands of the police they had gotten him quickly and quietly out of the country. It didn't matter. Everything had ended in the secret garden.

Footsteps on the path below. A man in coveralls stared up at him. "Got to come down, mate. Mortar's cracking up there, it's off-limits to the public."

Vasily descended the spiral steps. "A man once died up here."

The workman nodded somberly. "He fell, did he?"

"No, he went home. But he was never alive after he left here."

Vasily returned to the hotel, where he waited for the BBC to bring him news of catastrophe in America.

"Now you're scaring me," Claire said. She stood in the kitchen, her back against the counter, the fresh dough she was kneading temporarily forgotten. "What do you mean a trance?"

"That's what it felt like. How did I seem to you?"

Claire's fingers were sticky, so she brushed her hair back with her wrist. "You seemed quiet, maybe. And you were smiling, just a little, like you were in a good mood."

"Before or after the phone call?"

"What phone—oh, the crank call?"

"*I see the President,* that's what he said."

"You think that's why you did it? Because somebody said something silly?"

"I don't know, but everything after that phone call felt odd."

"You weren't . . ."

"What?"

She turned to the sink and began rinsing her hands. "What did Rodriguez say about the phone?"

"I didn't tell him."

"But if you think it's related . . ."

"I think it's coincidence. What were you going to say?"

She dried her hands and turned to face him. "Have you been drinking?"

"You think I'm sneaking martinis on the side?"

"I didn't say that."

"I am not my father, Claire."

They were silent. Bill's father had been an alcoholic. Until he joined Alcoholics Anonymous Dan Sullivan would suffer black-outs and wake up in cheap hotels or park benches in places like Wichita or Denver with no memory of how he arrived. It was a legacy that haunted Bill, whose intolerance to alcohol was even more severe than his father's.

"I'm sorry," Claire said.

"I made you a promise," he said stiffly.

"It's the only time I've known you to do something you can't explain."

She was talking about their wedding, the first one, the wedding that never was. Bill had missed it. He had broken his rule and went drinking the night before the wedding. A bachelor party Roy and some friends held for him. Rather than dampen their spirits, Bill nursed a beer until a dozen sips became a swallow, a dozen swallows and it was time for another mug. By the time they dropped him off at his apartment on DuPont Circle, his hands were numb and he could barely see. The last thing he remembered was tumbling headfirst onto his couch.

The wedding was scheduled for one-thirty Saturday after-noon. Bill woke up with a blinding headache and a ringing in his ears that was all too real. He was sleeping in the bell tower of an Episcopal Church in Hinton, West Virginia, hundreds of miles from Washington. He stumbled down circular stairs where the surprised pastor confirmed the awful truth: Saturday had disappeared and it was Sunday morning. Bill had missed his wedding, missed an entire day out of his life.

The car had been found out of gas and abandoned in a state park near Hinton, and Bill never mentioned to anyone what he discovered when he returned to his apartment: someone had torn apart all photographs of him, including those with Claire. Although the door was unlocked, Bill didn't believe anyone had broken into the apartment. The only other explanation—that he had done it himself—was too uncomfortable to contemplate. So he sentenced the vandalism to the limbo of the unknown and blamed his father, who had suffered the same blackouts and bizarre behavior before he joined Alcoholics Anonymous. Two months later he and Claire wed in a civil ceremony. She did not wear her wedding dress.

"All right," Claire said matter-of-factly. "You weren't drinking and you heard a window smash so—"

"No window. No smash."

"But you said—"

"That's what I told them. That's not what I heard."

"What did you hear?"

"Nothing."

"Then why did you leave the post?"

"That's what I'm trying to tell you. There was no reason to leave, no reason to open that door, but that's what I did. And when I saw the President, I thought he was a stranger, an impostor. An enemy, *that's* what I saw. That's why I drew the gun."

"You were going to shoot him?"

"I don't know. Dad went crazy. Maybe it runs in the family."

"When he was drinking, that's different."

"I'm glad you're sure."

"I am sure." She took him by the shoulders and stared up at him. "You remind me of the quarry where we used to swim when we were kids. The water was so still you could toss a rock into it and watch it turn color as it sank, a deeper and darker green until right before it disappeared it was almost black. That's you. There's always been something deep in you I can't see, but I know it's pure and clear down there. It's part of who you are, part of what makes you strong. Not crazy. You would no more shoot the President than you would me."

The phone rang. It was Roy and he sounded upset. "I just heard what happened. Why didn't you call me?"

"What for? I talked to Rodriguez, we reported it in the log. Craines wants an official memorandum tomorrow morning, I'm doing it tonight."

"Fuck Craines. He'll hang your ass out to dry quicker than candidates kiss babies. I want to see the O.M. before you turn it in. Take the morning off, meet me for lunch at Harbor Place. The restaurant facing the water, the Sequoia."

"I'm on duty tomorrow."

"Not anymore. You're taking a four-day vacation until you take over Liaison next week."

"I didn't request a vacation."

"You can do that tomorrow at lunch. I'll bring a request."

"Wait a minute, what are you saying? I'm off Protective? Why?"

"They confiscate your gun?"

"No."

"Take it out, look down the barrel and pretend you're the President of the United States. One o'clock tomorrow, the Sequoia."

The line went dead. Bill put down the receiver and leaned on it until his fingers ached. Three presidents knew him by his first name, but now, after thirteen years on the Protective Detail, this was how it ended. No recognition, no farewell party, no jokes and no goodbyes, just a log entry, indelible and permanent, to prove Bill Sullivan's last act at the White House was a mistake.

CHAPTER

8

Harbor Place is a complex of shops and restaurants spread along the Potomac River below Georgetown. It is not the usual meeting place for Secret Service personnel, which was probably why Roy had chosen it. Bill arrived early and stood waiting in a patch of sunlight. As always, his eye was drawn to potential risk—the balcony that would make a good assassin's perch, the cracked tile that might trip an unwary pedestrian, the possibility that the boy walking along the retaining wall might fall. Claire joked that he could find a needle in a haystack so long as it was about to puncture someone.

Roy appeared, wearing an overcoat and a plaid driver's cap with a button-down brim. His handshake was firm, his greeting perfunctory. As they entered the Sequoia, Roy said, "I hear this place has good seafood."

"I think you want Tony's."

"What?"

Bill indicated a restaurant across the courtyard whose name was hand-painted in white letters on a piece of driftwood. A clear-eyed waitress in a man's tunic approached. "Lunch, gentlemen?"

"You serve seafood?"

"Yes, sir. Would you like seating indoors or out?"

"Indoors."

"This way." Clutching two menus she started toward a distant table.

"What's the matter, Roy, you don't want to eat outside?"

"It's chilly."

"You mean after yesterday in the Oval Office?"

"Is that what you think?" He waved at the waitress. "Miss? Change of plans. We'd rather sit outside."

She took them to a table on a patio overlooking the Potomac, where heat lamps provided pockets of warmth. After handing her his hat and coat, Roy sat down. "There, I hope you're satisfied."

"You missed your calling, Roy. You should have joined the CIA."

He tapped the table. "Where is it?"

Bill handed him the two-page official memorandum. Roy pulled out his glasses and read it with an intense expression. Occasionally a frown flickered across his features like the shadows of circling seagulls that swept across the table. When he was finished, he looked up pensively. "A window breaking?"

"That's what I heard."

"Ummm."

"Problem?"

"Did it sound metallic? Like wind chimes or something? Because I talked to a friend of mine last night. He's a doctor. He suggested you be checked for tinnitus. You know—ringing in the ears."

Bill picked up his spoon and banged it on the metal table. "What did that sound like to you, Roy? Glass or metal?"

Rather than answer, Roy consulted the memorandum. *"I drew my weapon as I entered the Oval Office."* He glanced up, eyes skeptical. "Edgarton says you pulled the gun *after* you entered. Swears you looked right at the President as you did it."

"What does the President say?"

"He was reading a policy announcement. Door opened, when he looked up you had the gun."

"Which I holstered. You think I wanted to shoot him?"

A look of horror crossed Roy's face. "Christ, no, but remember what happened after your bachelor party . . ."

"You peed on a Rolls-Royce."

"Not that."

"Was it a Bentley?"

Roy frowned. "You know what I'm talking about. You disappeared, you lost an entire day."

"I drove to West Virginia."

"You didn't remember it."

"Did you remember driving home that night?"

"I remember the next day. I was at the church in my tuxedo waiting for you."

"What's the point, Roy?"

"Simple. I covered for you when we joined the Service. You didn't mention the wedding, I didn't mention it, but if it's a chronic behavior pattern I have an obligation to report it."

"Remember Tim Doherty? Standing post outside the Camp David library when he heard all hell break loose and broke a hinge off the door to get inside. Turned out the President overturned a shelf of books trying to reach his cat. It happens."

"Not when there's no bookcase."

They were silent a moment. A seagull strutted nervously and eyed the basket of bread on the table. The waitress returned, her arms dimpled from the chilly air. Roy ordered a seafood salad and glass of white wine. He was alert to Bill's response when she asked him, "Wine for you, too?"

"Pellegrino with a lime."

When she was gone, Roy leaned toward him. "There's something I have to ask—"

"No."

Roy looked as if he'd been slapped. "You didn't let me finish."

"I know what you're going to say and the answer is no, I'm not drinking."

"Did you expect me not to ask?"

"You've got your answer."

Roy blew on his fingers and rubbed his hands together. "You have to understand the way things work at G Street. There are no lone eagles, no cowboys at headquarters. If you're not on somebody's team you're on your way out the door. And you— I've let it be known we're friends, I've advertised my confidence in you. You're an extension of me. Whatever you do reflects on my judgment. You make an enemy of the Chief of Staff, you've made me an enemy. I've got enough battles to fight without putting out brushfires created by my own team."

He was part of Roy's team now. Bill rolled the thought around. He didn't like the taste of it. "Liaison wasn't my idea."

Roy removed his glasses and cleaned them before tucking them back into his pocket. "I'm not going to twist your arm, Bill. Is it something you want or not?"

"Do I have a choice?"

"Apply to a field office. Work out of Atlanta, St. Louis, Memphis, there're lots of openings."

Bill followed the gaze of a young couple at the next table who had turned to watch an elegant yacht pushing its way up the Potomac River. The white displacement hull and varnished superstructure called to mind an earlier era of gaslights, carriage houses and calling cards.

"Beatrice," Roy said. He was gazing at the yacht.

Bill shaded his eyes and read the name on the transom. "Looks like *Minerva*."

"Beatrice Corporation. They own it. Lunch and a sightseeing cruise for Congressman Rinaldi."

Leave it to Roy, Bill thought, to know who was currying favor with whom. Lunch arrived and they talked in generalities. Roy removed pieces of hard-boiled egg from his seafood salad and ate quickly. When he was finished he pushed the plate away and glanced at his watch. "You want coffee? I've got to run but you can stay."

"No, thanks."

Roy waved a credit card at the waitress. "Okay, here's the game plan. You're on vacation until Monday. Let me handle things at G Street. You don't talk about what happened. I know everybody and his brother's calling you, but the more you talk the longer it takes to blow over. I'll tell Edgarton we're investigating the matter, and by next week his shorts will be clean and he'll forget all about it. Come Monday you report to G Street and we start fresh. Just promise me one thing. No more surprises."

"Not planning any."

He shook his head. "You should have been a lawyer, Bill. You're like a chameleon. A wisp of smoke here, a little over there, everywhere and nowhere." He settled back and pushed the half-eaten salad aside. "By the way, you were right about this place."

"Lousy seafood?"

"I didn't want to be seen with you. Makes me realize what a political animal I've turned into working at headquarters."

"You were born a political animal, Roy."

"Think so?" He smiled at the thought. "That's sad, that's really sad."

Driving home, Bill felt little sense of triumph. He could add Roy to the list of those he had deceived, but lies brought him no closer to understanding what had happened. Last night he lay awake in bed while his mind replayed the day's events again and again, searching for answers. What disturbed him most was his momentary failure to recognize the President, a man he had known for years and saw almost every day. As if he were losing his mind . . .

He was in the curb lane when he stopped for a red light. A lean black man with a soapy squeegee approached to wash his window. *Go find someone else,* Bill thought. As he leaned across the seat to wave the man away he saw himself reflected in the broken side-view mirror on the passenger door. The car next to him, a white Mercury Cougar, was also visible. He could see the lone driver wearing sunglasses and a hat, see his arm come smoothly to eye level, outstretched, holding a pistol—

Bill's reaction was pure instinct. He threw himself across the seat and his right foot pivoted off the brake pedal and hit the accelerator. The car lunged into the intersection. There was a screech of brakes and sudden impact. Glass showered the front seat, the car spun ninety degrees and stopped. A car horn was blaring, tires squealed from the opposite direction, ending in a barely perceptible bump.

As Bill sat up, glass fell from his body. He was in the middle of the intersection, cars backed up on either side. The left side of the Mustang was bent inward by a black limousine, which had hit him broadside. On his right a Mazda Miata coming from the opposite direction had managed to stop just as its bumper touched the door.

Bill scrambled out of the car. The Mazda driver was a young man whose face screwed up in anger. "What the fuck are you doing, man? I had a green light and you just—"

The Smith & Wesson was in Bill's hand. The driver raised his hands and stepped back. Bill hardly saw him. His heart was pounding and his mind was fixed on the gun that moments before had been pointed at his head. A gun with a silencer. Beyond the limousine he could see the Cougar moving now, turning left, making a U-turn.

Bill leaped over the hood of the limousine and through a cloud of steam billowing from the radiator. Not enough room for the gunman to complete his turn. But instead of stopping, the Cougar lurched up over the curb and sped away in the opposite direction. Bill fired once from a crouched position. He felt like squeezing off every bullet in the cylinder, but there were too many cars, too many people. The Cougar disappeared.

Shaking with anger, Bill stood up. As he returned to the Mustang, people gave him wide berth. His shirt was torn, blood oozed from a cut on his chest, and he held the Smith & Wesson pointed at the sky. Aware of the threat his appearance inspired, he returned the gun to its holster. The door to the limousine was locked, so he tapped on the smoked glass window and displayed his identification. "Bill Sullivan, United States Secret Service. Are you all right in there?"

He could see a woman huddled in the backseat, but neither she nor the driver would unlock the door until the police arrived. The limousine had diplomatic plates and its occupant turned out to be the wife of the Chilean ambassador. Bill told his story twice, first to the responding officer and then to Detective Sergeant Dexter Carlyle, who arrived fifteen minutes later. Carlyle was a heavyset African-American with a bead of perpetual sweat along his upper lip. He wore a baggy suit with an American flag pin fixed to the collar and treated Bill with the grudging respect the metropolitan police reserve for federal agents whose authority overlaps and sometimes supersedes their own. He pulled out a minicassette tape recorder and made a show of reciting the date, time, and Bill's name, address and phone number, before asking questions.

"This man actually fire at you?"

"The gun had a silencer and as soon as I saw it I moved. Maybe he fired, maybe he didn't."

"You're sure it was a gun? Real one, not a toy?"

"I know weapons, I wear one every day."

"All right, was there anyone else in the car with you?"

"No."

"Anybody in the other car?"

"I didn't see anybody."

"And you didn't get a good look at the driver?"

Bill tried to recall the reflection in the mirror. "I saw the gun, I ducked. A hat and dark glasses, that's all I remember."

"What kind of hat?"

"Baseball hat, I think."

"What team?"

"Smith & Wesson."

Carlyle frowned and flicked off the recorder. "Is that a joke, Mr. Sullivan?"

"*Which team?* Is that a joke?"

"You're the one who saw him."

"For a fraction of a second in a mirror as big as your hand. You try it and see how much you remember."

Carlyle sighed and resumed taping. "Anybody else see the gun?"

Bill pointed to the window washer, who was telling his story to a group of onlookers. They turned as Carlyle ambled over. The window man put his squeegee behind his back and stepped in front of the bucket of soapy water. "Not breakin' any law, officer."

"What's your name?"

"Call me Rafe."

"I want your name."

"That's it, man. Rafael Jonah Watkins. You think I'm going to shine a brother?"

"What did you see, Rafael?" Carlyle pronounced each syllable: *Rah-fay-el*.

"Windshields, that's what I see, 'cause that's what I *look* for."

"You see the man in the white car, a Mercury Cougar?"

"I see but I don't see, you see what I say? Somebody stops, I scope it out, check if the glass be scummed up, covered with bugs, running dirt, that's all I care. Figure can I do the job before the light changes? This dude gonna pay or pee, that's what I'm thinking whenever I got—"

Carlyle's hand shot out and grabbed him by the belt. Rafe's hands flew up. "Hey, hey, hey."

"Did you see the man in the Cougar?"

"Yeah. Was a white dude, very Caucasian looking."

"What else?"

Rafe shrugged elaborately. "You know how it is with white people—they all look the same."

"What about a gun? You see one?"

Rafe pointed the squeegee at Bill. "Seen this dude wavin' a piece. He go wild, go after that car, pull off a couple shots, coulda hit somebody."

Rafe was no more help than the ambassador's wife or her driver. Carlyle interviewed a number of pedestrians, but none of them had noticed a gun. A white car had left the scene, but so did a number of other cars, including the Mazda that had hit the Mustang. With each interview Bill could see the detective's suspicion mount. By the time the tow truck arrived he was beginning to second-guess himself. *Had* there been a gun? He had no enemies, so why would anybody try to kill him? Or did the guy just go around pointing guns to scare the shit out of people? Bill imagined the man laughing as he drove away and felt a cold rage.

It took a tire iron to pry open the trunk of the Mustang so Bill could retrieve his briefcase and a windbreaker. The car was beyond repair, a total loss. At least the kids weren't here, he thought gratefully as the crumpled Mustang, front wheels in the air and rear tires scraping, was hauled away. It was one hour and forty minutes since he promised Roy no more surprises.

CHAPTER 9

Twenty-four hours after the activation signal there was still no news of the American President's death. Had the signal failed or was Sullivan still waiting for an opportunity? Vasily wished he had the Sorin file and knew the details of the training. His own participation had been deliberately limited. He decided to wait another twenty-four hours and try again. In the meantime there was Yelena.

She had opened a ballet studio near Seven Dials in Covent Garden. It was a renovated warehouse painted bright red, and clustered around each battered door were buzzers trailing electrical wires that rose up the side of the building like ivy. Vasily found Number 28 and read the list of tenants, mostly last names but a few organizations: Morrow Casting Associates, Blue Meanie Theatre Group, something called Peppy Temps, and the name he was looking for, Helen Lawrence Dance Studio.

Helen, as if she were Greek. And *Lawrence.* Even in death his rival mocked him. Jeremy Lawrence. She had taken her lover's name deliberately to spite him. Vasily stared at the building and then turned away before the temptation to confront her drove him inside. Preparation was crucial. And for his plans he needed Guy Jurmon.

When Vasily knew him so many years ago, Jurmon was a producer of pornographic films, usually featuring underage women, which was where their interests coincided. Vasily had blackmailed more than one diplomat or his assistant by baiting a trap with an underage girl and having Jurmon surreptitiously film it. He half suspected that the footage found its way into Jurmon's commercial releases, distributed to Europe and America. He had had no contact with Jurmon since he fled the country, but he was certain the man would remember him and equally certain he would still do anything for money.

He entered Bob Randi's videotape store, where a fat security guard lounged near the door. A Pakistani clerk eyed him speculatively. "Help you with something, sir?"

"I'm here to see Mr. Jurmon."

A mask slid over the clerk's features. "Maybe. What is your name?"

"Victor Frank," Vasily said, using the code name he once employed with Jurmon. The clerk nodded and said, "Wait please." He called something to the guard, then moved to a closed door where a buzzer sounded and he disappeared inside. Vasily looked around the place. The walls were lined with magazines and videotapes, most of them illustrated with genitalia or couples involved in various forms of sexual congress. Had there been a time when he and Yelena had delighted in such material? Now it seemed to him merely more evidence of the world's decline and his own isolation within it.

A customer in a dark blue suit entered, and with the same efficiency he probably analyzed financial results he gave his briefcase to the guard at the door, received a numbered tag in exchange, then went straight to the section that specialized in gay material. The British and their boarding schools, Vasily thought disdainfully, with their universal graduation requirement, a prick up the ass.

The Pakistani returned and behind him was one of the most unattractive men Vasily had a ever met. Guy Jurmon wore a purple turtleneck and a black velvet coat that flared over his thick hips. His hair was dyed a rich, artificial brown, and his skin fell back from his forehead in a series of folds, lidding his eyes and hanging from his nose and cheeks like melted wax. His lips, delicate and sensuous, were drawn in a feral grin. "Ahhh, it is you," he said in a raspy voice. "Come to my office, *mon ami.*"

Jurmon led him down a hallway where a thin, waiflike girl waited outside his door. She was dressed in a red spangled G string and matching bra. She spread her arms in exasperation. "Can we finish talking?"

"I have a visitor, Lynette. This is Victor Frank. Lynette Lamb, she's one of my stars."

"I'm seeing stars, Guy."

"Finish your shift. I'll talk to you later."

She glanced impatiently at Vasily as Jurmon shut the door on her. Guy turned with a smile, an effect of his teeth moving forward. "How old would you say she looked?"

"Sixteen, seventeen."

Jurmon's face fell. "She looks that bad?"

"How old is she?"

"The customers think fourteen but her birth certificate proves she's twenty. No tits, no hips, that's the key. Men who want to boff their daughters adore talking to Lynette."

"Just talk?"

"The girls are in booths, no touching allowed. But if they make a date . . . ?" Vasily wondered again if Jurmon was gay or straight, or if such an ugly man could attract anything other than his own five fingers. It was like trying to guess the sex of a frog.

Jurmon offered a cigarette and took one himself. The room was decorated with posters of X-rated movies, most of them made by Jurmon under the pseudonym Lance de la Rue. A hamster in a cage on the file cabinet ran in a wheel, which made a whirring sound. On the desk was an ashtray made of glass in the form of a woman's face, her mouth open wide to form the bowl where a half dozen cigarette butts stood at crumpled attention.

"I'm surprised," Jurmon said, the cigarette bobbing from the corner of his mouth. "When Abdul told me Victor Frank, I thought, impossible, there is no statute of limitations for what you did. But here you are. Have you come back to tease the police or has the Queen forgiven your sins along with those of your old government?"

Through a tendril of smoke Vasily caught the opportunistic gleam in Jurmon's eye. The man would turn him over to the police for the price of a pack of cigarettes. Better for them both if Jurmon thought he was still working for the Russian government and saw greater profit by their association.

"The situation in Russia changes but human nature does not. The value of certain information remains just as high today as it did when we worked together before. I was sent to discover if you could perform the same services for the new regime that you once did for the old. And for a comparable price."

The glitter of interest was unmistakable. "We are speaking pounds sterling, not rubles."

"Of course."

"Adjusted for inflation."

"It can be arranged."

"And for the greater risk."

"The risk was always great."

"You've been away a long time, my friend. The laws are more strict, the police more vigilant, the public more outraged by child prostitution. You think I'm making excuses to charge a higher fee, but I've been in this business over thirty years and I know what I'm talking about. Believe me, the cost is higher today."

And you are just as full of shit, Vasily thought. He was impatient arguing over the price of a nonexistent service, but it had to be done. If Jurmon knew that he was acting on his own and with limited funds his hand would find the phone as soon as Vasily stepped out the door. He forced himself to continue, named a junior staff member of the admiralty, and negotiated a price of seventy-five hundred pounds if the staff member could be filmed with an underage girl. Jurmon would provide the girl and the video camera while Vasily's people lured the target to the rendezvous. When he was satisfied that Jurmon's greed would insure his discretion, Vasily moved to the real reason he had come to see the man. "I need two personal favors, one simple, one more difficult."

"Begin with the difficult. What can I do?"

"I need a gun."

"That's not easy in this country."

"You don't run a place like this without a little protection. I'll pay a hundred pounds, revolver or automatic, fully loaded. Age, condition and accuracy are unimportant as long as it is in working order."

"Single shot?"

"Two, minimum."

Jurmon's lips worked each word. *"Mon ami,* I am going to accommodate you for old time's sake. Now what is the easy thing I can do?"

"A phone call." He explained what he wanted and gave Jurmon the background he would need. The man's eyes glittered. "What's it all about?"

"You know the rules."

Jurmon sighed and picked up the phone. Vasily said, "Remember, you've got to sound well educated."

"Too bloody right." Jurmon smiled. He thought it was funny.

Vasily dialed the number and leaned close to the receiver to hear the conversation. A soft male voice answered, "Helen Lawrence Studio."

"Is Miss Lawrence there? This is Doctor Sanger calling."

"Just a moment."

There was a pause. Vasily felt his stomach churn with anticipation.

"Hello?"

"Miss Lawrence?"

"This is she." The sound of her voice brought a thousand memories and Vasily closed his eyes.

Jurmon's voice sank to a gravelly low. "Miss Lawrence, this is Doctor Ralph Sanger. I have a daughter, Alice, who is fifteen.

She is intent on becoming a dancer. I tell you frankly I'd rather she went to university, but she believes her future is with the Royal Ballet. I'm willing to support her if she has real talent, but I don't want her to waste her life on a dream that can't be realized. I wonder if you'd look at a videotape I have of Alice and give me your frank opinion of her talent."

"How much training has she had?"

Vasily held up his fingers and Jurmon said, "Three years."

"Who has she trained with?"

"A private tutor from Canada. She really hasn't much training, that's why I'd like you to take a look."

"Rather than a videotape why don't you have Alice come down for an audition. I'd have a better feeling for her sense of dedication and personality than from merely watching a videotape."

"We're not on the best of terms, I'm afraid. Alice is in France with her mother. She feels I have no faith in her and I feel she's sacrificing her life to an insufficient talent. If you would give me some guidance on the matter, I'd be happy to pay you whatever you charge for a private lesson."

"I may not agree with your opinion of her talent."

"In which case she'll have my support instead of my criticism. Can we arrange something this week? I work until five-thirty, but I could meet you at six."

"How about Thursday this week or Tuesday next?"

Taking his cue from Vasily, Jurmon confirmed the Thursday date and rang off. "How was that? Did I sound posh?"

"Posh enough. What about the gun?"

"How soon do you need it?"

"Thursday at five-thirty."

Jurmon's eyes seemed to bulge as his eyelids rose in surprise. "Her? What are you going to do?"

Vasily stood up. The smell of cigarette smoke was making him ill. "I'll pick the gun up on Thursday."

He moved to the door, but Jurmon scrambled after him and grabbed his elbow. It was the first time they had touched and Vasily drew back instinctively.

"Wait, wait." Jurmon removed the cigarette from his mouth. "What does she look like? Is she attractive?"

"It doesn't concern you."

"Wait, listen." His voice sank to a raspy whisper. "Is she going to be eliminated?" Vasily stared coldly at him and Jurmon took a step back. "What I mean is, I have a client, an Austrian fellow who would pay dearly for a video. And a distributor in Amsterdam. If you're going to do her anyway why not make a bit of money? Never mind Moscow, this is you and me, personally. Could be worth two hundred pounds you want to record it. Two cameras, one a wide shot, one close on her face. You can do it yourself, wear a mask, fuck her first—or fake it, it doesn't matter—"

Vasily's hand shot forward, caught Jurmon around the neck and pinned him against the wall. A camera to film Yelena's death. And Jurmon watching it with beady eyes and sweaty palms . . .

"You bastard," he hissed.

Jurmon's face was turning purple. His arms flailed against the wall and tipped one of the framed posters to the floor. It hit with a sound of breaking glass that brought Vasily back to his senses. He released Jurmon, who sank to his knees, gasping and spitting.

Vasily looked around the room for some water but saw none. There was a television-size refrigerator in the corner of the room. Inside it he found half a turkey sandwich wrapped in foil, a box of suppositories, three bottles of Guiness Stout and two six-packs of diet Pepsi. He brought a Pepsi to Jurmon, who looked up fearfully at his approach. His breathing had returned to normal but he still had tears in his eyes. Jurmon took a swallow, coughed, then drank more.

"Sorry," Vasily forced himself to say. "But you must not be involved in this."

Jurmon picked up his cigarette from the floor. It was still lit. He took a few quick, shallow drags. Vasily helped him to his feet and then, to change the subject and the atmosphere, he said, "Is that a gerbil or a hamster you have there?"

"A hamster smells. Manfred is a gerbil. He's odorless, aren't you, Manny?"

Jurmon hunched over the cage, his back to Vasily, as he tapped the bars with his fingernail. "Manny's not a smelly boy, are you, Manny?"

Vasily wanted to leave, but he knew it was important to provide Jurmon an opportunity to regain some measure of dignity. "Shall I call you Thursday morning to confirm the gun?"

"You can have it now." Jurmon turned around. In his hand he held a small automatic pointed at Vasily's chest. Jurmon's eyes glowed with eager triumph. "It's already loaded," he said, working the slide and cocking the hammer.

He wants to frighten me, Vasily thought, and so he allowed his face to mirror the emotion. Jurmon looked down at the gun in mock surprise.

"What? Did you think I was going to shoot you? Sorry." He walked up to Vasily and extended his hand, palm up, the automatic resting on its side. "You know how to use these?"

Vasily kept his eyes on Jurmon. "Why don't you show me."

It was a game. Vasily had spent nine years as an instructor at the KGB's Special Weapons School, but he watched impassively as Jurmon ran through the loading and cocking procedure. It was a Bernardelli 22 caliber automatic, not a formidable weapon, but it wouldn't matter. By the time the little demonstration was finished, Jurmon had regained his sense of selfimportance and Vasily had the tool he needed for the first step of his plan.

CHAPTER

10

Every agent undergoes a thorough psychiatric evaluation when he joins the Secret Service. Those assigned the Protective Detail are given annual reviews by psychologists whose Evaluations & Counseling would review each agent's file and try to ferret out any psychological weaknesses while pretending to ask a few friendly questions. "Let's see here, I see you had another child last May. Congratulations. How's this affected the family? Any problems adjusting to the new baby?"

Like everyone, Bill had the appropriate answers ready. The White House detail was a high-profile, high-stress job, and it was common knowledge that any hint of instability would result in a quick reassignment to some distant field office. To work the prestige assignments you had to be impervious—or look that way. By tradition and by temperament Bill was not eager to talk with Dr. Stuart Birnbaum.

The psychiatrist met him at the door and personally ushered him into the office. Birnbaum was a loose-limbed young man whose jogging shoes were visible beneath his desk.

"Sit here." He indicated one of two comfortable chairs that faced each other over a small table. There was no couch. "Would you like coffee?"

"No, thanks."

Birnbaum crossed to the window, where a Mr. Coffee sat on the sill. He had exchanged his jacket for a dark blue sweater—the collegiate look, Bill thought. When he returned, he ignored his desk and sat opposite Bill, fixing his eyes on Bill's face with the dedicated stare of a visitor at a nudist colony. "So. I understand you've had a couple of unusual incidents recently. You want to tell me about them?"

"Incidents plural?"

"Entering the President's office without provocation and this automobile accident on Tuesday."

It had been too much to hope that the car crash would pass unnoticed, especially since it was the second time within a week that Bill had drawn his weapon. And fired it, this time at a car that hadn't been found and an assailant who hadn't been identified. The police report worked its way to G Street, where Roy had suddenly become unavailable. "Valley of death," he told Bill the one time he'd managed to get through to him. "You couldn't even wait twenty-four hours after we talked . . ."

"I don't need to see a shrink, Roy."

"Standard procedure if you're going to start target-shooting Mercury Cougars. Call me on the other side of the tunnel."

That was Wednesday morning. Since then, Bill had talked with an inspector from the Office of Investigations, a man so noncommittal he referred to himself as "we." Now he was supposed to reassure Stuart Birnbaum he wasn't crazy.

Sensing his discomfort, the psychiatrist said, "I know you don't like this, Bill, nobody does. Nine out of ten people who walk through that door do so under duress. But I've got a function just as you do. You wouldn't put up with me trying to guard the President, I wouldn't presume to do it. Unfortunately everyone thinks he can do a better job of counseling than a professional. If we can stick to the issues, we'll get out of here that much sooner."

"What do you want to know?"

"Let's start with the incident in the Oval Office. Tell me what happened there."

By now Bill had told the lie so many times it sounded like the truth. During his recitation Birnbaum encouraged him with noncommittal nods. When he was finished, the psychiatrist said, "You heard breaking glass. Has that happened before, a sound without apparent cause?"

"You think I'm hallucinating, is that it?"

"I don't know enough to think anything yet, Bill. What we're doing is gathering information."

Bill could feel his resistance rising. He had always hated the annual psychological evaluations and concealed his dislike by pretending they were a game. Tell them what they want to hear, show them what they want to see, those were the rules. Today it was impossible. Birnbaum wasn't looking for standard responses, he was searching for a flaw, a weakness, something he could name and hang a theory on. *Special Agent Sullivan is suffering from delusional paranoia manifested by hallucinatory images of threat and destruction.*

"What about it, Bill? Have there been any other instances where you've heard something or seen something nobody else was aware of?"

"I hope so. That's what I'm trained for."

Birnbaum nodded. "Good point. What I mean, of course, is instances where you've heard or seen things that were not subsequently validated."

"No."

"You're certain?"

"As I'll ever be."

"What about the automobile accident?"

"What about it?"

"According to the police, you said you saw a gun."

"I *did* see a gun."

"The police haven't been able to substantiate that. Why do you think that is?"

"A bullet in my brain would have substantiated it, but we wouldn't be having this discussion."

Birnbaum's smile was like a toupee of the wrong color, as perfectly fitted as it was false. He rotated his coffee cup in his hands until the Yale University emblem faced outward. "You feel secure that it was, in fact, a pistol the man had? And that he wanted to kill you?"

"He aimed the gun at the back of my head. I don't know if he wanted to kill me or scare me, but I wasn't going to wait and find out."

"Tell me what happened."

"You don't have a copy of the police report?"

"In your own words."

Birnbaum listened carefully, his legs outstretched, ankles crossed in an attitude that suggested warming himself before the fire. When Bill finished, he said, "Do you think it's likely someone wants to kill you?"

"I didn't say he was trying to kill me, I said he looked like he was trying to kill me."

"Point taken. Have you had any other incidents of anyone threatening you?"

"No."

"Do you think the two incidents are related, what happened in the Oval Office and the man with the gun?"

"The President was not the man in the car, if that's what you mean."

Birnbaum paused. "It's interesting you feel compelled to give a facetious response to what's really a serious inquiry. It's a form of distancing, a defensive mechanism. Isn't that what you're doing?"

"Not well enough."

Birnbaum began a rambling discourse on truth and pain and why discomfort was a sign of growth. Try telling that to Claire, Bill thought.

They had not mentioned the gun for fear of scaring the kids. Matt had seemed fascinated by details of the accident and at dinner he'd kept coming back to it. "But, I mean, how come your foot slipped to the right if that's the same way you were leaning?"

"I don't know."

Megan had said, "Because it was an *accident*, Matt. That's what an accident means, you don't know what happened."

"Were you driving the car, Megan? Is anybody talking to you?"

"Just be glad Daddy didn't end up in the hospital like people who fall off stupid skateboards."

The ensuing squabble had taken their minds off the wreck, but when Bill had gone to Matt's bedroom later to say goodnight the boy had said, "Dad, if you want to fix the Mustang, I can help."

"I think the Mustang is a total loss."

"But you're still going to drive, right?"

"Maybe more carefully."

"So I can go skateboarding again as long as I'm more careful?"

"I was wearing my seatbelt, you weren't wearing your helmet."

"I will, though. I promise."

"I'll talk to Mom about it."

But all that he and Claire had talked about that night had been the driver of the Cougar and if he'd meant to shoot Bill or scare him. Twice he'd caught her staring at him with a troubled expression. Each time she'd looked away quickly, but Bill knew she had been thinking about whether the gun had been real or not. He wondered which would frighten her more?

"Can we do that, Bill?" Birnbaum was saying. "I'll ask a simple question, you give a simple answer, is it a deal?"

"It's your office."

"Can I assume that's a simple *yes*?"

Childish, Bill thought, but he earned a nod of approval with, "Yes."

"Let's talk about your family for a moment. Your parents. Did either one of them suffer from periods of confusion? Any instances when your sense of the circumstance or perception of something that happened differed from theirs?"

Bill felt his anger stir. "What you mean is, does insanity run in my family? I wouldn't be wearing this if it did." He pointed to his lapel pin. "I wouldn't have gotten past the first interview, you know that."

Birnbaum leaned forward, elbows on his knees. "I'm not suggesting your parents were insane. People undergo many strains and stresses in their lifetime and they deal with them in different ways. Meeting a college sweetheart, the death of a family member, an affair, a divorce, all these things can alter our perceptions, sometimes in dramatic, if temporary, ways. All I wonder is if either parent had ever interpreted events in a manner you felt was at odds with your perception of them."

"No."

"Not even when your father was drinking?"

"I wasn't drinking when I saw the gun." Had Roy told Birnbaum about the bachelor party and the lost day of the wedding?

"Tell me about your father."

Bill sighed. "Do we have to go into all this?"

"Do you find it a problem?"

"I find it depressing. My folks lived in a depressing little town in the middle of the prairie. First their marriage died and then they died. Whatever my father's weaknesses were, they don't affect me so why go into it?"

"I would think you'd want to know your medical history. For your family's sake if not your own curiosity. There are genetic predispositions for illnesses like diabetes, Huntington's disease, even cancer."

"How about involuntary combustion?"

"What? Oh." Birnbaum blinked as he realized what Bill meant. "Do you often joke about your parents' death?"

"Only with people who can fully appreciate Freudian humor."

Birnbaum looked like he was going to pursue it, then decided not. "When he was sober did your father imagine hearing or seeing things?"

His father. Bill remembered him as a melancholy man given to periods of unnatural exuberance. He remembered how his mother used to send him to find his father and bring him home, first from the Roundup Bar and then later, after he stopped drinking, from the basement of St. Andrew's Church where he'd attended Alcoholics Anonymous meetings and denounced liquor with the same fervor he'd once drowned in it. Bill remembered the night he'd seen his Dad came out with his arm around Elsie Hunnicut. The same night he'd followed on his bicycle and watched them through Elsie's living-room window, their naked bodies lit only by the flickering gray light of the television, his father on his hands and knees above her face, his head buried between Elsie's legs while she took him in her mouth . . .

"What about it, Bill? When he was sober?"

"No, Dad didn't hallucinate."

"What about *his* parents? Your grandmother is still alive, have you seen her?"

"We send Christmas cards."

"She's still in Ireland?"

"She was last Christmas."

He and Claire had visited his grandmother the year after they married. It was like meeting a stranger. Bill hadn't seen her since his grandfather was still alive. He had been two years old and didn't remember it at all.

"And your maternal grandparents?"

"Their genetic defect is intolerance, not alcoholism."

"What does that mean?"

Bill explained that his mother's family was from Victoria, British Columbia, where they cultivated an English garden and British accent with equal fervor. They disowned their daughter when she ran off with and married a man they considered "half Irish, half bum." She was sixteen and pregnant. The animosity was mutual, and his mother had never spoken of her parents with anything but bitterness. Birnbaum listened politely, although Bill knew none of this was new, it was all part of his recruitment file. He suspected that the psychiatrist was simply testing his responses to see how candid he was. The questions continued and Bill struggled to recall the details of his childhood. Kansas seemed a lifetime away, its memories as dry and lifeless as dust. Finally Birnbaum said, "Your parents died in a fire. How did that make you feel?"

"How did Dr. Grinnel say it made me feel?"

He was referring to the man who'd given him the battery of psychological tests and interviews when he applied to the Secret Service. Rather than reject the question, Birnbaum paged through the file. "Dr. Grinnel suggests you're suffering from mild guilt because you attended a New Year's Eve party the night they died. Do you think you still feel that guilt?"

"I'm not a psychiatrist, I wouldn't know."

"It would be natural to feel that you could have saved them if you were home."

"Then I'm sure that's how I feel."

"On the other hand, they died of smoke inhalation, so it's equally possible you'd have been overcome as well."

"Sounds like an unresolved guilt complex. Maybe you can fix it."

"Are you comfortable your parents' death was an accident?"

Bill tensed. "I think uncomfortable would be more accurate."

"Have you ever imagined that someone started the fire deliberately?"

"The police know what happened. Faulty wire in a space heater."

"But what about you, Bill? Haven't you even imagined someone was out to kill your parents?"

"No."

The answer was too quick; Birnbaum's eyebrow raised. "Not even a malevolent fate?"

"What do you want to know? Have I ever *imagined* someone was responsible? Sure, I've imagined all kinds of things. A serial killer or some motorcycle crazy with a book of matches. I imagine dragging my parents out of the bedroom while a flaming roof falls in. I imagine shooting an arsonist before he can strike the match. Does that mean I feel guilty I wasn't there? Maybe so. But am I paranoid? Do I think somebody deliberately killed my parents? No." He sighed. "I covered all this with Dr. Grinnel."

"Do you find this discussion uncomfortable?"

"I find it useless. I don't believe in psychotherapy. I never have."

"Any particular reason for that?"

"I'm sure you'll find one and give it a Latin name." He stood up. "Are we done?"

"I can't make you cooperate, Bill. But it's a two-way street and I can't do this without you."

"I'm not in a cooperative mood this morning. Some days are like that. I don't want to share the toothpaste or take my son to swimming class or give another tourist directions to the Vietnam War Memorial. You've got my file, you've got the police report, there's nothing more I can add."

"Just so you realize that you determine the content of my report more than I do."

Bill hesitated. "So what will your report say?"

"That you exhibit a marked defensive behavior that appears out of proportion to the case under discussion. That I recommend further counseling before you return to active duty."

Bill stared at him and his disgust was so apparent that Birnbaum said, "I'm on your side, Bill. I wish you'd believe that."

"Lucky me." He sat down and they began again. Bill answered the questions simply and conveniently and with as little regard for the truth as his father had shown when he started screwing Elsie Hunnicut.

Juho Ryti stood on a pier extending into the Chesapeake Bay, holding the casting rod with both hands. He bent back, then with a quick flex of his arms brought the rod in an arc that ended abruptly and sent the silver lure flashing high into the air. He savored the frozen moment before the lure struck the water, then began reeling it in. The tang of salt water and the heave of waves against the pilings were not as familiar as the pine-scented lakes of his homeland, but the routine of rod and reel was the same and had a soothing effect.

It had been forty-eight hours since the abortive attempt on Bill Sullivan's life, and he was no closer now to understanding why things had gone wrong than he was when the Mustang leaped forward just as his finger tightened on the trigger. It was as if Sullivan sensed the attack, a phenomenon Juho had witnessed among animals in the wilderness but never among men. He wondered if it had anything to do with Secret Service training?

Juho was a perfectionist. He had missed his intended target only once before and quickly remedied the failure with the second shot. That he could not pinpoint his mistake with Sullivan irritated him like a scratch in the stock of a rifle where it rested against his cheek.

The masters in Moscow had been upset. "The package must be delivered immediately," they insisted. Juho wondered why the death of a Secret Service agent was so urgent, but he was too old and experienced to panic. The Russians would push him into making a mistake and then blame him for failure; he had seen it before. The next attempt would be far more difficult, the target was on guard now. That was why he had temporarily abandoned the surveillance, changed cars and hotels, and adopted a second set of false identification papers.

There was a tug, and the tip of the fishing pole bent toward the water. A couple of kids wandered over as Juho reeled in a small black bass. He immobilized the fish beneath his boot while he removed the hook. An unworthy trophy. He kicked it back into the water.

A crow on a piling white-topped with guano caught his attention with its raucous cry. The bird turned its head to one side and eyed him. Juho's mother believed crows were bad luck. Now, as the bird shifted its position without moving its gaze, Juho felt a presentiment of doom. It was as if Bill Sullivan were watching him through the eyes of the crow. He feinted with the fishing pole. The crow's wings lifted slightly, then settled back. Juho was annoyed. The bird should be more wary, just as Sullivan should have been less. He drew the rod back and snapped it forward. The silver lure spun through the air in a quick arc. At the last moment the crow seemed to tumble off the stanchion in its haste to get away. As the wings beat fiercely the hook snagged a black feather and rode it to the ground. One of the kids turned to him in astonishment.

"Wow, you almost hooked that bird."

"Next time," Juho said with a smile. He reeled in the line, removed the black feather and twirled it between his fingers. "Next time." He disassembled the pole and put away the fishing gear. It was time to go back to work.

CHAPTER 11

A gap-toothed goblin with eyes of fire watched Bill jog along the lake. It was night, and Halloween pumpkins carved into monstrous faces sat on every porch. It seemed to him they were laughing at him: *There goes Bill Sullivan, he's losing his mind.* That was the fear that haunted him. When Bill confronted the possibility he found it a double-edged sword: on one hand, it exonerated him from responsibility for his actions; on the other, it made him a threat to his friends and family. Wasn't that what the psychiatrist, Birnbaum, implied about his father? Not just an alcoholic but maybe crazy. For the first time in years Bill found himself thinking about his parents, looking for clues to their mental health. He was surprised how much he had forgotten. But there were others who might know, people in Kansas, friends of his parents, one in particular—Elsie Hunnicut.

He forced his mind past the aversion her name evoked and

considered it from an adult perspective. His father had had an affair. It wasn't a crime like robbing a bank or running down a pedestrian, only a sign of weakness. But Elsie could tell him things about his father's health, his father's life, that were lost to him now.

Bill returned to the house and went to the basement to make the call. The information operator in Kansas had no listing for Elsie Hunnicut, but Bill located her brother, Gus, who told him that she had married someone named Lloyd Fuchs. A few minutes later Bill had Lloyd on the line. The man had a flat, nasal voice and expressed no curiosity when Bill asked to speak to Elsie. When she answered, her voice brought no hint of recognition.

"Elsie Fuchs?"

"Yes."

"This is Bill Sullivan, Dan Sullivan's son. You remember me?"

"Billy Sullivan?"

"That's right."

"You got a lot of nerve calling here, Billy—if you *are* Billy Sullivan."

"I'm sorry if it's inconvenient, but I need some information about my father. We're trying to put together a medical history, and apart from his drinking problem, I don't remember much. I thought you could help me fill in some gaps."

"After the way you done me at the funeral I got nothing to say to you."

Bill had no idea what she was talking about. "Wait," he said quickly. "I'm sorry if there's any bad feeling about the past, Mrs. Fuchs. Can I ask you a few questions?"

"Let he who is without sin cast the first stone, that's all I got to say to you, Billy."

The phone went dead. He called again and this time Lloyd Fuchs told him, "She got nothing to say to you, mister. And don't keep calling here or we'll lodge us a complaint with the phone company."

That night when they were getting ready for bed, Bill told Claire about the conversation and Elsie's reaction. She seemed puzzled. "What is it you're trying to find out?" she asked, her words warped as she rubbed her cheeks with skin conditioner.

"Medical history, family background. Who my folks were as adults." *And if I'm going crazy.*

"You don't know what Elsie meant about the funeral?"

"No idea." He was already in bed, an unread Sports Illustrated draped across his chest. Claire stood up and unbuttoned her blouse.

"Call her Monday, she'll talk to you then."

"Think so?"

"Her husband will be at work. That's when wives talk about their old boyfriends."

As she spoke, she unhooked the bra with one hand and let it drop. Claire had a full, solid figure with a slightly rounded stomach and full breasts so white in contrast to her suntanned frame they seemed luminescent. She thrust her arms through a cotton nightshirt and was about to pull it over her head.

"Don't do that," Bill said.

Her eyes slid to the bedspread where his arousal was clearly evident. She let the nightshirt fall and approached the bed. Bill's eyes were drawn to the triangle of black pubic hair that grew toward the center, sculpted as if under the influence of opposing winds. As he moved to make room she said, "No, you stay there."

Ever since Matt's accident a new ardor had crept into their lovemaking, familiar bodies awakened to new alterations of mood and mind by the brush with disaster. This was not their usual routine. The magazine slipped to the floor as Claire pulled the sheets away. She crawled over his body, dipping her torso in a wavelike motion that caused her breasts to skim his legs. Her fingers slid to his chest, moved inward, down his abdomen, and toyed with his pubic hair. Bill murmured and strained upward. She lowered her head and shook it gently, cascading her hair like a thousand shivering fingers along his groin. Her head stilled, lowered, and he felt the warm outflow of her breath. He strained toward her, grazing her teeth. She lifted her head and smiled. "Want something?"

"You."

He held out his arms and she moved forward, straddled him, then leaned down to his embrace. They kissed and she kept her mouth on his to capture his groan of pleasure as their bodies fused. They began a slow rocking motion.

"Love you," he whispered.

"Bill, Bill . . ."

It was then, through half-closed eyes, that he saw the movement at the window, someone behind the drape, watching. With a yell he shoved out from beneath Claire, dropped to the floor and sprang up in a defensive crouch. The new silk drape, twisting in the wind, settled.

"What?" she said.

"I thought someone—You okay?"

She was massaging her arm where his knee had struck her. "I'll live."

He moved to the window, pulled the drape aside and looked out. At the end of the block a halo of moths gathered at a streetlamp and a Halloween pumpkin glowed from a neighbor's window. What caught his eye was the station wagon parked almost out of sight—the same unfamiliar station wagon he'd noticed earlier when he returned from jogging. And there was someone in it, he could tell from the steamed windows.

You bastard, he thought. I *am* being followed. He began pulling on his pants.

"Bill—?"

"Someone's out there. Watching the place. I saw him earlier when I was out."

He grabbed his gun. She sat bolt upright. "What are you doing?"

"I'm going to prove I'm not crazy."

"Call the police."

"The police don't believe me."

"What if he has a gun?"

"He won't see me coming."

She grabbed his arm. "Just let the police handle it."

"They don't believe me. Whatever's happening is happening to me and nobody else believes it, not even you."

"That's not true."

"Then trust me."

Bill's blood was racing, but his mind was calm. He had no intention of making himself a target. Not this time. In the garage he got a flashlight and rummaged through his toolbox for a valve-stem wrench. He left by the back door, forcing Ginger back inside when she tried to slip through his legs. He ran along the lake until he could cut through a footpath and regain the road at a point behind the station wagon.

Was the driver keeping an eye on the side-view mirror or only watching the house? Bill crouched and used the other cars to shield his approach. A car turned onto the street and in the glow of its passing headlights he saw a single occupant in the station wagon raise a pair of binoculars and train them on his house. Bill felt exultant. *I'm not there, you bastard, I'm behind you.*

He scuttled crabwise behind the station wagon. On his hands and knees he reached around the right rear tire, removed the valve cap, then used the valve-stem wrench to unscrew the one-way plug that held the air in the tire. At the first hiss of air he tensed but kept working, ready to grab the gun at any sign of alarm. In his haste the wrench slipped and dropped to the pavement. Bill switched the gun to his right hand and waited. Nothing. He recovered the wrench and after a few more turns the plug came out completely. The tire deflated rapidly. Bill shifted the flashlight to one hand, the Smith & Wesson in the other.

The tire was almost flat before the car rocked as someone got out. Bill remained in a crouch, glancing back and forth until the silhouetted figure appeared. Bill flicked on the flashlight, illuminating the gun he held pointed at the intruder's chest. "Hands on your head. Now!"

A teenage boy, eyes wide with terror, stepped back. "Don't shoot, don't."

"Hands!" Bill said, still energized by the expectation of threat. The boy's hands flew over his head. Bill grabbed him by the collar and jammed the muzzle against his temple. "Who are you?"

"Please don't, please . . ."

"Put your hands on the car and spread your legs."

"Are you a cop?"

"Just do it."

Bill kept the muzzle of the gun against the base of the boy's head as he checked for weapons. There were none. The boy was trembling. Bill removed the wallet from the boy's rear pocket and read the name on the driver's license. "Ross Terhoff. You're watching my house. Why?"

"Please, Mr. Fowler. I didn't mean anything."

"Who?"

"You're—aren't you Michelle's father?"

Then he understood. The Fowlers were his neighbors, the house with a light in the upstairs window where teenage Michelle Fowler lived.

"I'm not Joe Fowler, I'm a neighbor. I saw you out here and thought . . ." Thought what? Somebody meant to kill me? "We've had some trouble in the neighborhood," he finished lamely.

"Not me, sir. I swear to God I was just sitting here, that's all I did. Really."

"You seen anyone else out here watching houses?"

"No way. And if I'd known—I mean I won't come here like this again. I really won't."

The gun was heavy in his hand, and Bill realized that somewhere along the line he had pulled the hammer back and cocked it. I've got to stop this, he thought. I've got to find out what's happening to my mind.

When he returned to the house he and Claire did not resume lovemaking, but lay together in the darkness. "I know why the dream is back," Bill said. "It's not Matt's accident or the new job. It's what happened that night, the night they died."

"No, don't. It wasn't your fault."

"Then who moved the car?"

"What do you mean?"

"I passed out, slept in the car. But in the morning it was parked in a different spot. A block away from where it had been."

Claire spoke slowly. "Someone moved it?"

"I had the keys. They were still in my pocket when I woke up."

"You mean . . . you went somewhere that night?"

"That's what I have to find out, Claire. What my mind is hiding. I have to go to Kansas."

CHAPTER

12

Vasily Amenov sat before the window of his hotel room. The window looked out on an air shaft split by a narrow opening between two buildings. Through the cleft he could see the street, where vehicles and pedestrians appeared and disappeared so quickly they were mere flashes of color. It was his last day in London. He had attempted to activate the Sorin Project, but without success. The BBC News brought no report of catastrophe in the White House. He would have to go to America and see firsthand what was wrong. But first, Yelena.

Vasily bent over his work. He had a 22 caliber bullet braced against a windowsill thick with multiple layers of paint. Carefully he filed two notches into the lead tip at a right angle to each other. He used a metal fingernail file and periodically tapped it against the sill to clear the teeth of tiny shavings. The notches would insure that the bullet spread upon impact, causing maximum damage. When he was finished, he loaded the Bernardelli pistol and dropped it in his pocket.

He checked out of the hotel and took the Tube to Heathrow Airport. The flight didn't leave until that evening, but he didn't want to visit Yelena carrying luggage. He left the bag in a locker but not before removing his shaving kit and one set of underwear, including socks, which he took back to the city.

During his years as an instructor at the KGB Special Weapons School Vasily had learned that success or failure in most cases was determined before the operation began. The most exotic weapon was useless unless it was properly positioned and at the right place at the right time. Planning and preparation, that was the key. To insure that he had time to escape the country, he spent the afternoon creating a false trail for the police to follow. From a Salvation Army store he bought a cheap business suit that would have embarrassed even Guy Jurmon, raincoat, pair of worn shoes, alarm clock, sunglasses, and a suitcase. He then took a taxi to the Hilton Hotel, where he checked in under the name Jeremy Lawrence.

The bathroom featured a tub with a whirlpool jet that groaned when he used it. Vasily left a ring of dirt in the tub and a few strands of hair caught in the drain—something for the forensic experts, he thought with a smile. He left his shaving kit, including toothbrush with well-mashed bristles, in the bathroom, put the clothes in the closet and placed the alarm clock beside the bed. In the lobby he asked the concierge for a book of matches—the final piece of preparation to mislead the police.

Vasily arrived outside Yelena's studio at five-thirty, free of luggage. A group of Yelena's students exited the building, young men and women in sweatpants and jeans, laughing and touching one another. At five after six he entered the building and climbed the broad stairway to the third floor. Outside the studio he paused to listen: the sound of a radio but that was all. No sound of conversation or other people present.

The metal door handle tingled at his touch and his heart pounded unreasonably. He stepped inside and found himself alone in a lounge. There was a battered chrome couch with square-cornered plastic-covered cushions and at the far end of the room a cluttered wood desk next to a metal file cabinet. On one wall was a scheduling board. One door led into the studio, which was visible beyond the clear plastic panels that separated the two spaces. Sunlight streamed through a long row of windows and lit the parallel balance bars that ran the length of the opposite wall. Yelena was sweeping the floor. She wore jeans and a flannel shirt opened to reveal a leotard beneath. Her hair was not so gold as he remembered, but he recognized her body and the way she moved, even wielding a broom, with elegance and grace.

I can't do this, he thought. Then she turned and saw him in the shadows. "Hello," she called and waved. "Are you Dr. Sanger?"

The voice was familiar, but the words and the intonation were completely British now. Despite his hatred some part of Vasily had always believed that Yelena too must have felt hardship, must have doubted her decision, must have regretted what she had done to them both. But her greeting—the relaxed wave, the evident comfort of her life of betrayal—dispelled that illusion. Now it would be easy.

He stepped through the door into the studio. She was coming toward him, smiling politely. The features were softer than he remembered, the pointed chin not quite as firm, but the high cheekbones still dramatic and only the interplay of delicate lines around the corners of her eyes to indicate her age.

"I don't have a janitor so whenever I have a free moment . . ." She slowed to a stop.

"Hello, Yelena," he said in Russian.

The nostrils arched and she stepped back. "Vasily? But you—" She glanced behind him. "You can't be here. The police—"

In Russian he said, "Have you forgotten your mother tongue?"

She swallowed and this time spoke in Russian. "How did you get into the country?"

"Did you think the British police kept me away all these years?"

"I thought you were arrested. Put in jail."

He felt a surge of satisfaction. Yelena had heard of his involvement with the Gorbachev coup, which meant she still knew people in the motherland. She still kept track of him. "The sentence was commuted. The reformers think this proves they are superior to our comrades of the former regime. You should return, Yelena. It is everything you ever wanted—freedom without responsibility."

"Freedom *is* responsibility. That is what you never understood."

She walked to a closet and put the broom away. He sensed the difference in her. She was stronger now, a mature woman where once she had been a passionate girl. Yelena turned to face him, her chin raised, arms crossed, elbows cradled in each palm. "I have a client coming. You must go."

"You mean Dr. Sanger?" He moved toward her, saw the confusion cloud her eyes. "He's not coming, Yelena. He never was."

"You?"

"A friend of mine. I wanted an hour alone with you."

"I'm not interested in anything you have to say."

He could have grabbed her arm as she passed him, but he did not. "Why did you change your name? Out of shame?"

She turned at the doorway. "You must leave, Vasily. Or I will call the police."

"I thought you would like news of your son."

"You killed my son. Just like Jeremy, like everyone you come into contact with."

"Your bastard's not dead."

Her eyes flashed in anger. "I know what happened at Sandulov. I saw Mischa's death certificate. Yes, I saw it. Does that surprise you? A copy was smuggled out to me. Why else do you think I stopped my fight to get him back?"

"I thought because your British lovers didn't want a Russian bastard in the next room calling for Mommy while they were fucking her."

She stiffened. "I'm calling the police. Stay here and they will put you on trial for murdering Jeremy."

She went into the office and picked up the phone. Vasily followed, but she showed no fear as she dialed. From his pocket he pulled out a photo and tossed it onto the desk. "That's Mischa."

Through the receiver he heard the voice, "Police." Yelena hesitated.

"Look for yourself," Vasily said. "He has his father's face."

A metallic voice said, "This is the police. Is someone there?" Slowly she put down the phone, then picked up the passport-size photo of a young man. "This could be anybody," she said without conviction. "This could be a boy who looks like Jeremy. You're doing this to hurt me."

"It's Mischa at eighteen. A British bastard about to become a Hero of the Revolution."

"I saw his death certificate. I have the copy."

"Because you were meant to have it."

"What do you mean? It was smuggled out to me. I paid—" She stopped. "Never mind how I got it."

Vasily leaned close. "You paid two thousand pounds to your mother's uncle, Dr. Kulygin, who paid the money to a nurse at Sandulov who made a copy of the death certificate. She handed it to him in a copy of *Izvestia*. Do you think we were such fools not to know of your inquiries? You should have paid more attention while we were married, Yelena. You should have known me better."

She sank into her seat, but her eyes remained on him.

"Why?"

"So you would stop trying to recover the bastard."

She looked defenseless now, like the girl he had once known. "He never went to Sandulov?"

"Of course he did. The boy was insane, pathetic. He stopped talking, he put pins through his tongue. One day he lit matches and caught the bed on fire. He was a coward, used to cry over nothing, roll up on the floor and pee in his pants. That's why I gave him to the Sandulov Institute. That's why he went there."

She closed her eyes and hugged the photo to her chest, her voice a whisper. "Is he still at Sandulov?"

"They cured him."

"Thank God." She looked at the photo. "So handsome. When was this taken?"

"Years ago."

"What about now? Where is he? Does he know about me?"

"He knows you're a whore and a traitor."

"No!" She jumped to her feet.

"He knows you abandoned him in a foreign country."

"That's not true. You took him. You stole my son."

"You stole my life, Yelena. And now you pay the price."

"Vasily, please." She touched his arm. "Where is he? You must tell me."

He glanced at her fingers. "In dancers the age shows up first in the hands."

She released him and a look of distrust came to her. "He's not alive, that's why you came."

"He's alive. He works for the State, handles an important job, has a wife and children."

"Children?"

"You're a grandmother, Yelena, and I should be a grandfather. But he's not my son. You stole my life, stole my future—"

"*Your* life, *your* future—you haven't changed at all. Everything was always yours."

"Except you."

"I gave you my young girl's heart, Vasily, as much as I could give. But I was your Firebird, your little ballerina, to be kept in a cage for your delight."

"I loved you."

She shook her head angrily. "You couldn't. You never *knew* me. So many times I tried to tell you and what did you do? You smiled and kissed me beneath the ear and whispered 'my little Firebird'—do you know how I came to hate that name?"

Her vehemence surprised Vasily. *She* was the guilty one, but she showed no remorse. He said coldly, "What name did Jeremy call you?"

"This is useless. What about Mischa?"

"What about us?" Vasily yelled. "What about the sons and daughters we never had, the grandchildren you killed when you left me? You don't mourn them, only this bastard who destroyed us." He tried to grab the photograph from her, but she gripped it with both hands and hunched forward protectively. Vasily took her finger and began to bend it back. She bit his forearm and he released her. Yelena stepped back, eyes blazing. "Get out, Vasily."

The imprint of her teeth was visible, a ragged half-moon welt. He smiled. "Don't you want to know how to find Mischa?"

"I'll find him myself." She picked up the phone. "I'm calling the police."

He pulled the gun from his pocket. "No, you're not. Put the phone down, Yelena." She hesitated, analyzing him. He said, "We have an hour and the hour's not over."

Slowly and deliberately she said, "When I left you I left fear behind." She touched the button for the Operator.

Bitch, Vasily thought, but his anger was tinged with admiration. Her fearlessness had always been one of the things that attracted him. He stepped to the wall and yanked the phone cord free. She replaced the phone calmly and looked at him. "Do you intend to kill me?"

"I intend to kill the bastard."

"Mischa?"

"Don't think you can warn him. He lives under another name and I have his file. You won't find him, Yelena. By the time you find him he will be a corpse."

"Why? Why would you hurt him? He did nothing."

"I did nothing, but you betrayed me."

"I was in love, Vasily, it wasn't something I planned."

"And that is an excuse to discard your wedding vows and take another man into our bed, *my* bed, while I was at the embassy? To give me a child I thought was mine and then reveal the truth. You look at me with disgust and yet I still see the woman I love. I still remember the feel of your lips, your laughter, your fingers in my hair, the way our bodies fit . . ."

"You're talking about sex, not love."

"You were a KGB wife, a privileged position, you shopped at the *Beriozka,* studied with the Bolshoi, a car and driver, a passport, all of it mine. I gave you everything and now I take everything. Mischa will die unless you save his life."

"How?"

"*The Firebird.* Your audition piece for the Bolshoi. I want you to perform it now, for me. You must awaken the tender memories that will convince me to spare him."

She drew herself up to her full height. "No, you've made up your mind, I see it in your eyes. Nothing I do will change it."

"Once you couldn't wait to dance for me. Each new routine you wanted to show me. Now, not a single arabesque to save your own son?"

"You say you loved me once. If that's true, show it. Tell me where to find him. Give me his address."

Vasily turned away, moving to the photographs of students on the wall. In one, a haughty young man with bulging calves and pointed toes was caught in midleap. A *grand allegro.* The term popped into his mind. How avidly he had studied her world, how eagerly she once quizzed him, executing various steps and poses for him to identify. The photograph was inscribed, *To Helen, a wonderful teacher and friend. Love, Mark.*

A friend. That's what Jeremy was supposed to have been. And what about this friend? Had she slept with him? Behind the shadowed bulge at the dancer's crotch Vasily imagined the man's genitals, imagined Yelena naked on her knees before him, remembered his own pleasure looking down on her and watching the blonde hair shimmering against his dark pubic hair, the wonder he had felt the first time she . . .

The chunk and whine of a freight elevator interrupted his thoughts. He turned and found her watching him warily.

"I will make you this promise, Yelena. If you dance for me, I will not kill him. On the grave of my father I swear it. But if you refuse, I will walk out that door and send you a picture of his corpse."

"Will you tell me where he is?"

"When I'm safely back in Russia."

She nodded and without a word went into the studio. Vasily returned the pistol to his pocket. He followed her and watched silently as Yelena found a cassette tape of *The Firebird.*

"I will start it," he said.

She showed him the correct button, then moved away, slipped off the shirt and jeans, and stood dressed in her leotard.

He watched her replace her practice slippers with dancing shoes, noting that her limbs were still as supple and limber as a teenager's.

"The way you did it on our wedding night."

Yelena froze. "What do you mean?"

"Our honeymoon, remember?"

"You can't be serious."

"Do you think I would trade your bastard's life for anything less than our happiest moment?"

"That was the happiest moment, Vasily? *That?* You get the same thing in a burlesque house."

"But I don't get you, do I?"

"We do it this way," she said with finality and positioned herself with arms swept back, leaning forward. "Turn on the music." Vasily didn't move. "You want the audition, damn it. Here." She began dancing without the music, her feet scuffing softly over the wood floor. Vasily walked toward the door.

"Where are you going?" she called. "Vasily!" He didn't turn or stop. "All right! All right, have it."

He took a deep breath and turned. Yelena had already removed her top and was stepping out of the legs, which pulled free with difficulty over the dancing shoes. The leotard snapped into a tight ball, which she threw toward the wall. Yelena stood before him, her body caught in a band of horizontal light, brown nipples riding the crest of pale white breasts, the ridge of pubic hair a translucent gold. Vasily stood transfixed, caught between present and past, the dreams of yesterday and blasted hopes of today. Yelena crossed quickly to the tape recorder and turned it on. The music leaped to life, quick and strong, the entrance of the Firebird while Prince Ivan watches from behind a tree.

Yelena crossed the floor in a series of swiftly executed leaps and poses in an impression of flight. The solo climaxed with turns on point increasing in speed and intensity until her form blurred and the music reached a crescendo. She froze. In his mind's eye Vasily saw the Prince rush out to capture her, felt his own fingers twitch in anticipation.

Yelena dropped her pose. She retrieved her jeans and stepped into them, keeping her back to him. Vasily's breathing was quick and the vein in his temple was throbbing. He couldn't move or take his eyes off her. The faint swell of her right breast was visible beneath her arm as she slipped into her shirt. The leotard she gathered and stuffed into a pocket. The music swelled again, filling the room. Yelena walked to the recorder and turned it off.

Vasily blinked and swallowed heavily. Yelena removed the tape and came toward him, but he didn't move from the door. She offered him the tape. "Here, you can keep this as a souvenir."

He ignored it, reaching instead toward the bead of sweat that had gathered on her brow. Yelena drew back.

"The last dance," he said softly and pulled out the gun. She didn't scream, but Vasily read her intention as she tried to knock the gun out of his hand. He pulled away and she tried to lunge past. Vasily got his arm around her neck and they stumbled in a circle. The room echoed to squeaking shoes and the grunts of exertion as Vasily kept pivoting, swinging Yelena off balance, trying to throw her to the floor. His right foot shot out and blocked hers, a maneuver designed to trip her, but Yelena was wiry and agile. With a quick hop she was on the other side of his foot, blocking him now and throwing him off balance. Falling, he dragged her with him.

Yelena scrambled away on hands and knees and her foot struck his hand, knocking the gun free. He lunged for it, missed, then rolled onto his back, blocking the path to the door. As Yelena leaped over him he scissored one leg up, caught her ankle, and spilled her to the floor. She rolled, started to rise, but he grabbed her foot and pulled it sharply toward him. Yelena fell face-down, knocking her breath out. By the time she recovered, Vasily was on top of her, the muzzle of the pistol jammed into the crook of her right knee. He pulled the trigger.

She screamed.

With his ears ringing from the concussion, Vasily wrestled himself onto her left thigh. There was more time now, but he didn't hesitate. The second blast shattered the other knee. He swiveled around and placed his face close to hers. She was still conscious, the lips drawn back in pain, pupils of her eyes narrowing in shock.

"I won't kill Mischa," he said. "But someone else will."

He wouldn't have remembered the book of matches if they hadn't been in the same pocket as the gun. He dropped the matches between her shattered legs, a clue to mislead the police, then left the studio. A man in a black turtleneck was in the hall. "What happened?"

"She's hurt," Vasily mumbled. "I'm going for an ambulance."

He had already chosen his escape route, ducking down a narrow pedestrian alley to Barrow Street, where he dropped the gun down a storm drain and hailed a taxi. The cab was spacious, with plenty of leg room, but Vasily sat pressed against the door, hunched over his knees, shivering slightly all the way to Heathrow Airport.

CHAPTER

13

Juho Ryti was fastidious about his kills. He did not employ weapons of mass destruction that would sacrifice the lives of innocent victims along with his target. In part this was his craft; he had a passion for precision. Then, too, it cheapened the value of his services if he destroyed lives without compensation. Finally, it was a matter of principle. Just as he didn't shoot the deer he didn't intend to eat, so he didn't kill anyone who was not an assignment—which was why, when the Toyota Previa emerged from the garage, he knew he could not install the car bomb today. The entire family was in the car.

Juho followed them to the freeway, where they turned east toward Washington. Going to the city, he thought. But on the George Washington Parkway the Toyota continued south, past the bridges that crossed the Potomac, to National Airport. Juho watched as they pulled into the passenger loading zone. The target exchanged hugs with his family, took an overnight bag from the car and entered the terminal.

When the Toyota departed, Juho inched forward and caught a glimpse of Bill waiting in line at the USAir counter. Juho drove to the closest parking lot and jogged back to the terminal in time to watch Bill buy a ticket. Keeping well behind, he followed the target to the security checkpoint, where he disappeared down the concourse. Going where? Waving his wallet he returned in a rush to the USAir counter.

"Passenger Bill Sullivan," Juho called out. "Has he picked up his ticket yet? He left this in my car."

The agent said, "I just checked him through."

"What gate?"

She looked down at her video screen. "Twenty-three."

Juho found a video monitor displaying departure information. Gate 23 was USAir Flight 890, destination, Kansas City. He checked his watch. There was enough time to purchase a ticket, but he quickly rejected the idea. Sullivan might recognize him on the plane. Worse, without his custom-modified luggage there was no way to transport his weapons. No, he decided, the target had only an overnight bag, he wouldn't be gone long. But the delay bothered him more than he cared to admit. Returning to the car, Juho tried to ignore the feeling that Sullivan was like the wolf he once hunted who always managed to slip away until one day it simply disappeared.

Kansas City was only an intermediate stop where Bill changed planes and continued to Wichita. He had spent his first year of college here but felt no affinity for the place, could barely remember it. He rented a Plymouth Sundance for the ninety-minute drive to Goodheart. Summer still retained its grip on the Midwest and he drove with the windows open to the smell of sagebrush and silage that seemed more foreign than familiar. This was the no-man's-land he had hated as a child, the flat prairie interrupted only by water towers, one after the other, marching toward infinity. Despite its broad expanses, the prairie had always seemed to Bill claustrophobic, like a prison with walls of boredom and chains of small-town gossip. He was surprised at the vehemence of his memories, the aversion they evoked.

Goodheart was much as he remembered it, a four-block-long main street bordered by two- and three-story buildings built years ago when the town was more popular and prosperous. The Sears & Roebuck where his mother once worked was now the Home Decorator Center, but the Sunflower Cafe was still there, as was the Roundup Bar, a windowless cinderblock building that looked more dismal than he remembered. Most of the new businesses were near the freeway, which passed through a half mile from the town. That was where Bill took a room at a Days Inn Motel.

He found Elsie Fuchs's address in the phone book and remembered the streets well enough to find the place without asking directions. It was a tiny house with false brick siding and rusty red and white awnings sagging above the windows. The sidewalk was bordered by an ankle-high green plastic fence. His knock was answered by the yapping of a dog. When Elsie opened the door he saw that she had grown heavy except in the face where her clean features were now tight and made more colorless by obviously dyed hair. It was hard to imagine her with his father.

"Yes?"

"Mrs. Fuchs, I'm Bill Sullivan. I've come from Washington to ask you some questions about my father. May I come in?"

She looked him up and down. "Are you cleansed, Billy? Do you repent what you done to me at Danny's funeral?"

It was odd hearing his father referred to as Danny. "Mrs. Fuchs, whatever happened back then is history. I don't want to embarrass you, but I'm trying to put together a medical history of my parents. You knew my father, and I need your help."

Her eyes hardened. "No, you don't, 'cause you ain't Billy." She tried to shut the door, but he put his foot in it.

"Mrs. Fuchs, please."

"Who are you really?"

"I'm Bill Sullivan."

"Not unless you changed your shape. Satan can change his shape to suit an ill purpose, but I have washed my sins in the blood of the Lamb and the scales have fallen from my eyes. Now you'd best get your foot out of my door before my husband comes home."

A religious fanatic, Bill thought with a sinking heart. "Look at me, Mrs. Fuchs. Don't you remember me?"

"I never laid eyes on you."

"Bill Sullivan. Remember the last time we saw each other? My parents' funeral?"

A stubborn look crossed her face. "If you're Billy you tell me what you did at Danny's funeral."

"I threw the first handful of dirt, I remember that."

"What about me?"

"You wore a dark blue dress with white gloves."

She blinked, uncertain now. "Then what'd you do when you saw me?"

"I don't remember doing anything."

"I knew it." She tried to shut the door again.

"Mrs. Fuchs—"

Suddenly she was screaming. "You spit at my feet. On hallowed ground where the Christian dead lie in the bosom of the Lord you spit on me. Before my friends, my family, my neighbors you judged me, you—you—" Suddenly her eyes flew upward and she pointed at Bill. "I rebuke thee, Satan, and all thy works and thy followers, and cast thee from my heart and from my house. In the name of Jesus get out! Get out! Get out!"

With each phrase she banged the door against his foot while behind her the dog danced on its toes, pink mouth wide and yapping. It was useless, the woman was nearly hysterical. He removed his foot and allowed the door to slam shut.

Bill returned to the car and drove aimlessly, opening his mind to the random memories of the past. Names floated up as he passed certain houses: Parker, Lambert, Smith, Blaylock—each house had a face attached, a kid he'd gone to school with. He drove past his school and noticed a new addition filled with more windows. Without thinking, he traced his route home. The last time he'd seen it the place was nothing more than ash and burnt timber. Now there was a new house, one with a stucco exterior and varnished wood door boasting a stained-glass window the size of a pot holder. *The new house*—that's how he thought of it, but the storm gutter was bent and there were rust stains around the windows; it was already an old house with its own sad history of bleak winters and constrained lives.

On the house next door crudely crafted wood letters spelled *The Purcells*. Bill remembered them—Sally especially. She was a chubby tomboy whom he'd run around with while they were growing up.

A gray-haired lanky man was sitting on the front porch. He looked up and Bill recognized him: Hank Purcell, Sally's father. Along with the name came a memory of the time one of the Purcells' two dogs was poisoned and Hank stayed up all night sitting in the backyard with a shotgun across his knees. But the memory was vague and he could no longer recall if this was something he'd seen or something his father had described.

Bill parked the car and approached the old man. "Hi there. You're Mr. Purcell."

"Who're you?"

"I'm Bill Sullivan. You remember me?"

"Bill Sullivan?"

"Billy back then. I used to live next door."

"Billy," Hank said with a smile. "Sure, I remember you." They shook hands. "You lived next door."

"The house that burned."

"Yeah, sure, I know you."

He felt a huge relief. "Have you got a few minutes? I'd like to talk to you about my folks. What you remember about them."

"Sure, come on in. Billy Sullivan, it's been a long time, right?"

"Almost twenty years."

They went into the living room, which was much the way he recalled it. There was a radio playing a country-and-western tune and the smell of roast chicken coming from the kitchen.

"Sit down, put up your feet."

"I won't take up much of your time, Mr. Purcell. I'm interested in finding out more about the fire, the one where my folks died. Do you remember that night?"

"I remember everything some of the time and some things all

the time—that's what I say when people ask me about my memory."

"But you remember the fire?"

"Daddy, who're you—?" A woman entered from the kitchen and stopped short. "Oh, I didn't know there was anyone here." She wore tennis shoes, shorts and a light cotton blouse. A red and gold scarf held a shock of honey-brown hair back from her head. Bill recognized her. "Sally?"

She looked puzzled. "Did my father . . . ?"

"It's Bill Sullivan."

Her expression remained blank. "Who?"

"Billy Sullivan. From next door."

She smiled, revealing a warm, generous mouth. "If you're Billy Sullivan then I'm Marilyn Monroe."

Before he could respond, Hank pointed his finger at his daughter and demanded, "Who're you?"

She said absently, "It's Sally, Daddy."

Hank smiled. "Sally, sure. I remember you."

She gave Bill an apologetic smile. "I hope he didn't insult you or anything. Daddy has Alzheimers. He remembers his first BB gun better than he remembers what he had for breakfast this morning, don't you, Daddy?"

"A Daisy Model Ninety-four."

"See there?"

Bill was stunned, the momentary confidence he'd felt in Hank's greeting shattered. First Elsie and now Sally denied knowing him. The only one who recognized him didn't recognize his own daughter.

"I'm hungry," Hank announced to no one in particular.

"Dinner's ready. It's on the table in the kitchen. If you'll excuse us, Mister—?"

"I need to talk to you. Just for a moment."

"Maybe later."

"No, now." She stiffened. "Sorry, but I just flew in from Washington, D.C., and I can't leave. It's important I talk to you."

She regarded him for a moment, then turned to her father.

"You go ahead, Daddy. The food's on the table. I'll be there in a moment."

Hank glanced at Bill and said, "My wife is a snake charmer. You're my witness."

Sally took her father's elbow and turned him toward the kitchen. "Daddy, go on."

Hank jerked his hand away. "I'm not a load of cowshit. I know where the kitchen is. I know it."

She looked after him, embarrassed. "I'm sorry, he doesn't know what he's saying." Self-consciously she tucked an errant strand of hair beneath the scarf. "What is it you want from me?"

"Sally, I know you. I remember you. Don't you recognize me?"

She shook her head with a puzzled smile. "Nobody changes that much. Billy, he was skinnier in the face and the voice is . . . just not the same."

"I can prove it. Look." Feeling vaguely foolish, he brought out his wallet and showed her his Virginia driver's license. "I'm Bill Sullivan."

She took the license and inspected it. He noticed that her pink nail polish was worn and chipped. "So you're Bill Sullivan. All that proves is there's more than one of you by that name. We got us two Johnny Johnson's right here in Goodheart."

"What about the wagon you had? Remember when we got the sheet from your bed and made a sail? Got as far as the water tower and tipped over?"

A slow smile worked its way across her face. "You're a regular mystery man."

"We used to sit in your Dad's car—the Buick Skylark, remember? We'd turn on the radio and pretend we were driving to San Francisco? And what about the night we went out to the boxcars on the railroad siding and your parents locked you out?"

She shook her head slowly. "Maybe I'm losing my mind here because you're not the Billy Sullivan I remember. Not unless you had a plastic surgeon work your face over or something . . ."

From the kitchen Hank called, "Where are my peaches?"

"In a minute." She turned to Bill. "Listen, you couldn't know what you know without talking to Billy. If he's out in the car or

something you tell him the joke's over. Now, if you'll excuse us."
She opened the front door.

Bill said, "Did you keep your *Horizons*?"

"Beg your pardon?"

"The high-school yearbook? *Horizons*. I know what I wrote in
yours: *To Sally in the sky with diamonds, keep that smile forever,
Cowboy Bill.*"

She stared at him. "That's a lot of studying up for a joke without a punch line."

"I know you. I went to school with you and I can prove it. My
picture is in *Horizons* and I don't look so different. Get the book.
I'll show you."

"I threw that thing out the day I got divorced. But I know
somebody who has one."

"Who?"

"Oh, no, now it's my turn for a little mystery. You staying
around here?"

"The Days Inn."

"I'll find a yearbook and call you. One of us is in for a big
surprise."

The television was blaring at full volume as Bill left the house.
He got in the car and drove the familiar streets of a town that no
longer recognized him, a newborn stranger in a world growing
more alien by the minute.

CHAPTER

14

By the time he got back to the motel a message from Sally was waiting. They were to meet at the Roundup Bar at nine. Bill was half tempted to call her and suggest another place; he had enough unpleasant memories of failed efforts to lure his father home from the bar. But it would be a good place to meet people he had known before. A good place to find out the truth.

Returning to the Roundup was like stepping into a time capsule. Pockets of light from Schlitz and Budweiser signs washed against stained walls; the place smelled of stale sweat and flat beer. Sally wasn't there, so Bill went to the bar and ordered a ginger ale. The bartender, a muscular young man with curly brown hair held back in a ponytail, looked pained. "Just a ginger ale, that's it?"

"With ice."

Either it was still early or the Roundup wasn't attracting the same crowd it used to. Three old men sat around one table, and four teenagers, one with a cigarette pack rolled into the sleeve of his black T-shirt, were playing pool. Two men Bill's age were hunched over a pitcher of beer, one with his back to him, the other with a baseball cap canted low over his head. Bill didn't recognize them. In one corner of the room stood a Wurlitzer jukebox where, as a boy, he'd watched the bubbles rise in colored tubes. Now there were no bubbles.

"That'll be a dollar," the bartender called.

"You should get it fixed."

"What's that?"

"The jukebox. It used to have bubbles coming up the tubes."

"That's what everybody says, but the Wurlitzer man come through a couple years ago to put in CDs instead of the old 45s. Turns out this is the E model, E for economy. This one never had no bubbles."

"It did. I remember it."

"Yeah?" The bartender called to the two men. "Hey Lou, did this thing ever have bubbles coming up the tubes?"

"What tubes? What bubbles? You sound like my wife."

As soon as he turned around, Bill recognized the square face and petulant lips and the hair now thin that had once been a crew cut. Lou LaBounty.

"I'm talking about bubbles in the jukebox," the bartender said.

"She is?" Lou's friend in the baseball hat leaned forward, his words slurred. "Fuck man, get her out of there."

"Yeah, Johnny," Lou said to the bartender. "What's she doing in the jukebox?"

The friend said, "Looking for a tube, what do you think?"

"Hey, I got her tube right here." Lou slapped his crotch. Their smiles died as Bill approached the table. "You're Lou LaBounty."

Lou's friend, the man in the baseball cap, had long sideburns and a snake tattoo around his wrist. He leaned across the table and said, "He used to be Lou LaBounty. Now he's Bubbles Magoolie."

Lou held up his middle finger. "See this, Rob? See this?"

Rob grabbed at the finger, but Lou yanked his hand away. They were both grinning, floating in a beery haze of adolescent good humor. Bill stepped closer.

"I'm Bill Sullivan. We went to school together, remember?"

Lou stared at him with a sloppy grin. "Bill who?"

"Bill Sullivan. I used to live here. Fifteen years, maybe more. You're Lou LaBounty, we were in the same class in high school."

The expected flash of recognition didn't materialize. From across the table, Rob yelled at his friend, "Bill Sullivan, numbnuts. Don't you recognize him?"

"Hey, Rob, bite my crank."

A new name popped into Bill's mind. "Rob Foglia," he said to the man in the cap. "You were two years behind us."

Rob pointed at him. "You must be Bill Sullivan."

"I'm serious. Do you remember me?"

Lou said, "He wouldn't remember his own dick if it spit in his face."

"Fuck you, he's Bill Sullivan."

"You don't know shit."

"He looks like Bill Sullivan to me."

Lou reached across the table and yanked the brim of Rob's hat down. "You look like a fucking penguin to me."

Bill wanted to grab Lou and shake him. *Look at me.* Instead Sally walked in and all eyes turned toward her.

"Bubbles," Rob yelled. "There she is."

She was wearing a short skirt, a low-cut blouse, gold earrings and enough makeup to stand out even in the dim light of the Roundup. Under her arm she carried something in a canvas B. Dalton book bag.

Lou said, "Hey, Sally, you want a beer?"

"Not with you two nitwits." And to Bill, "You mind if we sit on the opposite side from the loony bin?"

Ignoring Rob's pleas for Sally to join him, they found a table covered with a plastic red-and-white-checked tablecloth. When the bartender asked what she wanted, Sally indicated Bill's glass and said, "Whatever he's having."

"Schweppes or Canada Dry?"

"What?"

Bill said, "It's ginger ale."

She wrinkled her nose. "Forget it. Just bring me a draft." She turned to Bill. "Sorry I'm late. I had to get Peggy from next door to look after Daddy."

He indicated the book bag. "Is that it?"

She pulled out the yearbook and handed it across the table. It was wrapped in a plastic jacket. Bill opened it to the row of senior portraits and turned to the page where he knew he'd find his picture. It wasn't there.

"Have you got the—?" *Right year,* he was going to ask, but already his eye had found the captions at the edge of the page. *Bill Sullivan, Track 3, Baseball 2.* He grabbed the book and looked more closely. The boy who stared back at him had the same blond hair but a thinner face, a crooked nose and a distinctive elongated chin. Not him. Not him at all.

"You still want to tell me you're the same Bill Sullivan as this picture?"

Bill turned to the cover. It was the year of his graduation, exactly the same as the one he had at home. But this one had been altered. He turned back to the portraits and scratched at the photo. Sally grabbed his hand. "Don't."

"Where did you get this?"

"Norma Levett. She used to be Rawson back then, see?" She pointed to the photo of a girl with a flip haircut and button nose.

Bill felt dizzy, light-headed. There was a roaring in his ears, and he shook his head to clear it. "It's a joke. You switched photos, you manipulated this book."

"You're the one who came here pretending to be somebody you're not."

He grabbed her arm. "Don't play with me. I've had enough games. Where did you get this? How did you do it? How?"

"Stop it." She tried to pull away, but his fingers were locked tight on her arm. "Ouch."

"Tell me!"

A hand landed flat on his shoulder. Sally jerked free and jumped to her feet, knocking the glass of ginger ale to the floor.

Bill pivoted out from under Johnny's grip. The bartender faced him, chin high, hands raised in a cautionary pose. "Easy, buddy, we don't want no trouble."

"This woman knows me. These people know me. There's something going on here . . ." He turned in a circle. "You all know me. I grew up here. This is my home, my school, my house, my parents are buried in the cemetery here . . ."

"Bill Sullivan!" Rob yelled enthusiastically.

He turned to the bartender. "I know this bar. I know you used to have a bear's head up there and the prices were on a chalkboard up there, and there was a 1936 calendar up there. I remember all that. And I remember *him*. He's Lou LaBounty. We went to school together. And Sally lived next door to me." The words were tumbling too quickly now. He stopped. Sally had backed away. He held out his hand to her, his voice strained, "We sat in your father's car . . . don't you remember?"

Rob was still yelling, "Bill Sullivan. Look, it's Bill Sullivan, I remember you."

Not true. None of them remembered him; he was surrounded by strangers' eyes, a world that had all the appearance of reality but which was dead to him. Johnny returned with a glass of whiskey. "Here, you need a little cooler."

The country-and-western tune on the jukebox ended and the place went quiet. The kids at the pool table were watching him. Bill felt as if he were going to explode. He grabbed the glass and downed it. The burning sensation raced to his stomach. He leaned on the bar. Sally watched him warily. "You okay?"

"You don't believe me."

"I believe you know a lot about me and this town, you proved that. But after that, you're a mystery man. If it's not a joke—"

"It's not."

"And you really think you grew up here—"

"I *did*. At least . . ." He shook his head.

"Maybe it's a case of one of those unsolved mysteries like they have on television. Maybe they'll do a program about you, how you came up with all these memories of another Bill Sullivan." She smiled and he didn't know if she was kidding him or not. "Let's see if we can figure it out. Come on back to the table."

He wanted to run down the street, screaming at the top of his lungs, but he was numb.

"Come on," Sally tugged his arm. "Let's talk this thing out."

She must have signaled Johnny, because as soon as they sat down he brought another shot of whiskey. I shouldn't drink, Bill thought, but the admonition had no force. Nothing made sense now, so nothing wasn't sensible.

Sally said, "Tell you the truth, I wish you *had* grown up here. The Billy you think you are, he was no great shakes, let me tell you."

"That jukebox. I used to stand there with my forehead against those colored tubes, watching the bubbles."

"Okay, Mystery Man, let's play this little game out. I'll ask you questions and you tell me what you remember." She lifted his glass. "Here, want another?"

"I've had enough." The alcohol had suffused his body, relaxing him, bringing a vague euphoria. Sally's head swam toward him.

"Tell me how long you went to school here?"

"From twelve until eighteen."

"What homeroom did we share?"

"I don't . . . think we did."

"Sophomore year. Mrs. Randal. Remember she got in trouble with her income taxes and we called her Scandal Randal? Now, how could you forget that if you were the Bill Sullivan who went to school with me?"

The shot glass was still in front of him, the nut-brown liquid glistening. Bill took a sip.

"You okay?" Sally said. "You don't look so great."

"I don't drink."

"Could have fooled me." She reached across the table and placed her palm on his forehead. "You're hot."

He moved away. "I'm all right."

"I won't bite," Sally said with a smile. She lifted her glass and shook it gently. "The school song, you remember it?"

Bill found the words with difficulty. *"Goodheart Union we'll remember, golden days of sweet September . . ."*

"Wait, wait—that's confusing, hearing you say it like a speech. Sing it to me."

"I've got a lousy voice."

"Oh sure, remember what you did in the Junior Talent Contest?"

"I sang 'Ave Maria' and took second place." The answer sprang forth of its own accord.

"And you've got a lousy voice? Come on, let's hear you sing the whole song."

"I forget the rest."

The truth was that he couldn't recall the song; the words were there, but not a single note of music. Not true, there *was* music, a tune he couldn't identify, but it wasn't the school song and the words . . . he couldn't quite get the words . . .

"All right," Sally said. "What happened to Mike Bickle?"

"He slashed his wrists in the boy's bathroom during third period our senior year."

"Remember what the note said?"

"Note?"

"The suicide note. Remember who he blamed?"

He frowned. "No."

"You know a lot, but there's a lot you don't know. Now let me in on the secret. Why are you really here? Are you really in the Secret Service?" She lowered her voice. "Is it some kind of scam? Are you going to confiscate all our money and call it counterfeit?" Her smile died when he didn't return it. "Hey, lighten up, Mystery Man."

Bill saw it then, the sparkle in her eye, the hint of calculation and temptation, her refrain of *Mystery Man*—she thought this was some kind of seduction. He should have seen it earlier. Would have seen it if he wasn't so focused on himself. He pushed the bottle of liquor away. Sally paused. "What's the matter?"

"Nothing." The pain was spreading across his forehead, lights and activity on one side, darkness and pain on the other.

"You want some aspirin?" She reached for her purse and pulled some out. The bar seemed to throb, and when he looked at the Wurlitzer he could almost see bubbles rising in the tubes.

"Open wide," she said, holding an aspirin at eye level. In her other hand she had a glass of water.

"I'll get it," he said, but the words were slurred and his movements clumsy. Her hand dodged his.

"You might hit your nose. Say *ahhhh.*"

He opened his mouth, out of control, near the brink of blindness, and she put the water to his lips. *I don't want this,* he thought. An echo now, the tune in the back of his mind, like a music box hidden in the closet. And words. When he reached for them they slipped away. He lurched to his feet. "Got to go."

"You're in no shape to drive. I'll take you to the motel."

She helped him to her car, where he sat hunched forward, gripping the dashboard, pushing the walls of oblivion that threatened to collapse around him. When they arrived, Sally walked him to the door. "Key?"

It was attached to a cutout of a sunflower. Bill fumbled it out of his pocket and dropped it. They both bent to pick it up, and he lost his balance and stepped into her. Without knowing how it happened, he had his arms around her, hips against thighs, her breasts pushed against his chest, her eyes swimming toward him on a sea of unfamiliar perfume. Their lips met. It was wrong. He pulled back. "No."

She cupped his face. "Bill."

"I'm married."

"I don't want to know." She stood on her toes and tried to pull him close, but he averted his face. "I don't care who you are," she whispered. "It doesn't matter."

Claire, Matt, Megan . . . he felt like a statue as she kissed him and ran her hands over his body, searching, trying unsuccessfully to entice a response. Finally she gave up. "It's not just your memory that's fucked up, let me tell you."

He held out his hand. "Key."

"I'll do it," she said in disgust. "You're in no shape to find a slot in the dark."

He could hear the music now, the tune clear in his head as he stumbled across the room and fell facedown into the cheap starched sheets, the sound of a woman's voice, familiar, soft and soothing:

Where have you been, Billy boy, Billy boy
Oh, where have you been, charming Billy . . . ?

He lost consciousness before the answer came.

CHAPTER

15

The pounding in his head became pounding on the door to the hotel room. Bill opened his eyes. The room was dim except for a strip of light from beyond the closed curtains. "Police, open up."

Police? He struggled into a sitting position and fumbled for the lamp beside the bed. The light pierced his eyes, and he shielded his face with his hand until his eyes adjusted. He was naked. His clothes lay on the floor next to the disheveled bed-spread.

A key in the latch and the door opened, flooding the room with light. Three figures in silhouette stood in the doorway, two in uniform. Someone said, "Looks like we caught him with his pants down." The biggest shadow stepped into the room. "Looking for Bill Sullivan, is that you?"

"Who're you?"

"I'm Sheriff Bobby Luckner. This here is Deputy Willis. Like to ask you a few questions."

Sheriff Luckner had a wrestler's build with a beer-drinker's stomach that stuck out in front of him like a shopping bag.

"What time is it?" As Bill picked up his pants from the floor he saw two foil-wrapped packages on the floor.

"Nigh onto seven o'clock. Would have waited but—Leave those there, sir."

Bill had picked up the silver objects, two shrink-wrapped Trojan condoms. "These aren't mine."

Luckner took off his hat and held it upside down. "Just drop them in here."

"What's going on?"

"In the hat, please." As soon as he had them, the sheriff handed the hat to the deputy, a cow-faced young man with a thin moustache, who used a handkerchief to remove them and place them in plastic evidence bags. By that time Bill had put on his pants and dragged his shirt, covered with dust and missing one button, from beneath the bed. He felt hollow, but his head was clear.

Luckner said, "Were you with a Sally Purcell last night?"

Images of Sally, the bar, fumbling for a key . . . "Did something happen to her?"

"That's what we're trying to find out. Were you with her?"

"We had a few drinks at the Roundup. Where is she?"

"When was the last time you saw her?"

"She dropped me off here last night." He heard a drawer open and turned to find Willis poking through the dresser. "Unless you've got a search warrant leave the drawers alone."

The sheriff said, "Bud gave us permission, didn't you, Bud?"

The motel clerk, who was peering around the room like a preacher inspecting a whorehouse, started when Luckner called his name. "That's right."

"Doesn't matter," Bill said. "A motel room enjoys the same Fourth Amendment privileges as a private home. Unless you're in hot pursuit or you've got a warrant, just keep your hands out of my stuff."

Willis looked for instruction to the sheriff, who said, "You a lawyer, Mr. Sullivan?"

"I'm with the Secret Service. What about Sally?"

"About Sally—Miss Purcell—what happened after she dropped you off? She come into the room here?"

"No." And then, recalling the condoms. "At least not as far as I know. I was asleep before I hit the bed."

"Did you have sex with her?"

Bill's mind cleared, as if by an arctic wind. "Did she say that?"

"How about you answer my question first. You two spend some time between the sheets?"

"No."

"Sheriff?" The deputy held up a broken heel from a woman's shoe. "Behind the door."

"That could belong to anybody," Bill said quickly and just as quickly regretted it. He had a good memory for details and he remembered the shoes. "Did Sally say she spent the night?"

"Not exactly. She said you raped her."

Bill was stunned. "That's a lie."

"She said you showed up in town yesterday impersonating a guy who used to live here, Bill Sullivan."

"I am Bill Sullivan. I'm with the Secret Service. You can confirm that with the field office in Kansas City."

"You got any identification?"

Bill pulled out his wallet and handed it to him. The sheriff held it up to the light and turned it toward his deputy. "Look at this, Tim. You ever seen a federal badge before?"

"We had an FBI instructor in K.C., but I never seen his badge."

The sheriff handed it to the deputy. "Check it out."

Tim disappeared, and Luckner returned his attention to Bill. "If that thing's real you put me in a bind. On one hand I got a complaint by a citizen of this town saying you raped her—"

"That's not what happened. I had too much to drink, she drove me here, and when I got out of the car she came onto me. We kissed. That's all that happened."

A slight smile. "Just kissed?"

"She kissed me."

"Twisted your arm, I'll bet."

"Nobody raped anybody last night."

"Well, that's not what Sally says."

"Then she's lying."

"You're saying this is a case of female revenge because you turned the woman down?"

"I don't even know what she said, I'm just telling you what happened."

"Then I guess we better go to the office and sort this thing out."

"Am I under arrest?"

"God, I hope not. It's too early in the day to start reading all those Miranda rights. Why don't you just come down for a friendly visit and help us clear things up. We got coffee, donuts, all the comforts of home. And maybe I can figure out between the two of you just what happened here last night."

Bill went to the bathroom, where he washed his face, combed his hair and noticed in the mirror what Sheriff Luckner must have already seen, a row of parallel scratches across his chest the distance apart of fingernails.

Bill finished dressing and accompanied Luckner to a police car whose rotating light was blazing for no apparent reason. Willis had already gotten a computer readout. The sheriff studied it and said grudgingly, "I guess you're who you say you are, all right. No warrants, no unpaid traffic tickets." He handed the identification card back to Bill. "Times like this, I wish I'd stayed in the Army. I've known Sally Purcell ten years now and never known her to lie."

"Let me talk to her."

"No problem there."

They drove in silence punctuated by laconic calls on the police radio. When Luckner lit a cigarette Bill rolled down the window, diffusing the smoke with damp morning air. The sheriff's office, which also housed the county jail, was an austere stucco building with a tall communications antenna extending from its roof. A woman in uniform at the front desk studied Bill with avid curiosity as they went to the sheriff's office. Sally was dozing, curled in a chair. She jumped up when they entered. What looked like a man's sweater hung over a blouse and skirt equally wrinkled. She looked hollow-eyed, and the overhead light illuminated the ridge where the back of the chair had left an impression on her cheek. Seeing Bill, she stiffened and her eyes narrowed. The sheriff said, "Have a seat, the both of you."

"Is it true?" Bill asked. "You told them I raped you?"

"Now you talk. Now you'll say something." Tears welled up in her eyes.

"Why did you say it?"

"Why'd you do it?"

"I didn't do anything."

Sheriff Luckner interposed his stomach between them. "All right, you two sit down. I want some coffee before we begin this thing. Anybody else want to put in an order?" When nobody responded, he nodded to Deputy Willis, who went and got the coffee.

The office was overlit, the desk spare, a bulletin board on one wall cluttered with Wanted and Missing Persons posters. The sheriff sat them on opposite sides of the desk, then said, "Sally, this here is the man you were with last night?"

"Yes."

"According to what he tells me, you were, shall we say, in the mood. Says you kissed him, is that right?"

"It's not the same thing."

"The way you told it, Sally, he just up and grabbed you, but now it looks like there might have been a little bit of mutuality."

She said slowly, "In the early part of the evening I liked him. He had all this confusion about who he really was and it was like a game. I didn't know if he was kidding or what. But we talked a lot and he seemed like he needed help."

She glanced at Bill and looked away quickly, but not before he saw the vulnerability that had taken her to the bar last night. Willis returned with two coffees in thick plastic cups dripping with coffee stains. After giving one to the sheriff, he stood near the window and listened with his brow furrowed in concentration. Luckner thrust a thick haunch onto the desk and slurped his coffee. "Sure you two don't want some?" When there was no response, he said to Sally, "What we got so far is you went voluntarily when this man invited you into his motel room, that right?"

Bill said, "I didn't invite her to my room."

The sheriff frowned at the intrusion. Sally said, "He was drunk. I took him to the motel and when he couldn't get the key in the door, I unlocked it. Then he passed out on the bed and I thought . . . I just wanted to make sure he wasn't going to choke or something. I moved the pillow, and that's when he woke up."

"Not true," Bill said. "I didn't wake up until half an hour ago."

Her eyes flashed. "You don't remember, is that your excuse?"

"It didn't happen."

Luckner said, "Wait a minute, let's get first things first. You say he woke up and then what?"

"He started whistling this little tune. And he motioned, like this." She curled her finger in a beckoning gesture.

No, thought Bill, that's crazy. Even the sheriff couldn't keep the skepticism from his voice.

"He whistled like this?" The sheriff made a two-tone wolf whistle.

"Not like that, it was a little tune. I don't know what it was."

"So he did this tune and you did what? You run away?"

She glanced at Bill and then down. "No."

"And then what? He grab you right away or . . . ?"

She sat silently, a big tear rolled down her cheek.

"He grab you, Sally?"

"I know how this sounds . . ."

"What did he do?"

"He kissed me."

A pause. "You kiss him back?"

Her voice was so low Bill had to strain to hear. "It wasn't that I didn't like him. It was okay until I told him we had to have protection. I didn't want to get pregnant or take any chances, but he wouldn't listen. Just kept grinning and pushing me onto the bed."

"Sally, what you're saying now is a horse of a different color from the one you rode in on. If you were willing to have sex with the man—"

"Not if he wasn't safe. That's my choice and I said *no* and he ignored me. Even when I gave him a rubber he just laughed and tossed it aside. At first I thought it was a joke, but he wouldn't talk, he wouldn't listen. I tried to push him off and finally I screamed and that's when he put his hand on my mouth. He had this wild look in his eye. I thought he was going to choke me. That's not making love, that's rape."

Bill was appalled. The events she described had nothing to do with him. He shook his head, "No, no, no."

"Admit it, that's what you did!"

"Sally, don't do this . . ."

"Do this? You're the one! You used me like a piece of meat, like I didn't count at all. You just turned on me like an animal . . ."

Luckner said, "All right, Sally, calm down."

"You think it's my fault. Because I went to his room I deserve to be raped. Does he have to kill me before you believe me?"

"Nobody says it's—"

She jumped to her feet. "You want to know why I didn't tell you everything at the beginning, this is why. This is why!"

She marched out of the room and slammed the door. The sheriff pointed at Bill. "You stay put."

Luckner left the room, and after a moment's hesitation, Willis followed. Through the window Bill could see them talking, the sheriff leaning with one hand against the wall, shielding Sally or blocking her exit, he couldn't tell which. Bill felt sick to his stomach. No matter how drunk he was, he knew he wasn't capable of the kind of callousness she described. And yet, and yet . . . there was the physical evidence, the condoms on the floor and his bruised pubic bone, the truth of his own body. And the tune . . .

Sheriff Luckner returned, pulled out a cigarette and offered one to Bill, who refused it. Luckner toyed with the cigarette, turning it slowly between his thumb and forefinger.

"She went to the hospital, did you know that? The doctor tells me they got a pretty good collection of physical evidence. Sperm, couple of pubic hairs, what looks like skin samples beneath her fingernails. If it's like you say, none of them will match the samples I'd like you to give us."

There it was, the trap closing like a vise. The samples would match. The sheriff stood up. "You want to come to the hospital voluntarily or do I have to get official?"

"First I want to talk to her. Alone."

"I don't think she wants to talk to you."

Bill pulled out a business card and wrote on the back, *Your father knows*. "Give this to her."

The sheriff inspected the note, pursed his lips and left without a word. A few moments later Sally entered and stood with arms crossed, regarding him distrustfully. "My father knows what?"

"He knows what it's like to stare at you and not recognize you. He knows what it's like to be told things he did that he can't recall. He knows what it's like to be betrayed by his own mind."

"My father has Alzheimers. Jesus, I don't believe you."

"Sally, you were there when I found out I wasn't the person I thought I was. You brought the evidence. Did you think it was all a game? Is that what it seemed like to you?"

"I don't know."

"I think you do. Think of the way you held my hands in the bar, kept me calm, did you feel any threat, any warning of what happened last night? Yesterday I thought this town was my home, I thought I was Bill Sullivan and I thought we'd grown up together. You tell me it never happened, and I believe you. Now I ask you to believe me, I have no memory of what happened last night. No, it's more than that. It's not me."

"Sure, just the whiskey."

"Not the whiskey. Don't you see? If I'm not Bill Sullivan, then I don't know who I am."

"That supposed to make me feel better?"

"It won't make either of us feel any better. But I swear by my wife and my children and everything I hold dear that I have no memory of anything that happened after I fell into that bed."

She glanced away. "You should have mentioned her at the house."

"Who?"

"Your wife. You didn't tell me about her until the Roundup, and by then I already . . ." She shook off some private memory.

Bill took a deep breath. "You're right, Sally. Tell the sheriff that physical samples won't be necessary. I'll sign a statement acknowledging your account of anything that happened last night."

A welter of emotions crisscrossed her features and she turned to the window. After a moment she said, "I even bought a new bottle of perfume for last night. Silly Sally."

She turned on her heel and left the room. By the time Bill followed her she had already passed Luckner, who scrambled to his feet. "Sally, wait. What about this complaint?"

"Forget it."

"Wait a minute, now. This may be our only chance to take physical specimens from Mr. Sullivan."

She stopped and turned. "He's not the one."

"What?"

"I don't know who he is, but he's not the same man who raped me."

She walked out of the building. The sheriff gave Bill an appraising look. "Slick as snake shit, you federal boys."

For the first time in his life Bill felt like slamming his fist into another man's face. Without a word he left the sheriff's office and walked blindly until he found himself at the cemetery. There was no confusion now, he knew exactly where his parents were buried. The graves were as he remembered them, overgrown with weeds now but marked with matching gray marble tombstones. He placed a hand first on one, then on the other. They were cool to the touch, substantial, real, solid. His fingers tracing the names etched in the stone brought forth little emotional resonance.

"Mom?" he whispered. "Dad?"

From as far back as he could remember he had felt superior to his parents, more intelligent, more capable, stronger of character. And when they died, he had buried their memories and become self-sufficient, a man formed of his own aspirations. He had never cultivated their influence in his life, and now that he needed them he couldn't find them. He ranged backward in his mind trying to find the crucial elements of his upbringing, but found only memories without emotional meaning and after that nothing, a terrible void.

Bill placed his forehead against the tombstone and closed his eyes. In the distance the rumble of diesel trucks on the freeway drifted across a graveyard as flat as the cloud-scattered sky overhead. *If I didn't grow up here, if these are not my parents . . .*

Something tickled his wrist. He opened his eyes. An ant crawling up his arm. He flicked it away with his free hand and in the momentary preoccupation with the mundane a new thought struck: *the background investigation.* During their recruitment, the background of all Secret Service agents was thoroughly investigated. Everything in his file would have been verified at the time he joined the Service.

Chaos receded. Here was something concrete he could depend upon. Memories still contradicted the facts of the past twenty-four hours, but the background investigation corroborated his memories. It had to. He walked to the Roundup, where he retrieved the rental car. Back at the hotel he took a shower, changed clothes, then made two phone calls. The first was to USAir, where he booked an afternoon flight home. The second call was to Claire, who immediately felt the tension in his voice. "What did you find out?"

"A lot of things. Can you meet me at the airport without the kids?"

"Bill, what happened?"

"Nothing that won't keep, but I want to see you before I see them. Can you do it?"

"If I can find a sitter."

"Do it. Find somebody. I need to see you alone."

CHAPTER
16

The Russian Intelligence Service had built a new headquarters south of Moscow in a suburb called Yasenevo. Designed by a Finnish architectural firm, the new buildings featured dark windows running in vertical stripes along pink marble facades and a rambling, campuslike atmosphere that detractors referred to as "Little Langley," because of its reputed resemblance to CIA headquarters in Virginia. Yasenevo was meant to reflect the KGB's new image in the post-Soviet world, Big Brother with a smiling face.

The three men who sat at a table in Secure Room Blue were not smiling. They were part of a group informally known as *Oara Oum,* or Black Sand, after the tons of distinctive dark cement used to bury the damaged nuclear reactor at Chernobyl. In this case, the contamination they sought to contain was that of the "old" KGB programs, which might prove embarrassing, costly or politically disastrous to the new regime. At the top of this list was the Sorin Project.

The man at the head of the table was a senior KGB officer named Iosif Repin. He was a florid-faced man whose moods were reflected in the color of his skin. Because of his aggressive demeanor he was known as the General, a nickname he encouraged by his attitude toward subordinates, an intimidating mixture of scorn and abuse. Right now he was directing his abuse at Yuri Ulovsky, a handsome young officer who had drawn attention to himself with the question, "Why would he shoot her in the knees?"

"Because he's a madman," the General barked. "Which we already know. The real question is why he didn't shoot her in the heart?"

Gennadi Khiza, recently returned from a brief trip to London, said, "I think he wants her alive when Sullivan dies."

"Amenov told her that?"

"What other reason?"

"That's what our mind reader is supposed to tell us. If he ever gets here." The General looked at his watch. "He's late." For the past ten minutes they had been listening to Khiza's account of his interview with Yelena Amenov. He looked back up. "And the British? You spoke to the police, what do they say?"

"Amenov left clues to mislead them into thinking he would return to a hotel. Now they think he left the country."

"If he's not in the country, then he's left it. This is the nation who gave the world Sherlock Holmes."

Khiza rubbed his eyes. He hadn't gotten much sleep in the past twenty-four hours, and he recalled fondly the old Secure Room in the Kremlin where a samovar of coffee was kept at full brew during these meetings. Secure Room Blue was one of two windowless high-security rooms, each submerged in a different color. The effect was supposed to be modern, but with its blue rug, blue chairs and table, and blue walls, Khiza felt as if he were adrift in an endless summer sky.

"What does the woman think?" the General demanded. "Does she know where Amenov is?"

"She thinks he's back here."

"In Moscow?"

"Amenov told her Mischa was working for the government. And promised Mischa would die. She interpreted that to mean he was working in Moscow."

"What else? The Sorin Project?"

"He didn't mention it."

"Unless she lied to you."

Khiza remembered the woman's expression, face framed by the pillow, both legs wrapped in casts; she even took his hand, moist skin, lambent eyes, imploring him, "Save him, please. You have to save my son." He could see why Amenov fell in love with her, but he couldn't imagine destroying her ability to dance.

"She has no reason to lie. In fact, she pleaded with me to save Mischa."

The General snorted. "What do you think, Yuri? Perhaps this woman is paying your Finnish farmer *not* to succeed."

Yuri Ulovsky was Juho Ryti's control, the man who gave Ryti his orders and received his reports. Right now Ryti was overdue with his next report—one that Yuri fervently hoped would contain only four words: *the package is delivered.* Until then he felt he had to defend his agent's integrity. "The Hawk has never failed us."

"The Hawk, my ass. Who coded him that name? Your fucking Hawk is a penguin, Yuri. We paid him hard currency for hard results and what do we get? Excuses. From a man who never fails."

"He'll try again."

"Before or after Amenov decides to activate Bill Sullivan?"

Yuri shifted uncomfortably. "We could tell the Americans."

"What?"

"If you're worried about the Hawk—"

"You mean the fucking penguin."

"—we could just tell the Americans what happened."

The General turned a shade darker red, but before he could respond a three-note chime warned them of a new arrival. A lock clicked open and the door swung on silent hinges, automatically admitting a bald man in his forties, wearing an illfitting suit.

"You're late!" the General barked.

The newcomer jumped. Dr. Pavel Tipkov had received his expedited top-secret clearance only two days earlier. "They searched me twice."

"It's a Secure Room, Doctor. What did you expect?"

"I had no expectations. I've never been in one before."

The General introduced Tipkov, referring to him as the "mind reader," which caused a slight frown to cross the doctor's features. In fact he was a KGB psychiatrist who had been given Vasily Amenov's personnel file and asked to provide a psychological profile of the man. Reflections glistened from the top of his head as Tipkov lifted a worn briefcase to the table and removed a thick file with a variety of colored tabs sticking from it. The General drummed his fingers impatiently. "Any time, Doctor."

"You don't mind if I stand?"

"Stand, sit, lie on the table, just tell us what to expect from Amenov."

Tipkov anchored himself by placing his fingers on the table. "To begin with, here is a man who should never have been accepted into the KGB in the first place. Almost a pure psychopath. When he was posted in London he beat his wife's lover to death with a cricket bat."

The General's finger's stopped. "A what?"

"Cricket bat. The game that the British—"

"I know what cricket is. Speak up, man, so I can hear you."

Khiza suppressed a smile. It was obvious that no one had warned Tipkov of the General's characteristic histrionics. It was a technique the old man used to take the measure of his subordinates; only those who kept their composure kept their jobs.

The doctor paused long enough to regain his composure and continued. "Comrade Amenov discovered the bat at a restaurant where he followed his wife to a liaison with her lover. He still had the handle when he returned to the embassy. There are photographs here, dried blood and brain tissue. In primitive terms, a trophy. Amenov was proud of what he'd done. Subsequent interviews confirmed pronounced psychopathic tendencies characterized by a high degree of rationalization and a lack of empathy for others. He saw his wife and his child as extensions of himself. His perception of the world—"

A high-pitched beep from the paging device on his belt brought Yuri to his feet. "It's him."

The General nodded, his expression grave. All eyes remained on the door as it closed automatically behind Yuri.

"Shall I go on?" Tipkov said.

"Get to the point, Doctor. Wave the magic wand and tell us what to expect from your psychopath."

"It depends on his perception of our organization. Throughout his career he requested a return to field work, but none was granted. His work at the Foreign News Analysis Division and at the Special Weapons School he perceived as demeaning. It may have been why he supported the August coup, a simple desire to indulge in covert activity. In any event, the subsequent prison sentence robbed him of his self-esteem and the advent of a terminal illness stole any hope for the future. A man in such a condition is a danger to himself, his family and his society."

General Repin's face had been growing redder, but Tipkov missed the danger signs. Now he burst out, "I've read the file, we've all read the file, what the fuck is the man going to do?"

Tipkov winced at the General's tone. "I think he would go to great measures to wreak the same kind of vengeance on this organization as he did on Jeremy Lawrence."

"We knew that when he stole the file. Why hasn't he done it yet?"

"He may well enjoy the feeling of power it gives him. Like a cat toying with a mouse, once the mouse is dead the game is over. If he doesn't know the theft has been discovered, he may be in no particular hurry to play his hand. He may want to pick the proper time and place. For instance, the anniversary of his prison sentence is three weeks away. For a man like Vasily Amenov, such a date is fraught with significance. I think there's an excellent possibility the American President will die on that particular date."

For the first time there was a feeling of discovery; this was something they hadn't thought of before. Before they could pursue the matter an unhappy-looking Yuri Ulovsky returned.

"Well?" the General demanded.

"Sullivan has gone to Kansas."

"Yes? And?"

"There was no way for the Hawk to follow. He's waiting for Sullivan to return."

"He's *waiting?* Your precious expert, this mighty Hawk is standing around with his thumb up his butt, just *waiting?*"

"Sullivan is not a danger in Kansas," Yuri said stiffly. "We have a reprieve."

"We don't need a reprieve, we need a solution. We need action. We need a bullet in the brain of Bill Sullivan. Where is that bullet? Why hasn't it been fired?"

It was a rhetorical question, but Tipkov was fool enough to offer a suggestion. "Why not tell the Americans?"

"Fine, Doctor, fine. But before we tell the Americans we'll have to tell our own President how we failed to safeguard the Sorin Project, and then failed to stop Vasily Amenov from leaving the country after he stole it, and then made a down payment of twenty thousand Swiss francs in hard currency to a man who *failed* to solve the problem and now—having put our country at risk while we failed again and again—now ask him to go crying to the Americans that we thought we might kill their President but now that we've changed our mind one of our men has set off to do it anyway and we can't stop him so can they please stop him for us? Is *that* what you think I'm going to tell our leaders?"

Tipkov's head had sunk into his shoulders during this outburst. "What else can you do?"

The General yelled, "We have our fucking assassin do his goddamn job!" He swung a finger at Yuri. "He's your man. You're his control. You tell your precious Hawk he has one day. Just one. As soon as Bill Sullivan steps foot back in Washington your man has twenty-four hours to eliminate him. I don't care how, why or where it happens. Twenty-four hours or I'll go over and do the job myself."

Beneath the bluster, Khiza detected a glint of panic in the

General's eye. The Hawk was a professional, but he was a prima donna. It had been too long, the whole thing. Yuri hastened from the room and silence fell. The fate of the American President had become their own.

CHAPTER
17

At the moment Vasily Amenov was under review in Moscow he had already arrived in Washington, D.C. Still traveling under an assumed name he rented a silver Chrysler LeBaron, the kind of respectable American car that would blend into any neighborhood, and took a hotel room at a Holiday Inn. On Sunday he was ready to see for himself where Bill Sullivan lived. His plan was simple. He would make one last attempt to activate Sullivan, this time from a phone booth close enough to the house so that he could monitor the results. If the activation worked, Sullivan would be killed or imprisoned. Vasily didn't care which. His satisfaction would be Yelena's pain and the desperate attempt of the Russian Republic's leaders to wriggle free of their responsibility for the event.

With a map of Virginia on the seat beside him he drove to a planned community called Lynwood. Townhouses and two-story homes bordered tree-lined streets with autumn leaves piled against round-shouldered curbs. A hand-scrawled sign posted to a tree advertised a garage sale. Who would buy a garage, Vasily wondered, except neighbors living close enough to make use of it?

He wound his way along curving streets until he came to Ernestine Circle. The map showed that the street ended in a circular cul-de-sac but he felt compelled to see the house itself. He drove slowly to the address. Feeling immune to discovery he pulled over on the opposite side of the street and surveyed the two-story home with its Toyota Previa van parked in the driveway. A row of stuffed animals looked out from an upstairs window. My grandchildren, Vasily thought. That's who they should have been.

A teenage girl entering an adjoining house gave him an inquisitive look. An insular community, Vasily thought as he drove away. Strangers would be noticed. If he wanted to watch Sullivan's house he would have to do it from a distance. He parked at the Lynwood Community Center and walked the asphalt path bordering the lake. Joggers passed him, a group of kids on roller blades and an old woman walking a stiff-legged poodle. Behind the Sullivan house he moved into the trees and studied it through the binoculars. Bedrooms upstairs, a frosted window—the bathroom—and downstairs, double doors leading from the living room to a screened-in porch, small windows for a kitchen, dining-room table visible through a large picture window . . .

A branch scraped and a handful of coins pattered to the earth, one of them bouncing off the binoculars with a metallic *tink*. He looked up. Two legs hung below a small wood platform. Then a face peered into view and Vasily felt a physical shock; it was the ghost of Jeremy Lawrence staring down at him.

"Sorry," the kid called. "You okay?"

"What are you doing up there?"

"Nothing."

Nothing but watching me and wondering what I'm doing down here, Vasily thought. And if the boy was who he thought he was . . .

"What's your name?"

"Matthew Sullivan."

Yes! The same copper hair and freckled face.

"They slipped out of my pocket," Matt continued. "It was an accident."

"I was not hurt."

"That's cool."

Something wary in the boy's attitude. Vasily improvised quickly. "Matthew, have you seen a . . . red canary?"

"A canary? No."

"His name is Jupiter. I lost him an hour ago and I've been following him around the lake. He flew this way and I thought he was on the roof of that house over there."

"That's my house."

"It is?"

"But I haven't seen any canaries."

"Why don't I give you the binoculars and you can take a look from up there. Would you do that?"

"Okay."

The boy climbed down, moving cautiously. When his tennis shoe was within reach Vasily imagined grabbing the boy's foot and yanking him from the tree. Matt leaned down from a low branch and Vasily handed him the binoculars. He could see now that the boy's face was broader and had more of a pug nose than his grandfather. Still, the resemblance was remarkable.

"Did you fall?" Vasily asked, noting the welt on the boy's forehead.

"On my skateboard. Not from up here."

A shower of bark drifted down as the boy returned to his perch. Vasily turned his face aside and said, "Be careful. If you fall from that height you might break your neck."

The boy searched the area with the glasses. "I don't see anything. There's a Schindler's finch that lives around here and you see him sometimes, but I don't see a canary."

"You know birds?"

"The ones around here I do."

"Do you know the Firebird?"

"What's that?"

"A magic bird. If you have the Firebird's feather no one can harm you."

"You mean a mythical bird like the phoenix?"

"It depends upon your definition of myth."

"But it's not like a real bird."

"I saw one once. I still have its feather."

An uncertainty crept into Matt's voice. "Well, I don't see your canary."

Don't make him uncomfortable, Vasily thought. He began to pick up the coins. "You have some money down here."

"That's okay, I can get it." The boy climbed down and Vasily helped him the final step.

"Thanks," Matthew said. He gave back the binoculars and began searching for his money.

Vasily opened his pocket watch and removed the strand of red hair. He held it between his fingers. "Is this your hair?"

The boy stood up and squinted. "I don't think so."

"Almost the same color."

"Whose is it?"

"A man I once knew. Let's see how close a match it is." He reached toward the boy's head, but Matt pulled back. Vasily said, "I'm just comparing it."

"I got to go now."

"You're not nervous, are you?"

"About what?"

"You have a comb?"

"Yeah."

"Let's compare the hair. They say nobody's hair color is exactly the same as anyone else's, but this looks like an exact match."

"Mine is lighter."

"Bring out your comb. Let's see."

"But then I got to go." Reluctantly he brought a black comb from his hip pocket. "Nothing on it."

"Run it through your hair."

With a nervous smile Matt did so and removed a couple of copper strands. "See, it's lighter."

"Wait." Vasily took the hair gingerly between thumb and

forefinger and compared them. "It's lighter now, but when you're twenty-eight this will be the color of your hair."

Matt made a face. "Maybe it'll turn brown."

"You don't like red hair?"

"No way."

"Neither do I." He spoke more coldly than he'd intended and the boy was clearly taken aback.

"Well, I'll see you."

Leaving, the boy jumped over a fallen log with a lightness and grace that reminded him of Yelena.

"Remember to watch for my canary," Vasily called. He placed the boy's hair with that of Jeremy Lawrence and tucked the strands back into the watch. By this time Matt had reached his backyard, where a young Irish Setter leaped against the fence in greeting. The gate was unlocked, Vasily noticed. Matt knelt, cupping the dog's face first one way then the other while it tried to catch his wrists. He glanced toward Vasily, a brief surreptitious look, as the Russian left the area.

Back in his car, Vasily circled the neighborhood until he found a hill topped by a small shopping center overlooking the lake. Behind a Minuteman convenience store was a spot that afforded a view of the Sullivan house. A station wagon was parked there with a man behind the wheel, probably a husband waiting for his wife to finish shopping. Vasily decided to return tomorrow to begin his surveillance from the same spot. If his mind hadn't been preoccupied with Matthew Sullivan's uncanny resemblance to the man he had killed, he might have wondered why the husband with his gray crewcut hair was waiting behind the store rather than near the entrance.

Returning to Washington, Bill's thoughts turned toward catastrophe. He imagined a bomb in the baggage compartment, a fire in the lavatory, the collapse of the floor due to an faulty cargo door, a wing breaking off when some critical bolt failed. He had gone to Goodheart fearful of discovering a history of insanity in his family; instead he had discovered he had no history. The world was infirm and nothing could be taken for granted, which was why he felt a surge of relief when he saw Claire in the terminal. He had been half afraid that she, too, might turn out to be a figment of his imagination.

"You had me worried," she said as they embraced. "What happened?"

"You better sit down for this."

Claire wore a blue skirt with an ivory silk blouse. Around her neck was the gold Van Cleef & Arpels necklace Bill had given her on their tenth anniversary. Her battle dress, he realized.

Bill steered her toward a bar, where they sat in a dark green booth. He ordered a Virgin Mary and insisted that Claire get something stronger. She reluctantly ordered a vodka tonic. While they waited for the drinks he told her the easy part—about his doorstep interview with Elsie Fuchs and meeting Sally at her house. When he told her that neither of them recognized him, Claire's first reaction was one of amused disbelief. "They didn't *remember* you? You haven't changed that much."

"They didn't *recognize* me."

"Same thing, isn't it?"

"No."

Her smile wavered. "I don't understand."

"I knew every street. I knew Elsie and Sally, but the only person who thought he recognized me turned out to have Alzheimers disease."

"Who was that?"

"Sally's father, Hank. He said he remembered me but he didn't. He doesn't even remember Sally's name unless she tells him."

"Was it a practical joke? How'd they know you were coming?"

"No joke. Nobody knows me. It's as if I never existed. I'm not even in the yearbook."

"I've seen the yearbook. You're there."

"In *my* yearbook, yes. But not the one Sally showed me. It was my name but the picture was someone else. A kid I never saw before."

"Hers must be wrong."

"I found two more people this morning, Allen Green and

Dick Rosemont. They were both on the softball team with me. Neither of them recognized me."

The waiter in his green jacket arrived with the drinks. Bill didn't touch his, but Claire drank half the glass in three quick gulps. Bill steeled himself for what had to happen next.

"There's something else. When I talked to Sally her memories were different. More complete than mine. On the plane I made a list of everything I could remember." He handed her three sheets of paper, the first two completely filled, the third with a gap at the bottom. "That's it. Two hundred and eighty-nine childhood memories, sixty or seventy of them so generic I can't recall the details. It's like a huge forest when I think about Goodheart, but when I step past the first trees that's all there is, a row of trees and nothing else."

"I don't understand."

"When I landed I wasn't even sure if you'd be here. If you were real."

She reached across the table and took his hand. "I don't know what's going on," she said softly, "but I'm real, the kids are real, our life is real." She stared into his eyes and saw it, the outline of the thing he was hiding from her. "There's something else."

"I love you, Claire. You know that."

She withdrew her hand. "What?"

"This is hard." At the other end of the room tiny figures in football uniforms danced across the television screen, everything so normal and unreal. "I went to a bar last night. Not to drink but to meet Sally. I hadn't seen the yearbook yet—she brought one with her. When I saw someone else's picture in my place, I don't know, it was so disorienting . . . I started drinking. You know what happens. I lost it. The whole night. Like waking up and finding out the bad dream is real. Worse, it's not even a dream. I don't remember it. I lost the whole night, you have to understand that."

"Don't tell me." Her face had hardened.

"Claire, you have to know."

"I'm not asking you to explain yourself. I made that decision when you disappeared on our wedding. You never told me what happened. You said you couldn't remember—"

"I couldn't. I still can't."

"And I had to accept it. Those were the rules. You laid them down and I had to live with them and I decided 'Yes, I can do that.' So when you're on the road guarding the President I don't ask questions. If I call a hotel and you're not in the room I don't worry about it. Whatever happens out there," her hand waved off the rest of the world, "that's not us. You say it doesn't matter so it doesn't. It hasn't. Don't change the rules now, Bill. Don't do that to me."

The ice tinkled as she downed the rest of the drink with a shaky hand. Bill was shocked. All these years that he thought Claire trusted him, there had been suspicion. She had merely closed her mind to it. The silence grew heavy between them, uncomfortable and unresolved.

"Claire . . ."

"No." She looked around the room, a smile of disbelief collapsing in on itself. "You tell me this here, where I can't get away . . ." She raised the napkin to her face and turned to the wall. Two businessmen at a nearby table looked over, obviously wondering what he'd done to provoke Claire's tears. The waiter drifted over and said intrusively, "Anything else?"

"The check."

Claire wiped her eyes and blew her nose. She wadded the napkin into a ball and placed it in the ashtray, fixing it there with her eyes. "With Sally?"

"I don't remember anything, Claire. Nothing."

"But that's what happened?"

"She helped me back to the motel, I remember that much. Then nothing."

"Until you woke up with her."

"No."

She looked up now, eyes full of hope. "Then how do you know it happened?"

"She told me."

"She could have been lying." He shook his head. "How do you know?"

"There were signs."

She realized what he meant and looked away. Bill said, "It's worse."

"She's sick."

"No," he said quickly, "not that."

"What then?

"She says it was violent. That I raped her."

Claire snorted. "Now I know she's lying."

"I don't think so."

"You're not violent. That's not you. Don't you see? She's lying."

"She has no reason to lie."

"Don't tell me that." Her voice carried again and the businessman turned to look. "Jesus," she said, "I can't do this in here."

She got up and left the bar. Bill paid the check and caught up with her in an adjoining souvenir shop where Claire was staring blankly at a display of Redskins paraphernalia.

"Did you get the kids something?" she asked absently.

"No."

They walked in silence until they reached the parking lot. When Claire spoke it was with an uncharacteristic undertone of bitterness. "So what does she want? Money?"

"She's not like that."

"Is that why you had to tell me?"

He stopped and faced her. "I told you because you're my wife and I need your help. I'm in trouble, Claire. I don't know one minute to the next if there's going to be a next minute. I don't know who I am. I could turn around and wake up in bed and maybe I'd have raped you or killed you—I don't know—"

"Kill me? Did you kill someone?"

"How do I know, Claire? How do I know anything?"

Her expression changed. "You're right, you're the one who's sick." *I'm not sick,* he thought reflexively. "We can get help," she continued. "You have to see someone."

He was shaking his head. "You still don't see. It's not a mental problem. I was backgrounded, remember? Fifteen years ago I filled out application forms and they checked all that information. I'm vetted. Someone confirmed everything I said then and everything I know now. That's the missing link, the investigator who did my BI check."

"Who was it?"

"That's what I'm going to find out tomorrow."

On the way home Claire asked questions, which led to more questions, which ended in questions that couldn't be answered, the same questions that had consumed Bill on the flight home. If he hadn't grown up in Goodheart why did he remember it? But if he had grown up there, why didn't anyone remember him? And if he hadn't grown up there, wouldn't the investigator have discovered it? Questions circling questions like eagles riding up-drafts searching for prey.

When they were a couple of blocks from the house Claire asked him to pull over. She opened the door and stepped out.

"Where are you going?"

"I need a few minutes alone." She took off her shoes and tossed them in the car. "I don't want the kids to know. Not just about *her*—about any of it." Then she was running lightly down the sidewalk, reappearing in pools of light cast by swannecked streetlights, brief images like memories of Bill's life surrounded by a vast and growing darkness, memories he could no longer be certain were his own.

CHAPTER

18

Vasily Amenov arrived early at his intended surveillance post but not as early as the Ford station wagon. He saw it while he was still on the road parallel to the Minuteman convenience store, the Ford parked in the same spot it had been the day before. Coincidence, or was someone else watching the Sullivan residence? He continued past and turned into a Chevron service station. Parking where he had a view of the Ford, he trained the binoculars on the car. As he suspected, there was a man behind the wheel. And as he watched, the man raised binoculars to his eye and trained them in the direction of the Sullivan house.

Vasily felt a quick rush of adrenaline. His career as a spy had ended abruptly with the murder of Jeremy Lawrence. Stuck in Moscow he had remained a student of covert operations all his life. It was not love of teaching but the opportunity to talk with agents fresh from overseas assignments that led him to become an instructor for the Special Weapons School. He had spent many an evening discussing techniques and tradecraft over a bottle of vodka, but now, finally, he was on the front lines himself. Friend or foe? Who was the man in the station wagon and was it the Sullivan house he was watching?

Vasily looked at his watch; he had almost forgotten the purpose of his early arrival. He drove to a pay phone and fitted a speaker from his portable cassette recorder against the mouthpiece. He cued the tape and then dialed the Sullivan home.

Bill and Megan were eating breakfast while Claire prepared lunch for the kids. Bill hadn't slept well. The events in Kansas divorced him from the familiar morning routines; he felt like a stranger in his own home. Matt clattered downstairs and came into the kitchen, his red hair slicked down with oil in an attempt to make it darker. He opened the cupboard and let out a wail of dismay at the white carton he discovered.

"This isn't Frosted Flakes."

"It's generic," Claire said. "Same thing for half the price."

"But it doesn't have my Doomed To Extinction collection." He was referring to a series of cards illustrating endangered animal species.

"Big deal, Matt," Megan said primly.

"How can I finish the collection if I don't have anything to trade?"

"Trade your own picture."

"Shut up, weegus."

Claire said, "I don't like that term, Matt."

The phone rang and Matt picked it up. "Sullivan residence." Pause. "Just a moment. Dad, it's for you."

Bill took the phone. "Sullivan here."

"I see the President and he's—"

A tug of resistance as his fingers began to tingle and without plan or premeditation, he exploded in rage. "Fuck you!" He slammed the phone with such force that a pushpin jogged loose from the bulletin board on the wall and tumbled with its message to the floor. In the silence that followed the only sound was the click of toenails as Ginger slunk out of the room.

"Crank caller," he said hoarsely.

"A crank call?" Claire repeated.

The rage evaporated as quickly as it had come, leaving him dizzy from the rush of adrenaline.

"That same one," he said knowingly.

Megan said, "You said a bad word, Daddy."

He took a deep breath. "You're right, Sugarbear. And I apologize. It's stupid to get mad at machines. Everybody ready to go?"

Vasily Amenov, listening to the words recorded a lifetime ago, still found it hard to believe that his own voice was the activation signal that would trigger a murder. But in this case it didn't. All these years, all the money spent, the super-secret Sorin Project and this was the result: *fuck you* and slam down the phone.

He needed a new plan. But first he had to determine who was watching Bill Sullivan and why? He drove back to the vantage point that gave him a view of the Ford. Sullivan would have to pass this way when he went to work, and Vasily could monitor the Ford's response.

At seven-forty-five the Ford moved to the exit and held its position until a Toyota minivan passed—black and silver, the same minivan Vasily saw in the Sullivan's driveway. When the Ford pulled into traffic a few cars behind the Toyota, Vasily knew his instinct was right. Who is watching the watcher, he thought with rising anticipation, as he followed the Ford.

The Toyota made two stops, each at schools where a child got out. Then Sullivan headed into Washington, but got off the freeway at Fairfax and drove to a modern building whose entrance faced a rock garden with a fountain. A sign identified it as Goldman Medical Associates Building. The Toyota disappeared into an underground parking lot, but the Ford continued around the block and pulled to a curb where it had a view of the Goldman building. Vasily pulled into an alley and positioned himself near a trash dumpster where he had a view of the Ford.

Now we wait again, he thought. But he was wrong. The driver of the Ford, whom Vasily had begun to think of as the Watcher, got out of his car. He was a thin man with crew-cut gray hair, dressed in dark slacks and a blue windbreaker. He wore sunglasses and carried a plastic shopping bag. Vasily didn't recognize him.

The Watcher bypassed the clinic's entrance and disappeared down the steep ramp into the parking lot. Vasily hesitated, then got out of the car and jogged into the building. There were two elevators and a stairway. He took the stairs to the first level of the parking garage, opened the door a crack and peered out. No one was visible. He descended to the second level and spotted the top of the Toyota above a row of parked cars at the end of the garage. There was nobody around it. Had the Watcher entered an elevator?

As he started toward the Toyota the squeak of tires from an arriving car caused him to turn back toward the stairs. What am I afraid of? he thought. Nobody cares who I am or what I'm doing. He started back toward the Toyota and saw with a shock that the Watcher had materialized beside it. Vasily avoided eye contact, continued his turn and headed toward the bank of elevators. *Just another driver entering the building*—that's what his body language said but his mind was racing. Where had the Watcher been? Inside the car? Why? He didn't dare turn around, but was acutely conscious of the Watcher's crepe soles squeaking as he moved up the ramp.

The elevator doors opened, a woman exited and Vasily stepped inside. He got out at the lobby and stood inspecting the list of tenants in the building directory while he kept an eye on the sidewalk. The Watcher emerged from the garage and turned left. Heading back to his car, but without the plastic bag he'd had when he entered the garage.

Vasily took the stairs back to the parking area and inspected the minivan. It was locked and the windows were intact. If the Watcher hadn't been inside the car . . . With sudden certainty Vasily knelt, peered beneath the car and saw it: a dark shape affixed to the underside of the gas tank. He recognized the bomb: it was built for terrorism, constructed entirely of foreign parts: the housing was a Panasonic PV-31 video camera with a working viewfinder but packed with U.S.-manufactured C-4 plastic explosive smuggled illegally into the Soviet Union. The concussion trigger was West German. Once the bomb was armed, all it would take was the jolt of a car door closing or the bump of a pothole to destroy the car and everyone in it.

Vasily lifted his hand carefully from the bumper. During the bomb's development there had been problems with the triggers—not sensitive enough and the bomb failed to ignite, too sensitive and the damn thing exploded at a whisper. The problems had been overcome before the Panasonic was deployed, but Vasily imagined his body engulfed in flames and shuddered. Now he knew two things: that the Watcher was acting on Moscow's orders and that the KGB had discovered his theft of the Sorin Project.

He stepped back cautiously and flinched at the squeal of tires as another car entered the garage. In his mind's eye he saw the thin strip of plastic, half the width of a credit card, which had been removed, allowing the two metal contacts to join, completing the circuit and arming the bomb. He walked calmly to the elevator and pushed the button for the fifth floor. Anything to achieve a moment of peace so he could think. The Watcher outside, Bill Sullivan somewhere in the building and a bomb beneath the car. He wished now that he had come first to America rather than London. That way there would have been time to figure out why the activation signal failed and come up with a new plan before the theft was discovered. Now it was too late.

The elevator door opened and two people stepped in. His mind racing, Vasily walked down a hallway bordered by glass doors, turned at the end of the hallway and caught a glimpse inside a doctor's waiting room. His impression was one of tasteful decor, framed collages on the wall, people on couches along the wall—and Bill Sullivan. Keep going, a voice urged, but he thought, what difference does it make? He stopped and watched as Bill stood up and followed a nurse into the doctor's office.

It was not a visit Bill wanted to make. He felt embarrassed and demeaned. This is not me, he thought as he entered Dr. Goldman's office. The doctor was a broad-browed man with a wide mouth tucked below a brittle mustache. He lunged across the desk to shake Bill's hand, waved him to a chair while he finished making entries in his previous patient's file. "So what's the problem?"

Bill discarded all the subtle, circular inquiries he had imagined while in the waiting room. "How soon can a person be tested for the AIDS virus after a contact?"

Goldman jammed the file into a rack and leaned back. "Have you had contact with someone who has AIDS?"

"I've had a contact—I don't believe she has it. I didn't ask."

"Were condoms used?"

"No."

"How long since the first contact?"

"There was only one. One night, forty-eight hours ago." Goldman frowned. "Is that bad?"

"Bad? What's bad? It's just that it's impossible to test until six months after the contact. The incubation period's that long."

"I won't know for six months?"

"Ninety-five percent of the population shows in three months, but if you're in the minority five percent you won't know until six. Until then there's no point doing a blood test."

"In the meantime I want to be safe . . ."

"Condoms or abstinence." He reached into his drawer and pulled out a brochure on safe sex. "Read that, it'll tell you everything you need to know. If you have any questions, give me a call."

The brochure didn't tell him anything he didn't already know, and Goldman's forthright response was more unnerving than reassuring. You get it, you get it, you don't, you don't—that's what he seemed to be saying. They must deal with AIDS all the time, Bill thought as he left the office and took the elevator to the garage.

He was still lost in thought as he approached the Toyota. He pressed the button on his key ring that deactivated the alarm with its familiar *chirp*. A trash bag caught his foot as he opened the door. He kicked it aside, slid behind the wheel and paused as he contemplated using condoms for the first time in his life. He couldn't help feeling it was a badge of disgrace. He grabbed the door and slammed it shut.

Juho Ryti was watching when it happened. The car bomb had not been his first choice of a weapon, nor his second or third. He carried the KGB-designed Panasonic primarily as a backup device and had used one only once, to create a diversion while he escaped after delivering a death stroke. Bombs, even one so sophisticated as the Panasonic, were the tools of fanatics and amateurs. But his Russian control had been adamant that the job be done within twenty-four hours of Sullivan's return, and Juho, who already had misgivings about the assignment, put his scruples aside and took the easy way out. He wanted only to be finished with this job, finished with the Russians, with the Americans, with all of them. So he had taken the radio and slipped it under the car where the four powerful magnets, one in each corner, held it to the gas tank. Once it was in place, Juho pulled out the plastic safety slide that armed the bomb and breathed a sigh of relief when it didn't blow up in his face. He returned to his car to wait. Half an hour later the Toyota minivan emerged from the parking garage.

Juho couldn't believe it. What had gone wrong? Closing the car door should have triggered the device. Fucking Russians, he thought, they could put a man in space but couldn't design a dependable trigger mechanism. He held his breath expectantly as the Toyota bounced across a speed bump at the exit, but nothing happened. How much of a jolt would it take? Keeping well back, Juho followed the Toyota. Despite his reluctance to contaminate the kill with unintended victims he found himself wishing someone would bump into the van at a stoplight.

He followed the Toyota onto the freeway. The longer they drove the more it bothered Juho that the Panasonic failed to go off. It was his experience that Russian goods couldn't be trusted unless they were made for the KGB, in which case they rivaled the dependability of German and Japanese goods. This bomb was one of three he'd received from his KGB control and the first had worked perfectly when he used it as a diversion. But this one had malfunctioned. Or else . . . He frowned. Was it possible Sullivan had discovered the bomb? What about the man he'd seen in the garage? Had someone become suspicious? No, not possible. The bomb would blow up if anyone tried to remove it. Only a demolitions expert could deactivate it, and Juho would have seen them if a bomb squad was called.

The Toyota pulled into the G Street parking garage below the Secret Service building. Juho continued down the street, went around the block and pulled to the curb. Now what? There was an element of ambiguity in the situation that Juho disliked. It was not his nature to improvise; planning was the watchword and planning had kept him alive all his life. He waited for ten minutes until he was certain Bill wasn't coming out before he put a quarter in the parking meter and walked to the garage.

The Toyota sat innocently in its parking stall, but Juho approached it as he would a wounded animal, with a healthy caution, alert for any sign of a trap. There was no one around, but instinct warned him to conceal his true interest. When he was a few feet away, he knelt and pretended to tie his shoe. Then, as he stood up, he glanced beneath the car and the hair rose on the back of his neck. The bomb was gone.

Juho resisted the urge to panic. He noted the license plate to confirm this was Sullivan's vehicle, then marched briskly away, expecting at any moment the police to spring forth or Bill Sullivan to materialize from a doorway with a gun. What had happened? Had the bomb fallen off? Without exploding it seemed impossible. But it was equally impossible someone could have removed it. He sensed a trap, but the city deadened his senses and the concrete buildings and asphalt streets offered no clues.

He did not return directly to the car but walked up one street and down another to see if he was being followed. He wished someone *was* following him; then at least he could give his enemy a face. This was like dealing with phantoms. I should not have taken this assignment, he thought. The day he left Finland the first early snow had fallen, but here the trees still burned to the brilliant colors of autumn. He felt as if he had jumped back six weeks in time, a man out of season.

Once he was certain that he was not being followed, Juho returned to the car. As he unlocked the door he noticed a white splotch of bird shit on the windshield. He pulled out a handkerchief and wiped it off. Then he slid into the front seat and pulled the door shut.

The light came first, a brilliant flash that etched the black shadow of his body across the headliner, followed the barest fraction of a second later by searing heat as the car lifted beneath him. Not here—that was Juho's last thought. Not for a man of distant lakes and silent snow, not here in the middle of a city surrounded by melting plastic and the scream of torn metal and disintegrating glass—

Not here.

CHAPTER

19

"Too late by an hour," said a cheerful Chinese-American named Benny Lin.

Bill said, "What do you mean 'too late'?"

"They checked out your file an hour ago. What's in that thing, map to a buried treasure?"

Benny's eyes disappeared as his smile broadened, but his humor was lost on Bill. Intent on discovering who had done his background investigation, Bill had come immediately to see Benny as soon as he arrived at Secret Service headquarters. Benny was the assistant director of personnel and widely regarded as more capable than his boss.

"Who checked it out?"

"Raleigh Moore from SISD."

"He tell you why he wanted it?"

"You know the SI boys—they don't tell their wives when they want dinner."

SISD was Special Investigations—Security Division. It was not good news. Bill took the stairs down to the eighth floor, where Moore's secretary told him the inspector wasn't in his office but would be back any minute. Bill sat down to wait. He hadn't slept well and the familiar hollow feeling reminded him of working the hectic presidential campaigns where time zones and tight schedules sometimes kept them up most of the night.

The phone rang and when the secretary answered she gestured to Bill and mouthed *It's him.* She jotted a couple of notes. "Yes, sir. And you've got an agent here to see you. Bill Sullivan." She held out the phone. "He wants to talk to you."

Bill didn't know Raleigh well, and the man's tone seemed overly effusive. "Bill, hey great, I was going to ring you up today. Listen, can you stay there about ten minutes?"

"You pulled my file. Why?"

A slight hesitation. "Okay. We can talk about that. Just hold on, will you? I'll be right there."

"Where are you?"

"Not far. Give me a few minutes, I'm on my way."

He hung up. Bill handed the phone back to the secretary, who looked puzzled when she discovered her boss had hung up. "I wasn't through talking to him," she said accusingly.

"Where is he?"

"I don't know. He's been all over the building today. When I arrived this morning he was already on the phone. Mr. Moore works late, but he's never early. It's unusual for him."

Bill focused his attention on her. An impeccably neat woman, long skirt, high-cut blouse and a knowing air she wore like a cloak. The kind of woman who would never reveal a secret except to prove she was privy to it. Bill adopted a confidential tone. "You probably know this, but he was in Personnel this morning. Talking to Mr. Lin about discrepancies in some of the background investigations."

She nodded sagely and lowered her voice. "Not just Mr. Lin, either."

Bill leaned close and cast a wider net. "I think his name is Harrison or something."

"The FBI man?"

"Harrison, Lincoln, Ford—one of the president's names."

She frowned. "Vincour?"

"Vincour, that was it."

"Not a president."

"Secretary of agriculture under Harding."

"He was?"

"Do me a favor. Don't tell Mr. Moore that I mentioned his talk with Mr. Lin."

She drew herself up. "Privacy is second nature to me."

"I'm sure it is." Bill got up and headed for the door.

"Aren't you going to wait?"

"I'll call him."

Bill wanted to talk to Roy Patchin before anyone else discovered what happened in Kansas. He was in the hallway when Raleigh Moore turned the corner. He was a slender Afro-American who spoke with the precise diction of one whose self-image was reflected in others' eyes. He started when he saw Bill, but recovered quickly. "I was just coming to get you."

"I'm on my way to see Roy."

Raleigh fell into step beside him. "He's in the conference room, waiting."

Bill paused. "Waiting for me?"

"Both of us." Raleigh almost touched his elbow as if to urge him forward, then didn't. When they reached the conference room he paused to let Bill enter first. Roy was there along with two other men, Mike Leahy from Legal Department and a stranger whose clothing and demeanor suggested the FBI. He had razor-cut hair, opaque china-blue eyes, and clothes tailored to an athlete's body. Bill took a wild guess and said, "Hello, Vincour. What's the FBI doing on this side of the Mall?"

The placid expression disappeared. "Have we met?"

"Have you forgotten?"

Vincour frowned and his eyes flicked over Bill like a snake's tongue. Roy said, "How do you know Special Agent Vincour?"

"How do I know I'm no longer getting State Department Liaison? Must be something in the air this morning, random answers to unasked questions like why are we here?"

Vincour continued to stare as Roy said, "We have a serious

problem, Bill. You know Raleigh, apparently you know Agent Vincour, and I think you've met Mike Leahy from Legal." There were nods but no handshakes. "Before we continue, I think I should inform you that this in an official investigation, a joint investigation between ourselves and our sister agency. Agent Vincour will be our liaison with the FBI, and Raleigh will handle the investigation at this end of the line. I'll let him take over."

Leahy pulled a microcassette recorder from his jacket. He wore a neatly trimmed beard that advertised his freedom from the dress code imposed on field agents. "We're going to tape this, Bill, just so you know." He held it to his lips, recited the time, date and place, and even a case number. Then in a formal tone he said, "Agent Sullivan, you are hereby informed that you are under investigation for falsifying statements made on your application form. Anything you say may be used as evidence in the event of departmental action or criminal charges. You have the right to have a lawyer present before answering questions. Do you understand this right?"

"Sure." He understood the wolves were circling for the kill.

"And do you care to exercise that right at this time?"

"What do you think, Roy? My head on the chopping block?"

"You know better than I do."

"Just tell me what's going on?"

Raleigh said, "What's going on is that yesterday afternoon a sheriff in Goodheart, Kansas, called to confirm your identity. It seems the Bill Sullivan people remember out there is not the person you are. Last night he faxed us photographs. These look familiar?"

He showed Bill the shot from the yearbook. Sheriff Luckner had been busy.

"Quality's not great," Raleigh continued, "but you can see this is not the same person. And these aren't the same fingerprints." He tossed first one set and then another down on the table. "First ones are from your file. Second set we received half an hour ago from the Department of Motor Vehicles in Kansas. Those were taken twenty-one years ago when Bill Sullivan applied for his driver's license. It doesn't take an expert to see they're not from the same person."

Bill closed his eyes and saw again the discolored pages he had discovered the night before. Pages where he appeared in photographs in yearbooks from high school and Wichita State University. False pages.

Raleigh said, "You're an impostor, Bill. The details are correct, but your face is the wrong one every time. Who are you really?"

"I don't know."

Vincour had been shifting his weight impatiently. Now he said, "You don't *know*? What the fuck does that mean?"

"If I said 'Bill Sullivan' would you believe me?"

"You're *not* Bill Sullivan."

"Then who am I?"

"You're asking *me*?"

"You've got all the answers."

"Wrong. I've got all the questions, starting with who the fuck are you?"

Bill turned to Roy. "I want to talk to you privately."

"Ah, that wouldn't be appropriate at this point. Anything you've got to say—"

"Jesus, Roy . . ."

"Let's cut the crap," Vincour said. "I've got a one-time offer, right here, right now, you want to cooperate I can deliver immunity from prosecution for all but a capital offense or accessory. You murdered the real Bill Sullivan you're on your own; anything else you're home free."

"Murdered?"

"The kid didn't just disappear into thin air."

It was a question that had been lurking at the back of his mind, which he had avoided until now: what happened to the other Bill Sullivan? "I want to talk to the man who did my background investigation."

"No." Vincour punctuated his words by jabbing a finger in Bill's direction. "*We* ask the questions, *you* answer them."

"You ask nothing. This isn't the Hoover Building, you're on the wrong side of the tracks, Vincour." Bill turned to Raleigh. "Who backgrounded me?"

"Dennis Riggs."

The name was vaguely familiar, but Bill couldn't place the man or the face. "I want to talk to him."

"Riggs is no longer with the Service. He left about ten years ago and joined the FBI."

Riggs of the FBI. The name came back to Bill and with it the feeling of falling off a cliff. Now he knew why Vincour was involved. "The one who defected to Russia a few years ago?"

"You *do* know him." Vincour said.

"I remember hearing about it. Nobody knew the details."

"Did Riggs recruit you? Was he your control?"

"You think I'm working for the Russians?"

"Prove me wrong."

"Give me five minutes with Riggs and I'll prove it."

"Give you wings and you'll fly. Riggs is in Moscow."

"They have phones in Moscow. I'll call him, you can listen on the line. His answers will prove I don't know any more than you do. You've got his number, right?" The men regarded him silently. "What? You think it's some kind of trick? Secret code or something? Tell me what to say. Tell me what greeting to use. Tell me anything, but I guarantee you he won't know me."

"Maybe not," Vincour said. "Maybe they placed you blind. Doesn't prove anything."

"Just give me the fucking number." His flash of anger brought a smile to Vincour's lips.

"Let's do it," Roy said suddenly.

Raleigh frowned. "Call Russia?"

Roy turned to Vincour. "Do you know where Riggs is living?"

"Let's finish the interview first."

Bill said, "The interview is finished until I talk to Riggs."

Vincour looked to Roy as if to say *Are you going to let him get away with this?* Roy said "I'd like to try it. We might learn something."

A tiny wrinkle of annoyance appeared between Vincour's eyebrows. "It's your show. Give me a phone and I'll see what I can do."

It took a half hour to set up the call. During much of the time Bill sat alone, waiting. At one point Roy returned and regarded him speculatively. "Sorry about Vincour. If you'd have come to me first . . ."

"I didn't know, Roy. Not until I went to Goodheart."

Roy smiled ruefully. "I think he suspects me too. Keeps asking me questions about college, what you were like, how many holidays you spent with us. Probably going to interview Mom and Dad. Hell of a thing, to think you know somebody and find out you don't."

"Try it from this side of the fence."

"Anything you want me to know? Privately, I mean. Before Vincour and the others come back?"

The solicitation was awkward and Roy's studied casual tone rang false. A setup, Bill realized. "What's Vincour's first name?"

"First name? Nick, I think." He dug a card from his pocket. "Actually it's Dominick."

"He's the bag of shit you said was coming over from the FBI?"

"What?"

"When you called this morning."

"I didn't call you." There was a note of panic in Roy's voice.

"Relax, Roy, I won't tell him about you."

"Tell him what? I don't know what you're talking about."

"Anything you want me to know? Privately, before the others come back?"

Now Roy realized what he was doing. He had the grace to look sheepish. "I do what I have to, Bill."

"If it makes you feel better."

"Not really."

He left without trading any more on their friendship, and Bill didn't ask whether the microphone was in the room or Roy was wearing it. Ten minutes later Bill was sitting at a table with a list of questions and statements to ask Dennis Riggs. He was framed by the three investigators and a Russian interpreter, a young woman who stood with a phone to her ear talking to an operator in Moscow. Her name was Andrea, and she had the collegiate look of the capital's recently arrived and inexorably ambitious. Listening to her chatter away in Russian, Bill's hands grew numb and he flexed his fingers. Raleigh noticed. "What's wrong?"

"Nothing." Bill placed his hands flat on the desk. The attention of the three men returned to Andrea as she replaced the receiver.

"No longer his number. He moved. To a dacha somewhere outside the city."

"Did they have his new number?"

"There is no number."

"Can you get an operator?"

"It wouldn't help. He moved only a month ago and it takes six months to get a new phone. Also, in the area he moved not all the houses have phones."

"You've been there?"

"I studied three summers in Moscow. I have friends in that area."

Vincour handed her another piece of paper. "Try this. Supposed to be something called the Maurice Thorez Foreign Language Institute."

Bill said, "Why there?"

Vincour ignored him, but Roy said, "It's where Riggs works. Teaching English."

This time the conversation was longer and more heated. It ended abruptly and Andrea made a wry face. "Dennis Riggs no longer works there. She says it's against policy to give out personal information."

Vincour turned to Bill, "How convenient."

Bill ignored him. "Did the person you called speak English?"

"I don't know."

"Let me try." He took the piece of paper and dialed the number. While the connection was being made he asked her, "How do you say 'Do you speak English?' "

"Vy gavariti pa angliski?"

The phrase echoed strangely, preceding rather than following her voice. Someone picked up the phone. *"Alo?"*

"Vy gavariti pa angliski?"

Vincour and Raleigh grabbed extension phones and listened as Bill was passed from one person to another. Finally a woman's voice said, "I speak English. How may I help you?"

"I'm looking for one of your teachers, an American, Dennis Riggs."

"Mr. Riggs is not here any longer."

"He doesn't work there?"

"No longer he does not."

"Do you have a phone number or his home address?"

"Teachers personal data is not public, I'm sorry."

"I'm calling from the United States and this is very important. Mr. Riggs—Dennis—is very important to me. I've got to talk with him."

He could hear the sound of a hand over the receiver and a muffled conversation. Then her voice, brusque and impatient. "You were told this before. Goodbye."

The three phones returned slowly to their cradles. Roy thanked Andrea and ushered her out of the office. Leahy slid a finger beneath his watch band and rotated it. "Whether or not you conspired with Dennis Riggs the evidence proves you are not the Bill Sullivan you pretend to be. Would you like to reconsider anything you've told us?"

"I want to see my file. Maybe there's something in it. A clue as to what's going on."

"I think what's going on is obvious," Raleigh said. "Are you carrying?"

"Yes."

"I'll need you to surrender the weapon. Keep it in the holster."

He turned to Roy, who shrugged and said, "Procedure, Bill."

Bill removed his jacket and slid free of the harness with the holstered gun which he handed to Raleigh.

"The radio, the handcuffs."

Bill removed the Motorola and the handcuffs from his belt and placed them on the desk. "You want to strip-search me?"

"No, but I'll need your speed-loader, travel coupons, the rest of the gear."

"I left it at home."

"I'll need you to turn it in. Will you do that tomorrow?"

"Is that all?"

Raleigh turned to the deputy director for the final piece of bad news. "Roy?"

Roy said reluctantly, "You're suspended without pay pending the results of the investigation. That's it."

"Not quite," Vincour said as Bill started toward the door. "The FBI has a mandate for counterespionage investigations. You're my fish, Sullivan, and this is my ocean. You're caught, you're already hooked, and the only way you're going to swim free is to lead me to the bigger fish. Immunity in exchange for cooperation. The offer is good for twenty-four hours. After that, you get flayed and gutted with the rest of them."

As soon as Bill was gone, Vincour took a walkie-talkie from his briefcase. "Skip, you there?"

"What's happening?"

"He's on his way."

"We're rolling."

As Vincour replaced the walkie-talkie, Roy said, "What happens if he doesn't contact anybody?"

"Then we'll have to get nasty, won't we?" The smile was false and his china-blue eyes were cold as ice.

CHAPTER

20

The surge of exultation that Vasily felt when the Ford station wagon burst into a fifty-foot ball of flame surprised him. He was sitting at a bus stop a half block away, and the concussion rattled windows and a moment later washed him in a surge of hot air. He watched in awe as pieces of flaming and charred wreckage rained down onto the street. All that was left of the car was a twisted frame and black engine that lay smoldering in a shallow crater. Two pedestrians lay on the sidewalk, injured or killed in the blast.

Vasily felt a great release. After years teaching others to use the KGB's most sophisticated weapons, this was the joy of destruction. He had ruined a credit card, split it in half lengthwise to create a makeshift safety slide with which he could disarm and arm the Panasonic bomb. As he drove back to Lynwood he imagined their faces in Moscow when they heard the news—

their killer was dead, the solution to all their problems had failed. He imagined, too, the Watcher's expression when he realized too late it was his own bomb tearing him a new asshole. Vasily laughed out loud and slapped the steering wheel in glee. You thought you could steal Mischa? He's mine, comrades. He's been mine since he was born. I decide when he lives and when he dies.

Filled with new confidence he drove recklessly down the George Washington Parkway, swerving from lane to lane, passing cars on the wrong side, until the excitement abated and he slowed down as he approached Lynwood. He would have to work quickly now. They would know in Moscow that he had discovered their plan to eliminate Bill Sullivan. What action would they take? Tell the Americans? It was always possible, although it was apparent their first choice was to control the situation, neutralize the threat. They wouldn't be so desperate if they knew the Sorin Project was a failure and Bill Sullivan no longer listened to the activation signal..

But there was another signal he would listen to, a voice more familiar than Vasily's, and cries of pain more compulsive than a simple phrase calling the President bad. But the plan he had in mind was complicated. He would need help. Someone to drive a delivery van and someone to guard Matthew Sullivan while Vasily was making phone calls. The only problem was that he knew no one in America and trusted no one whose weaknesses he didn't know. Which was why, as soon as he returned to his hotel, he placed a long-distance call to London.

Guy Jurmon was at his club. The man's voice was low, and Vasily thought he could hear the thick lips brush the mouthpiece as he spoke. "I didn't think I'd hear from you again. Not after what happened to Miss Lawrence."

Vasily ignored his smug reference to Yelena and dangled the only bait that might lure Jurmon to America. "I have a new proposition for you. How would you like to make that video you asked me about?"

"What video?"

"We argued about it. I didn't want to use that particular, ah, actress but I have another one who would be perfect. Are you interested?"

"Who is the actress?"

"Does it matter?"

"Is she young?"

"Remember the girl I met at your club?"

"In one of the booths?"

"No. The one who wanted to talk to you when I came to the office."

"Oh. Lynette."

"How would someone like Lynette serve your needs?"

"You're talking about a special kind of film?"

"Very special."

"We should talk about this in person."

"Just what I was thinking. I'll go to the airport and purchase you a round-trip ticket on British Airways. You can pick it up at Heathrow tomorrow morning."

"Ticket? Where are you?"

"Washington, D.C."

"You're joking."

"You can be here in five hours."

"I can't just drop everything and fly to America."

"In addition to the film we're prepared to pay you ten thousand dollars for your expertise. Our people over here don't have the background or the necessary contacts."

He could hear Jurmon puff on a cigarette. When he spoke, his voice was lower and the words rattled like gravel. "How long would this take?"

"I've got the girl picked out. How long do you need for the filming?"

"A day to rent the equipment, maybe another day to set up a studio, some place to shoot it. A day for taping and another for post—no, postproduction I can do back here . . ."

"I need you here tomorrow. Don't tell anyone you're leaving the country."

"Not tomorrow. I've got a dental appointment."

"Skip it."

"I have to find someone to look after Manny . . ."

"Who?"

"Manny. You met him in the office—little fuzz face I call him."

The fucking gerbil. Vasily didn't try to hide his irritation. "There are cameramen over here who would work for half what I offered you. If you can't delay a dental appointment for ten thousand dollars we'll get someone else."

"Wait, wait. All expenses paid, first-class ticket, a rental car at the airport. Otherwise it's not convenient."

Otherwise you don't feel like you've shoved my nose in shit, Vasily thought. "Agreed, but you won't need a car. I'll meet you at the airport. Tomorrow's flight. You pick up your ticket at the counter."

After he hung up, Vasily decided he would find out if the return portion of the ticket could later be refunded. That was Guy Jurmon's real advantage—the man was expendable. No need to leave a witness to the kidnapping and no need to pay the ten thousand dollars. The only one who would mourn Jurmon when he failed to return to London was a gerbil.

That night Bill dreamed again of flames, of the house burning, of running down the hallway, his hands flinging fire, everything he touched erupting in flames . . .

He awoke with a jolt, clammy with sweat. The house was dark. Claire turned and said sleepily, "What?"

"Fire dream," he whispered.

Once she would have looped an arm over his shoulders and snuggled, but now she turned on her side and pulled the covers close. Their relationship had been strained ever since he returned from Kansas. Yesterday evening Megan caught them arguing and asked if they were going to get a divorce.

"Of course not," Claire said. "Why would you think that?"

"Jenny says right before her parents got divorced they yelled at each other all the time."

"Do you think we're arguing all the time?"

"You are now."

"We're having a disagreement, that's all. Daddy's upset about some things."

Daddy's upset. The words still rankled. Bad enough he felt pulled in sixteen different directions, uncertain of the past and uneasy about the future—now every argument was his fault and instead of her sympathy it was Claire's back that greeted him when the nightmares began.

He went downstairs and peered out at the street, looking for the FBI surveillance team. He had spotted them yesterday after leaving his meeting with Roy and the others—a Buick LeSabre, two Fords and a Volvo station wagon surreptitiously playing tag behind him as he drove home. The Volvo was a nice touch, undoubtedly rented, since government agencies only purchased American cars, a policy Bill could be counted on to know. He might not have noticed had the Volvo not been the same model and color as the one he and Claire owned before they bought the Toyota.

Bill had gotten a couple of license numbers and called them in to the Service's Intelligence Division. It was a routine request and a half hour later he knew the cars were registered to the FBI. That's why Roy had placed him on suspension. The meeting had been designed to either force his confession or frighten him into making contact with whomever they thought he was working for. He was tempted to force a confrontation but decided against it. Vincour would only assign a larger and less visible surveillance team. Tonight the street appeared normal, but he knew they were out there somewhere.

The pressure on his brain had become constant, creasing his brow in a perpetual furrow. Without knowing how he got there he found himself in the kitchen, standing at the liquor cabinet. His hands seemed those of a stranger as he poured a glass of Bailey's Irish Cream. Mostly milk, it won't hurt you. The hand raised the glass to his mouth.

In the morning Bill woke to the familiar sounds of the house. It was seven-thirty and Claire was already downstairs. Brushing his teeth, he remembered the dream of fire so clearly that he thought he smelled sulfur on his fingertips. He leaned close to the mirror and looked deep into his own eyes and could almost believe he saw a stranger's reflection.

"Bill?" Claire was in the doorway, her face drawn in fear and alarm. "Someone's been in the house."

"Where?"

"Megan's room."

He was already moving. "Is she—?"

"She's still asleep. I went in to wake her up and when I saw what they did—"

Megan's room was at the end of the hall. It was painted white, with floral curtains, a neat white desk and shelves overflowing with dolls and toys. Megan was still asleep, breathing evenly, one leg characteristically flung outside the covers. But what drew Bill's attention was the design on the rug—tiny black marks surrounding the bed in a neat oval. That was the first impression, then he realized what they were: burnt matches.

"Unless you think it's Matt," Claire whispered. "Some kind of joke." She turned toward the bathroom.

"Claire?" He extended his hand toward her. "What do you smell on my fingers?"

Her eyes widened. "You?"

"Just tell me what you smell."

She took his wrist and sniffed. The change in her expression told him everything. "Why?"

"I don't know."

"If you did it, you know why."

"I don't remember doing it."

"You have to get help. From Roy, from Stuart Birnbaum, I don't care who, you have to do something."

"I will."

She looked at the ring of matches, then dropped to her knees and began gathering them. A great calm had overtaken Bill. He knew what had to be done now. If he couldn't save himself, he would save his family. He knew exactly what had to be done.

It takes only a half hour to reach the Chesapeake Bay from Washington, D.C. The two-hundred-mile-long bay is bordered by an irregular low-lying shoreline that settles gently into the sea. Here are farms, fishing villages, yacht harbors and beach-front cottages where Washington residents escape the humidity of the city during the summer. Now it was October and seasonal communities were deserted, which was exactly what drew Vasily Amenov to the area.

The sign at the entrance to the low-lying wood bridge said *Fox Island, Private Property, Owners and Guests Only.* Beyond the bridge a row of summer homes sat on a narrow sandswept peninsula. Another sign, hand-painted, read: *Off-Season Rentals Available, Inquire At Caretaker Cottage.* The arrow pointed the way to a small wood cottage sheltered from the wind by a haphazard ten-foot-high wood fence.

Vasily parked beside a battered pickup truck and pulled a frayed rope dangling from the gate. He was greeted by two women: Ruby, a big, earthy woman in overalls, with a good-natured laugh, and her friend, Anntek—"It's one word." Anntek's hair was buzz cut like a boy's. She wore a black leather vest over a khaki work shirt, and there were deliberate holes in the knees of her jeans. Men haters, Vasily thought. Hiding his disdain he told them he was a writer interested in finding a secluded place to work for a couple of weeks. They ushered him through a courtyard filled with pieces of driftwood sculpture into a cottage whose rooms seemed to tumble one into the other with walls made almost entirely of stained or leaded glass.

"Who's the artist?" Vasily asked.

"We're both artists." Anntek was staring at him like a crow eying a kernel of corn.

"He means the sculptures out front," Ruby said. "Those are hers."

"And Ruby does the paintings. Post-modern eco-feminist."

Which means what? Vasily thought. As if reading his mind, Ruby said, "I feminize and tropicalize primitive forms. Are you interested in art?"

"I used to be."

"She's having a show," Anntek said, shoving a brochure at

him. A glance at the text numbed his mind: ". . . a personal and spiritual journey expressed through such archetypal symbols as tikis, fecund female figures, serpents, spirals, crescents and the myth of the axis mundi."

"You don't have to read it," Ruby said dryly.

"I'll do it later."

"What do you write?" Anntek demanded.

"Corporate reports."

She couldn't contain a sneer, which was fine with Vasily. *At least I won't have them coming around to discuss incantatory images of mytho-poetic prehistory.*

He asked about homes for rent and was told that of the sixteen, over half were closed for the winter, some were used only on the odd weekend, but three were available. Anntek tossed a thick key ring to Ruby, who accompanied Vasily to inspect the houses. Heavy boards rattled as they crossed the narrow bridge. Fingers of sand clutched at the single paved road that ran down the center of the spit. One home, a grand old three-story structure with a garage, would have been ideal except for its location. It was just across the bridge from the caretaker's house, too close for the privacy Vasily wanted. The second was a tiny two-room cottage on stilts, but the third was an older and more substantial structure, a two-story home with wide porches and a patio separating a detached garage. The location was perfect, the next to last home on the narrow spit of land, nearly a mile from the bridge and the two buddy-girls' cottage. The neighboring houses were some distance away, shuttered and closed for the winter.

Ruby opened the double locks and led him on a tour across creaking floors past a fireplace whose chimney moaned with each shift of the wind. The place was furnished in an eclectic multigenerational style, the furniture heavy and mismatched, walls strewn with bric-a-brac and amateur oil paintings of the seashore. Coal oil lamps sat in brackets in each room, and for a moment Vasily thought the place, like some of the dachas outside Moscow, had no electricity.

"We lose power once in a while out here," Ruby explained. "But mostly people like them for decoration."

The price was $650 a month, an off-season rate that seemed

exorbitant until Vasily discovered the summer rates ran about $3,000 a month.

"You can make the check out to Fox Island Association," Ruby told him.

He pulled out his wallet. "Not really an island, is it?"

"At high tide the causeway disappears."

He paid her in cash, and she gave him a receipt and the keys. Later, alone at the house, Vasily donned a yellow ski parka and wandered across the beach while seagulls circled and screeched above him. He liked the isolation. It matched his mood. He dug a toe deep into the sand and kicked forward, the wind flinging damp clumps of sand toward shore. An easy place to dig a grave. Especially one for a child.

CHAPTER

21

Claire was teaching, so Bill had her drop him off at the Hertz Rent-A-Car office, where he picked up a car to use pending the insurance settlement on the Mustang. He didn't mention the FBI surveillance team that was following them. Returning home, he stopped at the Minuteman convenience store where he used the automatic cash machine to collect five hundred dollars and made two phone calls, one to book a seat on the first flight to Moscow, the second to Executive Car Service, where he ordered a car to meet him at an address in downtown Washington at one-thirty.

He returned home. This was the day he was supposed to return the Secret Service gear contained in the aluminum briefcase. Instead he emptied it of everything but the travel vouchers and filled it with a change of underwear, a fresh shirt, overnight kit and passport. The note to Claire was difficult. Afterward he stood before her closet and ran his hand lightly over her clothes in silent farewell.

Driving to Washington, Bill made no effort to evade the surveillance team. He parked at Secret Service headquarters and with briefcase in hand crossed to 17th Street and walked four blocks to Farragut Square. His shadow was a middle-aged man with a camera, supposedly a tourist, whose sunglasses were superfluous on an overcast day. Did the FBI really think someone who spent all his life reading crowds couldn't spot their man?

All right, he thought, you want something to report to Vincour? It was a childish impulse, but he had a half hour to waste so he entered a bookstore and bought a Merriam-Webster pocket dictionary. He found a park bench where, referring to the dictionary, he wrote a series of numbers on a small piece of paper. The "tourist" was keeping an eye on him, all the while feigning interest in the statue of Admiral Farragut. Bill folded the paper into a tiny square, reached beneath the bench and jammed it between the legs and one of the wood slats that made up the seat.

It was one-thirty. He went to a pay phone, called Executive Car Service and had them confirm by radio that the driver was waiting. Then he walked up 17th Street to the headquarters of the National Geographic Society. Former President Reagan had once spoken here in Explorer's Hall, and Bill had made the security arrangements. He was familiar with the layout, the original building along 17th Street separated by a plaza and fountain from a new, modern addition that faced 16th Street. He stepped across the bronze emblem set into the marble floor and entered an elevator. On the second floor he got out, ducked into the stairway and took the stairs two at a time to the basement offices. An underground corridor, its walls lined with aboriginal cave paintings, linked the two buildings. Moments later he walked out of the 16th Street building and got into the waiting limousine.

"You forget something?" the driver asked as they crossed the Roosevelt Bridge. It was the second time Bill turned to watch the traffic behind them.

"That's what I'm going to find out."

Satisfied that they were not being followed, he settled back and closed his eyes.

Claire didn't find the note immediately. She had stopped at the grocery store on her way home, and it wasn't until after the kids arrived from school that she saw it lying on her bed. As soon as she recognized Bill's handwriting she had a terrible premonition. Every nuance of their parting this morning returned with a rush—the hugs he had given the children as they went to school, the way he stood outside the rent-a-car office, watching her leave. Her heart knew what the note would say before her hand touched the envelope.

> Dear Claire,
>   Please forgive me for the pain and worry you must feel now. There has always been something hidden from me, deep inside, something I've felt all my life. I think you've felt it, too. I couldn't live with myself if any harm came to you or the children, and after this morning you know how close that danger is. This is a battle I must fight alone—for you, for Matt, for Megan and for my own sanity. Don't call Roy or try to stop me. I know that's what you will want to do, but if you're tempted, look inside this envelope and you'll know why you mustn't. Don't worry, I will keep in touch and let you know where I am. Believe in me, Claire, as I believe in you and with your support I'll come back whole and well and be the husband and father you and the kids deserve. Whatever happens you know I have loved you more than life itself. Be strong, my love.

Call the airport, her heart urged, stop him. She turned the envelope upside down and the burnt matches tumbled out. A sick feeling gripped her, and she clutched a fist to her stomach. In her heartbeat she heard his voice: *Have faith, have faith, have faith . . .*

Megan called from downstairs, but Claire couldn't respond.

He's right, she thought, I have to let him do this for himself. Tears welled up. Megan entered the room, holding a glass of milk. "Mommy, the cheese has fuzz on it."

Claire rushed to her daughter and embraced her.

"Mommy, watch out." Milk slopped over the glass to the rug.

"My fault," Claire said, trying to smile. She went to the dresser and grabbed a Kleenex. With her back to Megan she took a deep breath and resolved to be strong for the children.

"Hurry, Mommy, it's sinking."

Claire knelt and dabbed at the spilled milk. Megan said, "Why are you crying?"

"I'm not crying." She wiped her cheek with the back of her hand. "Daddy's gone away for a while, that's all."

"Back to Kansas?"

"That's right. Get me another tissue, will you?" She kept pushing the Kleenex against the wet spot until it was saturated and coming apart in her hands. Megan returned, carrying a hand towel from the bathroom. "This will work much better."

Despite her resolve, the tears came.

When Guy Jurmon stepped off the plane at Dulles International Airport, Vasily was there to meet him. Jurmon wore a black velvet sportcoat over a black silk shirt with the collar opened wide to display a gold chain framed by sagging sunlamp-darkened skin. Not the right man if you wanted to avoid attention, Vasily thought.

Jurmon was smug and excited about the flight. He had recognized an aging rock star and stolen a dinner knife, which he offered to Vasily as a souvenir. His clothing smelled of stale cigarette smoke and cologne, a free airline gift. It wasn't until they were in the car heading to the hotel that Vasily sprang his surprise. "Instead of a woman we'll be taking a kid, a twelve-year-old boy."

"Wait, wait a minute." The cigarette dangling from Jurmon's lower lip bobbed as he spoke. "You said you were going to do a woman. We can't do a boy, a child."

"Why not?"

"Because this is mass-produced merchandise, it has to appeal to the widest possible audience. The death of a woman, who knows? She's a whore, she's the mum who spanked you, the bitch ex-wife who fucked your friend, she deserves it. That's where the satisfaction comes from. She *deserves* it." He drew the word lovingly through his lips. "But not a child. No one pays to see a child die."

"You showed me magazines with children having sex."

Jurmon's lips formed a smiling V. "Sex, sure, it's natural, it's loving, it's a pleasure. The customer believes the children *enjoy* it."

"But they don't."

"There are worse things. Like having your knees destroyed."

This was accompanied with a knowing leer that made Vasily want to shove the little toad out the door. When you die, he thought, there will be no cameras running, no one will buy videos of your death. But for the time being he had to pander to Jurmon's warped sensibilities.

"We'll use the boy to trap the mother. Then you can do what you want with her."

"Why not just do the mother and be done with it?"

"You tell me—who means more to a man, his wife or his children?"

"By the time they have children, the children."

"That's why the boy comes first."

Jurmon continued to whine about "your little switcheroo" until Vasily agreed to double his fee from ten to twenty thousand dollars. It didn't matter. Jurmon wouldn't live to see the money anyway. In the meantime he could contact his pornographer friends and buy the gun they would need to intimidate the boy and defend themselves in case something went wrong. The same gun Vasily would use to dispose of Jurmon himself.

FBI agent Dominick Vincour stared at the coded message that Bill Sullivan had left behind. Actually a photograph of the original. As soon as he was alerted that Sullivan had escaped, Vincour ordered the message retrieved, photographed and replaced. The park bench was now under constant surveillance and whoever came for the note would be arrested. In the meantime, Bud Lipman in Cryptography was doing a rush job trying to decode it.

Vincour stared at the message, a series of numbers separated by dashes:774-2-12-336-1-3-480-1-1-176-1-18-490-1-25-754-2-14-593-2-2.

Twenty-one numbers, that was it. Was each number a letter, a word or a prearranged sentence? Was one of them someone's name? Or a meeting place, a plan of action, what? The code confirmed Vincour's suspicions about Sullivan. Unfortunately, the surveillance team had lost him, a failure that Vincour was prepared to argue was due to the recent manpower shortage. Since the demise of the Soviet Union, the FBI's Counterespionage Division had suffered budget and personnel cuts. Sullivan's escape could be used as an argument against any further reductions.

His secretary's voice on the intercom interrupted him. "Bud Lipman is here, sir."

That was fast, Vincour thought as the man entered. Lipman was young and energetic and, like many of those attracted to cryptography, could find meaning hidden in a stop sign.

"What have you got?" Vincour said.

Lipman wore an impish smile. "Everything. It's both the easiest and the hardest type of code to crack. Anybody can do it with the key, nobody can do it without the key."

"You discovered the key?"

"I bought the key." He tossed a thick paperback book onto the desk, the Merriam-Webster pocket dictionary.

"A book code," Vincour said with satisfaction.

"Right. As soon as your guys told me that he'd stopped at a bookstore, we went back and asked the clerk. She remembered Sullivan. He asked for the most recent edition. Made a point of asking, I think you'll see why."

Vincour glanced again at the series of numbers. "Page and word numbers."

"And a column number. Three sets of numbers for each word—page, column and number of words from the top. Take the first set, 774-2-12, you look up the page"—he opened the dictionary to a yellow tab and placed his finger on a word high-lighted in yellow—"and you find the twelfth word in the second column is *vital*."

Unable to conceal his impatience, Vincour said, "I know how it works, give me the clear text."

Lipman handed him a sheet of paper. Vincour frowned as he read it: *Vital Information Not Credible Only Unreliable Reportage*. The message seemed ambiguous. No indication where Sullivan had gone or what the plan was. When he looked up, Lipman was grinning.

"What?" Vincour asked.

"He's right, you know."

"Who's right? What are you talking about?"

"Your message. Not credible."

"What do you mean, my message?"

"It's addressed to you."

"Don't fuck with me, Lipman."

"Look at the first letter of each word."

Vincour's lips moved as he located the letters. He felt his face flush as his professional suspicion of Bill Sullivan turned to personal dislike.

CHAPTER

22

Bill arrived at Moscow's Sheremetyevo International Airport at eight-fifteen in the morning, just after watching the sun come up over an indistinct land of autumnal brown and gray. The terminal was sleek and modern with a black rubber-tile floor and a soaring ceiling of patterned gun-metal tubes. Before he could pass through Customs and Immigration, Bill had to stop at the tiny Intourist office, where he paid fifty dollars for a three-day "instant visa" and arranged hotel accommodations. When the moon-faced clerk asked the purpose of his visit, Bill said, "Pleasure."

"Good luck," the man mumbled.

The terminal was crowded with kiosks selling fur hats, CCCP T-shirts, painted wood dolls nested within one another—*matryoshkas*—the word slipped like a falling feather through his mind, then was gone.

Bill exchanged three hundred dollars at the *Vneshekonombank,* the State foreign economic bank, then ran a gauntlet of taxi drivers crowded near the door until he found one, a redfaced man with a sweeping moustache, who spoke English.

"What kind of car?" Bill asked.

"Mercedes, just outside. Best car in Moscow, good heat, four-speakers radio, nice car. What hotel?"

"The Ukraina."

"Wait here, sir, stay warm. My name is Anton. I am coming right away."

In less than a minute Anton drove up in a Mercedes of uncertain vintage. He jumped out and held the door open for Bill.

"Service," he said. "The first principle of capitalist economy is service."

"I think the first principle is capital."

"Is what?"

"Money."

Anton sneezed. "The principle before the first principle, maybe." He put the car in gear and they lurched forward. "You have money for gas?"

"We need gas?"

Anton pointed. The gauge was near empty. "You have money?"

"How much do you need?"

"Wait."

They left the airport and headed toward the Leningradskoe Highway, which would take them into Moscow. Just before they reached it, Anton turned right onto a small access road. Bill tensed.

"Is this the way to the Ukraina?"

"Shortcut."

Had someone known he was coming? Or was it a theft? He had no gun, no weapon of any kind. "Stay on the main road."

"Don't worry, sir."

They pulled into a deserted parking lot behind a warehouse. Bill took his keys from his pocket and held them so the tip of each extended between the fingers of his clenched fist, a primitive kind of brass knuckles. Anton turned with a wad of rubles in his hand.

"Change money. I will give you better than the official rate. How much? Fifty? One hundred?"

Bill relaxed. "No thanks. I've been to the bank."

"Bank is no good. I can offer full-service exchange." He quoted a rate five times the official one and it was only after Bill threatened to go to the police that he reluctantly shoved his rubles back inside his coat.

They regained the main road and drove five minutes to a gas station where they joined a six-car queue to get gas. Anton turned off his engine and pushed the car each time they moved toward the pump. "Saving of petrol," he told Bill, motioning him to relax.

"Second law of capitalism," Bill said. "Don't make the customer wait."

By the time they reached the city it was almost one o'clock. Moscow was dusted by a dry snow that had filtered into crevices and rimmed the curbs. It was a low city with only a handful of skyscrapers disturbing the skyline and a half dozen others under construction. The image Bill had of old women shaped like shopping bags and poker-faced men seemed to have dissolved with the old Soviet Union. Jeans, stylish skirts, sweaters, leather jackets—they might have been anywhere in Europe.

The Ukraina Hotel was a huge Gothic building with a churchlike spire pointing toward the heavens. The lobby was the size of a tennis court and contained a restaurant, souvenir shops, money changing booth and an Intourist Office. Bill surrendered his passport and received something called a *propusk,* or guest card, "which you will need to enter the hotel and receive the key to your room," the clerk explained.

The key was in the custody of a concierge on the seventh floor, a woman who fit the old Soviet mold. She sat behind a small table like a Sumo wrestler, huge thighs distending a formless dress, her thick features framed by a bright scarf. She held Bill's *propusk* up to the light as if to check its authenticity, then tucked it into a drawer and gave him a key to his room.

"Leave with me when you go," she ordered and returned to the book she was reading.

Except for its view of the Moscow River, the room was unimpressive. The double bed was made of two singles shoved together and the burnt-out bulb in the lamp was coated with dust. In the bathroom a tarnished brass shower head shaped like a sun flower hung below a ceiling dimpled with mildew. None of it mattered to Bill, whose only interest was in finding the man who held the key to his past, Dennis Riggs. He tossed the bags on his bed, splashed some cold water on his face and returned to the lobby, where a clerk whose smile seemed painted on her face found him a dog-eared computer-printed phone book. Russian phone books carried no addresses, so he had her call the Maurice Thorez Foreign Language Institute and write down its address.

The institute, located near Gorky Park, was a weather-stained concrete building decorated with plaques commemorating teachers who had died during the Stalin purges. The admissions office was cramped and overheated and smelled of steam heat and warm linoleum. A pert young woman no more than nineteen with shoulder-length brown hair smiled at him. *"Da?"*

"Is there someone here who speaks English?"

"I am speaking English."

"Good. I'm looking for an English instructor you have working here, Dennis Riggs."

Her expression dimmed. "I'm sorry, sir, he is no longer employed."

"Can you tell me where I can find him?"

"Perhaps a new job he has found. Who can say?"

"What about his house? Where does he live?"

"I have no knowledge."

"You have records, don't you?"

"We are not the dispensary for private information of our employees. Perhaps you wish to leave your name and number and someone can touch the base to him."

Bill placed a twenty-dollar bill on the counter between them. "I hate to wait. Perhaps you can find his address for me."

The girl eyed the bill. "You are a friend of his?"

"A very close friend."

"Wait here." Before she disappeared, the receptionist said something to a co-worker chalking names on a staff assignment board who flashed a gap-toothed smile whenever she caught his eye. Then the receptionist returned with a piece of paper, which she carefully placed over the twenty-dollar bill. "Simply give to this your driver."

When she lifted her hand, the twenty was gone. The first law of capitalism at work, Bill thought.

The note was written in Cyrillic, which looked exotic and meant nothing to him, but the taxi driver had no trouble following the directions northeast of the city to an area of tiny dachas bordering a trolley stop. Dwarfed by huge apartment complexes to the east, the wooden homes were barnlike in appearance with additions and extensions stuck out at odd angles. The gambrel roofs were tar paper or corrugated tin, many with ladders leaning against them. Riggs's house was more of a shack with mismatched windows, each frame a different color, obviously second-hand. There was a smell of wood smoke; a dark smudge hung in the air above the houses.

Bill gave the driver two Marlboro cigarettes and indicated with hand signals and broken English that he should wait. He went to the door and knocked. A pregnant woman wearing a worn sweater over a cotton smock answered. She had mousy brown hair drawn back from her face, large, sad, luminous brown eyes. A small boy, maybe four years old, tugged silently at her hand.

"Speak English?" Bill asked. She gave a noncommittal nod but said nothing. "I'm an American, a friend of Dennis Riggs. Is he here?"

Her eyes grew wary. She shook her head. "No English."

"Dennis Riggs. You know him?"

From inside a man's voice bellowed, *"Kto tam?"* After a short exchange in Russian a man stumbled to the door. His shirttail hung over baggy trousers held up with suspenders. He hadn't shaved and his hair was mussed. He squinted and blinked. "American?"

"That's right. My name is Bill Sullivan. Can I talk to you?"

"What about?"

"Your work with the FBI, for one thing."

Riggs glanced beyond Bill's shoulder to the taxi and frowned. "You have permission to be here?"

"From who?"

"Wait a minute, do I know you? Your face . . . Sullivan, Sullivan . . ." His face cleared. "The background investigation, sure. Bill Sullivan. You're one of us. Come on in."

Not one of you, Bill thought as he stepped past Dennis and caught a whiff of stale breath and alcohol. The house was messy with toys and magazines strewn over the floor. The television was on and ice dancers performed to classical music. The kitchen was tiny and crowded with a wheezing refrigerator and a two-burner gas stove. Fumes from an oil heater permeated the place.

"Here, sit down, make yourself comfortable." He shoved a blanket off the couch and an empty vodka bottle tumbled out. "The place is a shithouse, but so's the whole country. What do you want? Vodka? Tea? Better make it tea." He called in Russian to the woman, who put the toddler down and busied herself in the kitchen with occasional mistrustful glances at them.

Dennis smoothed his hair back with a gesture that left strands of it standing upright. "So what happened? You're blown or they brought you back as a cost-cutting measure?"

"I came here on my own."

"Here, meaning you're reassigned or you just came back to see what's left of the country?"

"Here to find you. I want to know about the other Bill Sullivan. The one whose files you falsified. Where is he? What happened to him?"

"Who knows? Who cares? For ten thousand dollars I gave you a clean bill of health. Beyond that . . ." He shrugged broadly.

"You never met him?"

"Saw his picture, that's all. A couple of the neighbors in that godforsaken town, what the fuck was it? Birdshit, Kansas, or something?"

"Goodheart."

"Goodheart. They should come here. This is Badheart. Badheart Russia and it's going to keel over with a heart attack any day now."

The woman—his wife?—brought a loaf of Russian bread. As she leaned past him Riggs bit her sleeve and tugged it, growling like a dog. She jumped back, spilling the bread, and the fabric tore. Riggs laughed. "She loves it, don't you?" He smacked her bottom as she moved away.

"If I'm not Bill Sullivan, who am I?"

"You're asking me?"

"You were the one who falsified the report."

"I altered it to *make* you Bill Sullivan. *You* know who you really are."

"Who told you what to do? Who recruited you? Who was your control?"

Riggs winced. "Who recruited me was this lovely little lady named Anne Serling. Lips and tits, that's how they got their claws into me. Then they turned me over to this guy named John Weigand. Looked like a shoe salesman, you know what I mean? All soft voice and telling me everything was fine, they'd take care of me if anybody discovered what I was doing. First few months my asshole was tight as a squirrel's cunt, but nothing happened. No knock at the door, no call to the director's office, no cars parked outside the house . . . I couldn't believe it."

"Did you ever hear anything about my file? Who I was? Why they were validating me?"

"I didn't hear and didn't want to hear. But now they had my balls in a vise and here comes a new plan—I'm supposed to quit the Service and get a job with the FBI, work my way into Counterintelligence. It all goes like clockwork until ten years down the line I realize my office is feeding me false information, setting me up for a bust. That's when I became an honorary citizen of the USSR. I arrived the week after Gorbachev took office, which had to be the most piss-poor timing in the world."

The wife brought a kettle of tea on a tray. Dennis glanced up. "Except for her. It was perfect timing for you, right, Nina?" He gave her a false grin and she smiled hesitantly. "She loves me. Loves my dick. My dick is the father of her baby. Maybe. My dick betrayed me and I betrayed my country. This fucking dick,

I'd like to cut it off, where's a knife—" He grabbed a bread knife and brandished it with one hand while he shoved his pants down and grabbed his penis with the other. The girl screamed and struggled with him, overturning the table. Bill pushed between them and wrestled the knife away. Riggs was on his back, laughing. "You see her face? You see those eyes. She believes it. Believes everything I say. Thinks I'm going to cut it off and she'll lose her pension. My pension. That's my reward, me and my dick, we get our pension and she shares it, don't you?" He made kissing sounds, but Nina ignored him while she replaced the table and picked up the dishes.

Bill said, "Ten days ago someone tried to kill me. I don't know who or why."

"So you came running back to Mother Russia, that's just great. Maybe they'll make you a colonel. They made me one."

As they spoke, Nina bundled her child in a thick coat and went to the door. Dennis called in Russian and she answered in a low voice, then, with a pleading glance at Bill, left them. Dennis shook his head. "Dumb *kulak,* never could teach her English."

Bill felt stifled as much by the tawdry life he was witnessing as the stale air in the house. But he couldn't leave until he was certain he had gotten as much as he could from Riggs.

"I want you to put me in touch with the people who brought you here."

"They probably already know you're here."

"How?"

"You're one of their boys, aren't you?"

"I don't know who I am, that's why I'm here."

"Don't worry, it doesn't matter. The great good game is over. Those of us like you and me can no longer eke out a luxurious living by playing one government against the other. Nobody gives a shit who you are—Bill Sullivan or Mickey Mouse or Comrade Shitabitch, take your choice. It doesn't matter. This country, they can't get batteries for transistor radios and vodka production is half what it was a year ago. In America you've got race riots and mass murderers making butcher shops of shopping malls. You want to stay here and be a starving hero of a lost cause, fine. Otherwise you can go home and keep being whoever you . . ."

He paled, lurched to his feet, stumbled into a bathroom and vomited copiously. The door hung open and Bill could see his back arching spasmodically. The stink drove Bill outside, where Nina and the little boy were playing ball. Nina's smile faded when she saw him.

"Nina? You speak English?" Her eyes flicked to the open door.

"Little," she said, and hurried inside. Bill breathed deeply, cleaning his lungs with the fresh air. The boy stood forlornly holding the ball. His sweater was held together by buttons carved of wood. Bill held his hands for the ball, but the boy hugged it close and squatted. Bill went to the taxi. The driver, who was dozing, jumped when he opened his door.

"I need this," Bill said, picking up the vodka bottle from the seat beside him. The driver put up a fuss until Bill gave him the pack of Marlboro cigarettes. Bill returned to the house, where Nina, seeing the bottle, tried to block his way. *"Nyet, nyet."*

"I need answers."

"Makes sick."

"I'm sorry." He pushed her firmly aside, knelt beside Dennis and let some liquid splash on his lips. Dennis opened his eyes and grabbed for the bottle. Bill pulled it back. "A name, Dennis. I need a name. Who do you know?"

Dennis regarded him balefully. "You're fucked."

"Give me a name."

"Peter Yevchetko, he's a colonel in the KGB—what used to be the KGB, they keep changing the name."

"Phone number."

"I don't know, it's . . ." He called to Nina, who drew a worn leather address book from a drawer. They spoke in Russian and she found the number, which she read out loud while Dennis translated. Bill left the vodka and walked out the door. He had almost reached the taxi when Nina caught up with him. She said something in Russian and then, with her hand extended, tried it in English. "Dennis sick. Needing medicine, needing food, *da?*"

He took out a twenty-dollar bill and gave it to her. Nina grabbed his hand and tried to kiss it, but Bill was sick of it, sick of the wreck of a man he'd seen in the house and the desperate need for money that ran like a taproot through the entire land.

CHAPTER
23

It was growing dark by the time the taxi dropped Bill at 2 Dzer-zhinsky Square, the old block-long headquarters of the KGB. Inside the building he spoke to a uniformed man who didn't understand English. Eventually someone who did speak English came out and told him the offices were closed for the day. Bill left a note for Colonel Yevchetko with the number of the Ukraina Hotel.

Outside there were people picketing. He remained on the outskirts of the crowd and stared up at the building, ten stories high, made of brick with rows of arched windows. Up there, in an office beyond one of the windows, was a man who knew the secret of his past. Someone who once planned his fate, stole his memory, made him a stranger to his wife and children. Perhaps he was there right now, working late, taking phone calls or filling in some meaningless form or plotting to steal someone else's life.

A man in a white shirt came to the window on the seventh floor and Bill stepped back instinctively, seeking shelter within the doorway of a building across the street. Someone tugged his sleeve and he jumped. An old woman seated on a stool in front of a scale laughed. She wore a white coat and a floral scarf wrapped around her hair. She chattered at him and motioned him up onto the scale.

"I don't speak Russian," Bill said.

"Good," she said with a thick accent and motioned again. "Your weight you."

He stepped onto the scale. With a practiced motion the woman slid the weights and balanced the pointer. She pursed her lips and nodded. "Eighty-three kilograms. You are British? American?"

"American." He handed her a kopek, then, indicating the crowd across the street, said, "Why are they protesting?"

She shook her head and the fat beneath her neck quivered. "Protesting government."

"They don't like the KGB?"

"No, they desire for KGB to take back government. Back to old ways, *da?*"

Back at the hotel Bill spent a half hour with the overseas operator before he managed to get through to Claire. He could tell by the strain in her voice that she had been crying. "Bill, where are you?"

"Moscow." He heard her quick intake of breath. "I'm okay, don't worry."

"Why didn't you tell me?"

"I couldn't leave if you said *no.*"

"But it's not you, it's like what happened in Kansas, it's the other part of you that wants Russia."

Bill felt himself drawing away, her voice grew distant. This was something he feared, this knowledge, that beneath the impulse to discover the truth there was something else . . .

"Bill?" There was an edge of panic in her voice.

"I'm here. I'm all right."

"Come back, Bill. Before it's too late."

"It's already too late."

"Bill . . ."

"Not until I find myself, Claire. It's not you, it's me. I have to know. I have to know who I am. Nobody's going to kill me. I'm okay now." He recounted his meeting with Dennis Riggs and his plan to find Peter Yevchetko. Claire didn't share his eagerness to know the truth. "I don't care who they say you are, I just want you back home."

"I'll call you tomorrow."

"Wait, where are you?"

"The Ukraina Hotel." He gave her the number.

"Don't let go of us, Bill."

The whispered words went unheard as he replaced the receiver.

Vasily Amenov had rented a second vehicle, a white Dodge van that would better suit a kidnapping and afterward remain in the garage. Jurmon was the driver, an assignment he accepted only grudgingly.

"This is the wrong side of the road for me," he whined. "You Russians drive on the right, you should do it."

"You want to deal with the dog?"

Jurmon scowled and fell silent. He had already told Vasily how much he hated dogs, the result of being bitten in the face when he was a child. They had just left the parking lot behind the Minuteman convenience store, the same spot Juho Ryti had chosen to watch the Sullivan house. Ten minutes earlier the Toyota Previa had left the garage, and a phone call confirmed no one was home.

Jurmon parked at a secluded area next to the lake. Vasily put on a jogging outfit, stuck a dog leash in one pocket and a handful of Milkbone dog biscuits in the other. He jogged along the lake, his breath bursting in white puffs in the chilly morning air, until he came to the Sullivan house. Rather than draw attention to himself by acting surreptitiously, he marched boldly up to the fence and called softly, "Here, doggie, come on dog."

Nothing. Had they taken the animal with them? He called louder and whistled. The Irish Setter burst through a doggie door on the house and approached eagerly. Vasily didn't even need the dog biscuits. He let the dog smell him and the paroxysm of tail-wagging was proof that she was friendly. "Want to go for a walk, girl?"

There was no lock on the gate. Vasily stepped inside and slipped the choke chain over her neck. Ginger—that was the name on the dog tag. She tried to bite his wrist playfully, then eagerly romped out the gate. Not much of a guard dog, Vasily thought. And not much taste in people, judging by the way she greeted Jurmon, pushing forward to nuzzle his hand. Jurmon drew back. "Keep it away."

Vasily deliberately relaxed the leash. "I think she likes you."

"Just give her the bloody sleeping pills."

"Too soon. The kid just left for school."

Jurmon pivoted away, raising a knee to keep Ginger from nuzzling his crotch. "Bloody pervert."

Vasily smiled. Jurmon's aversion to the dog's indiscriminate affection would entertain him while they waited.

Bill did not sleep well. He was haunted by figures and phrases in Russian, and he dreamed of a dark woman with Asiatic features who cradled him in her arms and sang a haunting melody: *Where have you been, Billy boy, Billy boy? Oh, where have you been, charming Billy* . . .

The woman's eyes became huge sad pools, coming down toward him, expanding like dark orbs covering the sky, blotting out everything, lips moving in a whisper, glistening with moisture: . . . *I've gone to get a knife which will end my baby's life* . . .

His muscles jerked and he woke up. The eyes were still there, hazel eyes framed by blonde hair, rosy cheeks, a young woman sitting in a chair watching him. Still dreaming, he thought, until she smiled and said, *"Doboye utro, Mischa."*

He sat bolt upright, remembering his gun at the same moment he remembered he didn't have it. "Who are you?"

Speaking English now she said, "My name is Lizaveta Treplova. I am surprising you, please forgive it."

"How did you—" Get in the room, he was about to say. He

had locked the door from the inside, but now the answer became apparent: the door to an adjoining room was open and in the doorway a video camera on a tripod was pointed directly at him. "What's that for?"

"I am watching your sleep pattern. Marina says you can learn a great deal from a man by the way he sleeps. *Vosne chelovek vyedayot sebya*—the sleeping body mirrors the mind."

"Who's Marina?"

"She made you. I am her assistant."

"She what?"

"What is the word? *Created*, yes. She created you and now she is waiting."

Bill placed his fingers at the bridge of his nose and pushed hard. When he opened his eyes Lizaveta was still watching with a quizzical half-smile. Not makeup, he noticed, but cheeks burnished by the sun. Her face had the natural flush of one who spent time outdoors. He realized suddenly that beneath the sheets he was naked.

"Is that thing on?" He indicated the camera.

"It is part of the documents."

"What documents? What are you talking about? And what are you doing in my room?"

"I am with the National Psychiatric Institute. Your responses are on recording."

"Turn it off."

"It is making you nervous?"

"You're making me nervous, *it's* making me angry." He grabbed a pillow and slung it across the room. The camera toppled over backward and crashed to the floor. Lizaveta ran to the camera and cradled it like a child. "Why do you damage fine equipment? Are you so violent?"

"Why'd you come into my room? What are you doing here?"

She wasn't looking at him, but was fumbling with the camera. Her hips and thighs were outlined beneath tan slacks, her upper body hidden beneath a plaid shirt over a turtleneck sweater. She was feminine without design, the only jarring note the leather boots. Details he had noted earlier shifted into focus and he said, "Bicycle or motorcycle?"

She looked up. "What?"

"What do you ride, bicycle or motorcycle?"

It was her turn to be surprised. "But how?"

"Your face has color except where there's a helmet. White hands mean gloves, so my guess is a motorcycle."

Before she could respond, someone began pounding on the door, yelling in Russian. Lizaveta unlocked it and two armed men in uniform stepped into the room followed by a short, wiry man in a business suit. He and Lizaveta exchanged a few quick words, then he said in heavily accented English, "Excuse our caution, but we thought you had attacked Lizaveta Ivanova. You are the man who came to Dennis Riggs yesterday and demanded the name of Peter Yevchetko, is it correct?"

"You're Yevchetko?"

"No. He is retired from the government service. My name is Major Gennadi Khiza. I can answer all your questions. Please put on your clothes."

"What about some answers first? Like who you work for and what you want with me?"

"It is you who want something from us, is it not? When you are ready we will go."

Bill noticed out of the corner of his eye that Lizaveta had removed the video camera from the tripod and now had it balanced on her shoulder, taping the scene.

"You want to tape me getting dressed?" he said.

"I do not mind."

"Well, I do. Why don't you people leave me alone for a minute."

Khiza said something in Russian and the two guards stepped out of the room. "We are waiting for you," Khiza said. He and the girl retreated to the adjoining room and closed the door. Bill threw on his clothes. He wasn't sure what to make of the situation, but it wouldn't hurt to let the embassy know what was happening. He picked up the phone, dialed 9 and waited for the operator.

"*Da?*"

"I need an outside line."

"All outside lines are busy." She hung up. They had isolated

him. Bill opened the door to the room and found what he expected: the two armed guards waiting in the hall. One raised a
walkie-talkie and spoke into it. Without smiling, the other man
said, "Hello."

So what am I supposed to do, Bill thought, kick him in the
balls and run? He had come to Moscow for answers and he
wouldn't find them by running from the people who had them.
He took a deep breath. "Tell your boss I'm ready."

CHAPTER 24

They were waiting for Claire when she returned home in the early afternoon. She noticed the dark blue car in front of her house, noticed the two men sitting in it and noticed the government license plates. As she pulled into the driveway they got out of the car and approached her.

"Mrs. Sullivan? Special Agent Vincour, Federal Bureau of Investigation. This is Agent Williams."

Williams was a young black woman with cropped hair, intelligent dark eyes and a guarded smile. "We'd like to talk to you if we could."

"What about?"

"Your husband. Do you know where he is right now?"

She smiled faintly. "I'm a Secret Service wife. One of the things I learned early on is that Secret Service wives don't talk about their husband's business."

"To the general public. I'm sure that doesn't apply to other federal agents. May we come inside?"

"Are you here to help Bill or to prosecute him?" A stupid question, she realized even as she asked it. What were they going to say? "I'm sorry," she added quickly, "it doesn't matter. I don't want to say anything until I talk with Bill." She started toward the door.

"Your husband is a defector, Mrs. Sullivan, did you know that?" Vincour's tone was tough and uncompromising. Claire turned. "What do you mean?"

"He had an appointment with us yesterday morning. Instead he avoided a surveillance team and flew to Moscow."

"You were following him?"

"Your husband is a security risk. Can you tell us why he went to Moscow?"

"He went to prove that what you're saying about him isn't true."

"How well do you know your husband, Mrs. Sullivan?"

"I know he's not a defector or a spy."

"I didn't say anything about his being a spy."

"The implication is clear enough, isn't it?"

"Let me ask you this. Did it ever occur to you that your husband could be the victim of blackmail?"

"For what?"

"That's what we'd like to find out. If you'd allow us to review your phone bills, your husband's bank records, correspondence, things like that, it might give us a clue to what's going on."

She stepped toward them. "I have children coming home from school, and I do not want them to find strangers pawing through their father's possessions. Please leave us alone."

Agent Vincour called after her, "We can always get a search warrant."

Claire faced them from the door. "When you do, you can give it to my lawyer."

She shut the door, punched the code to deactivate the security system, then watched through the window as the two agents returned to their car and drove away. The confrontation left her with a queasy feeling. She checked the time—3:10. What time was it in Moscow? Just after seven in the morning. She went to the phone and spent fifteen minutes before she managed to reach his hotel. The phone rang and rang without an answer.

Vasily Amenov and Guy Jurmon were waiting in the white van when Matt emerged from school. Keeping a distance, they followed him down the street to Oak Knoll Boulevard where he turned right, continued a quarter mile to the road leading into his neighborhood and continued past it.

"Where's he going?"

"I don't know."

Vasily swiveled in his seat and whistled at Ginger. The dog, lying in a cardboard box, raised its head. Vasily scratched the dog's ears and Ginger made a sloppy and unsuccessful attempt to rise, then collapsed. The sleeping pills had done their work well.

"Another school," Jurmon said.

Ahead of them was a block-long brick building with an American flag on a tall pole in front and yellow school buses waiting in a small parking lot.

"Elementary school. He's waiting for his sister."

"Nab them both?"

"We may have to." It wasn't ideal, but they already had the dog and it was too late to change plans. If there was going to be two hostages he was doubly glad to have Jurmon to help manage them.

When his sister emerged, Matt joined her. Vasily hoped they would walk alone, but the kids clumped together in small groups, four others walking with Matt and Megan. Impossible to do it without witnesses, but that shouldn't matter. The next step depended upon timing.

Knowing their destination, Vasily and Jurmon drove past the children and turned into the Sullivan's neighborhood. The street ran five blocks to Dunsmore Lane, which then intersected Ernestine Circle. It was in this five blocks the snatch would have to be made. They had practiced the maneuver earlier and no words were necessary as Jurmon continued past Dunsmore, made a U-turn and pulled to the corner where they could see the Oak Knoll intersection. While they waited for Matt and Megan to appear, Jurmon pulled out his nasal spray and snorted it noisily. Shut up, Vasily wanted to say. Working with Jurmon was more aggravating than he had anticipated.

"There they are."

Jurmon shoved the inhaler into his pocket and started the engine. Five blocks away the kids had turned toward them, coming up the opposite sidewalk. Vasily lifted the groggy dog to his lap. "Come on, Ginger, time for a little accident."

Now the kids were only four blocks away, but the men in the van couldn't make their move without one more element—a car to precede them. Jurmon's eyes were fixed on the side-view mirror. "Here comes someone."

The car passed them and Jurmon pulled into the street behind it.

"Close it up," Vasily ordered, his hands busy with Ginger, who was trying ineffectually to climb off his lap. They were three blocks from the kids, then two. Vasily opened his door. "Now."

Jurmon braked abruptly to a stop as Vasily pushed Ginger out the door. The dog yelped as it hit the pavement.

"Don't hit her," Vasily warned as Jurmon backed up. By this time the car they had been following was turning onto Oak Knoll Boulevard. Vasily leaped out of the passenger door, jumped over Ginger and ran up the street.

"Hey! You hit that dog. Hey!"

The kids, still on the other side of the street, were staring. Vasily turned to them. "Did you get the license of that car? He hit that dog."

Matt yelled Ginger's name and came running.

"You know this dog?" Vasily asked.

"She's our dog."

"You're Matt. We met the other day. You live around here, right?"

Matt and Megan were on their knees beside Ginger. The dog's tail slapped the pavement weakly. Apart from the effects of the pills, Vasily could see no damage. He said, "We better get your dog to a hospital or back to your house. Can you put her in the van?" He slid the cargo door open and their friends watched somberly as Matt and Megan carefully lifted Ginger into the van. Megan's eyes were wide with fear. "Is she going to die?"

Vasily said, "You ride with your brother and keep the dog quiet."

Megan hesitated, but Matt was frantic. "Hurry up, Ginger needs help."

She climbed in. A friend of Matt's pushed forward. "What happened?"

"It's Ginger, she got hit. Come on."

From inside the van, Vasily blocked the opening. "Too many people will scare the dog." He slid the door shut and the van moved away.

"Just turn around and go back the way you were coming," Matt told Jurmon. They made a U-turn and headed toward home. Matt and Megan sat on the metal floor, Ginger between them. The truck smelled new.

"Turn left on Dunsmore," Matt said.

The truck swayed as they made the turn.

"Then a right on Ernestine Circle."

They kept going.

"You passed it."

"That's all right," Vasily said. "Ginger doesn't look too good. We better get her to an animal hospital."

"My Mom'll be worried."

"You can call her from the hospital." Vasily bent down and patted the dog's head. "Poor dog needs a doctor."

Megan said, "Do you think she'll be all right, mister?"

"How old is she?"

"She's five months."

"I can't believe what people will do," Vasily said. "I think they aimed at her deliberately."

"They did?" Matt's face darkened at the thought.

Megan said, "Why would anybody want to hit Ginger?"

"You never know about people," Vasily said. "Maybe they were once bitten by such a dog. Maybe they didn't like the color of her hair. Some people don't like red."

"That's sick."

"I believe I got the license number." Vasily pulled out a form and read a Maryland number.

"Good," Matt said. "That means we can tell the police."

"Are the police particularly good here?"

"If you got the license plate they'll catch them."

"Does your father have faith in the police?"

The flash of unease Matt had felt when they bypassed his street returned. "He's not home right now."

"Where is he?"

Matt recalled they weren't to discuss his father's absence so he just shrugged. "On business somewhere. How soon will we get to the hospital?"

The man looked up to his companion. "How soon will we get there, Guy?"

"Not long now."

"We should call my Mom and let her know where we are."

"Does your mother worry about you?"

"Not us," Megan said, "other people. Weird people. She says there are too many sick people in the world."

"What do they look like?"

Megan shrugged. "I don't know. Just weird."

"Like my friend up there."

"I can't see him."

"His name is Mr. Jurmon. Say hi to Megan, Mr. Jurmon."

They were waiting at a stoplight. Guy turned and smiled. "Hello, Megan."

Vasily said, "What do you think? Does my friend look weird?"

She drew back. "He talks funny."

Matt said stiffly, "Are we almost there?"

"Soon."

A change had taken place in Matt. The boy was tense now, looking around the truck. "Can we . . . pull over a minute?"

"Why?"

"We should call before it gets too late. People might get worried, especially if they saw us drive away. You know, because they wouldn't recognize this car. They might even call the police."

Megan said, "Why would they call the police?"

"Well, you know they might be worried." The boy's voice cracked and he looked away. Yes, Vasily thought, he knows.

"What your brother means, Megan, is that your neighbors might not know we're going to the veterinarian and they might think we're kidnapping you. Isn't that right, Matt?"

"That's why I should call."

Megan was staring at Vasily. "How do you know my name?"

Vasily looked at her a long moment. His sister's name—that was what had alerted the boy. "Matt must have told me when we met the other day."

"Probably," Matt agreed, but his voice was weak and his stomach felt empty and his hands tingled because he knew he hadn't mentioned her name at all. I've got to get out of here, he thought. Got to get out. But Ginger lay heavy on his lap, and Megan was patting her and whispering, "It's all right, Ginger, it's all right." But Matt knew the truth: it wasn't all right at all.

When she couldn't get through to Bill, Claire called Roy, but he was out of the office. Something the FBI man had said weighed on her mind: *How well do you know your husband?* She remembered Bill's anger when she admitted that she'd never believed his account of his disappearance the day of their wedding. She went downstairs to Bill's office and turned on the light. She had rarely been here alone. Feeling as if she were betraying a trust Claire gingerly opened drawers until she found Bill's bank records. Better I should find out, she thought, before the FBI comes back with a search warrant. She inspected the bank book and was relieved that everything was normal. Looking through his correspondence, attuned for a hint of Sally's writing, she realized how deep her distrust of her husband had grown.

At three-forty-five the doorbell rang. It was Brian Fowler and a couple of the neighborhood kids.

"Is Ginger okay?"

She had been so preoccupied that she realized only now that she hadn't seen or heard the dog. "What about Ginger?"

"She got hit by a car."

"Where? Are you sure it was Ginger?"

"Yeah. They were going to bring her here."

"The people who hit her?"

"Matt and Megan. They went with the man who found Ginger."

"What man?"

"He had a white truck."

She grabbed Brian's shoulders. "Who had a white truck? What are you talking about?"

"I don't know, but Matt knew him."

The tightness around her heart eased. Someone Matt knew, good. But who owned a white van? She couldn't think of anyone.

"When did this happen?"

"Ten minutes ago. Up by the big intersection."

"And they were coming here?"

"I thought they were."

Another boy said, "Maybe they took Ginger to the veterinarian."

The phone rang. "That's probably them," Claire said as much to herself as the kids. How had Ginger gotten out, she wondered as she rushed to the kitchen. The FBI agents? She grabbed the receiver. "Hello?"

"Mrs. Sullivan?" An unfamiliar voice.

"Yes."

"I have to speak to your husband, but I understand he is out of town, is that correct?"

"That's right. Who's this?"

"Jeremy Lawrence. Not 'Jerry.' Bill will know me. We have business to discuss."

"He's not here, can I take a number?"

"I don't have a phone so I'll have to call back."

"I'm waiting for an important call, Mr. Lawrence, but I'll tell him you called."

"What do the children like for breakfast?"

She had started to put down the phone, but his words trailing into the air were loud as gunshots. "What?"

"They eat healthy food, is that right? Granola, a little milk, that's what Megan says but you know how children are, they take advantage of relatives or strangers, especially cute children like yours, people want to spoil them and I'm sure you don't want that to happen, you want them back as healthy and well-disciplined as when you took them to school this morning, isn't that right?"

Her voice was a whisper, "You have my children?"

"They're safe and they'll remain that way unless you go to the police. Or the FBI or the Secret Service—I think you understand me."

"Please, I'll give you anything you want, just don't hurt them."

"I have never hurt anyone who didn't betray me first."

"Oh, God . . ."

"Listen now," the voice continued calmly. "Their safety depends on you. If you bring in the police and make my life difficult then your children become expendable. You understand that? If you put me at risk, you risk your children's lives."

Claire forced herself to concentrate. "Yes, yes, just don't hurt them."

"They won't be hurt, but to get them back I need a favor."

"I'll do anything."

"No, only your husband can do the favor."

"He's out of town, I just told you that."

"Then I will call tomorrow at noon. If he's not back by then or if you have gone to the police or your phone is under surveillance you will never see Matthew or Megan again."

"No, wait, I can't get in touch with—"

A click as the line went dead. She jiggled the receiver. "Wait, wait, please don't go. Let me talk to my children!"

A loud *beep-beep-beep* was followed by a mechanical voice: *"Please hang up. There appears to be a line off the hook. Please hang up the phone now."*

Claire dropped the phone and went running out the front door, running up the street crying for Matt and for Megan, running until she reached the elementary school, where she breathlessly confronted one teacher, then another, none of whom had seen Megan after she left the building. "Is anything wrong?" they asked, but she had no words for them, not with the kidnapper's threat echoing in her ears.

"Ginger's gone," she said stupidly to the last teacher who asked. And then, hoping they had disobeyed instructions never to take the shortcut, she ran through the woods to the lake and around the shoreline until she was back home. The backyard was empty, the house empty, the phone on the floor silent as death.

"Help me," she whispered as she sank to the floor. "Help me, help me," as she clutched her knees and began to tremble violently. "Please God," as tears rolled down her cheeks, nose running, and words torn by sobs. She needed help and there was no one.

CHAPTER

25

Bill was right about the motorcycle. It was a BMW chained to a pillar outside the hotel. While the guards loaded the video equipment into a limousine Lizaveta donned a layer of weather-proof clothing, leather gloves and a black helmet. They left together, but as soon as the first red light loomed Lizaveta roared ahead before it changed. The guards whooped and cheered and gestured suggestively.

They drove north to the outskirts of the city where they arrived at a huge complex of buildings behind a ten-foot-high concrete wall. A guard perched inside a small shelter at the entrance waved them into a broad courtyard fronted by three buildings, an older one with arched windows, marble columns, and balconies covered in wire mesh, and two others more modern in design, one a concrete monolith, the other with a facade of gray slate and elongated windows. As they got closer, Bill saw that there were bars inside the windows of the older building. A prison, he thought. Then he saw a man and woman in white coats leaving the building and he understood: a hospital.

They entered the old building and Khiza spoke to the receptionist. Lizaveta had exchanged her motorcycle helmet for the video camera. She held it to her eye as she followed them up a circular flight of steps beneath a dirty skylight.

"What is this place?" Bill asked.

"The Sandulov Institute," Khiza said simply.

Lizaveta lowered the camera. "It used to be the palace of a prince before the revolution. In that time the city was still many kilometers away."

Easy-listening music was piped throughout the building and a Beatles tune, "When I'm Sixty-four," accompanied them down a wide hallway to a solarium where pale autumn light streamed across a cracked linoleum floor. There were two people in the room, an old man in a wheelchair and a woman in her sixties whose face suffused with joy when she saw him. "Mischa?"

"I'm Bill Sullivan."

"Billy, of course." She reached to touch his cheek, a gentle gesture that took him by surprise. He stepped back. The man in the wheelchair said, "Marina . . ."

The woman nodded, took a deep breath and said softly, "Yes, good, as it should be."

There was a video camera positioned in one corner of the room to record the proceedings. Lizaveta put her portable camera down and made introductions. "This is Doctor Marina Sorin and Colonel Andrei Guneyev."

Marina was a sturdily built woman with bright, intelligent eyes and dark hair tinged with gray. The man in the wheelchair had the upswept gray eyebrows and heavy jowls that Bill associated with Russian military. Marina said, "Sit, please. We will call for tea and see if we can make sense of what is going on."

Four chairs were arranged in a semicircle facing a fifth, a large armchair with cigarette burns scarring worn upholstery. Bill glanced behind him before he sat down: a solid wall, no one-way mirrors, but two husky men in hospital greens stood guard on either side of the door.

"What are they for?"

"This is a psychiatric research hospital," Marina said. "They will protect us from antisocial acts of unstable patients."

"What about unstable KGB agents?"

"I do not understand."

Bill said, "You're KGB aren't you? Or is it just the colonel here?"

Guneyev's English was not as good as the others. "Old KGB is gone. All of us, we are only as powerful as our nation so look. We are like dancing bear—no, not even so much. We are white mouse running in a cage. You think we are fearsome? No, this bear goes without teeth, without claws. Look at me, I am KGB. Can you be afraid now?"

Marina smiled. "You have nothing to fear from Colonel Guneyev or anyone else here."

"Then why'd you try to kill me in Washington?"

"No one tried to kill you . . ."

"The man with a gun wasn't one of yours?"

Marina turned to Khiza and unleashed a torrent of Russian. They argued briefly, and she turned back to Bill. "I'm sorry. I did not know."

"But *he* does?"

Khiza said crisply, "The Sorin Project was a danger to the Russian Republic. Now you are in Moscow, so the danger is gone."

"What's the Sorin Project."

"You are."

A blinding headache caused him to wince. He shut his eyes and pushed back at the darkness that threatened to engulf him. When he looked up, the Russians were on their feet, watching him attentively. Marina said, "Mischa?"

"My name is Bill Sullivan."

Marina directed an angry comment to Khiza, who responded in kind. The tension went out of the room as a heavy woman brought in a tea cart. She had the bunched features of the mentally handicapped; a gap-toothed smile lit her face whenever anyone caught her eye. She poured the tea from a battered kettle. Bill used the time to try and regain his equilibrium. *Mischa.* He could feel resistance to the name. Let it go, he thought. You came to discover the truth. Don't resist it. He forced himself to say the words that fought expression. "How can I be Mischa? How can I be someone I'm not?"

Khiza said irritably, "Tell him or I will."

Marina said, "Listen to me, Billy. You are fighting the truth of existence, so let us begin with the truth of birth. You will want to reject what you hear, but I ask you to open your mind, pretend that this is a hypothesis, pretend for a moment it is 1962 and you are Premier Khrushchev who is facing an inexperienced and unknown quantity in President Kennedy. It is the Cuban missile crisis and Kennedy is ready to risk nuclear war. Khrushchev must retreat. He emerges, having lost face and vowing that this will never happen again. He realizes that under threat of nuclear war any president might prove lethal to the Soviet Union. What is needed is a foolproof way of removing a president. A dark star in the heavens of the United States. An assassin."

"I'm not a killer!"

"A hypothesis, remember? Let your mind stay open. An assassin, yes, but only if he can meet three impossible criteria: he must have no link to the motherland, he must be activated anonymously, and he must pass the most sophisticated psychological tests known to science. An impossible task. But imagine the use of such an assassin. Imagine during the Patriotic War against Germany how many people would have lived had Hitler's barber or his secretary or a bodyguard been our dark star. Imagine the day in 1941 when the Nazi army crossed onto Russian soil: A simple telephone call is made. The next morning Hitler's barber cuts his throat or his bodyguard lifts a pistol and shoots Hitler through the head. Twenty-three million Russian men and women and children all saved by a single bullet in Berlin!"

Bill didn't want to hear, didn't want to listen. It was as if gauze were being stripped layer by layer from his eyes, broad outlines hovering, converging before him as Marina continued.

"The KGB had already done a study of personnel surrounding the American President. The White House itself has a staff of over two hundred—gardeners, ushers, cooks, maintenance people—but these people carry no weapons and an attack would be less certain of success. No, our study showed the ideal candidate would be—"

The words came unbidden: "Secret Service."

Guneyev shoved the wheelchair forward. "To find an American boy for substitution was my job. This was not easy, so many details. A young man nearing six feet, his physical condition good, he must be an only child, Irish background—a man whom the Secret Service would not refuse when he applied to join. This was most difficult."

"But not impossible," Marina said. "Not like our part of the program."

"You don't know," Guneyev said stubbornly. "Believe me, it was most difficult."

Marina made a placating gesture and continued. "My own challenge was to create a personality who could not be caught in a lie. Whose reactions to a psychological profile would indicate a healthy American man, whose responses to a lie detector would show he was telling the truth. An American personality worn like a suit of clothes—no, like the armor of the feudal times, you can see nothing of the man beneath—" She waved aside even this explanation as inadequate. "No, more than this. An independent but secondary personality designed to withdraw on command and give control to the murderous impulse, the urge to destroy, the killing force you once called Cain."

"You're full of shit, all of you."

"This is useless," Khiza said to Marina. "There is no more Mischa. Mischa is gone."

Marina stood up. "You came to Moscow to learn the truth. Come. I will show it to you."

But the truth was eating him alive, strangling him. He had the urge to hurl himself across the room headfirst into the reinforced solarium windows. I'll kill myself. But the image of Claire and Matt and Megan rose, and he felt the dark presence subside. I can beat this thing, he thought, even a battle for my own mind.

But first I've got to *know,* I've got to expose the enemy, see it in all its power. Only then can I overcome it.

Bill took a deep breath, focused his mind on Claire and said calmly, "Where are we going?"

"Home."

CHAPTER

26

They took the elevator to the main floor where Colonel Guneyev led the way in his wheelchair while Lizaveta circled with the video camera glued to her eye. With staff members and inmates trailing them down the hallway, Bill felt like a man from Mars. As they passed a recreation room he saw something which caused him to stop so suddenly that one of the orderlies stepped on his heel. Beyond the patients playing cards and watching television, a cow-faced young man sat on the floor, his forehead resting against a Wurlitzer juke box. It was an icon of American culture completely out of place here, but what drew Bill's attention was the same thing that held the patient's eye, the bubbles which rose continuously in arched, rainbowhued glass tubes.

"What is it, Bill?" Marina said softly.

"Nothing." Watching the bubbles . . . Bill pushed the memory aside. "Is this what you wanted to show me?"

"This way."

They exited the building into a courtyard the size of a town square where inmates of the hospital sat on benches or tended a communal garden. A few of them played soccer on a patch of open ground bordered by the wall that surrounded the entire complex. Bill was only vaguely aware of them. His attention was drawn to the rusting American cars—an old DeSoto, a Ford pickup, a Plymouth with flaring tail fins. They were parked in front of buildings whose forms looked familiar, a red brick two-story building with a bare flagpole, a single-story cinderblock building with square glass translucent windows and a rusted sign hanging over the door. Recognition came like a blow. The signs were gone but he knew the architecture of the Roundup Bar, the Sunflower Cafe, Castleman's Grocery.

Marina was watching him. "You recognize this place?"

"Not possible."

"Of course it is. You know it is." Bill closed his eyes, but Marina's voice continued. "You mustn't fight your inner self."

"Shut up." Bill felt a hurricane in his head, a confused welter of thoughts that settled like uneasy leaves after a gust of wind. He breathed out and opened his eyes.

Marina said, "Better?"

"You built . . . Goodheart?"

"Just a few of the buildings important to your early memories. The cafe, the bar where your father spent his time, the grocery store . . . not correctly positioned, of course, but with photographs and maps the orientation was complete. Come, look." She led the way down the street. There were benches where people sat bundled in sweaters, facing the sun. A man moved a broom along the sidewalk outside the Sunflower Cafe. A poster in the window, faded to shades of pink and gray, showed a PanAm 707 jet landing in some palm-tree paradise. Across the street the marquee of the Strand Theater was bare, but faded impressions of vanished letters spelled *The Exorcist*.

"Coca-Cola City," Bill said softly.

"What's that?"

"Rumors that the KGB built an American town. Coca-Cola City they called it."

"An exaggeration. Just a few American buildings and some cars. We kept them for the patients. They pretend to drive and it calms them."

A scrawny man wearing a baseball cap approached. He was pushing a grocery cart with a faded Safeway insignia hanging from the basket and tires worn to half their previous size. He stopped the cart and surprised Bill by saying in English, "How about those Mets?"

Marina said, "Hello, Mr. Johnson. Do you remember Bill Sullivan?"

The man held out his hand. "Johnson's my name and plumbing's my game."

Bill glanced at Marina, who said, "Mr. Sullivan used to live here. Do you remember him?"

"How's it hanging? Long time no see."

"He's harmless, aren't you, Mr. Johnson?"

"No such thing as harmless. The price of liberty is eternal vigilance." He thrust his head toward Bill. "Who'd you vote for?"

"I didn't vote."

"I like Ike. You got a cigarette?"

"I don't smoke."

"Winston tastes good like a cigarette should."

"That's enough, Mr. Johnson," Marina said.

"You deserve a break today."

"It's Sunday, Mr. Johnson. Your friends are watching a football game. Why don't you go find out what the score is?"

"No shit, who's playing?"

"You go find out."

"I can take a hint. Catch you later."

He moved off. Bill said, "He's American?"

"He's a partial. They're all partials here. People who didn't make the transition and remain caught between two personalities. Sometimes he thinks he's Arthur Johnson, other times he knows he's Boris Roskov, but no one can control the timing. He has other problems, too. The KGB's early attempts were unbearably crude, but then again, the early subjects were prisoners who had no future beyond a gulag. Now they exist in a permanent gulag of the mind."

"You mean *you* made him crazy."

She shook her head in irritation. "Not me, they were here before I arrived. Andrei can tell you."

The colonel was keeping pace in his wheelchair and overheard this. "I was not responsible for the practices they used initially. I was administration director, not a doctor."

"He says that now," Marina said in a low tone. "But when he ran the program, the KGB used sensory deprivation tanks where people stayed for eighteen months. Some went insane and others so malleable to suggestion that they had no ego, no identity at all. This is what comes of using adults. By the time the child is even a few months old a certain stability is established, a sense of the world that resists alteration. It is like sinking the foundation into the earth—once there, it is difficult to change it. Children. You must begin with children."

Her bright owl eyes watched him expectantly. Children. His mind veered away and focused on the Roundup Bar where the double doors had been replaced by a metal door with a dull brass lock. "What's inside?"

"This is now a storage facility. The buildings have different uses now, but at one time the interiors were exact replicas of the originals. I can show you pictures."

They turned a corner and there it was, the house he'd grown up in now magically restored before him. He half expected Dad and Mom to appear at the door.

"Welcome home," said Marina, and then, guessing his thoughts, "Yes, the real home burned to the ground, but this was your home during training. Afterward it became the residence of the director of the Sandulov Institute, who has generously permitted us to use it."

A bell rang, and uniformed attendants began gathering the inmates and leading them back into the hospital. Bill forced himself, one leaden foot at a time, up the steps. He hesitated at the door, then pushed past an invisible barrier in his mind and stepped inside. The shape of the living room had changed, a wall had been added and the furnishings were different, but otherwise it was as he remembered.

Marina said, "There was only one room we had time to recreate for your homecoming. I will show you."

They went upstairs to his bedroom. Everything was there, his Rolling Stones poster, the KLH stereo system with a stack of LP records, even the antique dresser from Ireland. He grew dizzy and sat on the bed with its familiar bedspread, brown with a raised rib pattern that called up memories of comfort and security. Moths had eaten tiny holes and it smelled faintly of mildew. The group of Russians watched him expectantly.

"Mom and Dad?"

"The people you remember as your parents died in the fire."

"Were they here?"

"Never."

"But I remember having dinner with them . . ."

"Memories, not real experiences."

"Memories of what?"

"Sometimes actors. People hired to play the part of parents whom you perceived as the people in Kansas. Sometimes memories only, constructed for a specific purpose and implanted in a susceptible mind. You are a collaboration between us—me standing here and Mischa who is trapped inside you."

Mischa. He felt it this time without the former panic, the stirring in his mind, no longer simply a force but now a form, an entity eager to be known.

"If that's true, then I don't know what's true or what's false. Maybe I'm not even here, how do I know this isn't a—what? A false memory?"

"Your hand on a hot stove would prove the present moment is real."

"What about Claire? Matt and Megan, I know they're real."

"Of course."

"But my parents . . ."

Marina shook her head. "You remember the day you arrived at the University of Maryland? That is the demarcation line. Everything before that is a manufactured memory, each impression separately placed like bricks."

"Then why don't I remember you placing these bricks?"

"You do. Or at least the person beneath the mask remembers

them. Mischa knows the frame that is invisible to you just as you know the picture that is invisible to him. In that separation lies his uniqueness and your success."

"You're saying I'm only half a person?"

"You are a complete personality who shares the same physical body with another personality. Unless you have eclipsed Mischa, which is what we must determine now."

She nodded and the guards reached for him. Bill bolted for the door and ran headlong into two men entering the room. He knocked one to the floor, but someone from behind caught him around the waist. For a moment they all careened around the bedroom, spilling the bookshelves and overturning the stereo. He jabbed an elbow into someone's solar plexus and kicked a guard in the head as they carried him to the floor. They wrestled Bill onto his stomach, a man on each arm and leg, another on his back. He heard Marina shouting as they tied his ankles, knees and wrists with elastic bandages. Then they carried him like a rug, bucking and twisting, into a room that had been stripped of furnishings except for a metal table bolted to the floor. They placed him on his back and held him while one of the men strapped him to the table.

Marina stood over him. "Try to relax."

"Let me up."

"Shhhh." She placed her hand on his forehead. Khiza came forward with a bottle of vodka which he poured into a plastic glass and handed to Marina. She peered down at Bill. "I'm sorry, Billy, but the project is over." She held out a glass of vodka. "Drink."

Bill jerked his head to one side and the glass tumbled to the floor. The next time, the guard held his head and Marina pinched his nose until he was forced to take a breath. One glass after the other they poured into his mouth. Some spilled over his cheeks, but some of it found its way down his throat. He coughed and the alcohol burned his eyes. Marina reached over with a towel and wiped his face.

"Your American personality is too firmly entrenched. Like removing a skin graft, the only solution is painful. It is time to take off the mask, Billy. It is time to come home."

Again and again they forced the alcohol down. He felt a warm buzz spread throughout his body and a presence now like a leopard creeping through the grass or a dark egg growing inside him, ready to hatch, eager to burst forth.

"How do you feel now, Mischa?"

"My name is Bill."

More vodka and time blurred. He became hot and flushed the way he always did when drunk.

"Mischa, come home."

"Claire, Matt, Megan . . ."

She began singing to him, the song of dreams and nightmares. *"Where have you been, Billy boy, Billy boy? Oh, where have you been, charming Billy . . ."*

A paralysis crept over him, extremities growing warm and then growing numb, no arms now and no legs, sense of self disintegrating into gyrating colors, red blood pulsating, blue onrush of air, yellow bile surging, a smell of ozone and the green crackle of electrical current, a billion neurons dancing up his spine. The alcoholic fog coalesced into a young man's face eager in anticipation rushing forward—

". . . I've been to find a knife . . ."

Bill felt himself falling down a narrowing tunnel, a wowing sound like the change in tone of a passing train's whistle, the world seen through the wrong end of a telescope, all sensations shrinking to a tiny pinpoint . . .

"No!" he shouted, but the word changed form as it flew from his mouth and he shouted, *"Nyet!"*

A sudden calm, space undefined and yet vaguely familiar, a tiny cave still warm from someone's presence, vibrations dying away even as he became aware of them, melting at the touch like tiny ice crystals caught in an eyebrow, the last thought of the former occupant, "Now see how *you* like it."

He was trapped inside his own mind.

CHAPTER

27

The Sorin Project
30 October 1962–23 November 1977
from the personal diary of Project Director,
Doctor Marina Sorin

I was made director of the Ipatyev Project. Yes! This at the command of Premier Khrushchev himself. I demanded the project be changed to my name. Such a risk. Thought he would strangle me but he agreed. They must be desperate. Colonel Guneyev must have accomplished nothing. The second happiest day of my life. The first will be when I complete the—I almost wrote Ipatyev—Sorin Project.

2 NOVEMBER 1962

This morning they gave me an oath of secrecy, then revealed the true goal of their experiments. Colonel Guneyev watched me closely. "The assassination of the President of the United States." I think he expected me to faint but I had already guessed. Why else does the KGB need an expert on Multiple Personality Disorder? Why else their interest in my juvenile patient with his English-speaking personality and the destruction anger which he commands?

Guneyev reveals they have been trying to create a dual personality for three years. We went to the Sandulov Institute for the Criminally Insane. Pathetic. Prisoners have been exposed to shock treatments, drugs, sensory deprivation, hypnosis, magnetic pulses—the result a collection of psychotics and grotesques fit only for a human zoo. They would have sought my help earlier if I were a man.

5 NOVEMBER 1962

Guneyev wants me to transfer the boy immediately to Sandulov, but I told him I must prepare the boy emotionally. Not really true, but with Guneyev it is necessary to establish my authority. He is angry that I have taken his title of director. He is a big man, somewhat overweight, with the drooping eyes of a hound. Why should a KGB officer with no scientific or medical training have the title? When he first approached me for advice he probably thought I would stand in his shadow and he would gain the glory. Now he feels betrayed.

"I could have taken the child without you," he reminds me. This is supposed to make me grateful, but I say, "Yes, and if you take the boy what chance of success would you have? After three years see what a forest of halfwits and gargoyles your team has created." He glowers. I should be silent, but it is not my nature.

8 NOVEMBER 1962

The destructive impulse manifested again today. Frustrated by a new toy, a blue steam shovel, the boy smashed it to pieces using fists, feet, finally a rock. In his fury he tore a fingernail but later had no memory of it and cried to discover his toy broken. Outbursts occur two or three times a week, the violence usually less than thirty seconds, often followed by a period of erratic behavior during which the boy will not speak or respond to outward stimuli. Afterward neither Billy nor Mischa can recall the incident. I must dissect this violent impulse, trace its origin, map its pathology, then develop a technique to control it. Or series of techniques. A puppet with a thousand strings, most of them still invisible and beyond my grasp.

15 NOVEMBER 1962

I introduced Guneyev to the Bill personality. I could tell it was Bill as we approached—calm demeanor, head high, none of the nervous mannerisms that Mischa manifests. Guneyev did not believe that the two personalities spoke different languages. I explained that such divisions of talent were normal in cases of Multiple Personality Disorder, but Guneyev believes nothing I tell him. When the boy wouldn't respond to Russian he talking louder and louder. I told him the boy was not deaf, and when Guneyev used English I saw the reason for his reluctance. His English is bad. He said, "How did you do, young boy?"

Bill's response, "Sing a song of sixpence," confused Guneyev. When I said, "Pocket full of rye," Bill recited the rest of the nursery rhyme, which confused Guneyev more. He cannot see how we can make sense of this child, much less make him an assassin. Too bad the funding for this project didn't come from the Ministry of Science rather than the KGB.

16 NOVEMBER 1962

A new problem. Mischa's mother is now claiming that the boy is the son of an Englishman, her lover. She wants the boy back and the British embassy is pressing the issue. I am adamant the boy not be taken. His psychosis is unique and we shall never find such a subject again. For once Guneyev agrees with me. He says he has a plan, but will not tell me what it is.

23 NOVEMBER 1962

The KGB lives up to its reputation. They put the boy in the hospital today with the symptoms of cerebrospinal meningitis. I don't know how they produced the symptoms, but can only hope some quack doctor doesn't get the serum confused and inject him with the actual bacillus. That would be typical of the thickheads at KGB.

24 NOVEMBER 1962

Mischa still "sick." I moved into an office at the Sandulov Institute. Facilities first-rate, but the head of the institute was less than cordial. I think he resents the secrecy surrounding my presence and my program. Fortunately I won't see him or any of the other staff on a day-to-day basis. We are located in our own building, separated by the grounds behind the institute. Over the next few months I will phase out my private practice to devote full time to the Sorin Project.

I still like the sound of it.

27 NOVEMBER 1962

Last night Mischa died. Tomorrow they cremate and bury ashes at St. Clements. Apparently they have a child's body, some boy from the state orphanage who died recently. This will end Mischa's official existence and put an end to Yelena Amenov's campaign to regain her son. Actually Mischa was brought to Sandulov last night at three in the morning. He was feverish but heavily sedated. He awoke around dawn as Bill. After giving him a glass of apple juice, I read to him and he slept. When I tried to wake him at ten he was groggy and spoke in Russian, so I knew he was Mischa. I argued with the nurse, a fat cow who I suspect may have given the boy too much sedative. She denied it of course, but not until 1420 did Mischa wake. He was confused and fearful but became more cognitive and relaxed as the day progressed. I fired the nurse. People had heard us argue.

3 JANUARY 1963

If we are to gain control of the Mischa/Bill shift we will need the boy's father, Major Amenov, but he is defensive, uncooperative. A tall man with deep eyes who carries his head well back, tension around the mouth not apparent in photographs where his smile dazzles. He hates the boy, doesn't believe multiple-personality diagnosis. "He speaks English to spite me."

When I asked why the boy loves nursery rhymes Amenov said it was his wife's attempt to turn the child against him. The man is a classic sociopath who sees the world only in terms of himself. He will not speak his wife's name, but refers to her as "the whore" or "Mischa's mother" or "the traitor," He will not discuss his relations with his wife or the reasons she stayed in England. "My son is sick, not me."

I want to tell him that his son is a symptom of his own sickness, but I refrain. The father's dysfunction not an issue here, only his cooperation. We get it under duress. Colonel Guneyev presents orders from the Kremlin. Amenov is assigned the Sorin Project. His reactions to his son will be either negative or positive at my direction. He will have an apartment at Sandulov and will be available at a moment's notice. Amenov angry, threatens to quit the KGB. Guneyev tells him, "That is not an option." I thought it was a joke, but neither man was smiling.

10 JANUARY 1963

Repeated interviews with Amenov develop a picture of the abuse pattern, less physical than I expect but more emotional, mental. Gives him a puppy and beats it when boy doesn't finish dinner fast enough; takes him fishing, then pushes boy overboard and rows farther away each time boy reaches for the boat; goes to circus and coming home holds him within inches of arriving subway train, etc. Guneyev disgusted when he reviews the transcript. "He drove the boy crazy."

I point out the boy is not crazy, that dissociation is a survival mechanism, an alternative to psychosis. He doesn't believe this any more than Amenov.

1 FEBRUARY 1963

Rereading Pavlov's journals I am astounded at my own vision. The type of behavior modification I intend is so far removed from his early experiments that it is like comparing the complexity of a rifle bullet to that of a rocket ship. I will evolve an interrelated web of behavior modification techniques—hypnosis and posthypnotic suggestion, environmental conditioning, positive and negative reinforcements, affective transference—

I place in both boys the posthypnotic suggestion that they will share a rotating schedule, each allowed out every other day. *Allowed* implies we have more control than we do. When Mischa is threatened he will disappear and Bill will come forward to protect him, but the reverse does not hold true. Apart from that single constant, their shifts are arbitrary and capricious. But this is the first step, the foundation for the future—until we achieve control over which personality is present we can do nothing.

6 MARCH 1963

On the spot. That's what Mischa calls it when he is in control of the body. He tells me this under hypnosis. The phrase has connotations of being exposed, vulnerable. This is how Mischa experiences the world and why he so often takes refuge behind Bill. I told Guneyev to think of it as a day worker and a night worker sharing the same bed; they both use it, but only one man can be there at a time. Such crude analogies satisfy him and waste less of my time. To do otherwise is like explaining algebra to a giraffe.

25 APRIL 1963

Each boy has separate bedrooms. Mischa fond of his accordion, builds model ships, watches cosmonaut cartoon show. Bill's bedroom decorated with posters of American comic heroes, Superman, Batman, a green man named Hulk—male fantasy figures Guneyev says are typical of American culture. Possible correlation between childhood dominance fantasies and American propensity for political confrontation?

2 MAY 1963

Bill took the spot on Mischa's day. I removed his toys and he spent the morning alone in his room without distraction or interaction. What more can we do? Bill is self-sufficient and impervious to coercion of any kind. In the afternoon Mischa finally took the spot and was rewarded. His father ate lunch with him, played soccer, helped build a toy train. Mischa alternated between joy and uncertainty. Once, when Major Amenov reached back to rub his neck, Mischa flinched, perhaps expecting a blow. By the end of the day the boy had begun to relax and Amenov was tense. I told the major afterward to smile more when he was playing the good father. "I'm an officer in the KGB, I don't take orders from you."

I had Guneyev talk to him. Now he takes orders from me.

19 MAY 1963

So little progress. I have hired a bilingual couple to provide a sense of stability for the two personalities. "Grandfather" Ivan and "Grandmother" Akulina will live on the grounds of the institute. They will be both family and teachers, since there is no school here. These people have no idea the true goal of the Sorin Project, but believe they are participating in an experimental program whose purpose is to develop an alternative therapy for victims of Multiple Personality Disorder—cooperation among the personalities rather than integration. They are unimaginative people who are happy to have the job.

20 JUNE 1963

Painful to watch. Today was Billy's day, but Mischa took the spot. To drive him away Amenov made him hold a match between his teeth. Then he lit it. This is his favorite cruelty. Mischa crying, the match shaking, until the flame crept close enough to burn his lips. Then Bill took the spot, his ability to block pain astonishing. He stared at his father with a cold and distant expression even while the flame seared his skin. I intervened quickly, blew out the match and gave Amenov the signal for positive reinforcement. It was an effort. He much prefers the role of negative father.

1 JULY 1963

Bill under hypnosis today and I reached the core of his rage, a two-year-old child he calls Cain, from the Bible story his mother once read to him. The boy howled, rocked back and forth, screamed, threw objects across the room and acted as one possessed. It was like opening the door to a blast furnace. Even Guneyev was shaken by the experience. Now we must harness this rage, control it, target it.

17 JULY 1963

Reviewing the KGB file on Major Amenov I note my own reaction to a photograph of Mischa's mother. A beautiful woman, no doubt. She is wearing a feathered costume from a ballet and stands with one foot placed against the opposite knee. This reminds me of Natasha K. the time we went swimming and I saw the sun on her legs and realized I would never be beautiful. The same jealousy now. The child within us never leaves.

8 AUGUST 1963

Under hypnosis Mischa is aware of Bill, but the reverse is not true. Bill under hypnosis is aware only of the entity he calls Cain. Asked to describe Cain, Bill says "burning, angry."

"Let me talk to Cain," I said. But terror overwhelmed the boy and the trance was broken. For now we will concentrate on establishing control over the Bill/Mischa shift and only after that seek control over Cain.

Guneyev actually read the American translation I recommended, a layman's account of multiple personality entitled *The Three Faces of Eve*. He says he found it illuminating. In a coal bin even a 15-watt bulb is illuminating. I gave him a copy of my presentation at the Zurich conference, "The Dissociative World: A Phenomenological Examination of Multiple Personality Disorder." I hope he has sunglasses.

22 NOVEMBER 1963

Amazing news, the American President shot today. I call Guneyev, who tells me the assassin is not one of ours. Would he know? Guneyev is not nearly so much of the inner circle as he pretends. What stays in my mind is the look in Premier Khrushchev's eyes when he assigned me the project. I think if the premier had a gun pointed at Kennedy's head on that day he would have pulled the trigger.

24 NOVEMBER 1963

Everyone nervous over possibility of war with United States if assassin linked to our country. If not, what will this do to our project? If a common assassin can so easily kill the President, what need will the Kremlin see for my work? Guneyev was reassuring on this point. Security measures are bound to be increased in America, which means that only someone capable of infiltrating the Secret Service would be certain of killing the president.

15 FEBRUARY 1964

The Amenov recording sessions continue this week. Every day he recites in English a variety of phrases, titles of U.S. government officials, names of animals and proper names. It bores him, but we do not tell him the purpose. At one point he asks, "The bastard is afraid of my voice, isn't he?" He seems proud of it. I wonder if he guesses that his voice will be the trigger for the Cain emergence? I look forward to the day we have no more need of this man.

18 MAY 1965

A terrible occurrence. Bill was on the spot and I referred to him as Mischa. What happened was that Mischa took this as an invitation and displaced Bill. I knew as soon as I saw the impish smile what happened. "You didn't wait for your day," I told him.

"You called me."

He was still smiling when I hit him. There was no other way. I had to keep striking him until he manifested Bill. It was horrible. My finger is cut from his teeth and the boy needed stitches. It was the most difficult thing I have ever done, but Mischa must remain dormant except upon the schedule we set. His own safety will depend on this.

7 OCTOBER 1965

While Mischa was on the spot he made a drawing of a bird and gave it to me. This is the first sign of risk taking and indicates the growth of a healthy ego. He has taken to calling me Aunt Marina—a sweet child, really. Given any form of affection, he blossoms. I must beware my maternal instincts coloring my objectivity. It is time to increase the periods Mischa remains dormant and Bill takes the spot.

4 NOVEMBER 1965

From Amenov's recordings I choose the trigger phrase. "I see——and he's been bad." The object of aggression will vary during the boy's training. We give Bill a goldfish and he names it Racer. At the same time the message under hypnosis continues to reinforce the response that must rule his universe: release Cain to kill the bad one or be punished yourself.

11 FEBRUARY 1966

Mischa must remain dormant. I use hypnosis to build a belief system for each boy. For Mischa: The world is a dangerous place and his safety lies in giving Bill the spot. For Bill the training is more complex: His father will always tell him who is bad. Bill must release Cain to kill the bad one as soon as he sees him. If he does this, the good father will reward him, if not, the negative father will hurt him.

This is basic posthypnotic transference, but Guneyev is full of doubt and many questions. Who is Cain? Why can't we talk to him? I explain that Cain is not a personality but pure emotion— anger, terror, rage—bottled up, withheld, compressed. Notice how carefree Mischa is, how calm and dysthymic is Bill? Few negative feelings reach them, thanks to Cain. I give Guneyev some credit; he is trying to understand.

13 AUGUST 1966

The boy was hurt, there was no other way. This morning the loudspeaker in his bedroom broadcast this message in Amenov's voice: "I see Racer and he's been bad." Billy went to the fishbowl, tipped it onto the floor, raised his foot but couldn't kill the fish. He began to cry, picked up Racer and put it in the bowl, which he was filling with water when I gave the signal for negative consequence. Amenov waiting in another room burst in and terrorized the boy, a beating first, then forced him to bite the fish's eyes, etc. Guneyev left the observation room and looked at me later with disgust. But what can I do? Not until Bill unleashes Cain on command can we adopt positive reinforcement.

20 AUGUST 1966

Billy calm, happy, the bruises almost gone. He doesn't recall the beating. Why? My hypothesis—Cain the repository of traumatic memories as well as the destructive impulse.

Atmosphere here is strained, and assistants grow silent when I pass them. The beating upset them. They like the boy and cannot divorce their emotions from our purpose here. Hypnosis five times a day, one hour each. The new turtle is named Tommy.

29 MARCH 1967

Great relief. Positive reaction this time from trigger phrase: "I see Tommy and he's been bad." Without hesitation Billy took the turtle outside, smashed it to the sidewalk, began to cry. Amenov appeared as good father, reassured him, took the boy to a magic show and later threw the football with him. Will continue with reptiles, one each month for six months, then begin white mice.

Mischa takes the spot only when Bill under hypnosis. He is dormant for longer periods of time now. I miss him.

12 NOVEMBER 1967

Guneyev and I were talking about being on the spot and I had to laugh—if anyone heard us talking this arcane language they would think we were from Mars. Which in a sense we are, since we have cultivated and strengthened the Mischa/Bill matrix rather than integrated it. In truth we are in a new world, one of Mischa's making and our molding.

After Guneyev's recent efforts to insure funding for the Sorin Project I give him more credit. Now that he sees the progress we are making he gives me more credit. Certainly he argues less. And his shirts are cleaner.

14 JULY 1968

It occurs to me we no longer need Major Amenov. Others are available to provide positive reinforcement, and it has been two years since we last needed Amenov's particular brand of sadism for negative reinforcement. Today proved the point. Bill received the trigger phrase in a telephone call: "I see Blackie and she's been bad." Without hesitation he found the cat, carried it to the toilet bowl and drowned it. Had been his pet for a full year. Amenov's imitation of joy was unconvincing, and Guneyev and I took over, rewarding Bill with a Chinese kite we flew from the river. Guneyev agrees: Amenov is now superfluous.

8 SEPTEMBER 1968

We dump Amenov. Guneyev says he expected a reward,
wants to be spy, join covert operations. Amenov threw a fit,
broke a window when assigned some kind of Special Weapons
teaching assignment. Guneyev was surprised at his reaction,
says Amenov should have known that participation in a top-
secret project made overseas assignments impossible. My reaction: the father is angry because his son is getting the assignment
he wants.

No farewell party.

7 MAROII 1969

An argument today regarding Bill's insertion into American
society. The KGB wants to use an actual American family, but I
resist. The past is memory, why not an imagined history—false
documents and memories planted by posthypnotic suggestion?
Guneyev explains there are such things in the United States as
Social Security registrations and Secret Service investigations
that require the validation of an actual family.

"If it's an actual family," I point out, "they will know the
truth."

"That will not be a problem." He would say no more, but
from his attitude I guess the truth. They plan to destroy an
American family.

12 JULY 1970

The search has narrowed to five American families. Each has
a single male child named Bill, each is a resident of a small community far from Washington, none have much contact with relatives, all are of Irish descent—research shows the Secret Service
is dominated by the Irish and such a heritage will increase
Mischa's chances of acceptance. There is only one problem: how
do we keep the boy from returning home and discovering the
truth?

"That's why they call it the Sorin Project," Guneyev told me.
He thinks he is clever.

9 OCTOBER 1970

The other day Billy was at the piano practicing Bach's *Solfeggietto* and the light fell across his upper lip where a delicate mustache has begun. He is entering puberty. I am losing my boy. Both of them.

My biopsy is tomorrow. I told Guneyev I was taking the day to visit my mother.

11 OCTOBER 1970

I solve the problem of the prodigal son's return. Coming out of anesthesia I remembered my grandfather lying in his coffin on the kitchen table, how they made me kiss him and afterward I wouldn't eat dinner at that table. An aversion memory for Bill. Fear or guilt of such magnitude that any impulse to return home will be stifled by acute distress. I made the nurse bring a phone and called Guneyev to tell him my solution. He was annoyed I hadn't told him about my surgery.

12 OCTOBER 1970

From the window I wave to Guneyev and Bill in the parking lot. The boy was holding flowers and later the nurse brought them. A woman from Patient Counseling came to talk about my body image. I mustn't think of myself as mutilated, my femininity is a matter of the soul, not the flesh, and had anyone reviewed prosthetic devices with me?

"What for?" I asked.

"You don't want to develop a negative body image."

"I never had a positive one, so I'm not worried."

She thought I was kidding, said she admired my spirit. The kind of woman who would take her breast home in a bottle.

4 APRIL 1971

Scratches from the cat became infected and Bill's arm is orange with disinfectant. Nothing serious, but today Guneyev showed him how to use a gun. A revolver of some kind. We went to the river, where they shot at balloons. Bill enjoyed it, was quite calm despite the noise. My ears are still ringing. From now on Cain's rage must take the form of a bullet.

The dog's name is Sonny.

5 MAY 1971

A massive construction behind Sandulov. A street is being created, the duplicate of one in a town called Goodheart. Also the Sullivan house. We have maps and photographs.

24 SEPTEMBER 1971

Humor, another milestone. Bill plays chess with his math teacher, Yevgeni Zhubov—or Mr. McKenna, as Bill knows him. The man has asthma. Last week Bill beat him for the first time. Today Bill was about to duplicate the victory, when Zhubov suffered a coughing fit and overturned the board. Bill's comment: "The McKenna defense."

His humor is dry, verges on sarcasm. Evidence of a confident, stable personality.

28 NOVEMBER 1971

Using hypnosis I can alter Bill's perceptions so that he perceives our actors as residents of Goodheart. I feel like a brain surgeon wielding a scalpel more fine than anything in the physical world while carefully inserting pieces of information into his memory. There is a high school in the town, and I have photographs of all the students in Bill's class. All but the real Bill Sullivan. Guneyev does not provide it and I do not ask.

3 FEBRUARY 1972

An unhappy incident. I found Guneyev sleeping on the couch when I got to work this morning. His clothes were disreputable, his eyes bloodshot, and in the bathroom there was vomit on the floor. He apologized. Apparently Olga has left him because of his drinking. He says it is not a problem, but I think his wife is correct. He has smelled of liquor on more than one occasion and has missed two meetings in the last month. I told him this and he grew angry. "You take her side because she's a woman."

"I tell you what I see."

"Then I say you need glasses."

With that he opened the door violently with the wrong hand and knocked himself out. They took him to the hospital and made three stitches. I think he will be in trouble with his superiors.

7 APRIL 1972

Calamity. An idiot named Vostik has been named in charge while Guneyev is at a sanitarium. Supposedly this is temporary, but meanwhile I have a sausage-faced kid running around questioning everything I do as if his career depended on it. There is no need for him to tax his intelligence—all I need is a liaison to the Kremlin. Vostik. He sounds like a space program. If he is temporary, why does he clear Guneyev's desk and put all personal items into storage?

15 MAY 1972

Is everything doomed to fall victim to liquor? First Guneyev and now the entire project. We have on the grounds an American bar called the Roundup. Bill was allowed to go there with his "friends"—two English-speaking actors his own age—where he was introduced to an American beer called Coors. After a single bottle he became loud, overbearing, and manifested impaired coordination and erratic motor control. He sang "Charming Billy," forgot the words, became loud and giddy. The idiot Vostik tried to stop the scenario, ordered Bill back to his room and grabbed his arm. At that point Cain erupted, hit Vostik, threw the beer bottle through a window and rushed out the door. This was at night. Security guards later found a ladder against the courtyard wall, so it appears he has escaped Sandulov. The police are on the alert and dawn is near.

Word just came. Vostik's nose is broken. Good.

16 MAY 1972

I do not believe it, cannot believe it. Bill found sleeping under the Granitnaya Bridge. When they woke him he insisted he was an American citizen, had no idea where he was and demanded to be taken to the American embassy. Of course they brought him here. Under hypnosis I suggest that everything that transpired was a drunken dream. He is asleep now, but Vostik, with his nose in plaster, has just announced the project canceled.

22 MAY 1972

Everything is on hold. Bill goes to school, the routine continues, but I have been told to prepare a defense of the project. Vostik has set himself up as an inquisitor, wanders around demanding explanations from anyone he encounters. "How much does this cost? Why do you need it? Who authorized it?" His nasal voice reminds me of a pig. In the sound lab I hold the Amenov tapes in my hand and indulge in useless fantasy. "I see Vostik and he's been bad."

This gives me an idea.

2 JUNE 1972

There were three of them from the Kremlin along with Vostik. All men, of course, and sitting at a polished table I'm certain was deliberately raised six inches above normal. Vostik took an hour detailing the great cost and expense of the program and the great failure—"a human hand grenade with a faulty firing pin." I scratched my head and pretended to clean dandruff from my fingernails. Finally it was my turn.

"What justification can you offer, Dr. Sorin, for continuation of this project?"

"Proof of success."

"How can you prove it," Vostik demanded, "except by having the boy kill the American president?"

"He can kill you."

Pandemonium and desk pounding, I sat silent as a rock. Finally they listened. Vostik will enter the boy's world as a house guest, a friend of "Grandfather" Ivan and "Grandmother" Akulina. Vostik will be called Little Larry—two of the words on the Amenov recordings—and will sleep on the couch for one week. At the end of that time a phone call of Amenov's voice: "I see Little Larry and he's been bad." Then we shall see what Bill will do.

Vostik squealed like a stuck pig at the idea, until I mentioned using a cadaver. Then he grew quiet as the other three turned to look at him. His expression—how I wished for my camera.

20 JUNE 1972

From the jaws of defeat I snatch success. Frightening success. Little Larry died on the family couch. Even I was impressed.

It was not Vostik, of course. The bent-nosed pig refused to play the role, so for the past seven days one of our actors played Little Larry. Each morning Bill found Larry wearing a sleeping cap, curled beneath blankets and facing the rear of the couch. This morning we switched to a cadaver dressed in the same nightshirt and cap. At seven-thirty Bill received a phone call: "I see Little Larry and he's been bad." Without hesitation he drew the gun from the drawer and walked to the living room. For a moment he trembled and I thought we were lost. Then he raised the gun with both hands, aimed and pulled the trigger until it was empty. For a reward I let him drive the DeSoto. The Sorin Project is safe.

15 JULY 1972

Guneyev is back. He drinks only mineral water in which he mixes sugar, a concoction certain to rot his teeth. The first day he is subdued, but apparently Olga has returned to him and he seems grateful. To me he apologized, says it takes a good friend to tell a hard truth, wants me to call him Andrei, not Colonel. All right, then—Andrei is back.

I told him about the fiasco with Bill at the Roundup Bar, how alcohol released Cain, and asked him questions about his own experiences. He was uncomfortable until we walked outside where he relaxed. He smoked many cigarettes and told me his daughter refused to believe his alcoholism was a disease, but Olga is supportive and he is grateful. He seems subdued. I am glad he has stopped drinking, but in some ways I miss the storm and fire of the old Guneyev.

6 APRIL 1973

The Choose/Illusion Test. Although the house is a duplicate of the one in Kansas the actors playing his parents look nothing like their real-life counterparts. Under hypnosis each day I introduce photographs of the Kansas originals with the statement that these are his parents. The result: given a set of a dozen photographs and asked to choose his parents, Bill points to the Kansas originals.

"You're either a genius or a witch," Guneyev told me. He exaggerates, but it is true that the fusion of posthypnotic projection with reality is quite seamless.

"Could you make him believe he was Peter the Great?" Guneyev asked.

"If you give me another ten years and build the Winter Palace."

10 OCTOBER 1973

Bill under hypnosis every day now. We stare at photographs of places and people, memorize names, reiterate anecdotes and make associations. The mother's face is animated but the smile is forced, while the father appears cocky. I'm uneasy looking at them, knowing what must happen. The KGB has a photograph of the real Bill Sullivan, but I still haven't seen it. Andrei shrugs off my request. "He looks like any American."

"I'd still like to see him."

"No, you wouldn't."

He knows I don't agree about sacrificing these people. I could have pressed the issue but didn't.

23 MARCH 1974

I have a co-worker quiz Bill. "Who's this?"

"Mom."

"What is her given name?"

"Betsy Winters."

"Who's this?"

"Dad."

"Tell me about your father."

"He runs the Chevron station out by the highway. Mom wants to move back to Denver, but Dad is waiting for the new freeway. He says they'll have customers coming out of their ears, but Mom says he's crazy, they're never going to build that freeway."

On and on it goes, the information comes from the KGB, and I plant it in Bill's memory along with an aversion memory strong enough to keep him from returning to Goodheart, the suspicion that he started the fire that burned his parents to death. The KGB instructed me on this. Now I know how the parents will die.

10 JULY 1974

The first test outside a controlled environment. Bill is sent to tour Italy as Bill Sullivan. The KGB has given him a false U.S. passport, and he has a full set of memories. He is going with an English-speaking friend, actually a KGB recruit who looks himself quite young. There will also be two KGB men following him, and I am not certain what they will do if Bill drinks or Cain erupts or Mischa takes the spot. Kidnap him? Kill him? Andrei laughs at me when I suggest such things. After all, Mischa has been dormant over a year now, accessible only through hypnosis, and Bill now refuses alcohol.

17 SEPTEMBER 1974

Olga Guneyev memorial service. I hadn't meant to go, but Andrei gave me an invitation and seemed to wish it. Had to buy a new dress since I had nothing appropriate. A size larger than I used to be. The dress felt ugly and I left as soon as possible. During the service I watch Andrei and consider the irony—he gave up drinking for her and she is killed by a drunk driver. Watching the children I tried to imagine Andrei teaching his son to ride a bicycle or tying a bow in his daughter's hair or sitting at the dinner table carving chicken. I learn afterward those are his grandchildren.

2 FEBRUARY 1974

I meet "Jack" and "Sandy" today. These are the American names of the KGB agents who will attend a college in Wichita with Bill Sullivan next year. They look very young to me—or else I am getting older—and speak American English. The girl is quite pretty. It is her job to become Bill Sullivan's girl friend while "Jack" will bend his efforts to achieve a male friendship. Their relationship will isolate Bill while they draw from him personal memories, hopes, and fears—elements necessary to prepare our Bill for the substitution. I reviewed with them the type of information I desire. They are highly motivated but I think "Jack" is attracted to "Sandy." We must counsel these people carefully. Too much at stake to risk jealousy within the ranks.

9 MAY 1975

They have set the date for insertion: July 4, 1976. Brezhnev himself picked it, some kind of joke, the two-hundred-year anniversary of America. The thought of losing them fills me with dread and I find it difficult to separate the reasons. Is it because I have become fond of the boys or is it because I fear for their safety outside our artificial world?

I protest to Andrei, but he says if not now, when? And then he reminds me that until Bill takes his station at the side of the American president, the Sorin Project is not complete. He knows me well enough to know which argument to use.

13 OCTOBER 1975

First reports arrive from Wichita. "Jack" has befriended Bill Sullivan by offering a cheap room in the house he rented near the college. The refrigerator stocked with beer and food which he dispenses freely. There are many parties, much male camaraderie. Report includes details of Sullivan's sexual conquests in high school, much exaggerated as we know from surveillance during the time in question. Only significant insight—subject shows an animus toward his father based on father's alcoholism, father's weakness. I begin planting this information during hypnosis sessions.

19 NOVEMBER 1975

"Sandy" has achieved sexual intimacy with subject. Transcript of conversations indicate Sullivan captivated, calls her Angel, dreams of becoming an airline pilot, taking her to California. Material is rich in personal detail, including subject's disgust with father's affair with another woman. Another aversion memory?

10 JANUARY 1976

The year of the insertion. I am filled with misgivings since Andrei admitted the Sullivan parents were killed by fire ten days ago. This shocks me more than I can say. Having presented these people to Bill in such detail I feel I know them personally. Haunted by the sense that everything we have accomplished has been tainted and the project is doomed.

19 FEBRUARY 1976

There is nothing more that can be done to prepare Bill. He is as fully integrated into this false American community as I can make him. The only memories missing are personal ones that can only be obtained from the real Bill Sullivan. This cannot happen until summer arrives and the original leaves his college. Andrei and I both know what must happen. We do not speak of it.

5 JUNE 1976

A huge transcript arrives from the KGB. Personal memories of Bill Sullivan. There is only one source for these, the boy himself. It sickens me to think of it. They must be using sodium pentothal or some more exotic truth serum. I do not sleep well.

4 JULY 1976

An impossible deadline. Luckily Andrei convinced them to delay the insertion for six weeks. We can now work up to the last moment when Bill is scheduled to begin his second year of university at a new school, they will not tell me where. Every moment now spent with Bill under hypnosis, carefully planting and reinforcing the personal memories gleaned from the original. I work long hours to keep from thinking where those memories came from.

17 AUGUST 1976

I hypnotized Bill and brought Mischa to the spot one last day. He wanted to see the State Circus. Andrei wanted to come, but I said no. This was unkind, but my feeling toward the KGB is not good. The truth was I wanted Mischa to myself. He is a handsome boy and I was proud walking with him down the streets of Moscow. He thinks the old people with their public scales are wonderful fun, and we cannot pass one without stopping to check his weight.

"Your weight does not change that quickly," I told him.

"The days do."

He is right of course. His days are separated by months and years. At the circus he saw a girl whose breasts he liked and asked to see them. When she refused, he touched them anyway and I had some embarrassing moments explaining to the irate boyfriend that Mischa was mentally impaired. Mischa was hurt. "I like breasts. Her kind, not your kind."

He is accustomed to having whatever he likes. Inside Sandulov he is privileged, but how difficult the real world. He cheered up once the circus began and the rest of the night I think he enjoyed. We had dinner and took the evening cruise along the river. Mischa took off his belt and tried to drag it in the water, but the boat was too high. In many ways he remains a child. I think he will always remain one. My child.

25 AUGUST 1976

They are gone, both of them. Bill was on the spot, although the term no longer seems accurate. His presence has been almost constant for years now. I suppose that made it easier. He was excited yet self-contained, as always. Since he didn't know that we won't see each other again his goodbye was cursory. After all these years I receive a hug and a kiss due a favorite aunt. I am feeling sorry for myself. His mind is a trap I have designed to snap shut when he arrives in America. All memory of Aunt Marina and everyone else here will cease, instantly replaced by the carefully constructed world of Goodheart, Kansas. Still, I cannot help feeling like his mother. When the plane is gone, I sit in the ladies room and cry.

26 AUGUST 1976

Andrei called last night to let me know they had arrived safely. The call was a surprise, against the rules. Afterward I slept.

2 SEPTEMBER 1976

A strange feeling of isolation.

7 NOVEMBER 1976

Today marks the anniversary of the Revolution. A holiday and for the first time in twelve years I am free to enjoy it. I thought to stay home, but Andrei insisted I attend as his guest. He says that Likacev is pleased with the program, although I don't really care what Likacev thinks. We walked along the river and watched the fireworks. He took me home and there was an awkward moment outside the door. Did he think I would invite him in?

10 JANUARY 1977

I have received the Order of Lenin, but in secret. They did not even give me the medal, but handed it to me and then made me give it back. I will never see it again although they promised to bury the medal with me when I die. As if this would reassure me. Still, it is an honor, even if no one knows of it.

3 MARCH 1977

My appearance discourages me. I look in the mirror with hair pulled back to count the gray. Perhaps I will get a rinse. My work at Sandulov seems routine without Bill and Mischa.

"It's like when your dog dies," Andrei said. "The medicine is to get a new puppy."

This angered me and we argued. I told him if he brought me even the picture of a puppy I would throw it in the river. This was cruel because he is right. I should have begun a new program long ago.

17 MARCH 1977

Bad news today. The Sorin Project far more expensive than planned. They cannot fund another. So my work with the multiples will be merely on a theoretical level. There will not be another insertion. When I ask Andrei for reports from Bill he will not tell me. Security is too tight. He let slip that his new superior does not like him. I don't think he is happy in his new position. He calls frequently.

27 AUGUST 1977

Andrei's retirement party today. I caught him with a glass of vodka and I think this embarrassed him. After that, only punch. Many of the people I did not know. One drunken official asked how long we had been seeing each other. I told him we were simply colleagues and he said something unsettling. "The way Andrei talks about you I thought you were lovers."

2 SEPTEMBER 1977

Today I picked up the phone and imagined what it would be like to call Mischa. Andrei told me in confidence that the boy is attending University of Maryland. But it is useless. Mischa is dormant, and Bill would not know or recognize my voice. On arrival in New York his memories became only his Kansas past. No, I must put him from my mind. I will no longer keep this journal but get on with life. Mischa is dead now. Cain will live one day longer, the day that he shoots the President. This time there will be no happy ending, no father to take Bill fishing or play ball with him, no Aunt Marina to take Mischa to the circus. This time their task results in death. The Sorin Project is finished and so is this journal.

23 NOVEMBER 1977

One last thing. Andrei Guneyev and I were married today. No one more surprised than I.

CHAPTER 28

Mischa Amenov burst back into the world on a carpet of pain. He had been unaware of the inchoate fury that had gripped his body for thirty seconds—the rage of Cain directed against the restraints that held him firmly to the table—and in the sudden calm that followed, Mischa inherited the body that had been a stranger for so long. There was a rush of air on his face, the shock of fabric against his skin, the fullness of flesh and bone and body. Senses that had been muted erupted into life: the smell of vodka, floor polish and cigarette smoke, images diffused and monochromatic suddenly kaleidoscoping into a world of color, and Bill's last thought echoing in his head, *Claire*.

"I want Mischa to take the spot . . ."

The familiar voice, heard only yesterday and yet from a great distance . . .

"Can you hear me, Mischa?"

The woman's face came into focus. "Aunt Marina?" He tried to move, but his arms and legs were bound.

"The straps, release him."

Mischa shrank from the grim men in their green coats, but Aunt Marina placed her hand on his forehead. "They won't hurt you."

Mischa's wrists were bruised. He massaged them as he got off the table. Marina stepped forward and embraced him. "Mischa, welcome home."

Staring at her face, he touched her hair in wonder. "You're old."

A quick laugh escaped her. "You have been away a long time."

They were speaking in Russian now, rich and guttural, with nasal sounds blending and leaping like waves on a windswept sea. Then Mischa remembered something and fear turned his stomach to quicksand. "He wouldn't release Cain."

"It's all right, it doesn't matter."

But Mischa felt a growing anxiety. He could access Bill's memories, could hear the words that released Cain, *I see the President and he's been bad,* and he remembered how Bill had resisted the proper response and knew the rule from childhood: kill the bad one or be punished yourself. "I've got to get back."

"You're free now, Mischa."

"He'll hurt me."

"No, the signal was an error, the bad person is dead."

But he was *not* dead. The American President lived, the destructive fury called Cain was thwarted . . . And then he felt it, the presence deep inside trying to wrest control of his consciousness. Mischa rushed to the window, opened it and breathed deeply the smell of autumn leaves, a heady, rich smell that anchored him to the earth and the present moment. A man in a wheelchair gripped his arm. "Are you all right, my boy?"

Mischa stared. The voice was familiar, but the bent frame, the sagging face . . . "Uncle Andrei?"

"Who did you think?"

"Were you in an accident?"

A short laugh. "An accident of birth called age."

Mischa's attention was caught by the ring on his own hand. "Look, Billy got married."

This provoked smiles. Marina introduced Mischa to the others, including Lizaveta Treplova, the most beautiful girl he had ever seen. Her hazel eyes drowned him, and her lips glistened where they framed delicate white teeth.

"We are meeting the second time," she said as she shook his hand. "It is very odd."

"Scars," he said, the word floating into his head with an image of her arm. "You had scars."

The girl pulled her sleeve back. A faint white scar ran from elbow toward her wrist. "A motorcycle accident," Lizaveta explained. "But how did you know?"

Mischa shrugged. "It just popped into my mind."

"Bill's memory," Marina said.

"But I didn't show him my arms."

"His training. He must have noticed the scars and it made enough impression for Mischa to remember." She turned to him. "How much do you remember of Bill's life? Did you ever take the spot from Bill?"

"No, but Cain did."

"When? Do you remember?"

"When Billy got drunk Cain took the spot."

Major Khiza said, "He took what?"

"The spot," Marina answered shortly. "The seat of consciousness."

Mischa shrank from Khiza's antagonism. Deep within he felt an alien presence eager to take control. He clenched his fists against his temples and pushed the invader back into darkness.

"What is it?" Marina asked.

"Billy. He wants the spot."

"But how?" Lizaveta said. "Billy is the manifest personality. How can he be aware of us if he's not on the spot?"

"The process didn't stop," Marina said softly, almost to herself. "Why would it? The world we created here at Sandulov has been augmented by twenty years of reality. Billy's roots have grown deep into his psyche, perhaps as deep as Mischa's. Perhaps deeper."

"Am I in trouble?"

Marina's features brightened, but her eyes remained clouded. "No, of course not. You've done well, Mischa. Everything we expected."

"Not quite." Khiza lit a cigarette.

Guneyev spun the chair on one wheel. "Would you rather he killed the American President?"

"I would rather he killed Vasily Amenov."

Mischa's eyes grew wide. "Kill my father? Why?"

"Major Khiza didn't mean it," Marina said quickly. "Major, why don't we leave the room while Dr. Edishervashvili examines Mischa. All of us, let's give the doctor some privacy."

Dr. Edishervashvili was an avuncular man with a fringe of black hair ringing his head like a tangled halo. As the others filed out of the room he stepped forward and said, "You remember the weekly exams Dr. Vrubel gave you? That's what we need to do now."

"Where's Dr. Vrubel?"

"He retired many years ago, but don't worry, I won't bite."

Marina was the last to leave the room. Andrei intercepted her in the hall. He could tell from her expression that she was still fuming over Khiza's interference.

"Take it easy," he said in a low voice.

"He has the understanding of a frog and the patience of a fly."

"I know, I know."

"What is his purpose?" Marina hissed. "Mischa is back now. We can begin a rehabilitation program. We don't need Khiza. He intimidates the boy."

"Better let me talk to him."

They joined the others who had gathered in Billy's old bedroom. Marina's mind buzzed with plans: first a period of testing and evaluation during which she would reestablish her control over the two personalities and the Cain impulse. Next a therapy to convert the three elements into a single personality. Here was the second half of the Sorin Project, unplanned and unexpected and exciting. No one else had explored this area of Multiple Personality Disorder. And now that the Cold War was over she could publish the results, suitably edited to eliminate any mention of the assassination scheme. Already she could imagine the excitement that her research would generate in the scientific community . . .

Marina fielded questions from her colleagues while Andrei huddled in a corner with Major Khiza. Her emotions seesawed back and forth, one moment thrilled by Mischa's return, the next furious that the stupid KGB bastards had tried to kill him. They hadn't mentioned that little detail when they first asked her help.

She and Andrei had been on vacation, taking a Black Sea cruise, when the priority phone call from the KGB reached them: Vasily Amenov had stolen the activation code. Was there a way to disarm the Cain response? Would Bill listen to her voice, could she counteract the activation code? By the time they returned to Moscow, Bill had arrived. Andrei's sources, his friends in the KGB, had not known about the assassination attempt. Not until Bill mentioned it a few hours ago . . .

Dr. Edishervashvili appeared. "He's healthy as a horse. Pulse elevated slightly, but I think that's due to stress." He shook his head with a smile. "This is one for the books. Here's a man in his late thirties who's surprised to find hair on his chest."

Marina asked Lizaveta to keep the others in the bedroom; she wanted some time to talk to Mischa alone. She found him staring out the window.

"How are you feeling?"

"Hungry."

"We'll get you something to eat." She turned to call an orderly, but Mischa said, "Can you make him go away?"

"Who?"

"Billy."

Perhaps I could, she thought. But the urge was prompted by the same sentiment that disliked dogs but loved puppies and wished cats would remain kittens. His childhood was no more appropriate now than her desire to prolong it.

"No, Mischa. Billy's been on the spot too long and he's continued to grow all these years. He's part of you and we can't eliminate him. And I don't think we should."

"Maybe Cain could kill Billy," he said wisely.

"Cain isn't a person, not like Billy. Besides, I think Billy is too strong now."

"Billy gives me a headache."

Major Khiza appeared in the doorway. "I hate to interrupt a family reunion, but he's got to check out of the hotel."

"If he's comfortable doing it."

Khiza gave Mischa a look that made him cringe. "Make him comfortable," he said flatly, then left the room.

Eat shit, Marina thought. But Khiza was right. They had discussed it earlier. Bill Sullivan couldn't simply disappear in Russia without sparking an investigation by the American government. The conversion to a single personality must be done without interference or political pressure. Andrei had explained what would happen: Once Mischa checked "Bill Sullivan" out of the hotel, the KGB would take his passport and, after altering the photograph, send an agent posing as Sullivan to Switzerland. He would return under his own name and the Americans could search Switzerland to the end of the century for all the good it would do them.

Mischa gripped his head and closed his eyes. Marina jumped up. "Are you all right?"

"He hates me."

"Who? Major Khiza?"

He shook his head as if trying to clear it. "Go away!"

She grabbed his arms. "Mischa, stay here. Stay with me now. Nobody's going to hurt you. You're safe." Mischa shuddered, but his face lost its terrified expression. She said, "Talk to me. Are you all right?"

"It's Cain. Make him go away."

Disintegrating, Marina thought. The training was disintegrating from too many contradictory compulsions. She could sense Mischa sliding toward the abyss of raw emotion, urges run riot, unchanneled and unchained like the molten core of the sun. She had to prepare and guide him through the conversion before he suffered a psychic meltdown.

"Mischa, listen to me. Nobody wants Cain, but he's there in

all of us. He's the angry part of us, where we keep frustration and jealousy, the ugly part we don't like to see in ourselves or in others."

"He's there in you?"

"Yes."

"But not in Lizaveta," he said with sudden assurance.

"Her, too, Mischa. Everybody who doesn't have your ability to isolate him, to name him and give him authority he doesn't deserve. And now it's time to take that authority away."

"I'm afraid of him."

"That's why you need Billy. He's become strong over the years. He can control the negative emotions you call Cain, but you have to give him the power to do it."

"Me? I don't have any power."

"You have your memories. That's what Billy needs to know— which memories are real and which are false. He needs your memories so he's strong enough to face Cain. He can't do it without you and you can't become well without him."

"I have to give up the spot?"

"Not give it up, share it."

He grinned in disbelief. "Nobody can share the spot."

"You did when you were born. You have a very special talent and you needed it for a very special purpose. Now you no longer need that talent. It's time to become one person, you and Billy. But you have to make it happen. It's not up to me anymore."

He said something in a voice so soft she had to ask him to repeat it. He said, "Will I die?"

She took his hand, which seemed too large and strong for the boy she remembered. "No, you won't die. You'll be different, that's all. You'll be the person you were born to be."

Mischa looked at his feet. "Do you like him better than me?"

"Who?"

"Bill."

She hugged him then and felt the boy within the man, the thin, lean body she'd sent to America so many years ago. "I love you very much," she whispered. "And that won't change even when you're integrated, when you're healthy." She was embarrassed to discover tears in her eyes. She took a deep breath and held him at arm's length. "You have to join him or you'll make yourself sick. You understand?"

"Do I have to decide now?"

"Of course not, we'll talk about it later. First let's eat lunch and then maybe you can return to Bill's hotel and check out using his name."

Mischa looked uncertain. "Alone?"

"No. You can pick anyone you want to go with you."

He glanced around the empty room, leaned forward and whispered, "Can *she* come with me? Lizaveta?"

Marina's heart lurched, but she kept her expression neutral and with only a slight quaver in her voice said, "Of course. Whoever makes you comfortable."

CHAPTER
29

They drove to the hotel in a Chaika limousine. Andrei had convinced Khiza not to accompany Mischa, but the major insisted on sending one of his KGB men, a big man named Oleg. Marina countered by sending an orderly one size larger than Oleg, a burly, good-natured fellow called Dmitri. These two men were on one seat, Mischa and Lizaveta facing them.

Mischa was excited. He craned from one side of the car to the other, fascinated by the most rudimentary aspects of the city. At one point he saw a candy seller on the street corner and demanded that they pull over. Lizaveta didn't want him to leave the car so she got out to buy the candy. Mischa watched the movement of her hips with obvious admiration. Oleg nudged Dmitri and said, "Do you like that, Mischa?"

"She's very pretty."

Dmitri, who had unsuccessfully tried to strike up a conversation with Lizaveta, said, "A cold fish. Don't get your hopes up."

"Or your cock," Oleg grunted.

Mischa looked down: was his fly open? Oleg laughed and grew quiet as Lizaveta returned with the stick of candy. Mischa took it, pulled the paper free and tasted it. "Ummm." He shivered with delight and turned to Lizaveta. "Do you like candy?"

"Sometimes."

"Taste this."

She stared at him a moment, aware of his unabashed interest in her body, aware of the overt delight he took in her presence. She reached for it, but he pulled the candy away. "I'll hold it."

She leaned forward and tasted it. "Good." Keeping his eyes on her, Mischa brought the candy to his lips where he deliberately licked the same spot. Oleg was grinning. "What about me, Mischa? Can I have a taste?"

"Sure."

Lizaveta caught his arm. "He is kidding you," she said. The KGB man burst into laughter.

They pulled up to the Ukraina, and Lizaveta had the door open before the doorman reached them. They entered the lobby, where Mischa slowed, captivated by the surroundings. He paused to inspect a poster advertising a band called Novi Samurai scheduled to play that night in the hotel lounge. "Look," he said to Lizaveta, "a rock music band, here in the hotel."

"There are many such bands now."

"And they play degenerate music?"

"It is no longer degenerate."

Mischa's English was marginal, so it was Lizaveta who told the clerk that Mr. Sullivan was checking out. Once in the room, Mischa fingered the clothes in the closet and discovered a calculator in Bill's aluminum briefcase. He turned to show Lizaveta and found her lifting Bill's underwear from the drawer. "What are you doing?"

"You must check out."

"Wait, wait, the room is paid for. *He* paid it already, let us use it, you and I. We will order dinner. For Oleg and Dmitri, too."

Dmitri, inspecting a magazine, said nothing, but Oleg, who was crouched in front of the television, looked up. "It's a good idea."

"No. I am to take him back to the hospital."

"But not tonight," Mischa pleaded. "This is my first day of freedom and I don't want to spend it in the hospital. I want to celebrate. I will order borscht and *pelmeni* and ice cream, whatever you want."

"I have a job to do."

"Your job is to take care of me, be near, speak of pleasant things in the mother tongue so that I am—what did Aunt Marina say?—reaffirmed." He took her hand and dropped his voice. "I need your reaffirming."

"You need your head examined," she said, pulling her arm back.

Mischa frowned and sniffed his underarm. "I smell terrible, I must take a bath."

"We must leave now."

"Not yet, not yet, not yet," he sang as he danced away from her and disappeared into the bathroom.

"Let him buy us dinner," Oleg called.

"Shut up."

Lizaveta stared at the bathroom door, wondering which of her instructions she should obey first, to get Mischa out of the hotel or to avoid upsetting him? Marina's caution had been specific. "He will do what you say because he is captivated by you. Avoid coercion or threat that might trigger the Bill personality." And how am I supposed to captivate him into the car? she wondered. Oleg turned on the television and began browsing through the channels.

In the bathroom Mischa's clothes lay in a heap on the floor. He stared at his body in the mirror, turning this way and that, surprised at his bulk, surprised at the blush of gray hair around his temples, the lines around the eyes. He moved close and touched his face, bared his teeth and moved his lips around. "Haaaaaa," he breathed on the mirror, then wrote his name with his finger, *Mikhail Vasilievich.* I am here, he thought, I am back, I am alive.

He saw an ingrown toenail and was annoyed. My body was perfect, he thought; Bill has neglected this toenail. And somehow this made him sadder than simply counting the sum of the days and weeks and years he'd lost.

"Poor toenail, I will have you fixed," he promised, and the next moment saw himself in the mirror and thought, *You look stupid, who cries for a toenail?* He stood up and pulled his stomach in until his ribcage stood out and his abdomen was concave. This is how he remembered himself. Not so much bulk. Seventy-nine kilograms, that's what I should weigh. He pounded his stomach. At least I'm strong. At least he kept my body healthy.

Mischa tried to turn on the water, but there was only one handle, a large one extending from a circular chrome plate set into the wall. This was odd—how could one handle control hot and cold water? Or was there no hot water? In such a fine hotel he had hoped for a hot bath, but now, twisting the handle, only cold water came out. Still trying to figure it out he pulled a lever and the water disappeared for a moment, then sprayed down from the shower head. He leaped backward. "Yah! Yah!"

Lizaveta burst in. "What is it?"

He looked at her, embarrassed. "The water only goes cold."

Ignoring his lack of clothing she showed him how to operate it. Watching her bent over the tub with her blonde hair and the fine swell of her breasts beneath the blouse, he felt a lightness in his stomach and a warmth of sweet anticipation spreading through his loins. Lizaveta finished her demonstration and stood up. "There."

He was grinning foolishly. "Look."

Her eyes flicked down, noted his arousal, then back up. "You are a child," she said, and left the room.

Mischa stared at the marvelous change in his body with admiration and wonder. He gripped himself and thought, No, not this way, I want a woman. Tonight I want Lizaveta. He stepped into the hot shower and closed his eyes as steam rose around him. So good to be alive.

Ten minutes later Dmitri tossed clean clothes next to the tub, and told Mischa to hurry up. By that time the room was filled with steam that felt as rich and luxurious as the thick towels

Mischa used to dry himself. Wearing jeans and a black turtleneck sweater he went into the bedroom. The bags were packed and Lizaveta was sitting cross-legged on the bed, smoking a cigarette.

"I called Dr. Sorin," she said. "She says we must return to the institute."

"First I want to dance. The band is playing tonight, the Novi Samurai. See?" He opened Bill's wallet. "He has money, we'll celebrate."

"Good idea," Oleg said. "You can buy us all drinks."

"No." Lizaveta said. "He is not strong enough."

"Strong? Look." Mischa flexed his biceps and Lizaveta smiled.

"I mean mentally and emotionally. There is much work to do."

The phone rang. Lizaveta reached for it, but Mischa grabbed it and held it away from her. "Promise we can dance?"

"Give me the phone."

Then he heard it, a woman's voice, vaguely familiar, "Bill? Are you there?"

A blinding headache. Bill, exploding outward, took the spot. The world altered as his perceptions superseded Mischa's—Lizaveta's physical allure faded, the two men became threats, the hotel room no longer a plaything but a trap, and above all the voice on the phone, not that of a stranger but—

"Claire?"

"Bill, thank God—"

"What's wrong?"

"They're gone, they took Matt and Megan. You've got to come back."

"What?"

"Someone kidnapped Matt and Megan. They were on their way home and they had Ginger, two men in a van . . ."

Lizaveta grabbed at the phone but he yanked it away. "Leave me alone."

He spoke in English and her eyes opened in surprise. "You are Bill?"

Claire was saying, "What's wrong? Who's with you?"

"The kids, what happened?"

"A man called. Jeremy Lawrence. He wants to talk to you. Why, Bill? Who is he? What's happening?"

Over Claire's voice came Lizaveta's cry of alarm as Oleg brought out a pistol, a Marakov automatic. Yelling in Russian, she grabbed Oleg's arm and for a moment they struggled. Dropping the phone, Bill lunged across the room as Oleg shoved Lizaveta aside. The hammer wasn't cocked; Bill grabbed the barrel, preventing Oleg from working the slide.

"*Stoi!*" Lizaveta yelled.

Dmitri came lumbering across the room. Bill gave the Marakov a quick twist. Oleg let out a roar of pain as his finger, caught in the trigger guard, snapped. The gun was Bill's. He leaped free, working the slide, chambering a round. "Hold it!"

Dmitri stopped in his tracks, eyebrows flying up in sudden terror. Oleg held his broken finger to his chest, teeth gritted in pain and anger.

"Up! Up!" He gestured with the gun. "Face the wall." The two men complied, but Lizaveta started toward him.

"You must give me the gun."

"You too—against the wall."

"Me?"

"You're with them, they're with the gun. Do it."

"But I am trying to protect you," she said as she turned to the wall.

"Like you did at the institute?"

"It was the only way we could reach Mischa."

"The wrong way." He ran his hands over Dmitri's shoulders, belt, ankles. "Who is this guy?"

"Dmitri, he is one of our orderlies."

"This one?"

"Oleg, a KGB man. You cannot hurt him, Bill."

"Want to bet?" He kicked Oleg's feet farther apart, forcing him to lean more firmly on his hands. Oleg grunted as his broken finger touched the wall. A search of the man's belt discovered a spare clip of ammunition and a pair of handcuffs.

"These meant for me?" Bill asked as he took them.

"Please, Bill," Lizaveta said, "Marina cannot help you if you make trouble for the KGB."

"She's helped enough." Lizaveta stiffened at his touch. His fingers found the small of her back, her chest, the cleft of her breasts, waist, legs and around the ankles. He stepped back. "Tell your boys to move to the window and open it."

Oleg was the threat: Bill could see it in the man's eyes, looking for an opportunity to attack even as he followed instructions. A guardrail outside the window protected anyone from leaning too far out.

Bill tossed the handcuffs to Dmitri and, with Lizaveta translating, had him snap one cuff around his right wrist and loop his arm over the guardrail, bringing the dangling open cuff back into the room. Now it was Oleg's turn. He glared at Bill but did as he was told, reluctantly fixing the second cuff around his own wrist. The two men were pinned together, the railing between them. Bill picked up the phone. "Claire?"

The phone was dead. He kept the gun on Lizaveta, who watched somberly as he dialed the switchboard. The operator gave him an insincere apology and asked if he wanted to order an international call.

"I want you to call back right now. While I'm on the line."

"The international line you must place the order."

The country could change names a dozen times, but the inefficiency remained constant. "Never mind, get me the number for the American embassy."

Now that the immediate threat was contained, he wanted only to get out of Russia, to get home and find the children. His first instinct was to make a run for the airport, but he knew it wouldn't work. Not unless he was willing to kill the three people in this room. Otherwise they'd raise an alarm and the police would be waiting at the airport. There was only one way out.

"United States embassy," a woman's voice said.

"Give me the regional security officer. It's an emergency."

Bill had dealt with RSOs before, during presidential visits to Germany, Japan and China. They were charged with the security of the buildings and safety of embassy personnel. The RSO in

Moscow was a man named Walter Redding. Bill didn't know him, but when he mentioned the names of other RSOs he had worked with, Redding's initial skepticism vanished. Bill explained that the KGB was trying to kidnap him.

"You mean arrest you?"

"I mean kidnap by physical force. The reason has to do with national security. I'll give you a full report as soon as you get me out of here."

"You say you're armed?"

"A Marakov pistol, KGB issue."

"All right, don't shoot anyone, Bill, you'll be in more trouble than we can get you out of. Just keep your cool until I get there. What's your favorite baseball team?"

"Orioles."

"That's the code. I'll call you from the lobby, tell you Oriole is here if it's safe to come down. I'll be wearing a baseball cap, the Giants."

"Hurry it up."

He hung up and turned to Lizaveta. "Turn around and put your hands behind your back."

"This is not necessary."

"Tell that to my children." He yanked the cord free of the lamp next to the bed. "Come on, let's go."

She said over her shoulder, "Your children? I do not understand."

"Who's Jeremy Lawrence?"

"I cannot tell you."

The answer infuriated him. Her hands were tied now, so he tugged upward, causing her to gasp in pain. "Don't fuck with me, lady. The man kidnapped my children. I want to know who he is."

"He kidnapped . . ."

Bill spun her around and held her by the shoulders. "That's what the phone call was. Jeremy Lawrence, who is he?"

"Your father."

It was like a physical blow. Bill stepped back, a thousand jagged pieces of broken, half-formed memories as Lizaveta sought to explain in a torrent of words, a forgotten history come to life:

Yelena Amenov and Jeremy Lawrence, his real mother and father, and Vasily Amenov, Mischa's stepfather, a coldblooded killer.

And kidnapper. Calling himself Jeremy Lawrence was a private warning: I killed your father, I won't hesitate to kill your children.

The phone rang. Bill forced his concentration to the present moment. "Hello?"

"It's Oriole. I've got a Mercedes at the entrance."

"Be right down."

Lizaveta said, "No, Bill, you must return to Marina."

No, Marina wouldn't save the children. He yanked the phone cord from the wall, tucked the gun out of sight and left the room. The concierge glanced at him as he passed, but didn't ask for his *propusk,* undoubtedly assuming that he wasn't leaving the building. When he stepped into the lobby Redding wasn't there. And then he saw him, standing outside the main door beside a black Mercedes, a tall man in a business suit with a baseball cap worn far back on his head. Bill moved through the lobby, alert for any sign of interference. At his approach a look of relief spread across Redding's face. "Didn't shoot anybody, did you?"

"Didn't have a chance."

Dogged by the feeling that he had forgotten something, Bill slid into the backseat, followed by Redding. The car moved toward the street, then braked suddenly as a Lincoln Town Car turned abruptly across its path, heading for the entrance. Bill caught a glimpse of its passenger, a man wearing a baseball hat. And then he knew. His hand slid toward his belt.

"Wouldn't try it, Bill," Redding said, sounding exactly like an American. The barrel of his gun was like ice against Bill's temple.

"Who are you?"

"Ivan Sergeievich Bulgarin. Now put your hands on the back of the front seat."

Bill could see it now, the insignia on the cap, St. Basil's Cathedral and the legend *Moscow*—a tourist's cap, available in any hotel lobby.

He placed his hands on the seat while Ivan groped cautiously for his gun. Everything had happened too fast; the next move was pure instinct. As the car bounced over a pothole, Ivan's gun hand lifted momentarily. Bill's right arm shot up and back, blocking the gun. The explosion left his ears ringing. The Mercedes braked violently, tumbling them both to the floor where they struggled for the gun, neither able to gain the advantage.

Ivan freed his foot and tried to kick him, but it was impossible in the cramped space. Slowly Bill twisted the barrel toward the man's face. The car stopped. Ivan's eyes bulged with fear as the barrel intersected his forehead. Bill tried to finger the trigger, but the Russian had his hand over it. And then, from above and behind, an arm around his neck. The driver, kneeling backward, had him in a choke hold.

Bill tucked his chin down, trying to block the forearm pressuring his windpipe, but he was too late. He couldn't fend off the driver without releasing the gun, couldn't release the gun without getting shot. He could see the cars passing outside the window, a trolley rumbling down the street. Didn't anybody see them?

His chest heaved, the pressure increasing. Bill had no air, no voice, his lungs burning. The world dimmed, his fingers numbed. Ivan wrenched the gun away. Through a dark haze he saw the Russian's face, teeth gritted in triumph as the muzzle of the gun fixed Bill between the eyes. Dimly he heard the driver's sharp warning. Then the world turned black and he lost consciousness.

CHAPTER

30

Night brought new desperation. Unable to contact Bill, Claire drove to Roy Patchin's house in Chevy Chase, Maryland. Roy's wife, Nancy, answered the door. If she was surprised to see Claire, she didn't show it. "Come in, Claire, how nice to see you."

"I'm sorry to barge in like this. Is Roy here?"

Nancy's smile tightened imperceptibly. "Is anything wrong?"

Everything is wrong, she thought. But all she said was, "I have to talk to Roy."

Nancy led the way to a study where the walls bore witness to lives in celebration of themselves: photographs of Roy and Nancy at a dude ranch, riding horses, skiing, relaxing on a beach, standing on the deck of a boat in skin-diving gear. A stereo system covering half the wall included a radio tuned to a classical music station. Roy had taken off his shoes. In his argyle socks he padded across the room to greet her.

"This is a surprise . . ."

"She has an emergency," Nancy said, then tactfully withdrew. Roy looked worried. "If it's about Bill . . ."

"It's the children, Roy. Someone's kidnapped them. Today. Coming home from school."

"Kidnapped the children?" Roy repeated dumbly. "*Your* children?"

Claire explained in a rush of words. At one point she mentioned the kidnapper's accent and Roy interrupted her. "Russian?"

"British, I think."

Roy frowned and Claire continued until she had told him everything. "I called Bill," she said, "but there was a commotion and we were cut off. When I called back the line was busy. I thought he was calling me, but after ten minutes I placed another call and they said he checked out."

"He left the hotel?"

"It doesn't make sense. He knows about the kids, he wouldn't leave without telling me where he was going."

Roy seemed about to say something. Then he got up and went to the bar. "The man who called you, Jeremy Lawrence. Do you know him?"

"I thought maybe you would."

"Jeremy, Jerry . . . doesn't ring a bell."

"He said unless he talks to Bill tomorrow the kids . . . Bill has to come back. You've got to help me find him."

Roy returned with a drink, which she tried to refuse. "No, I can't drink."

"Yes, you can."

It was a shot of brandy on the rocks. She swallowed it quickly and made a face.

"Better?" Roy asked.

"Can I have some water?"

He brought her a glass. The warmth spread and she did feel better. Roy sat opposite her, his expression grave. "You say that Bill didn't answer when you called back?"

"He wasn't there."

"As far as you know."

"What do you mean?"

"Claire . . . forgive me, but I wondered if you've considered the coincidence. Within twenty-four hours of Bill's disappearance the children disappear. A kidnapper calls, but won't tell you what he wants. He'll only talk to Bill, who isn't here, and he'll call back in twenty-four hours. Meanwhile you're not to call the police or alert anyone. You see the pattern, don't you?"

"No."

"It's an ideal scenario for someone who wants to get his children out of the country without interference."

"Get his children . . . what are you talking about?"

"The FBI thinks Bill has defected."

"That's stupid."

"Just wait now. The man in charge, Nick Vincour—I think you met him—"

"I wouldn't talk to him."

"He was in my office today. Asking about Bill, his relationship with you and the children. What kind of a father he is, how close he is to Matt and Megan, whether he'd move to Russia without them."

"You're implying that *Bill* is the one behind the kidnapping?"

"Apparently it's happened before, Claire."

"Not to Bill. He's not a spy. I don't believe you're saying this."

"Why did he disappear from the hotel?"

The question was the same one she had been asking herself, but coming from Roy it infuriated her. "Because he's in trouble, that's why I came here. I thought you were his friend, but I guess I was wrong."

As she walked to the door Roy called, "Claire, everything he told us about his past was false. You know that, don't you?"

She turned. "I know this—that if you were in trouble he'd do anything in his power to help. You think he's a traitor? Look in the mirror."

She left the house, trembling in rage. Roy came running into the street after her. "All right, Claire, you're right. We'll do it your way."

She turned, arms akimbo, tears of frustration blurring her

vision. "Don't you understand? If Bill isn't here tomorrow he's going to kill the children."

"I know someone at the State Department," he began, but Claire closed her eyes and turned away. "All right, wait. The kidnapper, this Jeremy Lawrence, does he know Bill?"

"I don't think so. He called him Billy."

"And he's going to call at noon?"

"That's what he said."

"Here's what we'll do. I'll try to locate Bill, but if that doesn't work I'll come over at noon and we'll find out what the kidnapper wants."

"He won't talk to you."

"He will if he thinks I'm Bill."

"You?"

"If he thinks he's talking to Bill he won't hurt the kids. And until we know what he wants, we can't get them back."

We. There was someone else involved, someone to share the burden. "All right. But you won't tell anyone about the children. Promise me."

"I wouldn't do anything to endanger Matt and Megan." Standing on the cold sidewalk in his socks Roy shifted his weight from one foot to another. "Come back inside. You can stay here tonight."

"No, I want to be home if they call again or if Bill calls." Or the kids escape, she thought, but dared not speak for fear of jinxing the hope.

Claire returned home and dozed fitfully until just before dawn when a noise on the front porch jolted her awake, heart pounding with fear. It was the morning paper, filled with news of the world but none of the news she craved, the news of her own children.

If they intended to kill him they would have done it in the car. That was the thought that gave Bill hope as he paced the cell. He had regained consciousness to find himself bound, blindfolded and pressed between two guards, one of whom he assumed was

Ivan. After a ten-minute ride they hustled him into some kind of holding cell where his belt and all his belongings were confiscated. No one offered him a receipt, and no one responded to his repeated requests to contact the embassy. They hadn't killed him, which meant they wanted something. But what?

He stopped in the center of the room and yelled, "I want to talk to somebody."

He had done this periodically since he suspected the room was under electronic surveillance. The cell was fifteen feet square, floor and walls of white fiberglass tile, a spigot on one wall directly above a waste hole. Uniform indirect lighting came from the recessed borders of the ceiling. He hadn't expected a response to his demand, but this time the door opened and Major Khiza entered, followed by two guards with snubnosed machine pistols.

"You can stop yelling," Khiza said. "The guard has turned off the audio to this cell."

"If you're arresting me I demand you notify the American embassy."

"You're in no position to give orders, Mikhail Vasilievich."

"My name is Bill Sullivan."

"You know that's not true."

"Look at my passport."

"You assaulted a security officer, stole a firearm, and caused damage to a government vehicle—a Mercedes, for which the State paid in hard currency. For these offenses you could be given a prison sentence of sixteen years. On the other hand, you might cooperate with us and we will drop all charges."

"I think you should file the charges and notify the American embassy."

"You are a Russian citizen, you understand that, don't you?"

"I don't accept it."

"Then you are a traitor. Even in America the penalty for treason is death. You would be better to do your patriotic duty and cooperate with us."

"If I did my patriotic duty you'd be dead."

Khiza smiled coldly. "I am glad you do not wish to cooperate voluntarily. Now you will speak to General Repin. Come."

They led him down a short corridor to a room dominated by what looked like a dentist's chair, complete with head and foot rests. A familiar face stood just inside the door, his right index finger stiff and bandaged.

"You remember Oleg," Khiza said as the guards grabbed Bill's arms.

Oleg stepped forward and slammed his left fist into Bill's stomach. Bill managed to twist to one side, but Oleg wasn't finished. Grunting heavily, he drove a knee into Bill's crotch. Pain ballooned outward and his legs gave way. The guards dragged him over to the chair and lifted him into it. A man in a white smock came forward and smeared Bill's wrists with a menthol-smelling grease. With his drooping mustache and thick-rimmed glasses the man looked like a computer programmer, but the leather straps he locked over Bill's wrists had metal electrodes the size of quarters embedded in them. Not a computer programmer.

The man repeated the process on Bill's ankles while the guards strapped his waist. Then came more familiar items: a pressure cuff around his arm, another around his chest, a heart monitor and galvanic sensors taped to his chest. It was some kind of lie detector. The pain had dulled, and the wave of nausea ebbed. The man in the smock took a syringe from a metal tray. Bill said, "What's that for?"

"Dr. Lagutov is giving you a vitamin shot," Khiza said with a nasty grin.

It took both guards to hold Bill's upper arm while Lagutov made the injection. The doctor's grasshopper eyes, enlarged by the thick lenses, flicked back and forth from Bill's face to the needle. At first there was nothing. Then he felt flushed and his heart began beating faster. The air turned colder and the lights grew brighter—or seemed to. He found himself squinting. A tingling sensation worked its way across his body like a thousand ants crawling across his skin. Hypersensitivity. Even the slightest movement of his clothes felt like sandpaper.

"You won't feel like breaking anybody else's finger," Khiza said. He drew a fingernail across the back of Bill's hand, a scraping motion so light it barely depressed the skin but felt like the bite of a saw. Bill gritted his teeth.

"Feel good?" Khiza asked.

"What is it?"

Khiza called in Russian to Lagutov, who now sat behind a small desk, monitoring Bill's responses. After a brief discussion, Khiza said, "The chemical is a synthetic norepinephrine—a neural stimulant. But we call it—how would it be in English?—the burned-cat treatment."

A large man in a wrinkled suit entered. He had a thin nose and delicate veins webbing his cheeks. He walked around Bill like a mechanic inspecting a car. "So, this is the famous two persons in one body."

"I'm an American citizen and I want to call the American embassy."

"I don't give a shit what you want. I am General Iosif Repin and you are here to answer my questions. You are being monitored by a polygraph—a lie detector. Doctor Lagutov will tell me if you are telling the truth or not. If not, the electrodes in the restraint cuffs will deliver a mild shock—mild under normal circumstances. To you it will feel as if your backbone is being torn from your body. There will be no marks on the skin, no electrical burns, no damaged limbs or long-term rehabilitation. I know your CIA has a process equally humane."

"I'll give them your name."

Repin frowned, then raised one finger toward Lagutov, who moved a dial on his control panel. Bill's skin felt as if it were under attack by angry hornets and his bones were like barbed wire. He writhed uncontrollably, the movement exacerbating the pain. Then the pain stopped.

"You understand the rules now?" Repin demanded. "You answer only the questions I ask. Answer honestly. Otherwise I can increase the voltage until your mind breaks from the pain. We begin with control questions. What is your name?"

"That's what I came here to find out."

Repin frowned and started to raise his hand. Bill braced for the pain, but the General paused. "Don't fuck with my patience," he warned. "What is your *American* name?"

"Bill Sullivan."

"Your address in America?"

The questions continued, all of them simple and straightforward so that the doctor could chart a baseline of normal responses. Bill answered honestly—there was no point not to. He was beyond the pale now, outside legal channels, outside diplomatic channels and beyond, he suspected, even the designated authority of the KGB. Their complete disregard for diplomatic consequence was ominous. Unless he could be of use to these men he might never leave this room.

"Do you know Vasily Amenov?"

"I know of him. He kidnapped my children."

The General, who had been watching the doctor for confirmation of each answer, turned with surprise. "What? Why do you say he kidnapped your children?"

"The phone call at the hotel was from my wife. Your people must have been listening."

A brief exchange in Russian with Khiza. The major went to the desk and picked up the phone. Repin turned back to Bill. "Did you meet with Vasily Amenov in Washington?"

"No."

"But you spoke to him on the phone."

"Is that a question?"

"*Did* you speak to him on the phone?"

"Yes."

"When?"

The questions became more pointed, and Bill began to sense where they were leading. General Repin was interested in Vasily Amenov and the results of his attempt to activate the killing response. Bill described the events in the Oval Office and his subsequent suspension. Some of this he felt Repin knew, since Khiza would have briefed him on Bill's meeting with Marina Sorin. Finally, in a tone too deliberately casual, the General said, "Was it apparent to the authorities in America that you meant to kill the President?"

Bill hesitated. He didn't want to give them an excuse to kill him to safeguard a secret. "Yes."

Repin frowned. "Then why did they not arrest you?"

"They're investigating me. Still gathering evidence."

"But they know that you are Mikhail Vasilievich Amenov and one of our agents?"

"Yes." Again the only answer that might save him.

From behind the desk Lagutov shook his head. Repin's face suffused with anger. "You think I have shit for brains?" he yelled. "If they knew this, you would not have come to Russia."

"Then why ask—"

Repin signaled Lagutov, and Bill's body arched. This time it was worse, the voltage higher, the fire ants eating him alive. When it was over he lay panting, the sweat like ice on his brow.

"I would offer you water," the General said coldly, "but the temperature and taste would be painful. Now I ask you again, do the American authorities know about the Sorin Project?"

Bill said nothing. Repin said, "No answer is the same as a false answer."

"I called my wife. I told her."

Repin gave the signal without even waiting for Lagutov's nod. Bill's body arched and sheets of fire rose before his eyes, then a jumble of images foreign and familiar, from his past and from another's past, contradictory memories, childhood in Kansas and childhood with a man, a father, who forced him to hold a match between his lips . . .

The current dropped. The smell of ammonia stabbed like an ice pick. The world returned to focus. Khiza was holding some sort of smelling salt. Bill turned his face away and inside his neck fiery thumbtacks scraped. Khiza would have happily jammed the capsule up Bill's nose, but General Repin pulled his hand away. "Are you back with us, Mr. Sullivan?"

"Yeb vas," Bill said. Repin looked surprised and Khiza stepped forward. "Now he is Mischa," he said in Russian.

In English Bill said, "Fuck you."

The two men stared at him. "Which one are you, Bill or Mischa?"

The Russian words had already faded. "Untie me and I'll show you."

"He is the American." Khiza said.

"I ask you again, Mikhail Vasilievich, do the Americans know about the Sorin Project?"

Bill knew he couldn't take another jolt of electricity, but the confirmation Repin wanted would be his death warrant . . . unless there was a reason to keep him alive.

"For the last time," Repin began.

"No," Bill said quickly, "they don't know about it, but Vasily Amenov will tell them. I can help you find him. He kidnapped my children, he wants to talk to me. Take me to Washington and you can trap him. You can keep your secrets, all I want is my children back."

"I am supposed to silence a man who might divulge the Sorin Project with a man who is the Sorin Project? You're an anachronism, Mikhail Vasilievich, an expensive piece of Soviet machinery as useless to the motherland as the Berlin Wall."

As he spoke, General Repin walked to the control console and leaned over the doctor's shoulder. Bill called after him, his voice rising in desperation, "The American embassy knows I'm here. My wife knows I'm here. If anything happens to me the investigation will lead right to the Sorin Project."

The General turned and smiled. "Not if you're killed by a fellow American."

His hand moved to the console, and the words Bill started to say became a scream of pain. The chair lurched as his body twisted spasmodically. The scream died as Bill's throat constricted and flames rose before his eyes, turning the world white hot before it evaporated and then nothing.

CHAPTER
31

Gennadi Khiza held up a shot glass and said in a loud voice *"Vashe zdorovje."* To your health.

His two companions clinked their glasses and downed the contents in a single swallow. Khiza slammed his glass to the table and grinned stupidly at Dennis Riggs. "So how does it go? 'To make a cat bark you . . . you light a match . . .'"

"First gasoline," Riggs corrected sloppily. "Give it a bath in gasoline and then light a match and the cat says 'Woof!'"

Khiza forced himself to laugh. He had been drinking all night, but he was not drunk. The waiter had been instructed to substitute water for vodka in the glasses he brought Khiza and his partner, Ivan Bulgarin. Only Dennis Riggs was drinking alcohol. Only Riggs was drunk.

Khiza was strangely exhilarated. During the Afghani war he had shot a captured rebel between the eyes when the man refused to answer questions. It was a heady experience, an omnipotence he hadn't felt again until now. Tonight he was in charge of two deaths, not ragged rebel boys but Americans, clever and dangerous. He thought of his wife, arms curled around a pillow and asleep by now, and fantasized returning fresh from the kill and making love to her.

"Woof!" Dennis yelled, and the Russians laughed again. He was having a good time. He always had a good time when someone else was buying drinks, and his two new friends had been buying all night. It didn't occur to him that not even a Russian found the same joke funny the fifth time around.

Riggs worked three nights a week at the *Restoran Skazka,* or Fairy Tale, where he sang rock-and-roll songs in English. Entertainment was expected in Russian restaurants, and Riggs alternated with a floor show featuring girls doing the French cancan. Usually he drank the night's pay in liquor before he got out the door, but tonight he had no such worries. He had made such a hit with these two Russians that they had invited him back to their rented dacha where they could continue drinking.

It was time to go. Riggs retrieved his guitar and said goodnight to Luka, the bartender, who gave him a bear hug and whispered, *"Ostorozhno."* Be careful.

Riggs felt a quick infusion of comradeship and said loudly, "You're all right, Luka, no matter what my wife says."

The men stumbled into the chilly night. "I'll come with you," Khiza told Riggs. "We'll follow Ivan."

Ivan climbed into a Mercedes-Benz and Riggs felt a stab of jealousy. In the aftermath of his defection the Soviet government gave him a Mercedes, but when his debts mounted, he sold the car in exchange for a Zhiguli, the Fiat design manufactured in Volgograd. Last year he sold the Zhiguli for a secondhand Zaporozhets, a car it was said that was built by the masses for men without asses. The car was uncomfortable and unreliable, and it seemed to Riggs that he spent an hour under the hood for every two on the road. Tonight it was cold and the Zaporozhets didn't want to start.

The possibility he would have to leave the car until morning actually appealed to Riggs; the Mercedes would have a good heater. He was almost disappointed when the engine bounced into life. As they drove north from the city, Khiza plied him with questions and Riggs found himself bragging about his past work for the government, giving broad hints that he was an intelligence agent. Beyond the outer ring road they passed through the village of Abramtsevo, its main street lonely and deserted.

"How much farther?" Riggs asked as they entered the country and the pavement narrowed. He didn't want to run out of gas. Or pay for it.

"Almost there. Ivan's dacha is just a few kilometers."

The Mercedes turned onto a dirt road where the trees crowded close. Khiza was still talking, but Riggs was only half listening. He couldn't recall any communities out this way.

For no apparent reason Ivan pulled to the side of the road and stopped. "I think he's lost," Riggs said as he followed suit. The interior of the Mercedes glowed as Ivan got out of the car. Riggs reached for the door, but Khiza put his hand on his arm. "Stay here. There's an accident."

"Where?"

"A man was run over and killed tonight. The funny thing is, he shot the driver before the car hit him. They were both Americans."

Khiza was smiling slightly. What was he saying? Riggs didn't understand—didn't want to understand. From the corner of his eye he was aware of Ivan standing between the two cars. Now Ivan tapped the hood of the Zaporozhets to get his attention. Riggs turned. The Russian was in silhouette and standing so close to the hood that it was hard to see the gun, or maybe Riggs didn't want to see it, wondering, now when it was too late, *since when does a civil engineer drive a Mercedes?* The explosion split the night. Two neat holes, one in the windshield, the other above Riggs's left eye. A spurt of blood as the body slumped. Khiza was already scrambling out the door.

Bill heard the shot. He lay bound and gagged in the trunk of the Mercedes. The massive electrical shock that had left him paralyzed with pain had worn off, leaving him beset by a maelstrom of impressions, memories and emotions in conflict, reality and illusion indistinguishable from one another with one crucial exception: Claire and the children stood out as fixed points in an incoherent world. Slowly, like sediment settling in a storm-tossed sea, the confusion cleared. The children were his beacon, Claire was his direction, all roads must lead home. He forced himself into the present moment.

He had been in the trunk for a number of hours, shivering in the cold despite the dusty wool blanket thrown over him. During that time his fingers managed to pick away at the duct tape holding his ankles until during the last few minutes, he had freed his feet. The dirt road had caused a coating of dust to settle over him, drifting into the compartment through the air holes his captors had punched in the rear wheel wells. His wrists were taped behind his back. He had just begun to rub the tape against a raised portion of the metal frame when the car stopped.

Not yet, Bill thought. He wanted his hands free, but there was no time. He twisted backward, found the swatch of tape he had removed from his ankles and patted it clumsily across the top of his feet where it would appear to his captors that the bounds were secure. And waited. A car directly behind them; he could hear the engine.

The shot was a surprise. For a moment he thought they were shooting through the trunk. Then a quick hope—someone rescuing him? But the muffled voices were familiar and dispassionate. The sharp sound of a key opening the trunk. Bill closed his eyes as light flooded the compartment. The blanket was yanked aside, fresh air washing over him.

"You awake in there?" Khiza said in English.

Bill's mouth was taped shut. He groaned, but kept his eyes closed.

Someone grabbed him around the knees, the other around the shoulders. Bill forced himself to remain limp. He wished now he had spent the time freeing his hands, which were still taped behind his back. As they lifted him one leg pulled free of the other and the clump of tape dropped to the ground.

A cry of alarm as Bill's eyes blinked open. He snapped a kick to Ivan's jaw even as Khiza released his shoulders. Bill fell against the fender and scrambled to his feet. He saw the gun in Khiza's hand and drove forward into the man's chest. Khiza stumbled backward, brought the handle of the gun down in a glancing blow. Bill kept moving, knocked Khiza aside and lunged into the dark safety of the trees.

Shots rang out, one, two, and on the third a spark from a rock where the bullet ricocheted into the trees. Bill was moving fast now, crouching low for balance, feet pumping, dodging between trees rimmed by fading headlights. Leaves and pine needles were slippery underfoot, bushes grabbed at his ankles, and he tripped twice over unseen obstacles. His pursuers were yelling at each other, following him, crashing through the brush.

Bill stumbled down a gully, rolling the last five feet into a tree trunk that knocked the breath out of him. Here, below the reach of the headlights, it was darker. He tried to control his ragged breathing, noisier still through his nose. He could hear them now, calling back and forth. Bill pushed his cheek against a pine tree, scraping the tape from his mouth. Beyond the crest of the gully came the snap of a branch and quick silence. Some one tracking him. He stopped moving, tape still covering half his mouth.

There was the sound of a car door closing. Were they leaving? Then he saw it—the sweep of a flashlight darting among the trees accompanied the sound of someone returning. One man had remained in the vicinity while the other had gone for the flashlight. Standing on a thick root, bracing his shoulder against the tree, Bill peered past the top of the gully. He could see them now, from the chest up, silhouetted in the moving flashlight beams, Ivan Bulgarin, who had impersonated Redding at the hotel, and Major Gennadi Khiza.

If I had a rifle, Bill thought . . . and free hands. The question was, had they pinpointed his location? The answer came a moment later when Khiza headed north along the top of the rise while Ivan began picking his way toward him. Bill shifted his position to use the tree as a shield. He cringed when a clump of dried leaves crackled underfoot, but the Russian was also making noise and didn't hear. The flashlight's beam bounced across the tree without stopping, moved south as the man headed away from him. Keep going, Bill prayed. Just keep on going.

Instead Ivan began a random pattern that brought him closer. Bill inched to the left, keeping the trunk between them, as the Russian approached to his right. He could see now what looked like a deer trail that passed within a foot or so of the tree. If Bill could keep moving he could remain hidden, but the closer Ivan came, the faster he had to move to stay out of sight and the more noise he made.

The Russian stepped into view sweeping the flashlight ahead of him while Bill held his breath just three feet to his right. *Keep moving.* The moment stretched to an eternity, then Ivan turned, light bursting into Bill's face—

The gun was visible, caught in the beam as Bill's foot connected with it and sent it flying from Ivan's hand. The Russian yelled and stumbled back. A sharp report not five feet away— the gun as it struck a rock and then slid to the earth. Bill dove toward the gun, which had come to rest at the base of a shelf of lichen-covered rock, even as Ivan's flashlight beam pinpointed the location.

Hands still behind his back, Bill had no choice. He sat down heavily, fingers groping for the pistol as Ivan charged him. He got his hands on the barrel and Ivan kicked him in the stomach. Bill doubled over, hands fumbling for the proper grip. Ivan brought the flashlight down full force, aiming for his head. Bill jerked to one side and took the blow on his shoulder. Numbing pain shot up his arm. The flashlight went out.

Ivan was groping for his throat now, sitting astride Bill, pinning him to the ground. Behind his back the pistol slipped into Bill's grip. He arched upward and in the moment that Ivan's weight was free of his body he twisted to his right side, bringing the gun free of the ground and parallel with his back. He fired twice, aiming by the feel of Ivan's body straddling him. The Russian screamed and fell back.

Bill rolled free and came to his knees. A thrashing in the forest. "Ivan?" The other flashlight was advancing toward him. Bill, still holding the gun, moved away from the body. Khiza heard the noise and called again, then advanced more slowly. Bill used his knee to shove the last of the tape free of his mouth. Cold air came rushing down his throat; now he could breath more quietly.

Khiza appeared at the crest of the gully. His light found the body and he froze. Then it swept wildly around the area and suddenly blinked out as the Russian realized what a good target the light made him. Then he started moving away, slowly at first, then running back to the road.

Bill leaned against a tree, aware of a sharp pain in his collarbone. Ivan groaned, but Bill didn't dare approach him. Not until he had the use of his hands. The sound of a car door and the Mercedes driving off at great speed. Bill moved up the depression until he found a rock where he could scrape the tape from his wrists. Finally the tape gave way. He massaged his wrists a moment, then picked up the gun and moved cautiously back to Ivan.

The Russian was lying quietly now, his head framed by an inky circle of blood. Keeping the gun trained on him, Bill picked up the flashlight, but it was broken. He lifted Ivan's hand and checked his pulse. Nothing. The man was dead. A quick search gained Bill a spare clip for the pistol and Ivan's wallet. He stuffed the two items into his jacket pocket and made his way back to the road where he surveyed the scene from the trees. A small car sat with its motor running, pale headlights throbbing. The Mercedes had disappeared. Had Khiza been the only other one? Or was someone left behind, waiting in the trees for him to show himself?

No, he decided, a larger group would still be beating the bushes, trying to find him. Still, he fired twice across the road to draw return fire. Nothing. Crouched low, he zigzagged to the car, paused and then, still crouched, threw open the door. And almost shot Riggs as the body slumped toward him.

"Shit," Bill whispered. Now he knew what the shot was that he had heard.

There was no way he could drive to Moscow with a body in the backseat, so he pulled Riggs from the car and into the trees. He removed Riggs's socks and used them to wipe the seat and steering wheel clean of blood. Tracks in the dirt road told him that the Mercedes had made a U-turn, so Bill drove the opposite direction.

He had no idea where he was or where he was going. The little car wasn't fast, but it wasn't a fast road. Occasionally there were farmhouses, but he passed no other cars. Whether it was the aftereffects of the drug or the emotions of the moment, he found himself alternately shivering and sweating.

After fifteen minutes the road intersected a paved highway. Bill didn't know which way to go, so he turned left. He came to a small town where the only lights were in the local drugstore. Just outside of town the car began coughing. A glance at the gauge confirmed his worst fears—the car was running out of gas. He picked a flat spot, turned off the road, and parked the car in the woods.

Silence. Headlights off. Darkness.

He would hike back to the town and find a bus or train to take him to Moscow. That was his intention, but now that he was free, now that he was safe, his emotions burst like a dam, flooding him with an onrush of memories long dormant and long denied that carried him, paralyzed and helpless, deep into the night and deeper still into his past. The conversion had begun.

CHAPTER
32

Tiny droplets eased down the moisture-laden windshield leaving behind transparent trails through which the morning sun fingered Bill's face, waking him. During the long night the confused welter of contradictory memories had distilled into two categories: real memories of actual events and the false memories suggested by Marina Sorin, which he now perceived as framed by the external stimuli of the Sorin Project. Yesterday was like a postcard of a faraway place, a simple graphic image without color or texture compared to the richness and complexity of the world he could survey now.

Bill sat hunched beneath a dirty blanket, his back against the door. The effects of the drug had worn off. Filled with a renewed sense of purpose he got of the car. Frost covered the earth where the sun's rays hadn't yet penetrated. A squirrel scampered up a pine tree and scolded him angrily. Bill stretched and took a deep breath. His body felt different, taller somehow, almost as if he could continue rising above the trees and walk home, crossing continents in a single stride . . .

The illusion faded. He had no wallet, no identification, no passport. He had murdered a KGB agent, and the police—*militia,* Mischa's correction slipped through his mind—were undoubtedly looking for him. He had to get to the American embassy, but dared not call now that he knew the phone line was tapped. Had the Russians posted extra police around the building? If not, there would be only a pair of militia men guarding the gate. If he took them by surprise he could make a quick dash and gain the safety of the Marine-guarded inner grounds. But first he had to get to Moscow.

Bill discarded his jacket, which had dried blood on it, and removed almost two hundred rubles from Ivan's wallet. He hid the wallet beneath a rock. The gun was a different problem. It was a Marakov, the Russian copy of Germany's Walther PPK, but with a thicker butt. Without the jacket it would be difficult to conceal, but Bill was reluctant to leave it behind. Apart from his present danger, he had carried a gun for twenty years and felt incomplete without one. Bill reached under the dashboard and yanked a couple of electrical wires free. After clearing the bullet from the chamber he tied the pistol to his ankle, barrel hidden beneath the sock. He tucked in his shirt, cleaned himself as best he could and made his way to the highway.

The sun told him which way was east; the increasing morning traffic told him that the city lay to the south. Planning to hitchhike to the closest town or into Moscow, he began molding a suitable explanation: *I had an argument with my brother and he ordered me out of his car . . .*

A new thought brought him up short. *Ya ni govoryu parusski.* I don't speak Russian. Except he did. His mind ranged quickly: What's this word? And this? How do you say . . . ? The knowledge came at first on demand, then materializing before he formulated the question. It was like rounding a bend in the river and discovering the ocean, the Russian language with its wavelike cadences spread before him, a sea of communication inherited on demand. There was more knowledge, too, the texture and feel of a culture that was both alien and familiar. Russia.

Bill took a hitchhiker's stance and held out his hand, fingers clenched, thumb outstretched. A car passed, then another, drivers staring at him curiously. Something wrong here. Didn't anyone hitchhike in Russia?

Wrong signal. Mischa's knowledge. Bill could feel him now, not as a separate entity but a diffused presence, another dimension to his own personality. More cars were passing. Bill opened his mind and the burst of knowledge came like fireworks on a dark night. You did not stick out your thumb in Russia but . . . He raised his open hand to shoulder level and made a single chopping motion. The second time he tried it the car stopped. It was a green two-door sedan with rust-eaten areas that had been patched and painted a color that didn't quite match. There was a couple in the front seat and two children in the back.

"Kuda ti yedesh?" the driver asked.

"Moscva." He pronounced it like a Russian, and for a moment it seemed normal and the awkward Westernization *mosscow* was alien; then the perception reversed and the Russian pronunciation sounded strange. The wife stepped reluctantly out of the car to let Bill into the backseat, where the two children slid over to make room. Their clothing had a hand-me-down look to it and the interior reeked of stale cigarette smoke.

"I am Feliks Yavlinsky," the driver said in Russian. "My wife, Sonya, and my children, Ilyich and Anna."

"My name . . ." They waited expectantly. "Mischa," Bill blurted. "Mischa Amenov."

Feliks said, "You have cigarettes, Mischa?"

"No, but I can help with the gas." He pulled out the wad of bills he had taken from Ivan. Feliks nodded, put the car in gear and sounded the horn furiously as he rammed his way back onto the road. He looked into the rearview mirror. "Where are you going in Moscow?"

Caution warned him not to say the American embassy. He recalled the map of Moscow and picked a spot not too far away. "Gorky Park."

As soon as he said it came Mischa's memory, a ferris wheel, carnival rides, green grass and trees along the river . . .

"It's out of our way but if you can pay for the extra gas . . ."

Bill didn't want to appear too eager or too careless with the money so he bartered briefly and settled on a fee of twenty rubles.

"So what are you doing on the road without a jacket?" Feliks asked.

"My stupid brother," Bill began, listening with a strange sense of disassociation as he invented an explanation in fluent Russian.

Roy Patchin's silver Jeep Cherokee pulled into the Sullivan driveway five minutes before eleven. From the window Claire saw him lock the car and set the alarm. He wore an overcoat and gloves, one of which he exchanged for a comb, which he ran through his hair as he approached the house. Claire felt a huge weight lift from her shoulders. She had the door open before Roy reached the porch.

"How'd you do last night?" he asked as she hung his coat in the closet. "Get any sleep?"

"Not much."

"No word from Bill?"

She shook her head. The only phone calls were ones she had made informing the school that Matt and Megan wouldn't attend class today. She led the way to the dining room, where the phone sat prominently in the center of the table.

"Did you talk to the State Department about Bill?"

"I was on the phone with them before I came over. Them and the CIA."

"The CIA?"

"Bill called the embassy. Must have been either right before or after you talked to him. He told them he was in trouble, that the KGB was trying to kidnap him. He talked to the regional security officer, a man named Walter Redding. According to Redding, Bill said he had disarmed his abductors and was holding them at gunpoint. Redding went with two Marines to give him safe passage to the embassy, but when they got to the hotel he had checked out. That was the story, anyway."

"He wasn't there?"

"Redding insisted on checking the room to make sure. I guess it took a little persuasion. A maid was putting clean sheets on the bed, but the towel in the bathroom was damp and the shower stall was wet."

Claire closed her eyes. "I don't believe this. Someone kidnaps the children and now the KGB kidnaps Bill."

"We'll get him back. The embassy is making enquiries, official and unofficial."

"What do they think . . . happened?"

"Too early to tell, Claire. Let's concentrate on Matthew and Megan. Is it too late for coffee?"

Her expression cleared. "I think there's some left. What do you take in it?"

"Sugar, just a touch."

She left him alone and went into the kitchen, where she deliberately left Bill's cup in its usual place and took another for Roy. The routine of setting the coffee tray calmed her. When she returned to the dining room she found Roy reading Bill's departure note. He thrust it aside. "Sorry. I saw it sitting here and just . . ."

"That's all right." She placed the tray before him. "Maybe now you'll believe he's not a traitor."

"Tell you the truth, Claire, I don't know what to believe. Those months we roomed together during college I don't think I ever really got to know him. Bill was always different, his own man even back then. Didn't talk about himself, didn't drink, totally focused on joining the Service. We had a nickname for him, he ever tell you?"

"Ice Man."

"Never got angry or excited, always in control. At least until he met you." Roy floated a smile, which wasn't returned. "That's when he began to loosen up, have a little fun, think about something other than getting assigned the White House Detail. You were good for him."

Roy added a bit more sugar, the granules turning brown as he lowered the spoon.

"They should contact Dennis Riggs," Claire said. "That's who Bill went to see."

Roy nodded. "They know about Riggs. Someone's been sent to interview him."

She turned to look at the clock and Roy glanced at his watch. Silence filled the room. Roy sipped his coffee and he heard himself swallow.

"At least they want something," Claire said finally. "I was thinking about it last night. It's not like people who take children to hurt them. They want something from Bill, so there's no reason to hurt them."

He reached for her hand and jumped as the phone rang. They both froze, eyes locked. Claire whispered, "Sullivan residence—that's how Bill answers."

Another ring. Roy picked up the phone. "Sullivan residence."

"Is that you, Billy boy?" A British accent with a guttural undertone.

"It's Bill Sullivan, who are you?"

"Don't you recognize my voice?"

Roy hesitated. What was the right answer? Was this someone Bill knew or not? Claire waved to catch his attention and mouthed *Matt? Megan?*

"Where are my children?" Roy said.

"They're safe and will remain so unless you do something foolish. It's time to make a trade, you and I. Two lives in exchange for one. You have the better deal in terms of quantity. By weight I think we will be the equivalent."

"Let me talk to Matthew."

A pause. "Who?"

"My son. I want to make sure he's all right."

"You call him Matthew or Matt?"

Claire's eyes were fixed on him, but she couldn't hear and could give him no help. "When I'm upset I call him Matthew. And I'm upset now. Tell me what you want."

A note of skepticism. "Is the phone tapped, Billy?"

"No."

"And would you tell me if it was?"

"No."

A chuckle of appreciation. "Now I believe you."

"What do you want? Money?"

"Not what I want but what you've earned. What's the price of betrayal, Billy? A little girl's life? A little boy's?"

A nut case, Roy thought, with a growing sense of alarm. What the hell is he talking about? "We can make a deal, whatever you want, but you have to prove the children are safe."

"*The* children?" Again the suspicion. "You mean *your* children?"

"You know who I mean."

"What a cold and distant father you are. Different from what I expected, Billy. The way the children talk about you—that is, *your* children—I imagined you the perfect father. *If* you are their father. Sometimes it's hard to tell. Sometimes a woman fools a man, a wife fools her husband, a man claims to be a father who is not. Have you had that experience?"

Slipping away, Roy could feel it, their deception emerging like an ocean liner from the fog. He made one last attempt to regain control. "Stop playing around and tell me what you want."

"Is your wife there?"

"Yes."

"Who else?"

"No one."

"You're telling me the truth, Billy?"

"There's just the two of us. Why?"

"Three of us. I see Claire and she's been bad."

"Never mind Claire, just tell me why you're doing this."

The voice hard and flat. "You're not Bill Sullivan." A click on the line.

"I am Bill Sullivan, I'll prove it. Ask me a question, ask me anything. Hello?"

Claire grabbed the phone. "Don't hang up, please, we'll give you anything . . . talk to me. Say something." She looked helplessly at Roy. He took the phone with new purpose, jiggled the cradle and said, "Did you get it? Try."

He replaced the receiver. Claire's heart was pounding, but her voice was low and controlled. "Who was that?"

He didn't meet her gaze. "We may be able to find out where he called from."

"Someone's on the line? Listening?"

He raised a hand, urging patience, and kept his eyes fixed on the phone.

"Who, Roy?"

"Doesn't matter."

"They're my children, don't tell me it doesn't matter. Who is it? The police? The Secret Service? Who?"

"An FBI technical unit."

"You called the FBI?"

"It's the only way to get them back, Claire."

She shoved him, a quick open-palmed smack on the chest that surprised them both. "How dare you."

He grabbed her wrist. "Listen to me, the likelihood is that after they get the money or whatever they want from you they'll kill the children. You told me yourself they got into a van with a stranger, someone they seemed to know, someone whose face wasn't covered. Do you think he'll let them live to identify him?" She pulled free as he continued. "I hate to say it, but you've got to face facts, Claire. The best chance to find them is before the kidnappers get what they want. *Before,* not after."

The phone rang and their hands collided reaching for it. Claire's voice was cold. "Is this still my house or did you turn it over to the FBI?"

He withdrew his hand. Claire lifted the receiver. "Sullivan residence."

"Uh, is Agent Patchin there?"

Sick at heart she handed Roy the phone.

"Patchin." He frowned. "That's all? Okay, we'll let you know."

He replaced the phone, his expression troubled. Claire said, "They didn't find him, did they?"

"A pay phone. They're on their way."

She said in a whisper, "Get out of my house."

"It's sophisticated equipment, Claire. There's no way any-body could tell they were—"

She pushed past him, banged open the closet door, grabbed his coat and threw it at him. "Get out!"

Her body was rigid, eyes glistening with fury. Roy went to the entrance, turned to say something, then decided against it. He closed the door as quietly as he would leaving the nursery of a sleeping child.

CHAPTER
≡ 33 ≡

The drive to Moscow seemed to take an eternity. Between bouts of browbeating his wife and cursing other drivers Feliks tried to engage Bill in one-sided conversations where he held forth on everything from the cost of toilet paper to UFOs. Bill was happy enough to let him ramble; it kept him from asking questions.

When Bill stepped out of the car at Gorky Park he went directly to the closest bus stop, where the driver of the first bus told him to wait for the Number 10. He could have taken the subway to the Smolenskaya station and walked to the embassy, but the bus would pass in front of the building and give him an opportunity to see if the place was cordoned off. If so, he would look for a disguise or seek asylum at the British or Canadian embassy.

Standing inside the plexiglass shelter, Bill was cold. He expected that without a jacket he might draw attention, but people were wrapped in their own problems and he·was ignored. When the bus arrived he paid five kopecks and settled gratefully into a seat still warm from the previous occupant. A five-minute ride brought them to the American embassy. The building was located on a wide, busy boulevard informally known as the Garden Ring Road. Offices and residences were bordered by a red brick wall that encompassed the entire block. There were no police other than the usual two guards crouched in a wood structure not much larger than a telephone booth. What Bill hadn't expected was the long queue of people presumably waiting to apply for visas. One man, a bearded protester, carried a sign demanding freedom for Russian Jews. Across the street a woman stood beside a small tank on wheels—*kvas*—the word popped into Bill's mind along with the knowledge that she was selling a citrus drink whose flavor he could almost taste. Mischa again, the merging of memories created a constant strain that dulled his senses. Otherwise he might have read the street scene differently and sensed the trap.

The bus stopped at a concrete island in the middle of the boulevard. Bill got off and started toward the stairs leading to a pedestrian underpass. At the end of the block a World War II veteran in an army uniform sat in a wheelchair playing a violin. Something about the music alerted Bill . . .

Where have you been, Billy boy, Billy boy?

An English song, a childhood memory, *mother* . . . Bill stopped. The army veteran was Andrei Guneyev. The old man recognized him, dropped the violin and pointed emphatically away from the embassy. Friend or foe? In another minute it wouldn't matter. Ignoring the stairs Bill started across the busy street, dodging traffic. Threat materialized from the crowd: the bearded protester dropped the sign and yelled. A young couple separated from the queue, their eyes following the protester's outstretched finger pointing at Bill. The *kvas* vendor lifted a walkie-talkie to her mouth.

A trap. Bill wheeled around and regained the island. A car horn sounded as the protester started across the street in pursuit. Bill ran to the end of the island, searching for an opening between onrushing cars. A BMW motorcycle turned the corner followed by a black Mercedes, siren blaring, blue light blazing. Bill clutched at his ankle, but the gun was tied with electrical wire and no time to release it. Andrei Guneyev was signaling frantically, pointing toward the motorcycle now coming directly at him—

Lizaveta. He recognized the helmeted figure as the BMW skidded to a stop. She was screaming his name, eyes wide with fear. Bill threw a leg over the seat and grabbed her waist. The BMW leaped forward. The protester was waving an identification badge. *"Stoi!"* Lizaveta squealed into a U-turn and raced down a side street. They passed a group of children playing on an empty pedestal and turned down an angled street that brought them back to the Ring Road and directly into the path of the Mercedes.

"Hold on," Lizaveta shouted. They swerved toward the river and turned left along the embankment road. The Mercedes, its siren wailing, fell behind. A traffic light turned red, but Lizaveta paid no attention. The BMW's horn sounded woefully inadequate as they swerved to miss a car starting across the intersection. Then they were safe on the other side. They leaned to the left as the embankment road curved to follow the river. At the end of the next block more blue flashing lights. Armed militia piled out of a *voronok*—a black police van.

Lizaveta skidded to a stop. With buildings on their left and the river to their right, they were trapped. A railway bridge of boxlike metal girders spanned the river. The cycle leaped toward it. No good, Bill thought. Over the river they would be easy targets. Already the militia were crouching, rifles at the ready.

"That way," Bill yelled as they reached the tracks. He pointed opposite the bridge to where the railway curved toward the heart of the city. Lizaveta made a hard left and Bill braced with his foot. Then they were between the rails, pounding across the wood ties. Brick walls rose on either side as the tracks curved to the right and entered a tunnel. Darkness and the far end of the tunnel where cars were passing at right angles. Something about the tracks caught Bill's eye, just as they disappeared from view, yellow reflections moving along the rails . . .

"Poyest!" Train.

The yellow reflections leaped upward into a glowing head-light as the engine appeared. It was twenty yards from the tunnel headed directly toward them. Too late to turn, their only chance was to reach the street before the train.

"Go, go," Bill yelled.

It was like riding a bucking bronco, thirty feet from the road, the BMW in a bone-breaking scramble across the wood ties. The engineer saw them and the shriek of brakes joined the blast of the diesel horn. Bill's legs were outstretched, feet kicking the swerving cycle into an upright position every time it threatened to overturn. A particularly hard jolt bounced his chin against Lizaveta's helmet. Twenty feet, now ten, the diesel growing large, the engineer staring down through the glass, eyes wide, teeth gritted for the impact. Sunlight swept over them as they emerged from the tunnel. The train, slowing, lumbered into the crossing. Pavement rose beneath the BMW's tires. A sharp turn to the right and they were in the street. Bill felt the thick push of air as the train rumbled past behind them.

Lizaveta turned down one street and then another until Bill was lost. He got his bearings when they crossed the river, then lost them again. They turned into a short alley without an exit. Lizaveta parked behind a fenced enclosure filled with trash bins. She removed her helmet, shook her hair free and grinned. Her face was flushed and her eyes shone with excitement.

"Did you see it, the engineer's expression? He thought he would hit us." Her smile faded. "You are all right?"

She was speaking English. Bill replied in Russian. "You tell me. Who are you working for?"

A puzzled look replaced her smile. "You are Mischa?"

"Bill."

"But . . ."

"He's given me the language, now I want some answers. Why did you rescue me and how did you know I'd be there?"

She was staring at him in wonder. "Marina said the conversion would begin soon."

He gripped her arm. "Never mind the conversion. Whose side are you on? How did you know I'd show up at the embassy?"

"We did not know." She jerked her arm free. "We only knew the KGB had placed a trap."

"They told you?"

"Of course not. Andrei Guneyev discovered it. He was making complaints ever since your disappearance. Andrei has many friends in the old KGB, and they heard about your escape and the trap at the embassy. You should be grateful—I saved you from arrest."

"I'll be grateful when I'm back in Washington." He started toward the street.

"Where are you going?"

"Don't worry about it." What he intended was to call Claire and then go to another embassy, somewhere the KGB wouldn't be expecting him.

Lizaveta came after him. "Wait, first you must talk to Marina."

"So she can get Mischa back? It won't work. He's part of me now. And I'm in control."

"You are in danger. Major Khiza has reported that you murdered two men, and the police have an order for your arrest."

"*Two* men?"

"Dennis Riggs and a KGB man, Ivan Bulgarin."

"No, they killed Riggs. I was next on the list." Bill peered down the street, a nondescript neighborhood of multistory apartments mixed with occasional offices and shops.

Lizaveta tugged his arm. "Listen to me. Even the embassy cannot help you. Our government will ask your extradition and put you on trial for murder. It is too dangerous. You must leave Russia."

"I don't have a passport."

"There is a way."

"How?"

"Marina. She will tell you."

Bill regarded her for a moment. Her expression was earnest and her eyes met his without blinking. She was right about one thing: Inside the embassy he would be safe, but he couldn't leave it without risking arrest. There were undoubtedly ways of sneaking him out of Russia, but whether the State Department would be willing to brave the political repercussions . . .

"Where is Marina?"

"The apartment of Colonel Guneyev's son." Lizaveta pointed to the massive building behind which they parked.

A groaning elevator, its discolored indicator lights blinking laboriously, took them to the seventeenth floor. Muffled conversations and television programs echoed down a dimly lit hallway. An old woman wearing a *babushka* made no secret of her disapproval of Lizaveta's attire. Jeans and a leather jacket didn't exactly insure anonymity, Bill thought.

There was a doorbell outside apartment 1709, but Lizaveta ignored it and knocked twice. A man's voice: "Who is it?"

"Me," Lizaveta called.

The door opened cautiously, then completely. A stranger whose bushy eyebrows looked vaguely familiar said, "Come in, quickly."

If the hallways suffered from neglect, the apartment itself was overdecorated in a way that reminded Bill of a furniture showroom. No table or shelf was without a vase or figurine or a bowl of fruit, and anything made of wood was so highly polished it looked wet. The Oriental rug was protected from the feet of the matching couch and chair by what looked like upturned jelly jar lids.

Marina waited just inside the door. She came forward eagerly. "You're safe."

He pulled back from her embrace. "Your friend Khiza tried to kill me."

"Not my friend. He—" Her eyes widened as she realized he had spoken in Russian. "Bill?"

Lizaveta said, "The conversion has begun. He knows the language."

"Is it true? *Te gavarati pa-russki,* Bill?"

"I have the language, and I've got Mischa's memories. I know what you did to a helpless child, I remember the Institute, I remember the training, and I remember you."

His tone was harsh. Marina stepped back and looked at him

as if he were a stranger. The man who let them in had been regarding him suspiciously. "*This* is the man?"

Marina spoke in a subdued voice. "I'm sorry, we have been rude. This is Sergei Andreievich Guneyev, Andrei's son. And his wife, Vera."

A large-boned woman stood in the doorway to the kitchen and greeted him warily, no more happy to see Bill than her husband was.

Sergei turned to Lizaveta. "Where is my father?"

"Hasn't he called?"

"No. Was he arrested?"

Lizaveta explained quickly what had happened: While Andrei watched the embassy she waited in a cooperative garage where automotive tools were rented by the hour. She pretended to work on the wiring of the BMW until she heard Andrei's signal—a tiny beeper activated by a radio signal.

"This," Lizaveta said, displaying a gadget half the size of a matchbox. "I had it around my neck."

Bill recognized it as a beeper meant to be added to a key ring as an aid to finding misplaced keys. Sergei wasn't interested. "What about father? You didn't see if he was arrested?"

"It was too crazy."

Marina said, "If I know Andrei he'll be all right."

"My father has always inspired confidence," Sergei said stiffly, "whether it was justified by circumstances or not."

Bill sensed a tension between them that was not new. He said to Marina, "I have to get out of the country. Lizaveta says you know a way."

"It is Sergei. He works at the airport . . . a catering company."

Bill turned to him. "Will you get me out?"

Sergei said pointedly, "If my father asks it."

"How?"

Sergei told him.

CHAPTER

34

Returning to the Fox Island house Vasily Amenov felt like the cat with a mouse beneath its paw. Claire Sullivan and a man impersonating Bill had tried to fool him and failed. But why? Why would Sullivan use an intermediary? Did they know about Cain and were afraid he could activate him? Or wasn't Bill there? The more he thought about it, the more convinced he became that it was the wife who was playing games with him. Claire. She thought it was clever to put an impostor on the phone. To mock his instructions and betray the arrangement they had made. Betrayal had its price. As the tires clattered over the wood bridge leading to the island, Vasily considered what that price should be.

When he arrived at the house he found Guy Jurmon perched on the couch in front of a low table covered with Polaroid photographs. The television was blaring, a game show of some sort that Vasily turned off. "Any problems?"

"What is the capital of Burma?"

"What?"

"That was the answer. The answer to the question on the telly. They give you a word—an answer, really—and you supply the question. The answer was 'Rangoon' and so the question is 'What is the capital of Burma?' "

No, Vasily thought, the question was how long I can put up with you? "What are you doing?"

"The kidlets and me, we're doing a project. A scrapbook, a photo essay like those picture books, *A Day in the Life of Australia*. We're making *A Day in the Life of a Brother and Sister*."

He pushed the album toward Vasily. There were a couple dozen Polaroid photos of the children going about their daily business: brushing teeth, sweeping the floor, eating lunch, doing dishes. They were caught in an electronic flash, bordered by sharp shadows thrown against the wall.

Vasily said coldly, "You unchained them."

"Only one at a time. And I had the gun." Jurmon gave him a wet-lipped smile of satisfaction that made Vasily want to hit him.

He had installed Matt and Megan upstairs in the master bedroom, attached by a thirty-foot chain. The ends of the chain were looped around each child's neck and padlocked. The chain itself passed through a circular design in the wrought iron bed frame. It was a clever arrangement that allowed the captives a certain freedom of movement, including access to the bathroom. It meant there was no reason for Jurmon to risk unlocking them, but the stupid toad had done just that despite Vasily's explicit instructions to the contrary. He half suspected Jurmon had done it simply to irritate him. As he started toward the stairs Jurmon called, "They're not up there."

"Where are they?"

"In the garage. Their reward for taking pictures, they get to feed the fucking dog. Bloody animal spent the morning scratching the paint off the door."

"You left them alone in the garage?"

"They're chained to a rafter."

"What about the tool cabinet?"

"It's locked. I'm not that big a fool."

Oh, yes, you are, Vasily thought. The only reason the dog was in the garage in the first place was because Jurmon was allergic to dog hair.

The garage was separated from the house by a small patio where lawn chairs and a propane barbecue huddled beneath a redwood lean-to. As he crossed the patio Vasily's anger mounted. What if the kids started making noise? Jurmon wouldn't even hear them.

He paused to listen outside the door, then opened it. Matt and Megan were crouched beside the dog, which wagged its tail hesitantly as Vasily entered. The atmosphere was heightened, their bodies tense, expectant. Something wrong. Something was going on here.

"Having a good time with Ginger?"

"Yes."

He glanced around the windowless room. The chain linking the children was intact and looped over a rafter. The garage door was locked, the washer and dryer in the same position, cans of paint still stacked neatly on shelves, and the tool cabinet closed and locked. Everything normal except the atmosphere. Vasily could smell betrayal. Staring at them and without moving he said, "What happened over there?"

"Where?" Matt said just a bit too innocently. It was the girl who gave it away—Vasily caught her surreptitious glance toward the tool cabinet. He started toward it.

"Can we go outside?" Matt said quickly. Now Vasily was certain. He fingered the lock on the cabinet and it fell free, the hasp still attached but the screws holding it to the wood dangling loosely. There were marks in the wood where something had pried it loose.

"What happened here?"

"It was like that."

Vasily nodded and opened the cabinet. Each tool hung before a matching silhouette painted on the wall. One was missing.

"The hammer is gone," Vasily said. "Have you seen it?" The girl looked at Matt, who shook his head. "You are not a good liar, Matt. Or is it Matthew? Which does your father call you?"

"It doesn't matter."

"I asked you a question—what does your father call you, Matt or Matthew?"

"Matt, unless he's mad at me."

"Thank you, Matt. You see, I call you Matt which means I'm not angry. Only lies make me angry. The truth makes me happy. Are you happy, Matt?"

"What do you mean?"

"Well, if you're happy I'll ask you to put the hammer back where it belongs, but if you're unhappy it might be dangerous. You might swing the hammer in anger and hit your dog or your sister or perhaps even me. Do you think you would be capable of that, Matt? Striking someone with a hammer?"

Matt shook his head.

"Good. Then why don't you put the hammer back where it belongs."

Matt pulled the hammer from beneath his jacket. "I wasn't going to do anything," he mumbled, and was instantly angry with himself. Such a wimp.

"He was fixing my shoe," Megan said.

Vasily smiled. The little girl was tough. "Return the hammer, Matt."

As he passed Vasily, Matt wished he had the courage to turn and smash his captor's skull. Instead he replaced the hammer on its hooks.

"Such cooperation deserves a reward," Vasily said. He released Matt and locked the chain so that Megan was still tethered to the rafter. He picked up a basketball from beneath the workbench. "You and I will throw the basketball. You can teach me."

They went outside and stood in the driveway beneath a hoop and backboard attached to the garage. Tossing the ball from one hand to the other, Vasily walked around the boy. "Mr. Jurmon showed me pictures he took of you. Did you mind?"

"It's okay."

"You wanted the pictures taken?"

"Not really."

"Tell him not to do it. Tell people what you think, Matt. Don't despise them from a distance." He stopped in front of the boy. "Come right up close, look them in the eye and tell them: 'I want to put a hammer through your skull.' "

Matt stepped back and said stiffly, "Are we going to play?"

"That's it. Assert yourself. This is America and all American boys like to play basketball. Even your father. He had a basketball hoop attached to the side of his house when he was growing up, did you know that?"

"You knew Dad in Kansas?"

Vasily tossed the ball to Matt. "Let's play baskets, is that how you say it?"

"Shoot baskets."

"Shoot?" He drew a gun from his pocket and Matt tensed. "Like this?" He aimed at the backboard and pulled the trigger. Chips flew and Matt flinched. Vasily smiled and held the gun out to him. "Would you like to try it?"

Over the ringing in his ears Matt heard Megan call his name from the garage.

"I'm okay," he yelled.

Jurmon appeared at the front door, flushed with alarm, a gun in his hand. "What happened?"

"We are shooting baskets," Vasily said.

"You're out of your bloody mind. What if someone hears?"

"Who, the seagulls?"

Jurmon's face contorted in a violent sneeze that sprayed mucus across his lip. He disappeared inside. Vasily returned the gun to his pocket. "So, we will shoot the basket in the correct manner. You will demonstrate."

"I don't want to." Matt tossed the ball back to him.

"I'm not asking you what you want. I'm telling you to shoot baskets."

"I'm no good."

"Show me." Vasily threw the ball as hard as he could into the boy's chest. Taken by surprise, Matt stumbled backward, his foot caught on the edge of the pavement, and he sat down heavily. Vasily recovered the ball.

"Get up. Here, show me how to bounce it. What is it called? Drizzle the ball?"

"Dribble."

"I see. I used the wrong word. You think I'm stupid, don't you?"

"You don't play sports much."

"No, Matt, I don't play sports, you are right. Show me how to dribble."

Matt reluctantly bounced the ball.

"Did your father teach you to dribble?"

"And we do it at school."

"Now shoot a basket."

Matt took aim and sent the basketball in an arc. It struck the rim and bounced free. He started toward it, then glanced at Vasily, who nodded. "Go, yes, get the ball."

I could just keep running, Matt thought. But he couldn't leave Megan and he knew that Vasily would catch him or shoot him if he tried to escape. He scooped the ball from the street. Vasily held out his hand and Matt tossed him the ball. He began to dribble slowly. "Tell me about your mother, Matt. Is she an honest woman?"

"Yeah."

"A brave woman?"

"I guess."

"What scares your mother?"

"I don't know."

"Think."

"I don't know."

Vasily flung the basketball at him. This time Matt blocked with his hands and the ball careened off the side of the garage. In two quick strides Vasily retrieved it. "Would she be scared of this ball?"

"No."

"Not even if it broke your nose? Here, put your hands at your sides."

"What're you going to do?"

"Put your hands down."

"I can't."

"You know what a psychiatrist once told me? A man can be made to do anything given either positive or negative motivation. People do things to feel good or to escape feeling bad. Right

now you have a choice, you can follow instructions and feel
good or I can make it painful and you will follow instructions to
escape the pain. How shall we play our game, Matthew?"

Matt lowered his hands from his face. He was trembling with
anger and fear. Vasily smiled and hefted the ball.

"You see, you can do many things if you are not a coward."

He swung the ball at the boy, but at the last minute lofted it
into the air. Matt's hands flew to his face. The ball dropped
through the hoop. Vasily watched the boy coldly. "You are afraid
of a basketball. What does your mother fear?"

"I don't know."

"You live with her. Of course you know. Tell me what she
fears." He began to dribble in a circle around Matt. "Does light-
ning make her cry?"

"No."

"What makes her cry?"

"I don't know." Vasily stopped moving and his expression
grew cold. Matt said quickly, "Sad movies, when King died,
when the china bell broke . . ."

The ball began bouncing again. "Who is King?"

"Our first dog."

"And the china bell?"

"It was a wedding gift. It sat on the breakfront until a baby-
sitter broke it."

"When did she cry recently?"

"When she caught her finger in the door of the car."

The ball stopped bouncing. "Her finger? When was this?"

"A couple of months ago."

"See how much help you can be when you want to be?" He
turned and walked away.

Do something, Matt thought. But he felt paralyzed. "Inside,"
Vasily called from the door. "The game is over."

Jurmon was in front of the television. Vasily said to Matt, "Sit
down."

"I want to go back to the garage."

Vasily pushed him into the chair and went into the kitchen.
Jurmon smiled at him. "Have fun?"

"No."

"I don't blame you. Exercise makes sweat, sweat makes you stink. We don't like stinky people, do we?"

Vasily returned with a roll of tape and a clothes line. He taped Matt's ankles, then tied one end of the line between his feet. He handed the other end to Jurmon. "Keep him here."

Matt's voice quavered. "What are you going to do?"

No answer. The fat man tugged the line. "Hi, doggie."

Matt craned to see Vasily, who had returned to the kitchen. He took a heavy carving knife and moved to the garage.

Matt jumped up and yelled, "Megan!"

Jurmon yanked the line, pulling his feet out from under him. "Whoa, doggie."

On the floor, Matt rolled to his stomach in time to see Vasily disappear. "Megan, watch out!"

He got to his knees, but Jurmon yanked his feet again. He was dancing around Matt now, tugging the line, calling "Whoa, doggie, whoa, doggie."

There was a yelp from Ginger, then Megan screamed. Matt grabbed the rope and pulled it. Jurmon stumbled forward. "Bad doggie!" He looped the rope over his shoulder and ran full tilt toward the opposite side of the room. Matt was leaning forward to untie the knot when his ankles were jerked away, flinging him onto his back. His head struck the floor and sent sparks pinwheeling before his eyes. Megan's second scream was a blood-curdling cry.

CHAPTER
35

Roy's failure to tell her that he had involved the FBI left Claire feeling more vulnerable and more alone than before. Resolved to find Bill herself, she made a call to the State Department, where one official told her that another official was at lunch and asked her to call back. No sooner did she hang up the phone than it rang. Half-expecting someone from the invisible surveillance team to ask for "Agent Patchin," she answered brusquely, "Who is it?"

"Claire?"

"Bill, thank God." Hearing his voice made her giddy with relief. "Are you back, where are you?"

"Still in Russia but I'm on my way out."

"You're not—"

"What about Matt and Megan?"

She told him in a quick rush of words. When he heard how

Roy's deception had failed his voice quivered with an anger she had never heard before. "You let Roy impersonate me?"

"We couldn't find you. I thought if we found out what the kidnapper wants—"

"Me, Claire. He wants me! And now he knows you tricked him, do you know what he's capable of? Do you know what he'll do to a child?"

"Then why aren't you here? Why aren't you—" Her voice cracked and she was crying. "Yes, I know what he's going to do, he's going to kill them, he's going to kill my babies—"

"Claire." The voice had changed. It was low, controlled, familiar. "Claire, listen. The man who took our children is not Jeremy Lawrence, his name is Vasily Amenov and he's . . . related to me."

"Related how?"

"Too complicated. It's dangerous to talk too long."

"Where are you?"

"I can't say. Now listen, does Amenov know I'm in Russia?"

"Who? Oh, he didn't give me a chance to tell him."

"But the kids know?"

"They think you went back to Kansas. That's why he expected you back when he called. And he hung up before I had a chance to explain where you were and that I couldn't reach you . . ."

"That's better. Better he doesn't know. When he calls back don't tell him where I've been and don't tell him you know his real name."

"He might not call again, Bill. That's what I'm afraid of."

"Yes, he will. He wants me and he'll call back until he gets me. When he does, tell him I'm on my way home from Kansas, I'll be there tomorrow morning."

"Is that true?"

"If it's not, someone will contact you with a message. Otherwise I'll be there. In the meantime I want you to call the American embassy in Moscow and tell them something. Tell them that I will give myself up to a representative from the embassy, and I want to formally charge a KGB major named Gennadi Khiza with attempted murder."

"Murder? What are you—?"

"Diversionary tactic, don't worry."

Her confidence returned. This was the Bill she remembered, acutely aware of his environment, thinking three steps ahead of all possible events.

"You want to accuse who of murder?"

"Attempted murder. Gennadi Khiza." He spelled it for her. "Call right away and get the ball rolling. Tell them I'm going to call you back in three hours, you don't know where I am, you have no other information, just keep them making arrangements, okay?"

"Just hurry up and get here."

"Keep the faith, I'm on my way."

I love you, she thought, but already he was gone.

The tea had grown cold and the footsteps in the apartment above had become part of the inconsequential background noise of the building. Bill and Marina were alone in the apartment. Sergei and his wife had left to pick up Andrei, who had phoned from a shop a few blocks from the embassy. Lizaveta had gone to buy Bill a sportcoat and tie for the trip home. For the past twenty minutes Marina had told Bill everything she knew about Yelena Amenov and Jeremy Lawrence—his real mother and father— and the man who had kidnapped his children, Vasily Amenov.

"Why?" Bill said tightly. "Why would he hurt them if it's me he hates?"

He sat on the couch, his eyes focused on a chipped piece of wood in the parquet floor. Marina was in the chair opposite him.

"For the same reason he caused you to hold a burning match between your teeth—to punish you."

The words drew forth a memory, his father's face, his expression set in stone, words dripping venom, ". . . you're going to hold it until the flame burns out . . ."

Not his father, he corrected. Vasily Amenov was his stepfather. A wave of hatred and fear washed over him, hatred for what the man had done to him in the past and fear for what he might do to Matt and Megan.

"If he hurts my children I'll kill him."

Marina's face clouded. "You should not have contact with him. Not until you have complete control over the Cain impulse."

"There is no Cain. No more Mischa. They're all part of me."

"As are the years of training. Vasily Amenov's presence, even his voice, these are powerful triggers that you need to disarm before you confront the man."

Bill jumped up and went to the window. "I don't know what you're talking about."

"Then why are you angry?"

"I'm not angry, I just want to get home and find my children."

"Your anger is there. So is rage, frustration, fear, terror, cruelty—emotions you never dealt with before but must recognize now as part of you. Otherwise you will remain a partial like Frank Johnson."

"Who?"

"The patient you met at the institute. You remember him?"

Bill recoiled at the thought of the old man pushing the Safeway cart.

"Delay your escape," Marina continued. "Forty-eight hours only. Give me time to analyze the effects of the electro-shock, give yourself time to recover from the conversion . . ."

"No."

"You don't know the danger."

"I know the danger to my children if I don't return."

"What if it's not you who returns? We don't know that the conversion is permanent."

Bill said slowly, "It may not last?"

"Your dissociative pathology was unique, Bill, as was our intervention. I don't know if the catalyst for what has happened was your own will or the—"

Before she could finish, the door opened and Vera stepped into the room, followed by Andrei, who was in his wheelchair with Sergei guiding it. A violin case sat on the old man's lap. He was grinning, his exhilaration at odds with his son's somber demeanor.

"You made it," he said to Bill. "And you are Russian now, this what Sergei says."

"I *speak* Russian."

Andrei slapped the arm of his chair in delight. "You should have seen the militia when you got away. They were wild with each other, pointing fingers and shouting blame, it was wonderful." His grin faded at Marina's expression. "What's wrong?"

"They gave him electro-shock. Bill and Mischa have integrated and the Cain impulse is no longer isolated."

"That's good, yes? That's what we wanted."

"Not using such methods. We cannot know what peripheral damage was done or if the conversion is permanent. We need time for testing and evaluation."

"I'm out of time," Bill said firmly. "And so are my children." He turned to Andrei. "Will you help me escape?"

Andrei looked to Marina. When she hesitated, Bill said, "With or without your help I'm leaving. Now."

Marina bit her lip and nodded. "One favor in return. If he is still there, may I speak to him one last time?"

It took him a moment before he realized what she meant. "Mischa?"

"If he can still take the spot . . ."

Bill closed his eyes, relaxed and sent a silent call for Mischa. Nothing. He imagined falling backward into a swimming pool with eyes closed and he sensed him then, Mischa, everywhere and nowhere. He opened his eyes. "I'm sorry."

She smiled sadly. "As I thought. My Mischa is gone now and I never said goodbye."

They waited another ten minutes until Lizaveta arrived with a coat and tie. The coat didn't match Bill's pants but it made him look more like a businessman and the tie covered the bruises on his throat. Andrei added a pair of reading glasses and Sergei gave him a knit cap, which was as much a disguise as Bill wanted. False mustaches and cheek inserts could sometimes attract more attention than an average face kept in the shadows.

Before they left, Marina gave Bill a worn, leather-bound journal with gilt edges. "Take this and put it in a safe place. Keep it secret and the KGB won't dare touch you."

"What is it?"

"The first journal of the Sorin Project. I have eleven of them, but this will tell you about yourself and the scope of our work. Your birth record, I suppose."

Bill gripped Marina's hand, warm and weathered with age but still firm. He saw her as a younger woman with black hair, bidding him farewell in an earlier time, her eyes filled with the same affection. Bill leaned down and embraced her. *"Tyotya Marina,"* he whispered. Aunt Marina.

Claire had already talked to two people at the embassy in Moscow when she heard the car pull into the driveway. She had the front door open before the messenger in his brown uniform reached the house. Behind him a station wagon with the name of a messenger service: District Courier. "Claire Sullivan?"

"That's me."

"Sign here, number six."

He held out a clipboard with a number of names on it. In his other hand he carried a small package wrapped in plain brown paper and tied with twine.

"Who's it from?" Claire asked.

"On the packing slip." He cocked his head and read: "Bill Sullivan, eighteen hundred G Street."

She signed for the package and took it to the kitchen table. Her quick surge of anticipation was overtaken by questions: What could Bill be sending her? When had he contacted Secret Service headquarters? Why hadn't he said anything over the phone? The twine was wrapped tight and she needed a knife to cut it. The paper peeled away and she caught her breath. An illustration from the Baby Sitter's Club, three teenage girls laughing: one of them white, one Oriental, one African-American.

Megan's plastic lunch box.

Don't open it. Claire backed away and stared at the box. Her hand found the phone and she called Roy at his office. When he came on the line his voice was low and tentative. "Claire? Did you hear anything?"

"Did you send me something?"

"What do you mean?"

"In Bill's name. I just got a package from 1800 G Street. Megan's lunch box."

"Her lunch box? Sent from this building?"

"That's what the packing slip says."

"When was this?"

"It just arrived. Did you—did someone find . . . Megan?"

"Claire, we haven't found anybody. What about the box? Is there a note?"

"I don't know. I haven't opened it."

"All right, listen to me, don't touch it. I'll have someone there in a few minutes. Just leave it alone, you understand?"

Claire wasn't listening. She placed the receiver on the table and ignored Roy's voice, tiny and imperative. *I have to know.* She was methodical and careful. She rummaged through her drawers and found a pair of gloves so as not to disturb any fingerprints. Then she unsnapped first one latch then the other and lifted the lid. Crumpled newspapers. She lifted them out until, in the center, loosely wrapped white tissue paper. As she unfolded it a discoloration appeared, a rust-colored line that followed the telltale ripple of paper once wet and now dried. The paper tore and two objects slipped to the table, one on top of the other.

Gloves, she thought, unwilling to recognize the truth until the blood-encrusted ridge and familiar red hair forced her to do so. She shut her eyes a long moment. *I will not be sick.* When she opened her eyes this time she knew what she would find: Ginger's ears.

CHAPTER

36

The plan was simple enough. Sergei Guneyev was a supervisor for AeroMar Catering, which provided Delta Air Lines its in-flight meals. AeroMar was relatively new, a joint venture between Aeroflot and the Marriott Hotel Corporation. Sergei could sneak Bill onto Flight 31, a nonstop to New York—if he would. Bill was beginning have his doubts. Sergei drove silently, hunched over the wheel, his expression grim. At a red light he slammed on the brakes; they stopped next to a police car. The movement was so abrupt that the officer looked over at them with a frown.

Here it goes, Bill thought, if Sergei is trying to get us caught, here's his chance. Sergei ignored the police and when the light changed he rocketed away. Bill said, "Are you trying to draw attention to us?"

He didn't respond but his driving slowed somewhat. Finally he said, "Did my father take you to his apartment?"

"No."

"The same apartment where I grew up. My mother died in that apartment. She loved flowers, but Marina has not the patience for them. Now there are only photographs. The bookcase is filled with them—pictures of me and my brothers and sisters, graduation pictures, a wedding picture of Marina and my father, grandchildren—but among them all is a silver frame without a picture. An expensive frame, always polished. She has time for *that*." He gave a sour laugh. "When people ask them 'Why an empty frame?' do you know what they say? 'A portrait of our fantasy child.' Because Marina was too old to have children. My brothers and sisters, we all thought it was a harmless illusion."

They stopped again at a traffic light and Sergei turned to look at him. "But an illusion would not endanger his life, would it?"

"Illusions can be stronger than reality. I think your father knows that."

"My father's heart condition is not an illusion. He will require bypass surgery, a dangerous operation in this country but standard procedure at the Stanford Medical Center in California."

"Is that where he's going?"

"I can get him a free ticket to America, but rubles will not pay for such an operation."

Bill regarded Sergei. With his florid face and features barricaded against expression he seemed a throwback to the oldstyle Soviet man. *Glasnost* had come to politics, but people like Sergei were still closed in mind and spirit.

"Help me get home, Sergei Andreievich, and I'll make certain your father gets the medical attention he needs."

A slight relaxation of tension around the mouth and eyes. They were on the open highway now. A ridge of autumn leaves, brown and dirty, lay windswept along the side of the road. As they approached the airport Sergei said, "I can't take you inside the security perimeter without identification. You will wait at a bus stop outside the terminal until I return with the service truck."

Sergei had already explained how it would work: Because the ramp area was undergoing reconstruction there were times when service vehicles found it quicker to take the public road from one end of the terminal to the other. This is what Sergei would do shortly before Delta's Flight 31 was ready for service.

Bill sat with a changing group of travelers hauling luggage on and off buses. He felt conspicuous carrying only a small canvas bag Lizaveta had given him to carry Marina's diary. Fifty minutes later Sergei returned in a silver truck with a wavelike logo in black. Bill climbed inside, glad for the warmth. The Russian was wearing a uniform whose flamboyance didn't match his mood: vivid purple slacks and sportcoat, white shirt and a burgundy tie.

"The cart directly behind me," Sergei said tersely. "Quickly or they will notice the truck is missing."

Too narrow, Bill thought when he saw it. The food service cart was like an oversize suitcase on wheels, four feet tall, six feet deep, with the inner walls lined with plastic lips for food trays. But unlike a suitcase, the door was a narrow rectangle.

"I put a blanket on the floor for your knees," Sergei said over his shoulder. "Can you fit inside?"

Bill tried, but found it impossible while the cart was upright. He lay it on its side and squeezed inside, his body as flat as a frog beneath a rock. He pulled Marina's diary after him. "Okay."

Sergei pulled to the side of the road. He grunted heavily as he lifted the cart onto its tiny wheels. Gravity wedged Bill against his left shoulder and knee. He should have removed the Marakov pistol, which, tucked beneath his belt, dug painfully into his abdomen. Sergei peered in at him. "All right?"

"Just make it quick."

"Remember your promise to my father. And no noise."

The metal door clicked shut, wrapping him in darkness. No noise? He could hardly breath, much less make noise. The ridges designed to hold the trays bit his ribs as the truck rejoined the traffic. From now on he could monitor his progress only by ear. They paused once, a muffled exchange, then moved forward. The truck felt as if it lurched over a log, although it was probably only some sort of speed bump. The road was smoother inside the perimeter.

The truck arrived at a loading dock. The rear door opened and light seeped around the frame of the cart. Sergei was the crew chief. Bill heard him giving instructions, felt the rattle and bump of other carts.

"What's that one?" someone called.

"Spare cart for the peanuts," Sergei said. "It's not going."

Bill listened carefully. Sergei had told him that loose supplies were often transported in a spare cart. More chatter, the muffled complaints and banter of workers who would never eat the meals they delivered, never fly in the planes they serviced. The cart shook as caterers climbed aboard and shut the doors. A different driver took them to the airplane, someone whose abrupt movements jammed Bill's head against the door and made it hard to breath. Already his left arm was numb from lack of circulation. There was no way to unlatch the door from the inside and he felt a new appreciation for the horror of children accidentally trapped and suffocated in abandoned refrigerators.

The truck stopped at the plane. This was where armed security guards collected identification cards from each person who entered the plane and returned them only to the same individual. A leftover card meant someone was still aboard the aircraft, a simple, failsafe system. Sergei would have no trouble getting aboard, but if Bill was discovered . . .

The slam and bang of the carts was reassuring. Someone maneuvered Bill's cart out of the cab onto a lift that jerked and whined its way up to the loading door. The tiny wheels banged across the threshold, jamming Bill so firmly he thought he would choke. *God damn it, Sergei.* But it wasn't Sergei who said, "Careful, Kulygin."

"Fucking cart's got a bum wheel."

"It's only peanuts."

"What?"

Now Sergei's voice, cold and brusque. "What are you doing? I told you to get the fruit plates."

"Boris has them."

"Then check the wine manifest. One of the seals is broken, we may be short."

"A seal broken?"

"Shit, another inspection . . ."

The cart was moving again now, quickly, bumping down the

aisle, away from complaining voices and potential discovery. It bumped against something, shifted back and forth, then stopped. The latch clicked open and light caused Bill to squint.

"Hurry up," Sergei hissed.

They were blocked from sight by the rear cabin wall, but the aircraft was alive with the sound of crew preparation and at any moment someone might appear in one of the two aisles. Bill felt like a turtle trying to push free of its shell. His left foot was numb and gave way as soon as he tried to stand. Sergei caught him, dislodging the Marakov from his belt. The gun fell to the floor. Sergei stepped back in horror, eyes flashing wildly to the aisles.

Bill knelt, tossed the gun into the bag with the diary and lurched into the closest lavatory. Without saying goodbye in word or glance, Sergei shut the door behind him. To lock it would signal his presence; all Bill could do was wait and hope that nobody in the catering crew felt the call of nature.

He lowered himself quietly to the covered toilet and massaged his ankle. If he was discovered now at least he was on board an American carrier. The Russians could keep the plane from leaving, but they couldn't remove him by force. Not legally, anyway, but Khiza and his KGB friends hadn't shown any particular respect for legal niceties so far. At least he still had the gun, although how he could use it he wasn't certain.

He waited. Every time someone passed the door he tensed. When the caterers were there he heard Sergei's voice ordering them around, keeping an eye on them. An American voice joined them, the Delta steward checking supplies and confirming Sergei's manifest. After that came the flight crew, American voices, relaxed, carefree, as out of place in Russia as a rose at the North Pole.

The passengers arrived. Bill tucked the gun out of sight, stood up and raised the toilet seat. For half an hour he stood there as if taking a pee. If anyone opened the door he might get away pretending he was a passenger. He waited until the aircraft's door bumped shut and they began to push back from the terminal. Then he opened the door and stepped into the path of a flight attendant. She blinked in surprise, but before she could start making deductions Bill took the initiative. He pressed a hand to his stomach and said, "Do you have anything for an upset stomach?"

Her eyes cleared of confusion, "I'll see if I can find something. Where are you sitting?"

A good question. Luckily the plane was only three-quarters full. "I was back here," Bill said, indicating the smoking section, "But I thought I'd change to one of those nonsmoking seats."

"We're all buttoned up so take your pick. I'll see if we've got some aspirin."

The plane was a Boeing 767, an American plane, American flight crew, lumbering down the taxiway to freedom. Bill took an aisle seat. As soon as they were airborne he took out Marina's diary and began a journey into his past while the aircraft climbed through the clouds to his future.

CHAPTER

37

On one of the most glorious nights of the year, with a spectacular view of cities marching past a few thousand feet below him, FBI Agent Dominic Vincour was in a piss-poor mood. For one thing, he was missing his parents' fiftieth wedding anniversary. For another, this afternoon's phone-call intercept of the kidnapper had been hopelessly screwed up by the Secret Service guy, Roy Patchin. And now Bill Sullivan had returned to the United States carrying a pistol instead of a passport and no identification at all.

When Sullivan left the country, the FBI had added his name to the computerized "watch list" that Immigration officers checked when processing United States citizens. When he showed up asking for a passport waiver he was taken into custody. It was a measure of the man's importance that Vincour had been able to requisition one of the Bureau's Bell Jet Ranger helicopters to fly to New York. The cities unrolled below like glittering beacons in the night—Washington, Baltimore, Philadelphia, Atlantic City—but Vincour was in no mood to appreciate them. A veteran of nine years in the Bureau's Counterespionage Division, it was his experience that traitors wanted one of four things: self-esteem, money, revenge or martyrdom. The fifth category—idealism—had died with the failure of communism. Nobody did anything for ideas any more, just ego and frustrated ambition. But Sullivan fit none of these categories, and with each new piece of information things made less sense, not more.

The copilot tapped Vincour's knee and pointed. The spire of the Empire State Building was visible surrounded by a sea of lights, Manhattan rising from the dark borders of its two rivers, the broad Hudson on the left, and the bridge-crossed East River to the right. The helicopter veered toward Long Island, where the running-ball approach lights pinpointed JFK International Airport.

Five minutes later Vincour was following the Immigration duty officer through a labyrinth of hallways in the lower level of the international terminal.

"Not even an airline ticket," the duty officer was saying. "The guy steps off a plane with a loaded gun in his pocket and that's it."

A uniformed airport security guard opened the holding cell, an overlit room with a couch, two chairs and a water fountain, all bolted to the floor. Bill had been pacing the floor. When he saw Vincour his distaste was apparent. "You? Where's Roy?"

Vincour still hadn't decided on a strategy, but in the face of Sullivan's belligerence he took an aggressive approach. "I'm in charge of your case, not Roy Patchin. You want to cooperate, I can have you home in two hours. Otherwise I can have you arrested, it's up to you."

"On what grounds?"

"False statement on your Secret Service application. Carrying a concealed firearm on board an aircraft."

"I've got a license."

"Not to carry a firearm without identifying it to the flight crew."

"My kids are in danger and you're feeding me this bullshit?" He moved to the door, but the duty officer blocked his path. Bill was running out of patience. All his life he had been a man on the inside, someone allowed where others could not enter, a man whose special responsibilities conferred special privileges. But now, with his children's lives at stake, they were treating him like a criminal . . .

"Get out of my way."

"You arrived without a passport and without identification, sir. We have the right to hold you until positive identification can be made."

"You heard *him*," Bill said, indicating Vincour. "He knows me."

The FBI man said, "I'm not positive yet. Suppose you answer a few questions to prove who you are?"

"Suppose you go fuck yourself," Bill said angrily. "My children are kidnapped and you're playing games with their lives."

"I know all about your children."

"Then you know I've got to be home when the kidnapper calls."

"Let me tell you something. The Bureau is in charge of two investigations—the kidnapping of your children is one, your espionage activities are the other."

"There are no espionage activities."

"You're either a traitor or a spy, Sullivan, that much is clear. Now why don't you—"

A hot anger erupted and before he could stop himself, Bill's hand flashed out and grabbed the FBI man by the throat. "You hurt my children I swear I'll—"

No good. Even as the duty officer moved toward him the burst of rage vanished. Bill released Vincour and stepped back, dismayed and angry at his own loss of control. *Cain.* Marina's warning came back to him

"You said I had no cause for arrest?" Vincour said as he

straightened his shirt. "How about assault and battery against an officer of the federal government? We even have a witness."

"What do you want out of me?"

"Answers. You want to go home? I'll trade you a free ride for some answers. Like why did you go to Russia?"

"To see your man in Moscow."

"He wasn't our—" Vincour caught himself. Was Sullivan trying to bait him? He couldn't quite get a fix on the man, who seemed different from their first meeting, more volatile, less controlled . . .

"Why did you want to talk to Dennis Riggs?"

"Same reason you want to talk to me, to find out who I am."

"What did you find out?"

"You won't believe me."

"Try me."

Rather than answer, Bill retrieved Marina's worn journal from the couch. They had confiscated the gun, but Bill argued the journal's return. He had spent most of the flight reading it, alternately amazed that he could read Russian and sickened at the incidents of abuse he discovered. He found them mirrored in the dark corners of his memory, events so charged with pain that he put the journal aside more than once to fight the black rage they inspired. The journal would be more compelling than anything he could say.

The FBI man opened it and frowned. "It's in Russian."

"A Russian wrote it, what do you expect? Now let's go."

Vincour shook his head. "This could be anything, cookie recipes, whatever. I want some answers—like what you talked about with Riggs and what happened to your passport and where'd you get the gun?"

"Talk to me after you read that."

"No dice."

Bill had no intention of trying to explain piecemeal something as complex as the Sorin Project. Each answer would generate ten new questions and only convince Vincour he was lying. "Then arrest me."

"Don't tempt me."

"Do it. You'll have to read me my Miranda rights and let me make a phone call which will be to Washington so I can let them know how badly you're fucking up."

"You're wasting your time. I spoke to the director before I came up here, he's already up to speed."

"I'm not calling him, I'm calling the President."

Vincour's eyes widened, then narrowed. "Bullshit."

Bill recited a phone number and said, "That's the White House switchboard. You want to dial it or shall I?"

The Immigration officer looked to Vincour, whose voice betrayed his uncertainty. "The President's not going to talk to you."

"I saved the family pet from eating rat poison, he signs his Christmas Card in person, my children had Easter pictures taken with the First Lady. You want to call or shall I?"

Vincour stared at him a long moment. "I get you home, you answer questions fully, completely and without reservation. Is it a deal?"

"As long as I'm there when the phone rings, I'll answer all the questions you want."

Vincour turned to the duty officer. "What do I sign?"

The bathroom was dark, with only a rectangle of light from the bedroom falling across the floor. Matt lay with his ear pressed to the heating vent. He had discovered that he could hear conversations in the room below. Vasily Amenov had just returned and Matt was hoping for some information about his parents or the kidnappers' plans. Instead, it was Jurmon's voice, raised in complaint. "How can I control them when you undermine my authority? You tell the boy he doesn't have to pose for photographs—"

"I don't want photographs."

"Well what am I supposed to do out here? It's fucking boring sitting around all day with my thumb up my arse waiting for you to make up your mind . . ."

The voices faded as the men moved to another part of the house. Matt knew what he was talking about. This afternoon, after Vasily left the house, Jurmon had appeared in the bedroom with his Polaroid camera. "We're missing a picture in our family album. Can you guess what it is?"

Matt and Megan said nothing.

"Come on, what do all little boys and girls do in the morning?"

Matt sensed that Vasily was the more dangerous of the kidnappers, but something about this man Jurmon made his skin crawl. He didn't like the way he looked at Megan, who sat on the bed, hands around her knees. To deflect Jurmon's attention Matt ventured an answer. "They eat breakfast?"

"Before that."

"Brush their teeth."

"Before that—*usually*."

"I don't know," Matt said woodenly.

"Take a pee," Jurmon announced triumphantly. "That's what's missing from our little photo essay, the essence of good health, eliminating poisons." His lips formed a reptilian Cupid's bow smile that galvanized Matt to a level of resistance he hadn't felt before.

"You can't take pictures of us anymore. The other guy said so."

The smile oozed shut. "The other guy's not here, is he?"

"Just leave us alone."

Jurmon thrust out his lower lip in a mock pout and turned to Megan. "Listen to how your brother talks. He's not being very polite, now, is he?"

It was then that Matt began banging his head against the top of the wrought-iron bedstand. He had overheard Vasily warning Jurmon not to touch him or Megan, so he kept on banging his head and repeating, "Leave us alone," until Jurmon backed out of the room and stood glaring from the hallway.

Thinking about it now, Matt felt a glow of satisfaction. He returned to the bedroom, the chain dragging behind him, one end locked around his neck. Megan lay curled beneath a blanket on the bed. Earlier she had told him what happened in the garage, how Vasily had kicked Ginger in the head, dragged the dog out of Megan's reach and stabbed it. The man's back was toward her and she hadn't realized that Ginger had been mutilated and Matt didn't tell her. The only reason he knew was because he had watched from the bedroom window when Vasily buried the animal beyond the perimeter of the yard.

"What are they saying?" Megan asked.

"Nothing much." The bedsprings squeaked as he sat down. Megan's neck was red beneath the chain necklace. "Are you okay?"

"I was thinking, if Ginger goes to heaven is it just a dog heaven or are people there too?"

"I guess there's people."

"She'll be scared of people now."

"Not people in heaven. She won't be scared of them."

"Will she remember us if they kill us?"

"They're not going to kill us," he said quickly. "Don't talk crazy."

"They killed Ginger."

"I'm going to get us out of here." He got off the bed and walked to the window, the chain sliding across the floor behind him.

Mist rose from the bay, blurring the lights on the far shore. It seemed so unfair that just a few miles away people were living normal lives, eating dinner, watching television, kidding around and laughing, without any idea there were people in trouble so close to them. The chain rattled as Megan came near. "Why are they different?"

"What?"

"Those blinking lights."

"They're buoys marking the ship's channel."

"I know, but they're different. See that one, it goes white then green, but that one out there just goes white and red back and forth."

"Red is one side of the channel and green is the other. I forget which is—" Matt stopped, struck by a thought. "Wait a minute, I got an idea. Go back to the bed."

"Why?"

"I need enough chain to reach the light switch."

The links rattled through the bedstand as Matt crossed to the switch by the door. He turned them off.

"Don't, Matt."

"Shhh."

"What are you doing?"

"Do you think they can hear this?" He clicked the lights back on.

"Leave them on."

"No, I'm signaling." He began intervals, three short followed by three long.

"Signaling who?"

"Whoever's out there. That house at the other end of the island." He continued working the light switch.

Downstairs, Vasily was doing his best to ignore Guy Jurmon, who was still complaining about the children. "I'm not a fucking baby-sitter, I came here to shoot a snuff film and we don't need two kids to do it."

Vasily sat as still as a statue in the living room, his eyes closed. The stomach cramps had returned, a sign that the cancer had renewed its assault on his body. He had used up the last of the medication he'd brought from Russia and was attempting to lessen the pain by willing it away.

"You hear what I'm saying?" Jurmon demanded.

Vasily replied without opening his eyes. "Do you have any painkillers?"

"What? Got a headache, have you?"

I have you, Vasily thought grimly. When he didn't respond, Jurmon moved closer and his tone became more calculating. "You don't look so good, you know that? White as a bloody ghost."

Vasily's eyes opened. "Do you have anything or not?"

"Got some Perkies and some Blue Moons, those ought to cheer you up."

Something about Jurmon's expression reminded Vasily of a child holding a grasshopper under water.

"Never mind," he said. He got up and went out to the front porch, where he breathed deeply and tried to imagine the damp, sea air cleaning his system of disease. A distant foghorn, low and mournful, was like a wounded animal calling his name. A faint illumination on the nearest sand dunes, then gone, the effect of the lighthouse at the eastern edge of the island . . .

But it didn't match the lighthouse code and the illumination wasn't coming from behind the dunes but from above, like the moon, but it wasn't the moon, not with that pattern. He stepped out from beneath the porch and looked up. The rim of the window of the master bedroom told the tale: light flashing three times quickly, three times more slowly, an SOS

Vasily took the stairs two at a time and burst into the room. The kids must have heard him coming; they were both sitting on the bed, anxious eyes on him as he grabbed a chair and advanced with it over his head. They scrambled out of reach, but his target was the overhead light. Vasily smashed it, then went into the bathroom and broke the light above the sink. He returned to the bedroom, where Matt tried to shelter his sister. Vasily reached past him, grabbed the lamp beside the bed and hurled it against the far wall. Without saying a word, he walked out and slammed the door, plunging the room into darkness.

Everything I do is wrong, Matt thought. He was trembling and tears of frustration stung his eyes. Everything I do is wrong.

In the caretaker's cottage Ruby was making tea. She stood at the counter, adding tea bags to a steaming ceramic pot. Through the window she saw Matt's signal, but at first paid no attention— just another light blinking off. And on. And then off again. She paused to watch. A short circuit? No, it was too regular.

"What's the signal for SOS?" she called to Anntek, who was in the other room. "Three long and three short, right?"

"That's what they taught us in Girl Scouts."

"Someone's signaling from the Chalmers place. What do you think?"

Anntek came into the room and peered over her shoulder. The light had stopped. "I thought it was an SOS," Ruby said uncertainly.

Anntek held up two fingers. "How many fingers."

"As many as I like."

It was a private phrase they used to mock society at large. Anntek playfully wriggled her fingers and turned away. Ruby lifted the soggy bags of Celestial Seasonings's Sleepytime tea and dropped them in the sink. It had begun to drizzle now, a fine mist that gathered on the window in tiny droplets and inched down the pane.

I'll check the place in the morning, she decided. Then she took the tray into the bedroom where Anntek waited.

CHAPTER

38

It was after midnight by the time Bill arrived home. He had convinced Vincour to let him call Claire from the helicopter, and she had the door open and was in his arms before the FBI agent was out of the car. Holding her close, feeling her body pressed next to his, inhaling the scent of her hair, Bill felt whole again. And yet he was aware of an alternate set of impressions—the thrill of a strange woman's body—which were not his but Mischa's, responses that spread like smoke before the wind as they were absorbed into his own responses.

Vincour coughed politely. "You mind if we go inside?"

Bill and Claire separated, but their fingers remained intertwined. Bill said, "It's late. We'll talk tomorrow."

"Tonight. That was the deal."

"My husband just got home," Claire said. "Can't you wait until tomorrow?"

"I'm on your side, Mrs. Sullivan, but what I've got to find out is what side your husband is on."

"It's all right," Bill said to her, and for the briefest moment Claire thought she saw in his eyes the kind of frank admiration men reserve for chance meetings with attractive women. Then it was gone and Claire decided it was only the jacket and tie that she had never seen before that made Bill seem unfamiliar.

There was another FBI agent in the car, a nondescript young man named Wilson who had met the helicopter at Dulles International Airport. He greeted Claire with a false smile and stiff handshake and stared into every corner as if memorizing the house. Bill waved the FBI men to seats while he and Claire sat on the couch facing them.

"I'll give you three things tonight," Bill said, "the rest after you read the journal. First, the fire in Goodheart that killed Dan and Betsy Sullivan was not an accident. It was murder."

"Your parents?"

"They weren't my parents. I never knew them." Claire's fingers tightened in his hand in surprise.

Vincour said, "Then you *are* an impostor."

"That's right, but I didn't know it until forty-eight hours ago."

"How could you—"

"Second thing. The kidnapper's name is Vasily Amenov, a Russian citizen who entered this country within the past two weeks, probably under a false name and passport."

Vincour whipped out a pen and notepad and scribbled quickly. "Do you have a description?"

No, Bill started to say, but Amenov's face rose before him along with a child's concept: *father.* He described what he remembered, adjusting as well as he could for a child's perspective. Wilson, who had been staring fixedly at Vincour's notepad, suddenly thought of something to say. "Do you have any idea why this man would take your children?"

"I know exactly why he took them."

Vincour looked up. "Why?"

"You'll find the answer in the journal."

"Never mind the journal, tell me what's going on."

"Are you married, Vincour?"

"What's that got to do with it?"

He turned to Claire, his expression so full and rich with love that it frightened her. Bill was more guarded than this. But no longer.

"We've been married thirteen years," he said, speaking more to her than to them. "But what I've discovered in the last forty-eight hours is going to affect Claire in ways I can't predict. What I've got to say is hers to hear first, and not as a byproduct of an FBI interview. Until she knows what happened, nobody knows."

Bill returned his attention to the FBI men. "Now we're going to bed. You guys want to spend the night, there's this couch and one in the basement. Spare bedding in the basement closet, bathroom behind the kitchen. If you leave, lock the door, otherwise stay on this floor or the basement—upstairs is off limits."

He took Claire's hand and led her from the room. Something was different, Claire knew it now, but her fear had vanished. His hand, his touch, his walk—everything about Bill filled her with an immense confidence. They were at the top of the stairs when Vincour appeared below. "You said three things."

Bill turned. "MPD. That's where it begins and ends."

"What's MPD?"

"Ask any psychiatrist."

They entered the bedroom and closed the door, leaving Vincour standing at the bottom of the stairs wondering why he felt as if he knew less now than he had when he went to get Bill Sullivan six hours ago.

In the morning, fog shrouded Fox Island. Neighboring houses were visible, but those farther away appeared like faint sketches on a pearl canvas. Vasily enjoyed the fog. Obscurity gave him a sense of security. Guy Jurmon complained that the damp air caused his sinuses to swell and the fog horn kept him awake.

The two men were eating breakfast in the kitchen. Vasily was already dressed, but Jurmon was lounging in a sweater over a purple silk dressing gown with a frayed hem. He was reading the *Washington Post,* his slender legs splayed out like a frog, red bikini briefs visible between the folds of the robe.

"Did you see this?" Jurmon asked. "A new strain of AIDS. It's mutating so fast they don't have time to analyze it before it's something else. Maybe it'll kill all the beautiful people, the ones who started it."

"What beautiful people?"

"Who do you think does all the fucking? Not poor people, not your ugly bloke with hairy fingers, no, it's the beautiful people tossing each other off twenty times a night, they're the living laboratories for virus mutation. Know what I think when I see some flower-faced cowboy or young bird with skin like honey and tits as hard as rocks? *You're next.*" A wolf's grin lit Jurmon's face.

Before he could reply, Vasily heard the sound of a car approaching. Both men tensed.

"Watch the kids," Vasily said. He went to the living room and peered out the window. A dune buggy with balloon tires and a roll bar stopped in front of the house. There was only one person: Ruby, from the caretaker's cottage. For a moment she stood there and let her eyes wander over the house. Was it his imagination or did she pause at the master bedroom? He moved quickly to the front door and opened it. Ruby had just gained the front porch.

"You're up early," Vasily said.

If he startled her, she didn't show it. "Sorry, did I wake you?"

"Not at all."

"Just thought I'd drop by with some fresh apples." She was holding the box, waiting for him to take them. Vasily gave her a searching look: the face was that of a farmer's daughter, clear-eyed and open, without a trace of duplicity.

"Just put them on the table," Vasily said. "I would invite you in, but I just started working on a project due the first of the week."

"No problem." The denim overalls stretched as she lowered the box to the picnic table. "Saw a light blinking out this way last night, was that you?"

She was not so simple as she appeared, Vasily decided. "Oh, that. I was walking on the beach and my friend was signaling that dinner was ready."

"This was late, around ten-thirty."

"When I'm working I often eat late."

"Well, just thought I'd check."

"I'm glad to know somebody's keeping an eye on the place," Vasily said with an icy smile.

Ruby went back to the vehicle, started the engine and turned to wave goodbye. Something caught her eye and she looked up. Vasily stepped outside and followed her gaze to the upstairs window where Matt was gesturing wildly. Then Jurmon's arm came around the boy's throat and yanked him back into the room.

No! Vasily thought, but it was too late. Alarm flooded Ruby's face.

"My stepson," Vasily called. "He's kidding around."

The dune buggy lurched into gear and raced off so quickly the rear tires fishtailed. Vasily drew his gun and fired twice. At the second shot the dune buggy swerved into the sand but regained the road and disappeared in the fog.

Vasily cursed and ran to the car. He had to catch her before the bridge, it was his only chance. He fumbled the keys from his pocket and pumped the accelerator until the engine roared into life. He raced after her. Homes appeared and faded into mist, empty homes, luckily, which meant there were no other cars on the road. There was no sign of the dune buggy. Vasily leaned forward, straining to pierce the fog that swallowed the world in white at one hundred yards. Had Ruby been clever enough to turn off the road? No, there she was, the dune buggy materializing up ahead. They were almost at the bridge.

Vasily shifted the gun to his left hand and tried two shots. A waste of bullets, impossible to aim, but the shots caused Ruby to panic. The bridge was visible now around a curve to the left. She veered off the road and cut across the beach where he couldn't follow. The new trajectory increased her lead, but brought her to the bridge at a sharper angle. The boards thundered. She was going too fast and yanked the wheel hard to keep from hitting the railing. The dune buggy rose on the two right wheels, wobbled for a moment, poised between control and disaster, then struck the railing. A crack like a gun shot as a piece of wood the size of a baseball bat flipped into the air. The dune buggy disappeared over the edge. A moment later a plume of water leaped skyward, then nothing.

Vasily slowed and stopped next to the demolished railing. He got out of the car and looked down. The buggy was on its side, almost totally submerged. Ruby's head was just above the waves, her face white, coughing. She tried to push free and cried out in pain. Then she saw Vasily. "Help me."

"You can't get out?"

"My legs . . ."

Vasily glanced down the road. There was no one in sight. He pulled off his shoes and set them on the bridge. Then he picked his way onto the broken pilings closest the buggy. He crouched above Ruby. A wave larger than most passed over the girl's head and left her coughing.

"Give me your hand," Vasily said.

She reached up. He took her hand and twisted, locking her arm tight. Ruby screamed. He put a foot on her neck and pushed her head below the surface. Ruby's head twisted as she tried vainly to wrench free. Bubbles escaped from her mouth and blood ribboned from cut lips. Vasily kept her arm locked tight, wedging her neck against his foot, his foot thrust firmly beneath the waves. At one point the backwash of a heavy surge brought her face momentarily above the water and she gagged weakly, but the next wave came like a blanket. The terror left her eyes and her face relaxed, the long brown hair spread over his foot like seaweed.

Vasily let go her arm, which dropped with a heavy splash. He stood up, his feet and pants soaked. He climbed back to the roadway. The houses were still lost in fog, the road deserted. He removed his socks, wrung them dry, put them in his pocket, then put on his shoes. There would be no wet footprints in case someone stumbled upon the scene or Anntek came looking for her mate.

He returned to the house, where Guy Jurmon waited anxiously on the front porch. "What happened?"

"She saw the boy."

"I know that. What about—"

"Why was he at the window?"

"What was I supposed to do?" Jurmon's voice rose in a squeal of self-defense. "He heard the car start and ran to the window. I grabbed him as soon as I could."

"Not soon enough."

Jurmon followed him inside. "What happened to *her*? Where is she?"

"She's calling the police."

"The police?" His eyes bulged.

"What did you expect."

Jurmon ran to his bedroom and began gathering his belongings, frantically shoving clothing into a suitcase. Vasily followed, amused and comforted by Jurmon's distress.

"The fucking kids was your idea," Jurmon blubbered. "We have to get the kids to trap the mother. Right. And now look. Why are you just standing? We're going to jail!"

Vasily smiled. "She had an accident."

Jurmon was tugging the zipper shut on his suitcase. He looked up. "What?"

"She had an accident. She fell off the bridge."

"You said—"

"Just wanted to see how fast you could move with the right motivation."

"Did she get away or not?" Jurmon's face was red, his hands shaking.

"She ran off the bridge and drowned."

"She's dead?"

"Trapped beneath the car, with a little help."

"We've still got to get out of here."

"We're not going anywhere."

"Maybe you're not, but I am."

"Sit down." Vasily shoved him backward onto the bed and stood over him. "Nobody saw what happened. If we run away we draw attention to ourselves, we arouse suspicion and what is now an accident begins to look like something else. *That's* when the police will come after us, so that's just what we're not going to do."

"I didn't come here to get involved in murder."

"I thought that's exactly why you came."

"That's business. This is . . . gratuitous." Vasily laughed but Jurmon continued, "You now what I mean. Controlled conditions, a purpose, every risk weighed before taken, that's what I'm talking about. This is out of control."

"Speak for yourself. You're the one who couldn't control a twelve-year-old boy."

"You try it when the bloody police come."

Vasily's expression hardened. He needed the children as leverage, but the boy was becoming a major problem. "We simply have to insure their silence."

"Then you better drown them, too."

Vasily gave him a contemplative look. "That's not a bad idea."

He went to the closet, where a row of empty coat hangers dangled. A few of them had cleaners' bags with the name of a local laundry printed in red and white. Vasily removed one and folded it into his pocket. With Jurmon following, he went to the master bedroom.

Matt was nursing a bloody lip, cut during the struggle with Guy Jurmon. He had never been struck before and it surprised him that the pain wasn't as bad as the shock. He was beginning to regain his confidence when Vasily and Jurmon entered the room.

"That was a stupid thing you did," Vasily said. "What does your father do when you do something stupid, Matt?"

"You're not my father."

"How would he punish you? With a hairbrush? A stick? A belt?"

Megan said, "Daddy doesn't hit people."

"Maybe you would be better behaved if he did."

The girl shrank at his approach. Matt said, "It doesn't matter. You're going to kill us anyway."

Vasily showed a heightened interest. "Why do you say that?"

Caution, Matt thought. Don't let them know that bits and pieces of conversations he overheard through the vent had convinced him they would never let him or Megan go.

"I don't know," he said.

"Did Mr. Jurmon tell you that?"

Jurmon was standing at the window, nervously watching the fog-blanketed street. He turned with a frown. "I said fuck-all."

Vasily ignored him. "Did he?"

"Maybe."

"Bloody little liar!"

"Shut up," Vasily snapped. He crouched next to Matt, who had backed up against the dresser. "You're right about one thing, Matthew. We'll have to kill you if you don't cooperate. Do you know what happened to that woman you waved at? She's dead. Her car ran off the bridge and she was trapped. I wanted to save her but I couldn't. You know why I couldn't? Because she knew about you. Your little game last night brought her here and when you waved at her this morning you signed her death warrant." His hand slid into his pocket. "You killed her, Matt. You drowned that woman. The water came down over her head like this . . ."

He pulled the bag over the boy's head. Matt tried to push free, but Vasily spun him around and shoved him against the bathroom door. There was a full-length mirror attached to the door. Matt could see himself struggling and Vasily behind him, pinning his arms, pulling the bag tight against his face. A tiny air passage collapsed when he tried to draw a breath. The harder he breathed the more the bag gripped his face. In the mirror, deformed through plastic, he saw Megan struggling against the chain to reach him. Vasily's voice was in his ear . . .

"This is what it's like to drown. This is what you did to her. An eye for an eye, Matthew, how do you like what you did to that woman? How does it feel?"

Matt's head was throbbing. He twisted violently, but iron hands locked him tight.

"How does it feel to drown, Matthew?"

Tiny metallic chips danced before his eyes and his chest heaved ineffectually, straining inward. His last sight was of himself in the mirror, face horribly twisted and distorted by plastic, a smear of blood discoloring his mouth like a gaping raw wound . . .

His muscles turned to water, then nothing.

CHAPTER

39

They had not expected to make love that night. Not with FBI agents downstairs in the living room, not after the jackhammer revelations that Bill delivered and not while their children's fate hung in the balance. It was not a night for love, yet it was love that had brought them safely back together and now brought new strength born of a relationship renewed.

They sat on the bed with knees touching, hands gripping one another, while Bill told the story of a little boy, child of an English father and a Russian mother, who was taken to Russia by a stepfather who hated him. A boy so physically and emotionally traumatized that he wrenched into creation another personality as a means of escape. A boy whose personal tragedy was exploited by the state, whose emotions were forged into an instrument of murder, whose technique for survival was turned to bitter purpose.

He told her about the Sorin Project, about Marina Sorin and Andrei Guneyev, about the Sandulov Institute and the training that now, no longer trapped within an artificial perspective, he could recall objectively. It was at this point that Claire surprised him by hugging him fiercely. "Thank God."

"For what?"

"I thought you were going to tell me that the dreams were real. But if you never lived in Kansas . . ."

Dreams? And then he remembered, the fire dreams and his nagging fear that he had caused his parents death.

"Memories," Bill said. "Like a movie of events that never happened. My life began when I met you, Claire. That's been the only reality I've known until now. You and the children have made me everything I am today. If it hadn't been for you I would have killed the President."

"No," she said softly. "No, you wouldn't."

"They made a robot, Claire. You made the man."

She whispered his name and her eyes were transparent with love. All Bill's fears—that he had changed, that Claire would no longer want him, that a relationship built on false pretenses could not survive—melted now as their lips met. They made love with a passion that transcended the physical press of skin against skin and became a private, powerful language of celebration and renewal. Their faith in one another had brought them this far and tonight, with bodies and emotions fused, their love was reborn.

Afterward Claire lay snuggled against his chest and listened to his heartbeat as they dozed and woke and held tight until the birds began to sing and a slow dawn returned color to the clothes crumpled heedlessly on the floor. Now it was Bill asking questions about Vasily Amenov, what he had said, how he sounded, what his reaction had been when he discovered that Roy had impersonated him. When he heard about the grisly package sent from G Street, Bill had to fight the black rage that rose within. Even Claire felt the change in his body and raised her head to look at him. "Are you all right?"

"Fine." He brushed the hair back from her brow. "Was Amenov there when the messenger picked up the package?"

"From what Roy said, he left it at the snack bar in the lobby. He told the cashier some story about the messenger being late and gave him five dollars to keep the package until he got there."

"Which messenger service?"

"District Courier Service."

"Did they do a sketch of Amenov?"

"I don't know. Roy didn't say." His eyes slid away and his expression became opaque. "What is it, Bill? What does he want?"

"He wants me to kill the President."

"Why?"

How could he explain the ugly memories that now lurked in the far corners of his mind? Memories that caused the parts of his personality once separate to stir again, Mischa drawing away in fear, Cain's fury unfolding . . .

She sat up and pulled the blanket close. "Roy was right. He's going to kill Matt and Megan, isn't he?"

"Not until I disobey him. They're safe until then."

"I don't understand."

Bill knelt behind her and wrapped his arms around her waist. "It has to be a punishment. That's how it always was—I didn't throw a ball far enough, didn't eat fast enough, didn't fold my towel into thirds—some imaginary transgression and the bad boy must be punished."

"Oh, God."

"It's okay, we'll get them back."

"How? You can't kill the President. . . ."

"I'm going to trap Amenov."

"He calls from a pay phone, Bill. Even when the FBI traced the call he didn't stay there long enough for them to catch him."

"The FBI doesn't know how he thinks. We're going to use his own mind against him just as he did to me."

From outside came the sound of someone pulling into the driveway. Bill climbed off the bed and peered from the window. Two men were unloading metal suitcases from a gray, windowless van.

"The troops are here," Bill said as he returned to the bed and began pulling on his clothes.

"You're hurt," Claire said, reaching to touch the mottled dark bruises on his neck. He intercepted her hand and raised it to his lips. The kiss was warm, but his eyes shone with cold purpose. "Come on." He helped her to her feet. "Let's find our children."

Faces staring down at him, Vasily's calm, speculative, and Guy Jurmon, thick-featured and eager.

"That's what death feels like," Vasily said calmly.

Jurmon raised a Polaroid camera and the electronic flash caused Matt to wince and turn away. He was lying on the floor of the bathroom, the plastic bag crumpled against the commode a few inches away. His chest ached and his ears were ringing.

"Get up," Vasily ordered.

Matt struggled weakly to his knees, braced himself against the counter and got to his feet. They returned to the other room, where he joined Megan on the bed. Vasily positioned himself in the center of the room, arms crossed. "All right children, the games are over. Here is what is going to happen. The police will come here sometime today to talk about the woman Matt killed. You will hope they can rescue you, but they cannot. If you make noise or signal them—if they discover you—then Mr. Jurmon and I will have to kill them, just as we did the woman who came here this morning."

Vasily drew his gun and crouched next to Megan. The girl drew back. "Megan, the policemen who are coming are just like your daddy, they want to go home and see their daughters and sons tonight, but if you make any noise while they're here I'll have to put my gun like this," he placed the barrel against his own head, "and shoot them through the ear because nobody can live if they get shot through the ear. And then you know what I'll have to do? I'll have to put this gun right here on your brother's ear and I'll have to shoot his brains out. All because you couldn't be quiet. You understand that?"

A big tear rolled down Megan's cheek.

He turned to Matt. "Everything I said to your sister applies to you, Matt. I don't need to tell you that, do I?"

Matt shook his head, but he was thinking, I don't believe you, I know we're dead anyway, you'll never let us go.

Vasily removed the locks and chains and directed the children into the hallway where fold-down stairs led through a trap-door to the attic. Images of escape fired Matt's imagination as he mounted the stairs, but even if he could get away what about Megan?

The attic was chilly and smelled of dust and damp cardboard. Light filtered from tiny windows set into the eaves illuminating the gridwork of wood beams and a floor of unfinished tongue-and-groove planks. Vasily looped the chain through a crosspiece near the apex of the roof and locked the ends around each of their necks in turn. His hands against Matt's neck were dry and cold. Jurmon arrived with two blankets and a pink plastic bucket, which he dangled in front of Megan. "Ever pee in a bucket before?"

"Put it down," Vasily said irritably. He turned to the children. "You may be up here all day. Mr. Jurmon will bring you food." Jurmon smiled. "When the police come there will be no noise. Remember what I told you—if you make me kill a policeman then each of you will receive a bullet through the ear."

The shadows of the two men descending the stairs were large against the roof. Then the stairs folded back on themselves and concrete counterweights lowered as the trapdoor swung shut. They were alone.

"There's spiders up here," Megan said.

"Shhh." Matt placed his ear against the floor and listened. He could hear their captors' footsteps descending the stairs to the living room. He got to his feet and moved as far as the chain would allow toward the cardboard boxes stacked in the corner. "Stand up," he said to Megan. "Give me as much slack as you can."

"Why?"

"Just do it."

With his sister standing directly below the crosspiece Matt was still five feet from the cardboard boxes. He stretched his foot toward them, but the chain, tight around his neck, pulled painfully at his jaw.

"What are you doing?" Megan asked.

"Trying to reach the boxes."

"Why? What's in them?"

"How do I know if I can't reach them?"

"You could use one of these boards we're standing on."

Matt looked down. The six-inch-wide planks beneath their feet were random lengths and held in place with a single nail at either end. They were tongue-and-groove but ill-fitted, as if the flooring had been an afterthought.

"You're a genius, weegus."

"Don't call me that."

Matt grinned as he braced himself over one end of a plank whose sides didn't quite touch its neighbor's. The single nail resisted his efforts until he got Megan to help him. It took them ten minutes working the plank back and forth before the nail came free. Another minute to lever the other end free and Matt had a board eight feet long with a bent nail at either end. Now he could reach the boxes, but they were stacked two high and it was difficult to pull them forward. He was tempted to pull the top box off but feared the noise would alert the kidnappers. He began to laboriously work a box forward on the bottom row, first one side, then the other, using the nail for better purchase. His hands grew cold and his nose began to run. It took a long time.

When Bill and Claire came downstairs they found FBI agents moving equipment into the basement and groceries into the kitchen. Vincour had disappeared, but Wilson was still there, his immaculate hair mussed and his shirt rumpled. He was drinking coffee from the "Super Dad" cup that Megan had given Bill on Father's Day. Wilson introduced them to the new arrivals, a hostage negotiation team under the leadership of a man named Tom Noonan. Behind a dramatically receding hairline Noonan wore his hair cropped short as moss.

"What's all that stuff?" Bill asked as one of the men took another metal case to the basement.

"Tape recorder, digital keypad, a voice stress analyzer, multifrequency filters and a few other classified goodies. You'd be surprised how much we can learn about the hostage-taker and his environment. What we'll do is set up in the basement, try to keep out of your hair."

Wilson drained the last of his coffee and drifted toward the kitchen.

"If you're going for a refill," Bill called after him, "use a cup without my name on it."

He was feeling less cordial this morning after Claire's account of how the FBI had tapped their phone without letting her know.

Noonan pulled Bill and Claire aside to explain how he planned to handle the situation. He had the voice of a radio announcer and manner of a group therapy leader. Every so often he fixed his gaze on them through smudged glasses and said, "Does that make sense?" and continued talking. He pulled a six-page form out of his briefcase and said, "What I'd like for us to do now is begin a psychological profile of the primary hostage-taker." He read from his notes. "Jeremy Lawrence, a.k.a. Vasily Amenov." He looked at Bill. "What do we know about this man?"

"That he wants to destroy me. And he's using the children to do it."

"We don't know that yet. It's important to let the hostage-taker's motives speak through his own words and actions. For instance, when he calls I want you to remain as calm as you can, avoid confrontation in favor of investigation. Probe, ask questions, see if you can draw him out. We've got a voice stress analyzer and a series of questions I want you to ask him. If he balks don't insist on it, let him determine the pace, but try to keep the conversation going. Don't answer questions with a simple yes or no but expound on them. Don't understand too easily what this man Amenov wants. I don't want you to sound stupid, but when you can, ask for clarification. When you answer a question, ask a question back. Make sense?"

"What's the point?" Bill said impatiently. "He's not going to wait around for you to trace the call and get a car out there."

"We might get lucky."

"He's an ex-KGB agent, you're not going to get lucky."

"You're probably right, Bill, but that's not the only reason for extending negotiations, it also helps create a rapport. The more he sees you as an individual the more difficult it is to hurt you."

"He already knows me as an individual. He's my stepfather."

Noonan blinked. "No one mentioned that."

"Listen, I appreciate your motives, but if you want to help Matt and Megan, here's what the FBI can do. Contact all the messenger services in the Washington metropolitan area. Give them a sketch of Amenov and put them on the lookout for anyone who wants a package delivered to this house or gives his name as Lawrence or Sullivan or any derivation of them."

"You expect him to send a package to you?"

"He'll have no choice after I demand proof that the children are alive. A photograph of them holding the front page of today's *Washington Post*."

Noonan's face clouded. "Ummm, I wouldn't advise it. It sounds too much like an ultimatum."

"It is an ultimatum."

"That's a mistake. An ultimatum is perceived as a challenge to the hostage-taker's authority, an attack on his self-esteem, and it's liable to produce exactly the result we don't want."

"The result we don't want is exactly what is going to happen unless Amenov is stopped. You want to alert the messenger services or do Claire and I have to do it?"

Noonan turned to Claire. "Mrs. Sullivan, they're your children, too. My experience in these matters tells me that this approach will raise the stakes and increase the risk unnecessarily. A flexible, persistent approach is the safer path to follow."

Claire rested her hand on Bill's arm. "We left the safe path a long time ago," she said.

They were both aligned against him, and Noonan saw that his authority in this hostage situation would be limited. He replaced the Risk/Threat Profile in his briefcase. "I'll talk to headquarters."

CHAPTER
40

"I found a gun," Megan said. She and Matt had managed to drag five cardboard cartons within reach. Matt moved to her quickly. "Let's see."

"Not a real one," Megan said as she removed a yellow plastic water pistol from a box labeled *Freddy's Toys*. "Maybe it will fool them."

"Does this look anything like Dad's gun? Get real, Megan."

They continued emptying the contents of each box, then re-packing it. One of the boxes contained letters addressed to someone named Freddy Chalmers. The address was Number 4, Fox Island, Maryland. The date on the letter was two years ago and the letter detailed a teenager's summer.

"This is where we are," Matt whispered, pointing to the address. "Fox Island."

A tap on the floor caused them to jump. It was the kidnappers' signal that someone was coming and they should be silent. They held their positions. The air in the attic had become warm and stuffy. There was the muffled thump of a car door, faint voices that faded.

"Is it the police?" Megan whispered.

"I don't know. Here, let's repack the boxes before they come back."

"They'll hear us."

"Not if we do it quietly. And when we hear the car leave we'll shove them back into place."

As they began replacing articles Megan reached for the squirt gun.

"Not that," Matt said. "Give it to me."

He pulled up the leg of his pants and stuffed the gun into his sock. "Don't tell them," he warned.

"But it's not real."

"No kidding? Duh, I didn't know that."

He continued packing. Megan glared at him. "You'll just get us in trouble."

"We're already in trouble, weegus, in case you hadn't noticed."

She punched him in the ribs. "Don't call me that."

"Cut it out, they'll hear us."

"My name's not *weegus*."

"Just put the stuff back in the boxes."

She crossed her arms stubbornly. "Who are you talking to?"

"Megan," he said grudgingly. She began to help.

The sheriff's car was green and white. Vasily was watching from the window when it arrived. The sheriff got out, adjusted his Smokey the Bear hat and approached the house. Like all American police he was armed. Vasily touched the revolver in his jacket pocket. He had taken a piece of styrofoam packing material from the Polaroid camera Jurmon had purchased, cut a hole for the barrel and used it to conceal the shape of the weapon.

"How many?" Jurmon whispered.

"Only one of them. Relax."

It was like telling ice to melt in the arctic. Jurmon had been nervous and anxious all morning. Vasily considered putting him in the attic with the children, but he assumed that Anntek had told the police about the blinking lights last night and he needed Jurmon for an alibi.

Vasily waited fifteen seconds after the doorbell, then opened the door. "Yes?"

"Officer Perkins, State Highway Patrol. Are you Jerry Lawrence?"

"Jeremy."

"Mr. Lawrence, I'm here to investigate a vehicular accident involving Miss Ruby Dalworth. I understand she came to see you this morning?"

Perkins was a burly man who hadn't shaved quite far enough down his neck. As he spoke he peered over Vasily's shoulder.

"Would you like to come in, Sheriff?"

"Thank you, sir."

They stepped inside, where Vasily introduced Guy Jurmon as a friend visiting from England and hoped the sheriff wouldn't notice the dark patches of sweat that had appeared beneath Jurmon's arms.

"Were you also here this morning?" the sheriff asked.

"I was sleeping late," Jurmon said, a bit too defensively.

"What's the trouble?" Vasily asked.

The sheriff explained that Ruby had been found trapped and drowned in her car. He consulted a spiral notepad. "Her friend, Miss Anntek, says that Miss Dalworth came to see you this morning?"

"That's right. She saw Guy's signal last night and thought it was an SOS. She stopped here this morning to see if anything was wrong."

"And was it an SOS?"

"Guy suffers from asthma. He had a rather severe attack while I was walking on the beach so he signaled me."

"The other homes are vacant," Jurmon added. "We didn't think anyone would be alarmed."

The sheriff scribbled in his notebook. "You under a doctor's care, sir?"

"Dr. Oldenfield. Got an office in Picadilly."

"Where?"

Vasily said, "He's from London. Give him your card, Guy."

Jurmon stiffened; clearly he hadn't expected this. "Don't think I've got any left."

"I think I've got one," Vasily said. He pulled out his wallet and drew out Jurmon's card. "Here we are. If you ever get to London you might stop by Mr. Jurmon's club. It's a good show. Beautiful women, just beautiful."

The officer nodded. "You mind if I keep this?"

"Not at all."

Jurmon's covert expression said that he minded quite a lot, but Vasily didn't care. If the police decided to check anybody's background he preferred it to be Jurmon's. Sheriff Perkins slipped the card into his pocket and said, "How long did Miss Dalworth spend here?"

"Not more than five minutes. We were eating breakfast, and after we explained what happened and apologized for alarming her, she left."

"What time was that?"

"A little after eight."

"Notice anything unusual? Did she seem upset or irrational in any way?"

"To tell you the truth she had rather a glazed look, but it was nothing new. You've talked to her, uh, partner? The one who calls herself Anntek?"

"I've spoken with her."

"They're artists and you know how artists are."

"How?"

"Let me put it this way. If an autopsy showed traces of marijuana I wouldn't be surprised."

With any luck, Vasily reasoned, the sheriff had noticed the same faint smell of marijuana that he had noticed in the caretaker's cottage. There were a few more routine questions, but Vasily could tell that the seed of doubt he planted had found fertile soil. The sheriff felt more comfortable with him than with a spike-haired lesbian artist grieving for her lover.

The phone call did not come at noon but was an agonizing fifteen minutes late. Nick Vincour arrived a half hour beforehand. He was unshaven, but had found a clean shirt and came armed with questions for Bill. There hadn't been time for a written translation of Marina's journal, but he'd gotten the essence of it and knew that MPD stood for the clinical diagnosis of Multiple Personality Disorder.

"It's like saying 'The Devil made me do it,' " Vincour told Bill. "In this case, someone named Marina Sorin. She's your Devil and she's given you this journal to prove it. Why?"

"She knew that otherwise people like you wouldn't believe me."

"Why should I believe the journal? Because it's written in Russian?"

"Have her authenticate it when she comes to this country."

"When's that going to be?"

"As soon as you arrange coronary bypass surgery for her husband."

"Me? Who are you talking about?"

"Whose budget is it coming out of? I don't know. You guys, the CIA, maybe the Secret Service—it all depends on who's got the most to gain from discovering how the KGB planted an assassin in the Secret Service and how badly you want to prove that the KGB killed the original Sullivan family."

Vincour stared incredulously. "Are you making deals for these people?"

Not deals, Bill thought. Repayment. Andrei and Marina had saved his life, returned him home to fight for his children and he would do no less for them. Before he could respond, Noonan interrupted them. "Ten minutes, gentlemen. If we could go over the guidelines one last time . . ."

They gathered in the living room, Bill and Claire and the entire FBI team, including the technicians from the basement. Bill only half listened. It wasn't Noonan's voice he sought but one from his past, the father of his memory, joyfully lifting him high into the air one moment, coldly pouring water up his nose the next. It was to Vasily Amenov that he tuned his senses.

At twelve o'clock the technical crew stood ready in the basement while Bill, Claire, Vincour and Noonan gathered around the phone in the dining room. The two FBI men wore radio headphones through which they would monitor the conversation. Noonan presented Bill with a series of hand signals—palm out, patting the air, to indicate a softer approach; a fist to indicate a hard line; a circling finger to mean play stupid and ask more questions. As the minutes ticked away, Noonan did exercises, twisting back and forth with hands on his hips, rolling his head around his neck to reduce tension.

The phone rang. Noonan held up one finger, two, three, then pointed at Bill to pick up the phone.

"Sullivan residence."

"Billy, is that you?"

"This is Bill Sullivan. Are my children safe?"

A dry chuckle. "A father's distress is a terrible burden."

"I want my children back. Let them go and I'll do anything you want."

"You know what it is I want you to do."

"Tell me."

"What you were trained to do. Cherish the good and punish the bad. I told you who was bad but you ignored me."

"The President?"

"You *do* remember." The playful tone became more business-like. "His life in exchange for your children. You have until noon tomorrow, Billy."

Bill said quickly in Russian, "On one condition Vasily Dmitrievich Amenov. First prove my children are safe."

A pause, then in Russian, "Is that you, Mischa?"

Vincour waved angrily at Bill and pointed to his ears: *What are you saying?* Bill turned away. "There is no Mischa but I have his memories. I remember you. And I believe you murdered my children the day you abducted them."

"They are unharmed."

"Then send me a photograph of them holding today's newspaper headline. If you speak the truth, I will trade the President's life for theirs."

"So easily as that? Are the police listening, Mischa?"

"What do you think?"

"I think Megan's ears look just like her grandmother's."

The line went dead. Bill put the phone down slowly. The technician looked up. "Lost him."

Bill was shaken by Amenov's last words. Had he gone too far, said too much, pushed too hard?

"What the hell did you say?" Vincour demanded.

Bill was still looking at the phone. They all turned to look at it. The long wait had begun.

Vasily felt the sense of excitement and heightened awareness. Bill was no longer a pawn, an unthinking finger on a trigger. He spoke Russian. He knew who he was, who he had been—he knew who Vasily was. What had happened to the much-vaunted training the arrogant Marina Sorin gave him? All those years, the massive expenditure of time and money, the waste of Vasily's own career, and for what? When it was time to activate him Mischa didn't react, no more dutiful now than he had been as a child.

But would he kill the President? Could he? Not if the police were watching him. Was that why he demanded proof that the children were alive—a way to stall, to draw things out, a way to avoid responsibility for their deaths if Vasily failed to provide the proof?

No, Vasily thought, you won't escape responsibility that easily. As he approached the bridge to Fox Island he saw Anntek and two other women draping black crepe around the fence surrounding the caretaker's cottage. Anntek turned to stare at him, a black look. She must have said something to her friends; as the heavy American car clattered over the bridge, which was still missing part of its railing, a glance in the side-view mirror revealed all three of them staring after him.

———

Crouched at the window, Matt pointed his gun at Guy Jurmon's head. Jurmon was cooking hamburgers over a propane barbecue on the patio. He wore an apron embroidered with the legend *Chief Cook and Bottle Washer,* which was too big and hung on him like a dress. Matt pulled the trigger and imagined a bullet spinning Jurmon to the ground.

But there were no bullets in the water pistol, not even bleach or kerosene. That was his plan, to load the pistol with bleach he had seen in the garage or with the kerosene in the coal oil lamps he had seen throughout the house. Except that the kidnappers had removed the lamps from the bedroom, and when Matt tried to talk Jurmon into taking them to the garage he wouldn't do it. Ever since the woman's death the man seemed preoccupied and afraid of defying Vasily's instructions.

The chain rattled as Megan came toward him. "What are you doing?"

"Nothing."

Megan glanced at his hand. "You're just going to get us in trouble if they find that stupid gun."

"Then why don't you get me some bleach to put in it?"

"What for?"

Matt pointed the gun at her. "Right in the eye. Know what that would do?"

She was shielding her face with her hand. "Don't point guns."

Matt swiveled back toward the window, aiming the gun at Jurmon. As Megan returned to the bed she said, "Just use soap and water."

Matt blinked in surprise. Why did she always think of things first? He went to the bathroom, filled the sink and massaged a bar of soap until the water turned milky. He held the gun below the surface and watched the bubbles froth the surface. When it was full he stuffed the rubber plug into the gun, wiped it dry and hefted it. The increased weight gave him a feeling of strength.

Now what? Simply putting soap in someone's eyes wouldn't free them. They would need the keys to the locks holding the chain. Who had them? And how could he wrest the key away even if Jurmon had soap in his eyes. It had to be Jurmon, he knew. He would have no chance against two men, and Vasily was far too dangerous. It would have to be Jurmon, and he would have to do more than squirt soap in his eyes, he would have to hit him, knock him unconscious . . .

The sound of a car's arrival drew him back to the window. Megan called, "Who is it?"

"The other one. Shhh!"

Matt eased the window open two inches so that he could hear. Vasily mounted the porch, carrying a white plastic bag with a newspaper sticking out of it. "Get your Polaroid," he told Jurmon.

"Why?"

"I want pictures of the kids."

"When *I* took them you raised bloody murder."

"These are for daddy. Kids holding this to prove they're all right."

Matt risked a peek. Amenov was displaying the front page of the *Washington Post.*

"Put them on the phone, let them talk."

"I don't want them out of the house. Here's more film, I didn't know which size so I bought three. Get the camera."

"The hamburgs are almost done."

"I'll watch them . . ."

Matt didn't wait to hear any more. He hurried back to Megan, who sat on the floor endlessly braiding her hair to pass the time. "It's Dad, he's back and he wants pictures of us. I just heard them talking."

"Pictures?"

"To prove we're okay. We're going to be holding a newspaper."

"Outside?"

"What difference does it make?"

"Maybe if they see the lighthouse behind us Mom and Dad will know where we are."

"Maybe if we held up a sign saying *Fox Island* they'd know. Come on, weegus, you think they're that stupid?"

Megan gave him a dismissive gesture in sign language: *You stink.* Matt signed back, *No, you,* and turned away before she could respond. And it was then, staring out over the dunes with

"Fox Island" echoing in his brain and his fingers still bent with the memory of what he'd just said, that Matt had an idea.

"I know how to do it, I know how to tell Mom and Dad where we are."

"How?"

Matt ran to the bathroom and returned with a hand towel. "Come on, pretend this is a newspaper. Hold it up like I'm supposed to read it."

She did it. Matt nodded, his eyes shining with excitement.

"All right, here's what I want you to do."

He began to position her fingers.

CHAPTER

41

They waited. There was nothing else they could do. The Secret Service building was under surveillance in case Amenov was insane enough to leave another package for pickup in the lobby. Messenger services throughout the area had been alerted to contact the FBI if anyone ordered a package delivered to 16 Ernestine Circle, and a helicopter stood ready on a moment's notice to provide airborne surveillance. The only question now was: had Amenov taken the bait?

The minutes ticked past. They weren't hungry, but Bill and Claire forced themselves to eat some soup and crackers. Vincour was eager for more information about the Sorin Project, but Bill found it difficult to concentrate on anything but what might be happening to Matt and Megan. Underlying his worry were Vasily's final words, which he hadn't mentioned to Claire: *Megan's ears look just like her grandmother's.*

The phone rang five times that afternoon, people asking about the kids, who were supposedly visiting grandparents, and inquiring about Claire, who had called in sick for her teaching assignment. Claire found it hard to maintain the pretense of normalcy. The most cruel moment came late in the afternoon when the familiar clatter of a skateboard coming up the driveway caused her heart to shout: *Matt!*

She was already at the front door by the time the doorbell rang. Teddy Smith, one of the neighborhood kids, stood staring up at her. He wore a backward baseball cap and faded denim jacket, the emblem of youth. "Is Matt back yet?"

"He's still visiting his—"

She stopped. It wasn't a single skateboard that Teddy held balanced on its nose but two of them back to back. The second one was familiar. The second one was Matt's.

"Teddy, where did you get that?"

"Dr. Kane asked me to bring it to Matt."

"Who?"

Bill had appeared in the doorway. "What is it?"

"Matt's skateboard. The one he had with him when—"

Instantly Bill was on his knee beside the boy. "Where did you get it?"

"I didn't do anything," Teddy said uncertainly.

Bill inspected the board. There was a quaver in Claire's voice as she said, "It's all right, Teddy, just tell us where you got the board. You said a doctor gave it to you?"

"Not a real doctor, a veterinarian. He's taking care of your dog."

"Claire, look." Taped to the underside of the skateboard was an envelope. Bill pulled it free and opened it. Two Polaroid photographs, Matt in one, Megan in the other, each holding today's front page of the *Washington Post*.

"Thank God," Claire whispered as she inspected them.

Bill felt equal parts relief and rage. Amenov was here, or had been only a few moments ago. Teddy was backing away. Bill grabbed him by the shoulders. "Wait, where did you get this?"

The quick flash of fear in the boy's eyes sparked an answering memory of Mischa's fear. He lowered his voice. "Listen, Teddy, we need to find the man who gave you Matt's board. We need your help, okay? Just tell us what happened."

Slowly the story came out: The kids were skating down Mongo Mountain when a man calling himself Dr. Kane offered five dollars to anyone who would return Matt's skateboard.

"He said when Matt brought your dog to the hospital he forgot his skateboard. Dr. Kane tried to return it but he had the wrong address, so when he saw us . . ."

"What kind of a car was he driving?"

"I didn't see any car."

"You mean he just walked up?"

Teddy nodded. By this time the FBI men had joined them and when Teddy identified the police sketch of Amenov as "Dr. Kane," Vincour quickly deployed his forces.

"Frank, get out there and see if anyone saw what kind of car he was driving. Tom, alert the locals, tell them the subject is leaving the area, probable direction east toward Maryland, possibly driving a white van. Get Lopez airborne and have him fly the area, special attention routes 50, 66, here to the Beltway."

They returned inside, where Noonan insisted that Bill and Claire wear cotton gloves while inspecting the photographs. Claire was puzzled. "There's something wrong . . ."

"Matt's lip," Bill said. "It's bruised."

"The way they're standing, the way they're holding the paper."

Noonan said, "Body language is stiff for both children. I'd say that's normal under the circumstances, but we'll have a medic take a look."

"Give me a loup," Vincour said. Noonan handed him a translucent cylinder an inch or so long with a magnifying lens at one end. He positioned it over the photo. "Lower lip appears swollen, the little girl's holding her right hand awkwardly, maybe hurt her hand."

Bill knew what he was talking about: the way Megan's fingers curled over the paper, awkward thumb position, three fingers straight in one hand, the little finger upraised in another . . .

"Bill?" Claire said. "I think I need to lie down."

"You all right?"

"A little dizzy . . ." She stuck out her hand for his arm. Her body said *dizzy,* but her eyes said something else: She wanted to talk to him alone. As they went upstairs he heard Vincour give instructions for checking fingerprints in the mobile lab. At least the FBI van was in the garage, so if Amenov had passed the house he hadn't seen it.

In the bedroom Claire shut the door and her weakness evaporated. "Bill, did you see their hands? Their fingers?"

"They were awkward but—"

"Not awkward at all. They were talking."

As soon as she said it the perspective shifted and he knew. "Signing."

"An address, Bill. Numbers and letters. Matt's right hand like this, the symbol for nine while his left hand . . ."

"A zero."

"And Megan . . ."

"X and I."

"Nine zero X I? Ninety X I?"

"X could stand for executive or express . . ." Or execute, he thought but didn't say it. Searching for another interpretation he said, "It could be the letter O, not zero, couldn't it? They're the same."

Claire's eyes lit up. "Maybe not a nine, either. Matt's thumb and forefinger are behind the paper. Maybe they're like this." She shifted her thumb-forefinger interface.

"F," Bill said immediately. The visible fingers, third, fourth, and fifth, were held the same way for F or for 9. What distinguished them was the way in which the thumb met the forefinger, in Matt's case hidden by the paper.

"F-O-X-I? Foxey? Doesn't mean anything."

"Maybe the name of the other man, the one who was driving the van—"

"Mr. Fox?"

They tried different combinations and tested other letter and symbol possibilities for signs that might be corrupted by having to hold the newspaper, but nothing made any more sense.

"They're signing," Claire said. "I know they are. But it's got to be some kind of code or some kind of shorthand. Maybe symbols instead of letters."

Claire half-closed her eyes in thought. Sign language employed many symbols and the manual alphabet was only a small part of the language. The problem was that most symbols took two hands, the passive one acting as a frame or fixed point for the active hand, which often incorporated a movement. But the newspaper separated their hands and you couldn't see movement in a Polaroid.

Bill tried another approach. He brought out four maps, three of the adjoining states—Virginia, Maryland and Delaware—and one of the metropolitan area. He spread them on the bed and placed his finger on Lynwood, west of Washington. "We're here, but they traced the phone call to Maryland." He drew his finger east toward the Chesapeake Bay while Claire studied the city index. They found it at the same time.

"Bill!"

"Fox Island."

"You've got it?" She peered to where his finger touched the tiny spit of land along the eastern shoreline. Claire said, "Megan's using the newspaper as the passive hand, which means . . ." She made the sign for *island* by holding her left hand flat, palm down, and placing the letter I, formed in her right hand, on top of it.

Bill handed her a different map. "You check Delaware, I'll do Virginia, and we'll see if there's any other *Fox* it could be."

There was only one other possibility, a tiny town called Fox Run in western Virginia, but it was a good two-hour drive from Washington. Their eyes returned to the blue Chesapeake Bay and Fox Island.

"How do you want to handle it?" Bill said. "If we tell Vincour he'll be out there with six SWAT teams, half the Coast Guard and a dozen helicopters."

"What are you thinking?"

"I go out and—"

"*We.*"

A slight smile. "*We* go out there, do a little reconnaissance, find out if that's where the kids are and make a decision."

The sound of a car pulling into the driveway caused them both to turn. Bill went to the window and looked out. "It's Roy."

"Don't tell him anything you don't want Vincour to know."

Bill thought for a moment, then a slow smile spread across his face. "Here's what we're going to do . . ."

Five minutes later Bill came downstairs alone. Roy was seated opposite Vincour at the dining-room table. He half stood to greet Bill, obviously ill-at-ease. Noonan was in the kitchen. He had a glass of Coke and was now rummaging the freezer for ice. "How is Claire?" he called to Bill.

"She's okay."

Vincour said, "Good news. We've got three partial prints on the photos and a complete right thumb on the skateboard."

No, Bill thought, bad news. Amenov was a professional, and if he didn't care about leaving fingerprints it hinted at something Bill hoped wasn't true: that Amenov didn't expect to survive.

Roy said, "Nick tells me the kidnapper's demand is that you shoot the President." He shook his head. "The man must be insane."

"How would you handle it, Roy?"

"What?"

"If you had kids? Would you trade the President's life for theirs or turn it over to our friends here and let the FBI handle it?"

Roy looked puzzled. "Trade? You can't—what do you mean?"

Claire arrived with a large, soft leather purse over her shoulder. She greeted Roy coolly, leaned over Bill's shoulder and said, "I'm going to the drugstore. You need anything?"

"No."

Vincour said, "Why don't you let one of the men drive you?"

"I'd rather have them looking for Vasily Amenov."

As the door closed behind her, Roy adopted a confidential tone. "She still angry about the other day?"

"Would you be?"

"It was a judgment call, Bill. You weren't here, Claire was

intimidated by this man's threats—and I understand why—but somebody had to make a decision that would give us the best shot at finding those kids." He held out his arms. "You want to crucify me after the fact—"

Bill stood up. "I'd like to talk to you about it. Let's take a walk, go down by the lake."

"You'll stay in sight of the house," Vincour said to Roy. And to Bill, almost as an afterthought, "We want you around in case Amenov calls."

You want me around in case you decide to arrest me, Bill thought. He grabbed a windbreaker; Roy donned an overcoat, which he didn't button. It trailed behind in the breeze as they walked through the leaf-strewn backyard. Roy adopted a tone of mild reproof. "You know what the FBI guys are saying about you? You gave them a journal that proves you're a Russian agent. That can't be true."

"Why not?"

"If you're a Russian agent why would you come back from Russia? Doesn't make sense. On the other hand, if you've got problems—I mean beyond the kids, of course—"

"Matt and Megan. They've got names."

"What's the matter with you? I'm on your side, Bill. I don't believe everything the FBI tells me, but I hope that anything of significance to the Service you'll tell me first."

"You carrying, Roy?"

"What kind of question is that?"

"Simple enough. You bring a gun?"

"No. Do I need one?"

"Maybe I'm a Russian agent named Mischa Amenov, born in England, raised at a KGB training school, inserted into American society a year before I met you, assignment to assassinate the President on Moscow's command."

Roy stopped. They had reached the border of the lake. Three ducks swam toward them, hoping for food. Bill kept walking, then stopped. "What's the matter."

"I almost believe you."

"You should have believed Claire when she told you not to call the FBI." He continued walking. Roy rushed to catch up.

"I told you, I used my best judgment."

"It sucked."

"All right, you're angry. Is that why you gave this journal or whatever it is to the FBI instead of to me?"

"There's more where that one came from. All you need is two tickets from Moscow and help with a heart operation. Check with Vincour, maybe you guys can split the cost." Bill glanced at his watch. It was too bad Roy didn't have a gun; he would have enjoyed taking it from him. "Come on, let's jog around the lake."

"We can't, I told him we'd stay in sight of the house."

"I didn't." He picked up the pace and Roy ran to catch up. "Slow down, I can't do this."

"Who do you think's in better shape, Roy, the FBI guys or us?" He put on a burst of speed.

"Hey, Bill! I'm supposed to . . . Jesus . . ."

Bill kept going, knees high, feet flying. The path curved easily along the lakeside and Roy fell steadily behind. Bill last glimpsed him stopped and leaning forward, breathing heavily, hands braced on his knees.

Claire was waiting at the Minuteman convenience store. "Did he have a gun?" she asked, moving aside to let him behind the wheel.

"Nope."

"That figures," she said darkly. A momentary smile flickered across Bill's face. They were on their own.

CHAPTER

42

Bill pointed to the sign advertising summer rentals. "Bulls-eye."

In fact they had almost driven past it. It was sundown and the lights on the sign hadn't been turned on. Beyond the wood bridge a slender asphalt road bordered by summer homes and sand dunes disappeared in the dusk. The homes looked deserted, which wasn't a good sign since it would make them more conspicuous. They pulled up to the caretaker's cottage, where a number of cars were parked. The place was brightly lit but black crepe paper lay scalloped across the wood fence and the only sound was wind chimes. Not a noisy crowd, Bill thought.

A somber young woman in a gingham dress and Earth shoes greeted them at the gate. "If it's about a rental could you come back tomorrow?"

"We're looking for a man who may have rented one of these homes." Bill showed her the FBI sketch of Amenov. The girl barely glanced at it. "I don't know, I don't live here."

"Is there someone we could talk to?"

"It would really be better tomorrow."

Claire stepped forward. "Someone kidnapped our children. We think they may be in one of these homes."

She peered at them a long moment. "For real?"

"Let us talk to someone. Please."

She led them to a glass-enclosed porch. "Wait here, I'll get Anntek."

Inside the driftwood-paneled living room half a dozen women and two men sat in a circle, talking softly. The smell of incense and marijuana drifted across the porch. The dark-haired girl returned with a woman with spiked red hair whose eyes were red and puffy, as if she had been crying.

"I'm Anntek," she said. "Mimi says you're looking for somebody?"

"This man." Claire handed her the sketch. Anntek held it to the light and her eyes hardened. "I knew it. I knew it wasn't an accident."

"You *do* know him?"

"This bastard killed Ruby."

Mimi clutched her friend's arm. "Don't say that."

"Ruby wasn't reckless and she knew that bridge. We replaced some of those planks ourselves. It's this man Lawrence."

Then they were all talking, asking questions and answering them so quickly that five minutes later Anntek was ready to call the police.

"Not yet," Bill said. "He'll kill our children if he sees the police. We want to look at the place. See if there's a way to get the kids out. Do you have a floor plan of the house?"

"No, but there's a photo and a description in the rental catalog."

Anntek took them to a room that served as an office. It was surprisingly neat, with information on the rental properties tucked into a file cabinet whose surface had been sanded to the metal and varnished. The description of the Chalmers property listed four bedrooms, two baths, living room, kitchen, dining room, sun porch and a detached garage. They studied the photograph and Anntek pointed to a window on the second floor. "That's the master bedroom. That's where Ruby saw the light."

Claire said, "But the police inspected the house?"

"This morning. The sheriff saw two men, Lawrence and some friend of his I never met."

"What's his name?"

She turned to Mimi. "Do you remember?"

The dark-haired girl screwed up her face. "Jorgan? Jurgon? No, I'll think of it . . ."

Bill said, "Are both men there now?"

"The car came back around five. I only saw Lawrence—or whatever his name is."

"And there's no other way off the island?"

"Only by boat."

"Guy Jurmon," Mimi said triumphantly. "That was his name."

They all turned to Bill, but he had no memory of anyone by that name. "Who else is on the island?"

"The Sheens arrived this afternoon. They're the fourth house down. There'll be more people over the weekend."

"Do you still have the shotgun?"

Anntek blinked. "How did you—?" And then she realized. Hanging on the wall among framed collages was a photograph of her with Ruby, each cradling a shotgun. It had been taken the day they shot a nesting squirrel that had chewed holes in a half dozen of Ruby's paintings. They were posed as cowboys, Ruby in suspenders and straw hat, Anntek in cowboy boots, jeans and a leather vest. Ruby was holding the squirrel by the tail, a mockery of hunters and their trophies.

"You can have Ruby's Remington," Anntek said. "The Ithaca was my grandfather's, and I'm keeping it."

The Remington was a poor weapon for the circumstances, the barrel too long for cramped quarters and its double-barrel design meant that he would have to manually reload every two shots. Anntek gave him a box of ammunition. Bill dumped the shells into his pockets. She also provided a pair of binoculars and two bicycles. They left with the understanding that Anntek would call the police if they didn't return within ninety minutes.

Bill and Claire pedaled silently through the night. The only sound was the rhythmic boom of the surf and an occasional crunch as they passed over a patch of sand. The air was damp and tasted of the sea. Two hundred yards from the Chalmers house they pulled the bikes into the dunes and continued on foot. There was no light in the master bedroom. The driveway was empty, but the garage door was open. Claire touched Bill's arm and pointed at the white Dodge van visible beside a Chrysler LeBaron. As they approached the house the sound of a television reached them. The kids? Would they be downstairs watching television?

"I'm going to circle the place," Bill told Claire in a low voice. "Stay low, stay out of sight if cars come."

With the shotgun in one hand and the binoculars around his neck, Bill began working his way around the house. As he suspected, the curtains were pulled except for the kitchen window, which faced the garage across an open patio. The kitchen was dark, but through the doorway in the living room he could see someone's feet propped up on a table in front of the television. Which one? Amenov or Jurmon? Or were there others?

By using the garage to shield him from view he moved close to the house and peered around the corner. The new angle gained him nothing. He ventured across the darkened patio. Halfway across someone turned on the light in the kitchen. Bill ducked back behind the propane barbecue and felt something warm brush his ear. He jerked back. The metal housing. They must have cooked out here tonight.

Through the kitchen window he saw a man cross to the sink. Bill raised the binoculars and got a close look: a squat little man, unattractive, with jet black hair and heavy lips. Guy Jurmon. Not a fighter by the look of him, but the thought of him touching Matt or Megan was repellent.

Jurmon rolled some pills into his mouth and downed a glass of water. Then he returned to the living room, turning off the light in the kitchen. So where was Amenov? And where were the kids? Bill continued working his way around the house, but the other rooms were either dark or had their windows covered. When he reached Claire she couldn't keep the strain from her voice. "Where were you?"

"I saw the other one. Guy Jurmon. Little man with black hair. I wanted to see what he was up to."

"What about the kids?"

"I didn't see them. Or Amenov."

"Do you think he moved them?"

"If he did, Jurmon will tell us. I think I know a way to flush them out, but it's not a sure thing. We could lose them, Claire. If you'd feel better letting Vincour handle it . . ."

"What do you think?"

"He'll never surrender. He'll die first and take them with him."

She stared at the house. "You said last night your life began when we met. So did mine. Whatever happens, let it be us, not somebody else."

Bill covered her clenched fist with his hand and gave it a firm squeeze. "I'll need your jacket. There's a propane barbecue on the patio. Still warm, they must have used it tonight. We're going to start a little fire and with any luck Amenov will come out. If we get him we can negotiate with the other."

"Why my jacket?"

"It'll smoke and stink, something to draw their attention without announcing our presence." He placed the gun in front of her. "Shotgun. Double barrel, two triggers, you have to load after the two shots are fired."

"You're giving me the gun?"

"I might have to. You might want it." He showed her the safety and how to cock, load and fire. "If you fire both barrels, take cover before you reload. First out of harm's way, then reload. Don't think of it as a shotgun. You'll be standing too close for the charge to spread. Pretend it's a rifle and aim it just as accurately, muzzle pointed between knees and neck at all times. You okay with this?"

She took a deep breath and let it out. "Let's get the children."

———

All day long Guy Jurmon had kept the television tuned to the local station, where periodic news reports reassured him that Ruby Dalworth's death was considered an accident. Vasily Amenov, on the other hand, had three times tuned in to CNN Headline News, which made no sense to Jurmon. Dalworth's death wasn't significant enough for the national news. But Amenov had been in a state of heightened anticipation all night and Jurmon didn't know why. Partly to irritate the Russian he turned on a show called *Wheel of Fortune*.

"Tell me if they interrupt your program for a news bulletin," Vasily said as he left the room.

"What kind of bulletin?"

"You'll know it when you hear it."

The world would know it, Vasily thought as he went upstairs. He looked in on the children in the darkened bedroom and played a flashlight over them. They stared at him like deer caught in headlights. "Go to sleep," he said. "I spoke with your father. If he obeys his instructions, tomorrow you can go home."

"Where is Dad?"

"Perhaps they will tell us on the eleven o'clock news."

The abdominal cramps had become constant now and he felt like a matador twisting on the horns of a bull. What had the doctors told him? Red blood cells dying, replaced by white blood cells until the system collapsed. Vasily ran a hot bath, something he found eased the pain and helped him focus his thoughts. He had just pulled off his shirt when he thought he smelled smoke. His skin prickled with foreboding. Pistol in hand he moved through the upstairs rooms trying to place the smell. Then he went downstairs. Jurmon peered over the television at him. "What's wrong?"

"Smoke. You don't smell it?"

Jurmon snorted noisily and shrugged. Of course not, Amenov thought, with your allergies you wouldn't smell shit if you sat in it.

Vasily moved to the kitchen area and saw something drifting over the patio. Fog? When he turned on the outside light the fog became a stream of dark smoke coming from the barbecue. He was both relieved and irritated. He went back to Jurmon and yanked the plug from the television. "You trying to burn down the house?"

"What?"

"The fucking barbecue, you didn't turn it off."

Jurmon looked. "Bloody hell . . ."

"Keep it up and you'll have the police out here in no time," Vasily said as he returned upstairs. Jurmon glared after him, then got up and went outside. Although he was dressed in heavy socks and a sweatsuit, the sea air was damp and chilly. I wonder if it's dangerous, Jurmon thought as a whiff of smoke caused him to turn his head aside. Cursing Vasily for not doing it himself Jurmon waved at the smoke and reached blindly for the knob. His hand touched hot metal and he danced back, waving his fingers . . .

Without warning something gripped his sweatshirt, yanking him forward against the twin barrels of a shotgun jammed against his throat. "Don't make a sound," said the face at the other end of the gun.

Gagging with fear, Jurmon was pulled into the shadows behind the garage. "Hands on your head," the man hissed. Jurmon felt someone searching him from behind, patting his shoulders, waist, legs. He didn't realize it was a woman until they forced him to kneel, his back to the wall. "Don't hurt me," he whimpered.

The gun was gone now, replaced by the man's hand, which closed like a vise around his neck. "Shut up and listen. Matt and Megan, where are they?"

He realized then who these people were, who they had to be: the parents, Bill and Claire Sullivan. They must have followed Amenov . . .

The hand tightened. "Where?"

"Master bedroom. I didn't hurt them. I never touched—"

The man banged Jurmon's head against the garage. "Where is Vasily Amenov?"

"I don't know. Upstairs."

"How is he armed?"

Jurmon was shivering now, telling them everything they wanted to know, praying they wouldn't kill him, searching their faces for pity and finding none. When he felt the warmth spread across his thigh he thought they had stabbed him. Then he realized he had pissed on himself.

"Here's what you're going to do," Bill said. "You're going to call Amenov down here. Tell him you can't put out the fire, you need his help. If you try to run or warn him—"

A girl's scream tore the night.

"Megan," Claire whispered, already running toward the house.

"Wait!" Bill called, but she paid no attention. Jurmon saw momentary indecision harden into resolve and the butt of the shotgun blurred toward his face. He jerked back and the blow missed his temple but caught him on the forehead, knocking him to the ground. He was aware of Bill running after Claire, then a single shot. The answering roar of the shotgun made Jurmon flinch.

Bill disappeared and Jurmon was alone. He stumbled to his feet, ducked behind the opposite corner of the garage and ran toward the dark safety of the sand dunes. Then he saw the open garage door and remembered that he had left the keys in the van. He stopped, caught between the urge to crawl into darkness and a chance to escape the island. How far could he get on foot and where could he hide on an island if the police mounted a search? In the van he could get away, drive to the airport, go home . . .

Clutching his damp pants and whispering encouragement to himself, Jurmon scurried toward the garage.

CHAPTER

43

His fear of Jurmon's ineptitude worked in Vasily's favor. He imagined the little pornographer throwing water on burning grease and splashing flames onto the garage wall, which was why, when he reached the bathroom, he glanced out the window to check his partner's progress. His view was partially obscured by a patch of condensation that created the illusion of two figures on the patio. Vasily wiped it clear and the two figures became reality: Jurmon, his head tilted back, eyes white with fear, the muzzle of a shotgun jammed beneath his chin, dragged behind the garage by a man in a blue windbreaker whose face passed momentarily through the light. *Mischa.*

For an instant Vasily stood stunned in disbelief. Now the figures were gone, the patio empty as if they had never been there. But they *had* been there. Mischa. Bill Sullivan. But how? Thoughts crowded one upon the other as Vasily, still shirtless, raced to the bedroom and grabbed his gun from the dresser. He had been followed, the police had surrounded the house, any moment the windows would shatter under the impact of tear gas grenades and men in body armor and automatic weapons would break down the doors . . .

Vasily flattened himself against the wall outside the children's bedroom. The only sound in the house was stupid laughter of a television audience from downstairs. Vasily kicked open the door and lunged into the room, gun at the ready. The children, who had been talking quietly, jumped apart. He lowered the gun and recovered from his combat crouch. No police, no rescue team, nothing. What were they waiting for? Why hadn't they rushed the house or called for him to surrender?

The shotgun. There was the clue and suddenly everything made sense. A shotgun was awkward for close work. Why didn't Bill use a pistol? Only one answer: he didn't have one. He was alone. Which meant no police, no one with a proper weapon. Vasily felt a surge of exhilaration. It was one against one now. Moving with quick confidence he unlocked the chain from around Megan's neck. "Stand still or I'll kill your brother."

Matt said, "What are you doing?"

Vasily ignored him. He locked the free end of the chain around the bedstand, then pulled the girl by the wrist into the adjoining bathroom. Matt was yelling his sister's name. Good, Vasily thought, help draw your father into the killing zone. A quick glimpse out the window; the patio still empty. It had been only moments since Jurmon's capture. Was Bill still beyond the garage or had he rushed the house? There was one way to find out.

"Scream," he told the girl. She shrank from him. He grabbed her hair and banged her head against the wall. "Scream!" He twisted her hair and her cry split the night. Vasily's eyes flicked from patio to the doorway and back—there! A figure running toward the house, a woman, and as he pulled the trigger Vasily recognized not Anntek or one of her brood but Claire Sullivan. She fell, clutching her leg. Vasily saw the shotgun's twin barrel flash into view. He ducked back as the blast shattered the bathroom window. Excruciating pain in his temple and right eye.

Vasily cradled his forehead and his hand came away smeared with blood. Megan lunged from his grip and bolted out the door. He swung the pistol but a red film blurred his vision and the shot went wild. From outside another blast of the shotgun tore a patch of plaster from the ceiling.

Vasily scrambled after Megan, his head tilted to one side, the only way he could see clearly. At the bottom of the stairs his foot caught the rug, and he stumbled against the wall. His outstretched hand knocked a kerosene lamp to the floor, shattering the delicate glass chimney. The back door slammed; the girl was gone.

Vasily fought down a wave of nausea. Every time he blinked pain tore the interior of his eyelid. He peered into a mirror on the wall. Beneath his bloody brow a thin shard of glass was embedded in his right eye. Gripping the glass between his thumb and forefinger he yanked it out. Pain made him dizzy and he leaned against the wall. At his feet a curved piece of broken glass from the lamp caught one drop of bloody viscous fluid, then another. A few feet away the sturdy reservoir filled with kerosene had not broken. It gave him an idea.

"Trial by fire," he whispered as he picked up the reservoir. He returned to Matt's bedroom, unscrewed the cap with its wick and splashed the kerosene along one wall. He got the lamps from two other rooms and repeated the process.

"Where's my sister?" Matt said.

"Trial by fire, Mischa."

"My name's not Mischa. What are you—"

Vasily struck a match, hesitated when he heard the sound of a car starting, then tossed the match into a corner. The kerosene was not as volatile as gasoline; there was no explosion, only the slow spread of flames, circling the room in a growing ring of fire.

Matt grabbed a pillow and started hitting the flames while Vasily moved to the window in time to see the Dodge van exit the garage and careen into the street. Jurmon? Or someone trying to save the little girl? He fired twice at the retreating van, then drew back from the window as flames inched up the wall. Matt was still trying to put out the fire. Vasily crossed to the bed and began pulling the chain hand over hand, drawing the boy back until his head was tight against the metal frame. Matt's fingers were at his neck, trying to keep from choking. Vasily turned toward the broken window and screamed, "Come get your son, Billy."

"No, Dad, don't do it."

Vasily turned on him, gory eye glistening in the firelight and blood draining down his bare chest. "He has no choice."

Bill didn't realize that Vasily was wounded. His first shot, quick and instinctive, had been to protect Claire. The second shot was meant to intimidate the Russian while he pulled her to safety behind the garage. Claire was pale, her features tight with pain. "The kids," she gasped. "Get the kids."

Bill reloaded the shotgun, noting as he did that Jurmon had disappeared. Out of control, everything was out of control. He bent over Claire's leg. The bullet had grazed her outer thigh, leaving a bloody furrow, but hadn't struck a major artery.

"Take off your belt," he said in a low voice. "Use it as a tourniquet. Can you do that?"

She nodded and reached for the belt. The back door slammed. Bill grabbed the shotgun and turned in a crouch. Was it Jurmon going back inside or Amenov coming to attack? His finger tensed then leaped away from the trigger as a backlit figure came running into view. "Megan!"

He cradled her with his left arm, shotgun outstretched in his right. "Shhh, shhh, it's okay. Here, stay with Mommy."

Claire reached for her. Megan was crying. "He hit my head."

"Where's Matt, honey?"

"He's in the bedroom and he's going to kill him."

Bill scanned the area, eyes flicking back and forth, trying to anticipate the direction of any new threat. "Where is he? The man who took you?"

"I don't know, he was bleeding."

"He's hurt?" Bill coaxed quick answers from his daughter until the sound of a car starting interrupted them. Bill circled the garage in time to see the van bounce over the curb, scraping its muffler as it raced away. He raised the shotgun, but two shots from the house caused him to pull back. Two shots—Claire and Megan? He scrambled around the garage and found them safe. "Jurmon," he explained. "He got away."

"The shots?"

Bill shook his head, but he knew what Claire was thinking. Had the two bullets ended Matt's life? And then Vasily's voice above the distant crush of the surf: "Come get your son, Billy."

And then Matt, his words indistinguishable except one: *Dad.*

Bill peered around the corner of the garage. The downstairs windows were brightly lit, the upstairs windows dark except that of the master bedroom, where the walls reflected a flickering orange light and a tendril of gray smoke eased like a snake from the broken window.

Fire. Paralyzing fear gouged his stomach and turned his legs to water. The memory of a lit match held between his lips and Amenov's face, eyes like ice, wavering beyond the flame, ". . . you're going to hold it until the flame burns out." The acrid smell of singed hair and eyebrows, smoke in his eyes, the flame searing his lips—

"My God," Claire said. She had crawled beside him and was staring at the master bedroom where a tongue of flame had appeared along the windowsill. Bill pushed his childhood terror aside and handed Claire the shotgun. "If he comes, you'll have to kill him."

"What about you?"

Bill glanced at the burning window. "I'll be all right."

But he had never been able to hide anything from her, not in his eyes, not in his voice. She grabbed his arm. "Bill, no."

He put his hand over hers and his eyes reflected the lifetime of love that they would never share. "Save our children," he said in a whisper that to her was loud as thunder. And then he was gone, zigzagging in a low crouch across the patio to the house. Without looking back he disappeared inside.

"Bill," she whispered. Megan pressed against her shoulder. "Where's Daddy going?"

"To get Matt," she said, but her voice quavered. "Get back, honey. Stay behind me."

Claire gripped the shotgun and waited.

_____

My kingdom for a horse, Jurmon thought gleefully. Hunched over the wheel he drove furiously, afraid of a bullet in the back until the lights of the house grew as small as those of the buoys at sea. In a moment of euphoria he made rash promises to the fates: see him safely home and he would never leave Britain again, he would stop smoking, he would give Lynette and the other girls a raise, he would stop cheating his business partner . . .

As he approached the bridge someone moved into the road. His heart lurched—the police—but the headlights picked out a woman with spiked red hair and gaunt features, an apparition from hell. She held up a hand for him to stop. *Not on your life, bitch.* Jurmon leaned on the horn and stomped the accelerator. He expected her to leap out of the way. Instead a shotgun materialized in her hands, barrel swinging in an upward arc directly toward him.

Jurmon danced on the brake pedal. "Stopping!" he shrieked while his mind echoed the frantic refrain, *Stopping, I'm stopping, please wait, I'm—*

The blast sheared off the top of his head and sprayed his expensive hair implants across the ceiling. Anntek jumped aside. The railing was already missing and there was nothing to stop the van when it vanished over the edge and plunged into the outgoing tide.

It was the stuff of Bill's nightmares: the burning house, the sense of frantic helplessness, loved ones killed in his own attempt to rescue them. Except in this case the agent of destruction was not the fire but the man who started it, the man whose hatred had smoldered for decades until it brought them to this place on this night, to kill or be killed. Bill was prepared to trade his life for his son's safety, but the dark memories of his childhood warned him that Vasily Amenov meant to destroy them all.

Moving through the kitchen, he opened one drawer, then another, until he found a carving knife. Not much of a weapon but better than nothing. He approached the stairs. The rug was disturbed, broken glass on the floor and a bloody handprint on the wall next to a mirror. Amenov was hurt, but how badly? As if in answer he heard the Russian's voice raised in song above the laughing television audience:

> *Where have you been, Billy boy, Billy boy?*
> *Oh, where have you been, charming Billy?*

A father's voice filled with mockery . . .

> *I've been to find a knife*
> *Which will end my baby's life*

. . . filled with threat.

> *He's a young thing and cannot leave his mother.*

When he heard the lyric *been to find a knife,* Bill was seized with a guilty certainty that his father could see him, knew his betrayal, knew his every thought . . .

Not my father. He pushed aside the fear that rooted him in place. Using the handle of the knife, Bill smashed the mirror, then picked up a piece the size of a saucer. He started up the stairs, mirror in one hand, knife at the ready. Bill had a terrible vision of Matt chained to a burning bed, his screams of pain lost in the crash of collapsing walls. Amenov had stopped singing. "Is that you, Billy?"

Not my father. Bill kept climbing. On the second floor smoke was crawling across the ceiling. The voice grew louder. "You should have followed orders, Billy. You should have done what I told you."

Bill held the mirror at a forty-five-degree angle and extended it beyond the wall. An inferno greeted him: The walls crawled with flames, heaving dark smoke obscured the ceiling, and he could feel the heat against his hand. Amenov, bare-chested and bloody, sat on the bed using Matt as a shield, one arm locked around the boy's neck while he held a gun to his temple. He was smiling.

Bill yelled, "Matt, you okay?"

"Don't come up, Dad, he's—"

The sinews of Vasily's forearm bulged as he choked off Matt's words. He called out in Russian, his voice raised above the snap of flames, "Trial by fire, Mischa, remember? Do you think your son is any more brave than you? He's crying now, do you think his tears can put out the flames? Come get him before he burns to death."

. . . Searing heat burning his lips, the smell of singed eyelashes . . .

The mirror quivered, giving Bill an imperfect image of the room. Matt seemed to be struggling, his right leg contracting as his hand worked its way toward his foot. Whatever Amenov's wound he showed no sign of weakness. *Father.* No, not his father, this was the enemy. Bill called in Russian, "Vasily Dmitrievich Amenov, it's me you want. Let my son go."

"Throw out your weapon."

"I don't have a gun. I'm unarmed."

"Prove it. Show yourself."

"Take the chain off my son first."

Vasily took out his key and tossed it midway across the room. "Here's the key, Mischa. Come and get it."

Out of time, out of options. Amenov would kill him if he rushed the room, would kill Matt if he didn't. *Just give me my son.*

And then he saw that Matt's movements were not random. The boy was pulling something from his sock. The mirror made it hard to see the object, but the position of Matt's hand as it slid slowly upward, tilting toward his captor, was unmistakable—a gun. Matt had a gun.

"I'm coming out," Bill yelled in English, hoping to distract Amenov and warn Matt. He tucked the knife into his belt and stepped into the hallway. From deep inside came Mischa's fear—*Don't hurt me*—but buried within the fear was something else, an insight into Amenov's personality: *Whatever the punishment, he wants me to see it.* Instantly Bill began waving at the smoke. "I can't see."

"Lean over, Billy. Keep your head low."

Bill moved into the bedroom, squinting, coughing. Flames raced up a window curtain. Matt had the gun close to his shoulder now and Bill caught the reflection of what should have been the barrel but looked like yellow plastic—*was* yellow plastic. A toy gun. An inner voice screamed in disbelief. Like a diver who sees too late that the swimming pool is empty, Bill knew he was dead.

Amenov said, "Welcome home, Billy boy." The pistol shifted from Matt's ear toward Bill. Ten feet away, too far and too late, Bill launched himself across the room, his hand reaching for the knife. If he was lucky his momentum would carry him crashing into Amenov even if bullets tore into his heart and just maybe the knife would land a fatal blow and save his son.

But Matt was moving, too. Leaning to one side he shot a silver stream of water into Vasily's eyes. No good, Bill thought as the first shot exploded. An invisible sledge hammer spun him to the left. He kept moving, kept his balance, but his shoulder burned, his right arm wouldn't respond, and the knife skittered across the floor.

The next shot should have killed him, but Vasily was clawing at his eyes with his free hand. Not water, Bill realized as the Russian fired two shots blindly before Bill slammed into him. His right arm useless, he grabbed Vasily's gun with his left hand and kept it pointed at the ceiling as they stumbled across the room.

"The key," Bill yelled to Matt. "Get the key."

Vasily had both hands on the gun now, trying to wrench it free, but Bill held on with the Devil's grip. The men were face to face. One of Vasily's eyes was collapsed, the other, blinking spasmodically, tearstained and red. As his sight returned, Vasily began pounding Bill's wounded shoulder. Pain spread in waves. Bill drove a knee into the Russian's crotch, but the man turned aside. The bed lurched as Bill pushed Amenov across it, forcing him backward against the bedstand. The Russian clawed at his face and dug his fingers into his eyes. Bill released the gun to defend himself, but he knew the danger. Stepping back he met the descending wrist with a snap kick that sent the gun spinning to the floor. It landed between them.

Bill dropped to one knee and recovered it, but Amenov's foot smashed into his stomach. Bill rolled with the blow and came to his knees with the gun pointed at the Russian. Amenov stopped in his tracks. For a moment they were all frozen in position, Matt trying to fit the key into the lock beneath his chin, Bill with his finger tensed on the trigger, Amenov with arms outspread, body leaning forward, momentary surprise giving way to an expression of cunning triumph. Slowly and distinctly he said, "I see Matthew and he's been bad."

Bill's hand went numb. *Pull the trigger.* His arm trembled, his head turned toward Matt. The boy stared in alarm, a mirror of Bill's own fear, his own weakness. *Kill the weakness.* A great hatred rose within him, hatred for the timidity and helplessness he despised, for the whipped puppy quivering in fear, dribbling pee, eyes huge and supplicating, fit only to be punished and punished again, *I see Mischa*—

"Dad!"

Matt's cry was like a searchlight, illuminating the darkness called Cain which rose from the poisons of his past. And he saw the gun in his own hand, now turning toward Matt—

"No!" Bill threw the gun across the room as Amenov charged like a bull. The Russian slammed into him and Bill stumbled back, tripping over the chain that linked Matt to the bed. Bill's head hit the floor, momentarily stunning him. The Russian was on top of him, pummeling him with his fists. Bill tried to wriggle free and they twisted across the floor. A fist smashed his temple, another hit him in the mouth. The taste of blood, the blur of another fist. Bill turned aside and saw the knife beneath the bed. He grabbed at it and missed. Amenov clutched his hair and began slamming his head against the floor.

Bill struck back with his good hand, but the Russian tucked his chin against his neck and kept up the attack. Silver confetti danced before his eyes and Bill felt himself weakening. His flailing hand brushed something, returned and found the knife. With his ears ringing from the sound of his own skull hitting the floor, Bill thrust upward. Amenov grunted and grabbed at his stomach.

Too low, the knife had missed its mark. Amenov winced as it pulled free but he kept both hands locked around Bill's, trapping the knife, twisting the blade downward. Pain stabbed his shoulder as the Russian rocked forward, his knee gouging the useless right arm. Bill was on his back and bits of flaming ash drifted from the ceiling, burning his eyes. Amenov had two hands, he had only one, and despite the blood pulsing from the Russian's stomach, the blade descended slowly and inexorably until the tip was at Bill's throat.

Amenov's cry of triumph was cut short by a single explosion. He jerked and Bill felt the pressure release. Amenov tumbled sideways, tried to crawl, then collapsed. Matt stood five feet away, both hands gripping the pistol just as Bill had taught him at Beltsville. For a moment his face remained a study in cold hatred, then his eyes widened in shock.

A fiery section of the ceiling plummeted from the dense smoke and exploded between them. Bill rolled to his feet, leaped the burning debris and grabbed Matt. The heat was intense now and dark clouds billowed after them as they stumbled downstairs and out the front door. Running into the yard a horrible scream tore the night followed by the crash of breaking glass. Bill turned.

Framed against the starlit sky came a falling angel of death, fire flowing from arms outstretched to engulf them. Bill shoved Matt aside and dove the opposite way. He felt the earth shudder and the wave of hot air. Then he was on his feet—"Matt!"—dodging the writhing mass of flame—"Matt!"—until he found his son safe beyond the reach of the man whose hatred had consumed him long ago.

EPILOGUE

Matt Sullivan stood with his skateboard at the top of the concrete embankment they called Mongo Mountain. He was surrounded by the grinning faces of friends and the awestruck gaze of younger children who dodged elbows and legs to watch the fun. A November afternoon, the air was bright and cold, and the word had spread: Matt Sullivan was running Mongo Mountain.

He stared down the hill and for a moment felt the old fear, the voice inside that promised, "You're going to fall, you're going to get hurt." It was the same voice he'd heard five weeks ago when he'd lost control of the board and ended up in the hospital. But the world had changed since then and so had he.

Matt closed his eyes, took a deep breath and called up images of the past month, days both strange and wonderful. A new family history, the Kansas grandparents who weren't really related and the grandmother they had never known in England.

Grandma Lawrence, although it was hard for Matt to imagine a grandmother who was a ballerina. Mom and Dad had already been to London to meet her and next month she was coming to visit after her legs were healed. Vasily Amenov had hurt her, too, and that was the other part of the past month, the more difficult part, trying to understand the dark unknown of this man and why he wanted to hurt them.

"Some people live charmed lives," Mom told him a few days ago, "and others seem to pay the price."

"Like Dad?"

She glanced out the window where Dad and Megan were playing with their new dog, not an Irish Setter but a Cocker puppy named Weegus. "Dad paid for his happiness. The rest of us got it as a gift."

Looking down now from Mongo Mountain, Matt could see his family watching him, Megan in black jeans beneath a puffy ski parka, Mom in her long coat and Dad wearing his Secret Service windbreaker. The bandages were gone, but Dad's arm was still stiff and he was doing exercises to loosen the muscles.

Mom caught his eye and her hand moved to her heart and outward, signing "I love you." Matt waved self-consciously, but already she had leaned close to Dad to share some private thought. That was another weird thing, the way they were acting with each other, like they were teenagers instead of normal adults. Some evenings they would leave after dinner to walk around the lake. "Going to feed the ducks," Mom called it, but half the time they didn't take any bread with them and usually ended up on the footbridge, leaning against one another, holding hands and talking.

And Dad was different, too. Matt felt a warmth of approval flowing from him he'd never known before. The Secret Service had assigned him to a special research project that involved a bunch of other agencies including the FBI and CIA. An old Russian couple had come to America to help him, and Matt always knew when they were on the phone because Dad spoke their language.

Someone in the crowd yelled, "You going to stand there all day, Sullivan?"

Matt looked down the hill. The concrete path began gently, then sloped more steeply until it made a precipitous drop before intersecting the path bordering the lake. Matt positioned the board and placed his foot on it, rolling it back and forth, testing the feel.

"Wipe out, wipe out," the kids began to chant. Matt ignored them, concentrating on the board, extending his body to make it part of him. He dropped his eyes and pushed off. Expecting the worst he overcompensated and almost lost control. Then he was centered and running, the spectators a blur of colored sweaters and jackets. The vibration increased, creeping up his legs, trying to turn his legs to jelly, threatening his stability. Somebody stuck a foot out and pulled it back, but not before Matt veered away, too abruptly, at too great an angle, heading for the grass.

"No way," he shouted to the gods of defeat. He bent his knees, leaning against the threatened spill. The ragged edge of grass tugged at the wheels, but Matt was ready, shifting his weight backward. He regained the center of the path and went into the final drop. For a moment he was floating, skimming the air with a feeling of invulnerability. He let out a whoop of joy so loud the crowd fell silent, turning with him as he piloted the board straight down, no hesitation, hands pumping, the wind tugging moisture from his eyes.

The lake rose off to his left, a final pull of gravity as he leaped the border and shot onto the path where Mom and Dad and Megan stood cheering and waving. He imagined himself as they might see him, swooping like an eagle from the sky, proud and strong as he had always wanted to be. Like his father now, free of fear at last, Matt Sullivan flew home.

RICHARD AELLEN is the author of *Flash Point, Redeye* (currently in development as a major motion picture), and *Crux*. Aellen, who served as a Navy photo intelligence specialist aboard the U.S.S. *Enterprise* during the Vietnam War, is a former professional pilot and instructor, and was president of the Berkeley Film Institute. He makes his home in New York City.